C000193650

Deanne Anders was [...] friends were still read[...] knew she'd hit the jac[...] of Harlequin Presents in her local library. Years later she discovered the fun of writing her own. Deanne lives in Florida, with her husband and their spoiled Pomeranian. During the day she works as a nursing supervisor. With her love of everything medical and romance, writing for Mills & Boon Medical Romance is a dream come true.

Rachel Dove is a writer and teacher, living in West Yorkshire with her husband, their two sons and their animals. In July 2015 she won the *Prima* magazine and Mills & Boon 'Flirty Fiction' competition. She is also the winner of the Writers' Bureau Writer of the Year Award in 2016. She has had work published in the UK and overseas in various magazines and newspaper publications.

Also by Deanne Anders

Florida Fling with the Single Dad
Pregnant with the Secret Prince's Babies
Flight Nurse's Florida Fairy Tale
A Surgeon's Christmas Baby

Also by Rachel Dove

Falling for the Village Vet
Single Mum's Mistletoe Kiss
A Midwife, Her Best Friend, Their Family
How to Resist Your Rival

Discover more at millsandboon.co.uk.

UNBUTTONING THE BACHELOR DOC

DEANNE ANDERS

A BABY TO CHANGE THEIR LIVES

RACHEL DOVE

MILLS & BOON

All rights reserved including the right of reproduction in whole or in part in any form. This edition is published by arrangement with Harlequin Enterprises ULC.

This is a work of fiction. Names, characters, places, locations and incidents are purely fictional and bear no relationship to any real life individuals, living or dead, or to any actual places, business establishments, locations, events or incidents. Any resemblance is entirely coincidental.

This book is sold subject to the condition that it shall not, by way of trade or otherwise, be lent, resold, hired out or otherwise circulated without the prior consent of the publisher in any form of binding or cover other than that in which it is published and without a similar condition including this condition being imposed on the subsequent purchaser.

® and TM are trademarks owned and used by the trademark owner and/or its licensee. Trademarks marked with ® are registered with the United Kingdom Patent Office and/or the Office for Harmonisation in the Internal Market and in other countries.

First published in Great Britain 2024
by Mills & Boon, an imprint of HarperCollins*Publishers* Ltd,
1 London Bridge Street, London, SE1 9GF

www.harpercollins.co.uk

HarperCollins*Publishers* Macken House, 39/40 Mayor Street Upper,
Dublin 1, D01 C9W8, Ireland

Unbuttoning the Bachelor Doc © 2024 Denise Chavers

A Baby to Change Their Lives © 2024 Rachel Dove

ISBN: 978-0-263-32160-9

05/24

This book contains FSC™ certified paper
and other controlled sources to ensure responsible forest management.

For more information visit www.harpercollins.co.uk/green.

Printed and Bound in the UK using 100% Renewable Electricity
at CPI Group (UK) Ltd, Croydon, CR0 4YY

UNBUTTONING THE BACHELOR DOC

DEANNE ANDERS

MILLS & BOON

This book is dedicated to Beth Diamond,
one of the most dedicated and caring L&D nurses
that I ever had the privilege to work with.
Small in stature she might have been,
but she was mighty in her love for God, her family,
and her friends.

CHAPTER ONE

SKYLAR BENTON HURRIED to the last seat available around the large conference table. It was the first Thursday of the month and she wasn't surprised to find the room crowded. Everyone who worked at Legacy Women's Clinic, from the medical assistants to the four physicians employed at the practice, wanted to be present for their monthly meeting. Lori, one of the other midwives, believed that it was the dedication of the staff that was responsible for their attendance. While Sky wouldn't argue that they had one of the most dedicated OB-GYN offices in Nashville, she was pretty sure that it was the dozens of hot, delicious doughnuts that their office manager, Tanya, brought in for the meeting that was the true draw.

"You look rough. Didn't you get any sleep last night?" Lori asked from beside her.

"Thanks a lot. I'll be sure to remind you how awful you look next time you have to pull an all-nighter." Not that it would be true. Her friend couldn't look bad if she tried to.

"It's just all part of the glamorous life of a midwife," Lori said, bumping her shoulder against Sky's.

Sky didn't feel very glamorous, sitting there in rumpled scrubs that she'd worn for the last twenty-four hours. It was great having a thriving midwifery practice, but it wasn't the same as an obstetrician's. A midwife worked with their patient for hours before the birth, sometimes acting not only as the provider of care but also in some ways as a doula who provided more hands-on support through the labor process. That was how she'd spent all of last night with three of her patients that were in labor.

And she still had one more delivery to do before she could go home and crash. Unfortunately, it was her patient's first baby and things weren't progressing as quickly as either one of them would like.

The smell of freshly baked doughnuts drifted down the length of the table as one of the boxes came closer. Her hand reached for the soft, glazed pastry before her brain could scold her on the lack of nutrients in her vice of choice. Closing her eyes, she embraced the rush of sugar as the doughnut all but melted in her mouth. Holding back a moan as she licked the sticky sweetness off her lips, she opened her eyes and froze. Across the table, dark brown eyes met hers and held. How had she not noticed him when she sat down? Refusing to be the first one to look away, Sky took another bite and chewed slowly while she tried to figure out what was going on. Dr. Jared Warner usually made a point of avoiding her, just as she did her best to get his attention. It had turned into a game of sorts between the two of them. One she had begun to actually enjoy.

Unable to help herself, she licked her lips again. Jared's eyes darted down as she made a point of dragging her tongue all the way around her mouth. His eyes met hers once more before he looked away.

"Chicken," Sky said, too soft for the man to hear her.

"What?" Lori asked.

"Nothing," Sky said, suddenly remembering where she was. Glancing around the room she was relieved to see that no one had been watching as she'd done her best to rock her stone-cold coworker.

Of course, she normally was more aware of her surroundings and made sure not to get caught teasing him, and she'd never gone this far with her teasing. He was just so much of a stick-in-the-mud, never wanting to step out of his well-beaten, boring path. He was always work, then more work. He didn't joke. He didn't tease. He never wanted to play. He was missing all the fun there was to have in life. Why that irritated her so much, she didn't know. Maybe it was because she saw herself, the person she'd been before she'd came to Nashville, in him. Or maybe it was because of the first time she'd seen him smile in a delivery. Picturing him with that big grin on his face, holding that screaming baby, still warmed her heart. It had been so natural. And so unexpected from a man who had always hid his emotions from not only her but everyone around them. After that, watching him return to that stony, totally boring exterior, she'd decided to make it her job to crack him open and see what was really inside. And so had begun her game of "shock the doc."

There were times when she just couldn't keep herself from ruffling his feathers with some silent nonsensical gestures. What was the harm? She'd even caught him smiling a few times when she'd flashed him a silly face. So what if she made herself look foolish. He had a really nice smile and it was a pity that he didn't let people see it more. Still, he was her boss's son, and she didn't want to ever disappoint the senior Dr. Warner with behavior he might not approve of, so it wasn't something she would normally do in a crowded room of her coworkers.

As Sky tried to concentrate on finishing her doughnut, making sure to keep her eyes to herself now, the door to the conference room opened and the elder Dr. Warner rushed in. With his silver hair combed back and his kind baby blue eyes, he looked like someone's favorite grandpa. "Good morning, everyone. I hope you are all doing well on this beautiful spring morning."

He took his seat at the front of the table and Tanya handed him a tablet. "Thank you, Tanya, I know each of you has a busy day today, so let's get started. First off, I'd like to welcome two new colleagues. I hope you've all met our new resident midwife, Brianna Rogers. She's a recent graduate of Vanderbilt and came to us highly recommended."

"Go Commodores," yelled one of the med techs from the other side of the table.

Everyone laughed at the man's shout-out for Nashville's largest university, which the majority of the staff had attended. Sky waved down the table at the young woman that had joined the practice a few days earlier. While Lori would be Brianna's primary preceptor, there would be times when Sky would be helping, and secretly Sky was hoping Brianna would stay after her residency was done. Their practice was growing, and it would be nice to have a third midwife on staff.

"Also, I want you to welcome Dr. Knox Collins, who will be filling in for Dr. Hennison, who, I'm sure you all know, just welcomed another baby boy."

As Dr. Warner began going through the monthly budget, Sky nudged Lori's arm and shot a sideways glance at the dangerously hot man sitting to Dr. Warner's left. How was it possible that she had missed seeing him? It had been all the office had talked about since they'd discovered that Nashville's own bad-boy doctor was going to be their new ad locum doc. With both his parents legendary country music stars, Knox had been covered by all the local media growing up. Sky just hoped that once it got out that he had returned home the media would not be hounding the office.

"And lastly, I'd like to share with you a special opportunity that has just become available to the practice." Dr. Warner handed the tablet back to the office manager and looked around the table, stopping when his eyes met Sky's. "It seems one of our midwives has been highly recommended to one of Nashville's rising stars. As most of Nashville is aware, Mindy and Trey Carter have recently relocated here from Chattanooga and are expecting their first child in just three months."

"They're the ones with the reality show, right?" asked the medical assistant sitting next to Sky.

"I've seen that show," Tanya said. "Cute couple and very talented."

Sky knew of the couple too. They'd made big news

when their debut album had hit record sale numbers. With their reality show beginning to air, there probably wasn't a single person in Music City that hadn't heard of the young couple.

"I've met them personally and they are a lovely couple that are very excited about the birth of their first child. Both Mindy and her husband plan to be very involved. Of course, as always, everyone will be expected to keep our patients' information private. Also, as an added bonus, the couple has requested that their midwife and doctor be involved to a certain point with their new show."

Everyone around the table started talking at once, some excited about the prospect and some of the staff shocked by the request. Their practice had cared for high-profile patients before, including famous musicians, but this was different. This was big and exciting.

"Yes, yes... I know this is an unusual request, but it comes with a very large donation to Legacy House," the senior Dr. Warner said, silencing everyone in the room. Legacy House was the home for pregnant women in need that Dr. Warner had established not long after he'd opened the Legacy Clinic after seeing that some of his younger patients didn't have the support at home that they needed during their pregnancy and postdelivery. While the home depended mainly on donations, everyone in their office played a part in supporting it with their time and talents, doing everything from tutoring to home repairs. Still, Sky knew the home provided care for a lot of women and it wasn't unusual for their budget to run short some months. Sky had always suspected that Dr. Warner personally covered those months. She also suspected it was one of the reasons the doctor was still practicing instead of retiring, or at least cutting back on his hours, as other doctors his age often did.

"So, as you can see, this is an opportunity that we are lucky to be able to accept. *If* we accept. As always, we all need to remember to keep our patients' information private." Dr. Warner stood, signaling that their meeting was over. "Thank y'all for coming today. Jared and Sky, can the two of you give me a few more minutes, please?"

Jared looked from his father to Sky. He wasn't sure what his father was up to, but from the meeting he had an idea. A really bad idea that included the midwife sitting across from him. The same midwife who only a few minutes earlier had made him squirm in his seat. The same one who seemed to love to annoy him. The same one who enjoyed playing silly games instead of taking life seriously.

"Isn't this exciting?" his dad asked as he walked over and took a seat next to Jared, his eyes dancing with a joy for life Jared had never understood, considering all the man had been through, with the loss of a child and then later his wife.

Exciting? It was more like a nightmare. "Maybe you should tell us exactly what the plan is. I take it that the three of us are going to have something to do with this new VIP patient and her husband?"

"I'm so glad that you are ready to jump in here to help, Jared. I knew I could count on you and Sky," his father said. With anyone else, Jared would have thought he was being sarcastic. But not his father. No, Dr. Jack Warner didn't do sarcasm. He always chose to see the best in others. It was part of his charm and sometimes it made Jared wish he was truly his father's son. Maybe then he'd be able to relate to his father's optimistic nature.

But after spending two years of his life in and out of foster homes, Jared's eyes had been permanently opened to what really went on in the world. There were no rose-colored glasses in his life.

"Excuse me, Dr. Warner," Sky said, "I'm sorry to interrupt, but I need to get back over to the hospital. I have a primigravida that has been laboring for several hours."

"How many hours? Has her water broken?" Jared asked. The risk of infection increased significantly during prolonged rupture of membranes.

"Her water broke spontaneously at four centimeters, only four hours ago. She's afebrile and the baby's heart tones are fine. Anything else, Doctor?" The fire in Sky's eyes warned him that she was ready to ignite, something Jared didn't appreciate. Even though Sky worked independently, if something went wrong and her patient required a cesarean section, it would become his responsibility. His questions had been appropriate.

"Just keep me updated. I took over call at seven and I will start making rounds as soon as we are done here."

"Okay, then," Jared's father said, plainly trying to act as peacekeeper, "let's get on with it. I met with Mindy and Trey yesterday, along with their manager, and they are all very nice people. I think working with them will be a pleasure." His dad looked across the table. "Sky, it seems that you took care of one of Mindy's band members, Jenny Mack, during her pregnancy and delivery a few years ago and she has, almost literally according to Mindy, sung your praises to her boss."

"I remember her. She had to schedule her appointments around rehearsal and gig dates. I don't think she was with the Carters then."

It always amazed Jared how Sky could remember her patients so clearly. He tried to remember his patients' names, but between his obstetrics practice and the gyn surgeries he performed, he found it impossible unless something really stood out about the patient. It wasn't how he had planned his career, but it was what it was. He was doing his best to build a practice and hopefully take over for his father someday. He had to see as many patients as possible, which sometimes limited their interaction more than he would like.

"Well, she seems to remember you too, and Mindy is very excited about meeting you. She is determined to have a midwifery delivery. Her husband, on the other hand, has some concerns. That's where you come in, Jared. In order to give this young couple the delivery they both want, I'm going to need the two of you to work closely together."

"What exactly do you need me to do?" Jared asked. He definitely wasn't one to discourage an expectant father from having a doctor oversee the birth of his child.

"I need the two of you to work as a team. This couple has a lot of pressure on them right now. They're new to the superstar level of country music and from what I can tell, the reality show is causing some…shall we say *stress* on the two of them. It's not good for either one of them, especially Mindy and the baby. Her last pregnancy ended in a miscarriage at nineteen weeks." Turning to him, his father looked him in the eye. "I know I can trust the two of you to do what is best for this couple and work together as the professional colleagues that you are."

Jared glanced at his dad and then over to Sky, who had gone unusually quiet. There were dark rings under her eyes and strands of blond hair hung loose around her face where it had come out of the band she kept it tied up in. He hadn't noticed that this morning. It had been all he could do to keep himself on his side of the table when all he'd wanted to do was lick that sticky sugar off those luscious lips of hers.

"What about the reality show? Do they really expect us to be part of that?" she asked, and Jared wasn't surprised to see a flicker of excitement in her tired eyes. She was the outgoing, flashy type of person they usually had on those kinds of shows. Not that he had any intention on being on the show himself. He didn't care for all that "reality" drama. He'd had enough drama as a child. Just the thought sent shivers through him.

"From what I can gather, you would only be there on the sidelines as you interact with them as providers for the pregnancy," his father said. "And don't forget what this will mean for Legacy House. Things are tough financially for a lot of people right now. Some of our regular donors have had to cut back on their giving. This donation would cover the rest of this year's budget. And then there's the possibility that they will tell others about the work Legacy House does. The two of you might even have an opportunity to tell others about it."

Sky's phone vibrated with a message, and she got up from the table as she read it. "I need to get back to the hospital."

She reached for the last doughnut left on the table before standing and heading to the door, then she stopped and looked back at his father. "Is it really that bad, Jack?"

The reassuring smile that was as much a part of his father as breathing faltered. "It's not just the lack of regular donations that's straining our budget. A lot of people are struggling right now, which means more young girls are coming to us for help. We are close to having to turn them away for the first time in twenty years."

Sky's eyes locked on Jared, then narrowed. Her chin went up and he felt like one of those unfortunate ants caught under a magnifying glass about to be zapped. "Whatever they need us to do, we're in, aren't we, Jared?"

Jared's mouth dropped open to argue, but then he shut it. How could he get out of this without looking like a jerk? It wasn't that he didn't want to help Legacy House. He'd been helping out at the home since he was a teenager. But working with this free-spirited midwife who acted like life was just another game would be a disaster. Look at how she'd resented him asking basic questions about her patients. How could they coordinate their care of their patient if she reacted that way every time he asked a question?

And then there was her unprofessional teasing of him.

Those big warm smiles and sassy winks rattled him. How much worse would it be if he had to work even closer with her?

Without waiting for his agreement, she spun around and headed for the door, the doughnut still in her hand.

"Well, I'm glad that's settled," his dad said, taking off his glasses and laying them down on the table.

"Why me?" Jared asked. "You know I'm not good at all that schmoozing with people. Wouldn't it make more sense for you to do this? Wouldn't the husband feel better having someone with your experience?"

"You're fine with people when you want to be. You just hold yourself back. You need to relax more. You're thirty-six years old. It's time you get out in the world and experience life instead of spending all your time working."

"You're one to talk. You've been going strong for almost forty years now. If anyone needs to slow down, it's you."

"When I was your age, I was married and building a home for me and Katie. The years we had together were the best years of my life. And when you came into our life you made us the family we always wanted to be. I want that for you, what I had with your mom, because no matter what you think right now, there will come a time when you'll need someone. Someone that understands you and will be by you no matter what happens."

His father suddenly looked ten years older than he had when he'd been rallying the troops at their monthly meeting. Was it the memory that he'd once had a family that didn't include Jared? Was it the memory of the little girl he'd lost? Jared knew he'd never taken the little girl's place in his parents' hearts. Not that he had wanted to. The Warners had been good to him and had treated him like their own. He had no resentment of their daughter, though at times he knew he'd disappointed them by not being able to be the outgoing, happy child they'd deserved. Maybe if in his younger years he'd been surrounded by the secure love they'd always given him, things would have been different. Maybe he would have been different. But that wasn't his reality. The life he'd lived being raised by a sickly grandmother and then later in foster homes had made him who he was. He couldn't change his past.

But it wasn't the time for them to get into an old argument that he knew he wasn't going to win. Jared lived his life just like he liked it: drama free. He worked hard and in his off time enjoyed the peace and quiet of the home he'd built for himself. He didn't need anyone else in his life. And he certainly didn't want to ever rely on another person for his happiness. Everyone he'd relied on as a child had left him or sent him away. By the time he'd been adopted by Jack and Katie, he'd learned his lesson. Not that he didn't care for them. They had been the best thing that had ever happened to him.

"But back to the Carters. You're overthinking this, Jared. I have full confidence in both your and Sky's professionalism. I know the two of you will make a great team."

He could see he wasn't going to get out of this. His dad had made up his mind. As Nana Marie used to tell him when he had to do something he didn't want to do, *Boy, put on your big boy pants and get it done.*

And so it was time for him to accept the inevitable and make the best of the situation. His only hope of getting out of this would be for Sky to refuse to work with him, and he couldn't count on that. Still, it wouldn't hurt to talk to her. Unlike his father, she would see that the two of them working together could only lead to disaster. He just had to find a way to get her to agree with him.

CHAPTER TWO

"YOU'RE DOING GREAT," Sky said as she wiped Liza's forehead with a cool rag.

"No, I'm not. I'm so tired. And I gave in and got an epidural after I swore I wouldn't need one. My sister is never going to let me live it down," Liza said.

"Well, I'm not telling her," Sky said, then looked pointedly at the young man at her patient's side. Waiting for him to take the hint was almost painful. Liza's husband almost looked as bad as she did. "No one will ever know, will they, Eric?"

"Oh, no, no...of course not," Eric said.

Liza looked over at him, disbelieving. "You're going to keep a secret? You are the worst blabbermouth in the whole family."

Eric shrugged his shoulders and looked up at Sky from the chair at his wife's bedside with a look of guilt that belonged more on a five-year-old child's face than that of a grown man. Sky looked away before Liza could see her grin.

"The most important thing is that you're fully dilated now. We could start pushing, or we could turn you over on your side and let you rest for half an hour." Sky was hoping that Liza would choose to rest a while. The baby hadn't progressed down as much as she'd like before they started pushing. Sky was tired and she knew Liza was even more tired at this point. The two of them could both use a power nap while the contractions did their own magic of bringing the baby down lower.

"Is that okay to do? Won't the baby's head end up funny shaped?" Eric asked.

"It's perfectly fine. Your baby's head has to mold as it comes down the birthing canal. That's why baby's heads sometimes look funny when they're born, but they don't stay that way." Sky found the things that new dads worried about amusing.

"And Baby Stella's heart tones are perfect. It will give the baby some time to move down now that Liza is relaxed, and a little rest will help when she's ready to push." Sky was a strong advocate of letting the patient's body tell them when it was time to push unless there was concern for getting the baby out quickly.

"I'd like to rest a bit, if it's okay," Liza said.

Tammy, the labor and delivery nurse, came into the room and they discussed their plan to give Liza a break. After positioning Liza on her left side to rest, Sky lowered the lights in the room and stepped outside.

"Dr. Warner was looking for you," Tammy said, then clarified, "the young one."

So much for a power nap. Sky reached down deep and tried to find the patience she would need to deal with Jared in the moods they both were in. She was tired, and he was aggravated about being forced to work with her.

If she hadn't been so tired, she would have looked forward to their interaction. She'd enjoyed placing him in a situation where he couldn't refuse the opportunity his father had given them. Seeing the uptight doc squirm was always entertaining. He was so cute when he was flustered. And those rare times when she made him smile, those she treasured.

But that wouldn't be the reason Jared had followed her straight over to the unit. He'd said he was on call, and he always rounded on the patients he was covering whether they were his patients or one of the midwives' patients. But while Dr. Hennison and the senior Dr. Warner usually just checked in with her or Lori, trusting them to share if there were any concerns or complications with their patient, Jared took it a couple steps further. He made it a habit to check the midwife patient's medical records and ask questions of the nurses taking care of them, as if Sky was withholding some information from him.

She had never understood why Lori wasn't bothered by this as much as Sky was. The relationship between the doctors and midwives in their practice was a collaboration and she believed sometimes Jared came close to crossing the line. Of course, as there was an understanding that if there were complications in the labor process the practice's doctors would assume care for any necessary procedures, such as surgery, it could be said that Jared's level of interest was reasonable. But still, all of his questioning made her feel as if he didn't believe midwives were equal partners in the practice. There was even a rumor that he had tried to talk his father out of hiring midwives into the practice, and it made her more than a little bit defensive when she had to deal with him, just like she had been earlier that morning when he'd questioned her in front of his father.

"Tammy told me that your patient was complete. Why isn't she pushing?" Jared asked the moment she took a seat in the nurses' station.

Sky looked at Tammy, who cast an apologetic smile her way. There was something about Jared, even though he could be as prickly as a porcupine, that made the staff trust him. Maybe it was the way he always had their backs when the staff was negotiating with the hospital administration. Or maybe it was the fact that Jared never left the staff to handle a difficult patient on their own. Or maybe it was simply that he didn't talk down to them, instead he respected them for the job they did.

If only Sky could get him to respect the midwives the same way. If only he could see that they had a place in the delivery room just as much as he did. There was a story there, and someday she would find out what it was.

"Liza just got an epidural and has chosen to rest a few minutes before we begin pushing." Sky wouldn't let him make her second-guess herself. She had done this hundreds of times. "As you can see on the monitor, the baby's heart tones have good variability along with accelerations."

"See, this is why we can't work together. You resent every question I ask," Jared said, turning toward her, his voice too intense for her lack of sleep.

Sky looked at him and blinked. Was this about her patient or was this about them teaming up to care for Mindy Carter? "I guess you couldn't talk your dad into taking over the Carters' case?"

His eyes refused to acknowledge that she'd seen right through him. His lips straightened into a flat line, but not before she saw him grimace. She'd seen it many times when she'd tried to get a rise out of him. It was as if the man was trying to convince her that he was above having human emotions. But she knew better. She'd seen the way his eyes had watched her lips that morning in their meeting. Was it possible that Jared was as curious about her as she was about him? Was there even the possibility that he was more than curious? Was the way he watched her this morning a sign that he might be interested in her in other ways?

Or maybe not. Maybe it was just her that felt that electric buzz that seemed to arc between the two of them. The only time she ever got any type of response from Jared himself was when they were playing one of their silent games, which just mostly seemed to annoy him. This morning could have been nothing more serious than the man was hungry.

"I simply voiced my belief that it would be better for my father to be the one that represented the practice with such a high-profile case. Don't you agree?"

The truth was she did agree with Jared. Even though she enjoyed her game of irritating him, the two of them had never worked well together. She resented his overpowering need to meddle, and he didn't trust her. It would probably be a nightmare, but she still understood why the senior Dr. Warner wanted his son to be the one to take the lead in this collaboration. It was a known fact that Jared was being mentored by his father to take over the practice someday. It was better to find out now if Jared could take the pressure that was sure to go along with the job.

"I respect your father enough to believe he knows what he is doing," she replied, though she did wonder if she was the right midwife for this job even though she had been highly recommended. The Carters had become unbelievably famous and certainly more well-to-do, as her grandmother would have called them. Sky had been raised in a simple two-bedroom house along with her six siblings and her grandmother in Tennessee's rural mountains. She'd had little to no training on how to behave with people like the Carters.

"Look, Jared, your father has made his decision, and for the sake of the practice and for Legacy House, we have to go through with this no matter how much you don't like me." There. Now the real problem was on the table for the two of them to address. The only way to deal with this was head-on. If the two of them couldn't be friends, the least they could do was learn to work together. Otherwise it was going to be a miserable three months.

"I didn't say I didn't like you. This has nothing to do with how I feel about you." Jared's brows crinkled with confusion. "I don't even know you that well."

"And we've worked together for over three years. Doesn't that seem a little strange to you?" The wrinkles in his forehead got deeper as he stared at her. Was he really this disconnected from all the staff? Or was it just her?

"I know you are a good midwife," Jared said, which coming from him was a huge compliment. Maybe there was hope for them after all.

"And I know you are a very thorough doctor." She'd had her patients' records combed through by him so many times that there was no doubt of that. "So let's start there and maybe by the time this is over we will both have learned more about each other."

His forehead relaxed, but his eyes narrowed as if he suspected that he was being tricked somehow. Maybe it hadn't been such a good idea teasing him so much in the conference room this morning. But it had been fun, and she figured fun was something Jared could use more of in his life. And what could be more fun, or more disastrous, than being on a reality show together with a couple of country music stars?

"How about we go to the first meeting with Mindy and Trey and their manager and see how it goes? It might be that once they meet us they decide we're not a good fit for them. Will you at least agree to that?" Sky looked over to the monitor displaying the laboring patient's fetal heart tones. Liza's tracing was beginning to show signs of head compression, a sure sign that the baby was progressing down into the birth canal.

"I've got to get back to my patient," she said as she stood to leave. "Let me know what you decide. Instead of looking at this as a form of punishment, maybe we should look at this as a great way to do something different and unique. Who knows, you might find that you like being in the spotlight. It might even be fun."

Without waiting for him to give her an answer, she walked out and headed to her patient's room. Somewhere in her pep talk she'd found herself getting excited about working with the music stars despite having to work with Jared. At least she told herself that it was the hobnobbing with the rich and famous that excited—and scared—her. She didn't want to admit that she hoped she might finally tear open that cold box Dr. Jared Warner hid inside of.

And who knew? Maybe she'd find the man wasn't made out of ice. Maybe she'd find the man was just waiting for a chance to come out and play.

CHAPTER THREE

JARED HAD KNOWN this was a mistake the moment Sky had gotten into his truck. They were both headed to the same place, so it had only made sense for the two of them to share the ride. But once the car door had shut, he'd been at a loss for what to say to the one person he'd done his best to avoid since she'd come to work at the practice.

There had always been an awkwardness between the two of them. It was something he didn't want to examine, because it might lead to a more uncomfortable problem. Awkwardness he could handle, but sometimes this felt more…personal. As if something unsaid between them,which made it very important that he avoid her as much as possible. Of course, that wasn't how Sky approached him at all. She was always pulling one of her silent pranks, flirting with him like she'd done at the last staff meeting or winking at him across a nurses' station when no one was looking, all of which he knew she did just to make him uncomfortable. It was those times when he wondered exactly what her intention was. It was like she was just having fun with him, while he was squirming with adult responses that he had no right to be feeling for a coworker. Not that she was acting that way this morning. No, there was none of her usual cheekiness. None of her teasing or her laughter. This morning she was so subdued that he worried she might be sick.

Not that he was complaining. The last thing he needed was to walk into a room with their new patient and have Sky pull one of her stunts, throwing him off his game.

The morning traffic had been heavy as the Nashville workforce started their day. They had been on the road for almost thirty minutes by the time they left Nashville and headed out of town on I-24 toward Clarksville to the ranch where the Carters had recently relocated. He'd spent his time concentrating on getting them safely through the snarl of traffic, but now that they had left the city, the silence surrounding them was deafening. He needed to say something, but he didn't know what. He wasn't a casual conversationalist. He spoke when he needed to. He greeted the office and hospital staff every day. Sometimes he even joined in on the Monday morning college football debate. He even knew which staff members to avoid if Vanderbilt had lost their Saturday game.

But this one-on-one stuff? He wasn't good at it. And, like so many other things in his life, he had learned to avoid it.

"Have you ever met anyone famous?" Sky asked. Even though her question came from out of the blue, he was glad that one of them had finally broken the silence.

"I operated on the mayor's wife a few years ago," he said, though he'd be more likely to recognize the tumor he had removed from her than to recognize the woman, even if her picture was plastered on a roadside billboard.

"Hmm," Sky said. He glanced over to see her staring down at her hands. Her top lip was poked out and she was chewing on her bottom one. Seeing this vulnerable side of Sky bothered him. He was used to feeling out of place. Being shuffled from foster home to foster home after his grandmother's death, he'd never felt that there was a place for him. Even now, after being adopted by the kindest couple in the state of Tennessee, he still didn't know where he belonged. It was like something was off with him but he couldn't put his finger on what it was, nor could he figure out how to correct it.

"Nervous about meeting the Carters?" he asked, though that didn't make sense. She was always so confident.

And why was he suddenly so worried about Sky and her feelings? He didn't do feelings. Feelings just complicated things. It was just another sign that this plan of his father's for them to work together was doomed.

"I just don't want to embarrass the practice," Sky said, before turning toward the window.

"I'm sure they put their cowboy boots on the same way everyone else does," he said as he followed his car's GPS instructions and took the next exit.

"Maybe," she said, still sounding nothing like the midwife he was used to dealing with.

"What's wrong? I thought you were excited about this," Jared said, though he told himself he needed to stop with the questioning. He had already passed the point of casual conversation.

"I am, kind of. I just don't know what to expect. What if they're not the nice couple everybody says they are? What if they're really stuck-up? What if they don't like me?"

"Why would you think that?" Was it possible that the flamboyantly outgoing Sky was having some type of confidence crisis? "Your patients always love you. That's why we're here today."

"I'm being silly. Of course they'll like me," she said before letting out an exaggerated sigh. Jared wasn't sure if she was trying to convince him or herself.

Then she sat up straighter and seemed to relax as she continued to stare out at where the cityscape had turned to open fields. "Oh, isn't this pretty? It's hard to believe we're only a few miles from the city."

Jared took his own deep breath, relieved that she'd moved on from all her misgivings. He had enough of his own to worry about.

"This must be it," she said, straining her neck to see the sign stating they had arrived at The Midnight Ranch. A plain dirt road ran between two fenced-in fields, then disappeared around a curve of trees. "Look, they have horses."

Three horses, one black and two a rusty brown, stopped their grazing and watched the car as it passed. Sky turned around in her seat to admire them, her body almost vibrating with excitement. This was more like the Sky he was used to dealing with.

"I've always thought that horses live a great life. Just look at the three of them. Wouldn't it be nice to have the freedom they have?" Sky asked.

"I guess they have a good life. Most are fed and cared for. Of course, they're really not that free. It's not like they are let loose to roam. They have to stay behind a fence." Jared had never given a horse's life much thought, but Sky was probably right—if their owners cared for them, they had a pretty safe life.

"I hadn't thought about that. I wonder if they resent looking over the railing at the pasture next door and not being able to get to it," Sky said, turning back around in her seat.

Jared hadn't meant to take away her enjoyment of seeing the horses. "We all have to live with boundaries."

"But most of the time, at least when we are adults, we set our own boundaries," Sky said, her voice dropping to almost a whisper. "I think that's worse than having others do that to us."

The pain in Sky's voice surprised him. If anyone lived life without boundaries, it was her.

A few yards farther down the winding drive they came to a wrought iron gate.

"Smile for the camera," Jared said as he rolled down the truck's window to punch in the code the Carters' manager had emailed to him.

Before he could stop her, Sky undid her seat belt and crawled over the truck console, her body brushing against his as she leaned out of his window. She was almost sitting in his lap and his body reacted immediately, his arms coming around her waist to keep her from falling out onto the road. The smile she gave the camera was one of her one-thousand-watt smiles. It was the same smile she would send him across the nurses' station that he knew she gave him to make him uncomfortable. It was a smile so beautiful that it took his breath away. His body hardened under her, and his arms tightened around her on instinct. "Don't you think you should at least wait for the reality show before you start performing?"

"I was just having a bit of fun? Maybe you should try it before you start criticizing me. You might find you like it," she said as she moved back into her seat, his arms falling away from her and his body suddenly cold without the warmth of hers.

He'd regretted the words the moment he'd said them. She was right. She was just being her normal self. It wasn't her fault that he'd responded to her the way he had. He straightened in his seat, refusing to let himself dwell on that unwanted need he'd felt to close his arms around her. It didn't make sense. It was almost laughable.

And laugh was what she'd do if she knew just what having his hands on her had done to him. Halfway around the next curve, he was glad to see the house come into view. He needed to get out of the truck and put some distance between the two of them.

It was two stories with an outside balcony running the length of the top floor. With large cedar posts and a front porch that ran the length of the house, Jared could tell that the architect had tried to create the look of a simple country home, but the size of the house made that almost impossible. Just the grandeur of the tall, double-glass front doors spoke of luxury that was way out of Jared's price range.

"Wow," Sky said, her voice low as if someone might be listening. "If my grandmamma could just see this."

Jared didn't know anything about Sky's grandmother, but he knew his own grandmother would never believe that he had been invited to a house this grand. Still, he'd give anything to have been driving Nana Marie up to this big house. Just to be able to show her that he'd done it. He'd made something of his life. Not that this represented his life... His life was more simple, quiet and safe. But most of all, *his*. He'd never have to worry about someone taking his home away from him. And that was the most important thing to him.

But still, his nana would have enjoyed this. All of this. She'd followed all the country music stars when she'd been alive, yet she'd never met one, even though a lot of them lived just minutes away from her. She was too busy working and raising him. Then she'd been too sick to leave the house, but somehow she'd still taken care of him. He'd once told her that when he was grown and rich he'd buy her the nicest house in Nashville. His five-year-old brain hadn't even known someplace like this existed.

As his truck came to a stop behind a black SUV parked in the circular drive, a woman whose gray hair was piled as high as the heels she was wearing rushed down the front porch stairs toward them. With bright red lipstick that matched her suit, she marched toward them with an intensity that made Jared want to put the truck in Reverse and speed back down the road toward town.

"Who do you think that is?" Sky asked, showing no signs of being intimidated by the woman.

"A fire-breathing dragon?" Jared questioned as he unbuckled his seat belt and opened the door.

Sky looked over at him and laughed as she undid her own buckle. Her eyes danced with the humor she was known for. "Don't worry. If she starts spitting fire I'll protect you."

He was pleased to see that she was back to her normal ridiculousness after recovering from her earlier dip in confidence—which didn't make sense, as he'd always found this flirty, flippant side of her irritating.

Before the two of them could make it around to the front of the truck, the woman in red bore down on them, waving a stack of papers in their faces. "I need your signatures on these nondisclosure forms before I can allow you inside."

"Marjorie, can you at least let them come inside before you start hounding them with all that privacy nonsense?" a young woman called after her.

Jared looked up to the front door, where a young woman, no more than twenty-five or -six, stood with her arms resting on her rounded abdomen. Dressed as she was in jeans and a T-shirt, with her long, blond hair flowing over her shoulders, he could have passed her on the street and never known she was one of country music's fastest rising stars.

"It's not nonsense, Mindy. You have to stop thinking

like an amateur singer. The information these two will have could be worth a lot. We can't have them going around spilling information about you and Trey to the public."

"I think the physician-patient relationship covers that," Jared said as he headed up the stairs to meet their new patient, ignoring the irritating woman and her papers who had just insulted both him and Sky with her demands.

"I'm sorry," Mindy Carter said as she held out a slender hand to him and then to Sky, who had followed him up the stairs.

"Marjorie means well. It's just that all this," the young woman said, holding out her arms, "came at us really fast and we haven't been able to catch our breath in the last few months. She takes her responsibility as our agent very seriously."

"It's very serious business," the woman said when she caught up with them, her breath labored as she climbed the last step. "You can't trust everybody here like you could at home. And the reality show is just making the media more gossip hungry."

"Aunt Marj, it's okay. The Legacy Clinic has a great reputation," a man Jared recognized as Trey Carter said as he stepped outside to join them.

"That's right, Miss Marjorie, and the two of us are thrilled to have this opportunity to take care of your family." Sky stepped toward the woman and offered her hand, her smile showing none of the dread that Jared felt.

"Look at us keeping the two of you standing out here. Please come in and I'll get you both something to drink,"

Mindy said. "We appreciate you coming here to talk to us. I know most doctors don't make house calls anymore."

"How about I get us all some iced tea and you sit down and rest?" Trey suggested, holding the door open for them to enter.

Jared stepped into the foyer, following Sky, and was surprised to see that it opened straight into a sitting area surrounding a massive stone fireplace. Across the room there was a table that could fit twenty easily, but still the room seemed comfortable enough with no sign of the glitz and glamour he had been expecting.

"You are not allowed to mention anything about Mindy and Trey's home to anyone until after the latest reality taping is aired tomorrow night," Marjorie said as she followed them into the sitting area and took a seat, not waiting for them to sit before raising those insulting forms at them again. "These aren't just to cover Mindy and Trey. The producer of *Carters' Way* is insisting on them too."

"Oh, we understand perfectly your concerns," Sky said, her voice dripping with a sweetness he hadn't known she possessed. "We'll be happy to take them with us and have the practice's legal team review them. But I think we can all agree that the most important thing we discuss today is Mindy and her baby. Don't you think?"

And as if Sky had performed a miracle, or an exorcism, the woman's eyes softened and she smiled for the first time. "Of course, nothing is as important as Mindy and the baby."

The doorbell rang and the woman immediately sprang

into action, flying off her seat and heading to the door. "That should be the party planner."

"I know she's a bit much," Trey said as he set a tray with the tea glasses down on the short table beside one of the couches, "but she's just being protective. Once she gets to know you, she'll calm down. And if she likes you, she'll be just as protective toward you. She's really just a super animated teddy bear. Her bites are rare and her love is genuine."

Jared stared at the man, taken aback by words that could have described the grandmother he had just been thinking of earlier. "I understand. You're lucky to have her."

"So, Mindy, how have you been feeling?" Jared asked, changing the subject when Sky turned toward him, uncomfortable with the way she was studying him.

"I'm good," Mindy said, rubbing her hands over her abdomen.

"We received your records from your doctor and they show your due date as August 1, which would make you almost twenty-eight weeks. Does that sound right?" Sky asked.

"I'll be twenty-eight weeks this Thursday," Mindy said, moving to sit closer to Trey as he took the seat next to her.

For the next half hour they discussed everything from Mindy's medical history to her birth plan. When they came to her history of a miscarriage the year before, Jared saw Trey wrap his arm around his wife. It appeared that Trey's aunt wasn't the only one in the family that was protective. It was very evident that the relationship the couple shared wasn't just something they pretended for the cameras. They seemed to have the kind of bond that Jared never understood. In theory, yes, he understood the human need for companionship. But to trust someone with that much of yourself? To risk losing someone again? No, that was definitely not something he was capable of doing.

So why did looking at the two of them make him feel empty in a way he'd never felt before?

"They're a cute couple," Sky said, as he started the truck to head back to town. "I don't think we'll have any trouble working with them."

"I guess," he said.

"Didn't you like them?" she asked. She'd turned toward him. It always made him feel uncomfortable, being the focus of all her attention.

He'd watched her with Mindy while she'd done most of the questioning, which had really been an informal health review. She was naturally good with people. He wasn't sure if she interacted with other people like she normally did with him, though somehow he doubted it. It seemed he caught most of her unwanted attention whenever they were in a room together. She just couldn't help but try to get a rise out of him, as if there was some perverse part of her that liked to make him uncomfortable, though he didn't understand why.

But she hadn't been that way today. Today she'd acted professional, something he very much appreciated.

"It's not important that we like them. It's just important that we give Mindy and the baby the best of care, which is something I'm sure we will do."

"Thank you," Sky said, giving him one of those big smiles that always sent a spark of unwanted pleasure through him.

"What are you thanking me for?" He forced his eyes back to the road that led off the ranch, but not before he saw the lovely way her eyes mirrored her smile.

"For trusting me. For having faith in me. In us. I know you have a problem working with midwives."

His hands tightened on the steering wheel. He didn't want to relive the reason he had trust issues with midwives. Did Sky somehow know his history? Did she know that it had been a midwife that had delivered him? That while he'd taken his first breath his mother had been bleeding to death? He didn't want to expose that secret part of his life. It was his own private pain to endure. "I don't have a problem working with midwives. I just want to be available and prepared if I'm needed."

"Whatever," she said, shrugging her shoulders as if it didn't matter that he didn't want to discuss it with her. "What did you think about the request to interview us on the reality show? I think it would be a great chance to give Legacy House a plug if we can work it into the conversation. It could bring in donations from all across the country."

He was glad she'd changed the subject, though it was another one he didn't want to think about. He had to agree that it would be good to get more revenue coming into the home to lift some of the pressure from his father. And with everything his dad had done for him, it was a small thing to have to answer a few questions for the show.

"I don't understand why they call it a reality show. In what world is the Carters' life a reality? If they want a real reality show they need to have a show about an exhausted mom and dad who go to work every day for minimum wage so they can come home and sit around the table with their kids and worry about how they are going to pay the bills." At least, that was the reality that he'd seen when he was a kid in foster care. He hadn't been dreaming of a big house with huge fireplaces and horses running around in pastures. He'd just wanted to know there was someone out there who'd make sure he got his next meal.

"I guess people wouldn't find that entertaining enough. Though if they'd had a hidden camera at my grandma's house when me and my siblings had been growing up," Sky said, her voice filled with laughter, "we could have entertained the whole country with our antics at the dinner table. My grandma could have won an award just for all the ways she could cook the deer sausage my uncle Ben brought us. Not that we complained. We were just happy to get a meal."

"What about your parents? They wouldn't have wanted to be on your reality show?" he asked.

Sky's laughter died and Jared knew he'd asked the wrong question. But then, as suddenly as her laughter had stopped, it started again. "My parents couldn't take the reality of raising seven kids. If it hadn't been for my mom's mother we would have been homeless."

Jared sat up a little straighter. Was it really possible that he and Sky had come from such similar situations? Yet here she was laughing about her childhood while his memories before the Warners had adopted him were anything but humorous.

"How do you do that?" he asked, before he could stop himself.

"Do what?"

"You talk about your parents leaving you when you were a child, and it sounds like things weren't easy at your grandmother's house, but you just laugh it all off. How can you do that?" Maybe the question was a little personal, but he couldn't help himself. He had never understood Sky's happy-go-lucky lifestyle. For some reason, now that he'd learned more about her, it was suddenly very important that he did.

Sky didn't answer him for more than a few moments, and he wasn't sure that she was going to. He looked over to see her chewing on her bottom lip again, deep in thought. Then she took a deep breath and began. "I can't deny that at one time I was bitter about my childhood. I acted out as most teenagers do, I think, but now that I look back on it, I was mostly just angry. Living in a small town where everyone knew that we had been dumped by our parents wasn't easy on me or my siblings. Not that times had been easy before my parents left us.

"No one wants to feel that they were unwanted. But my grandmother was a special woman. When our parents left us, I was angry and scared. We didn't know her well. Our mom had only taken us to see her mom a couple times that I could remember. But from the moment we got there she acted like having us dumped on her was the best thing that had ever happened in her life."

Jared could definitely relate to that feeling. "So you just got over it?"

"I wouldn't say I got over it as much as I decided that I wasn't going to let their actions determine how I spent the rest of my life. Not that it was something that happened overnight. Life isn't that easy. Right when you feel like everything is going your way, there's always something, or someone, who decides you don't deserve to be happy."

Jared looked over to see Sky staring out the window. "Why do I feel like you are leaving something out?"

Sky turned and gave him a smile that was filled with more sadness than happiness. He'd never known that a smile could be so sad, and he didn't like seeing it on her face at all.

"I'm sorry. I didn't mean to make you uncomfortable."

His words sounded ridiculous even to himself. All his questions had been uncomfortable. He was asking her to share things with him that he didn't have the right to know. What had he been thinking? Was he so self-absorbed in trying to figure her out that he'd not considered her feelings? He certainly hadn't wanted to drag out all his own painful history for her to sort through.

"It's okay. And it isn't something I left out. It's someone." Sky sat up straighter beside him. He saw her chin had gone up and her eyes were staring straight ahead.

She looked like someone preparing for a head-on battle. "I was engaged, or at least promised to be engaged, to my high school boyfriend. After graduation, he wanted to go off to college but all I could afford was community college. I thought everything was going great. I had gotten into the local nursing school and he was in pre-med. We had made plans for the future. Then, suddenly, he changed. The calls and messages just stopped. His first visit home, he brought a girl with him."

Jared glanced over at her. Her eyes had gone from hurt to hard and her lips were sealed so tight that he wasn't sure she'd ever smile again. "When I cornered him and asked him what was going on, he seemed shocked to think I had really expected him to abide by all the promises we had made to each other. Apparently, I wasn't good enough for the new life he'd planned. He didn't need a backwoods wife. He needed someone he could be proud of."

Jared's hands tightened again on the steering wheel. He'd had enough humiliating remarks aimed at him as a child to recognize the pain she felt. And he knew it didn't go away. You carried those scars with you for the rest of your life—though looking at Sky you would never know that she had been hurt that way. "You know that he was wrong, right? Any man would be proud of you."

"Maybe. But I know something even better now. I know it doesn't matter what a man thinks of me. What matters is that I'm proud of myself."

Jared's hands relaxed. He liked her observation better than his own.

"So yeah, that's my sad story. I've had some knocks in life, but haven't we all? I just choose to not let them hold me down. Life is short. I choose to enjoy it as much as possible and I think the key to that is having a positive attitude. And if some days I don't feel like smiling, I smile anyhow. There's a reason they say fake it till you make it. Besides, even though most people would think my life was hard, I wasn't alone. You're never alone when you have as many siblings as I do."

He spent the rest of the ride home listening to Sky tell stories of her and her family's escapades in the Tennessee mountains. She'd been more open and honest with him than he'd ever been with anyone. He'd never even confided about his life before the adoption to his own mother, the most caring woman he'd ever met. How was it that Sky could reveal such a painful thing about her past so easily?

Once they arrived back at the office, Jared was glad to get to work. Their house call to celebrity music stars had the office backed up with patients, so he grabbed a chart off his first examination room door and went to work.

It wasn't until later that night when he'd finally finished rounds and made it home that he let himself think about what Sky had told him about her family. For some reason he'd always assumed that Sky, with her over-the-top, happy-go-lucky nature, had come from one of those picture-perfect worlds. Somehow, finding that she'd survived the life she'd described that morning, while laughing through it all, gave him a new respect for her, though he wasn't sure about her statement about faking it. That didn't seem healthy to him. How long were you expected to fake it? Wasn't it better to deal with your feelings?

Not that he'd dealt with his own in a very healthy way. He didn't need a counselor to tell him that he let his past hold him back—his father had been telling him that for years. Yet now, hearing Sky's story, he found himself wanting to move past all those barriers he'd sealed himself behind.

But what then? What would happen if he let go of all the pain and loss he'd experienced as a child? What could his life be like if he chose to live like Sky? Jared had faced a lot in his life, but he knew that the possibility of letting go of the past and moving forward was the scariest thing he had ever considered doing.

CHAPTER FOUR

Sky stared with more interest than was appropriate as one jean-clad leg followed the other one down the ladder from the Legacy House attic. She didn't need to see the brown head of hair that eventually followed the hard muscled body as he climbed farther down the stairs to know that they belonged to Jared. She'd seen his truck outside when she'd arrived. She'd known he was here. But knowing that Jared was here and then being treated to this version of Jared was not the same. This version of Jared looked nothing like he did in his white lab jacket, which was always neatly pressed and buttoned all the way up to its stiff collar. This Jared was much more interesting.

As he wiped his dust-covered hands against the sides of his jeans, she had the outrageous urge to reach out and brush those streaks of dirt off him. When he turned toward her, she clasped her hands behind her back just in case they decided to go rogue and get her into trouble.

"Good morning, Jared," she said, making sure her voice was filled with as much of her normal morning cheer as possible even while her heart rate was climbing up into the danger zone. She stared up into those deep brown eyes that were always so serious and couldn't help but wonder if she would ever know the real Jared. Even today, with his clothes covered in dirt, there was a tense line etched between his eyes as he studied her. After all she'd shared with him earlier in the week, she'd thought he'd be more relaxed around her.

"What are you doing here?" he asked.

"I brought some donated maternity clothes that I received from one of my patients. What about you? Looking for ghosts in the attic?"

He lifted an eyebrow. Yeah, it was a stupid question. Jared wasn't someone who would spend his time ghost hunting. It was more something that Sky herself might do. Well, maybe not ghost hunting, but she would enjoy going through any old trunks that might be stored in the attic.

"There's a problem with one of the electrical outlets in the living room. It looks like a squirrel or a rat might have gotten in and chewed on some wires. I'm going to get an electrician out here today to deal with it."

Okay, maybe searching through the attic wasn't a good idea.

A girl carrying a laundry basket came through the hallway and Sky moved to the side to let her get around them.

"Hey, Jasmine. How are you feeling?" Jared asked, the lines between his eyebrows coming together into a small knot now as he concentrated on the girl. Sky looked closer at the young woman who couldn't be more than eighteen. There were dark shadows below her brown eyes and her face had that puffy, swollen look that no midwife wanted to see. Her stomach was rounded and by its size she appeared to be in her third trimester.

The girl gave Sky a look that wasn't very trusting. "I'm Sky. I'm a midwife that works with Dr. Warner."

"I'm fine," Jasmine said, her voice flat. With her experience dealing with teenage patients, Sky knew that the word *fine* was used to give only the most limited amount of information. There was something off with Jasmine though. Her eyes weren't just tired, they were empty, something that Sky didn't normally see in healthy young girls who were expecting.

"Are you taking the blood pressure medicine I prescribed?" Jared asked.

"Yeah, Ms. Mason gives it to me every morning and checks my blood pressure twice a day just like you asked. But it makes me feel tired," Jasmine said, shuffling her feet and hitching the basket onto her hip.

"I'll talk to Maggie and see if she can bring you in to see me tomorrow. I might need to adjust your medications," Jared said, once again aware of how lucky they were to have someone as devoted to her job as house manager as Maggie Mason. "And we'll get another scan on the baby."

Jasmine's lips turned up in a half smile at the mention of the baby before she walked past them. She got to the end of the hall, then turned back toward them. "Thanks, Dr. Warner."

Sky waited till Jasmine had turned the corner and disappeared. "What's going on with her?"

Jared folded the ladder back up into the attic opening. "Physically, her blood pressure has been climbing for the last month. Mentally, I'm not sure. I can't get her to talk to me about it. I've asked her if she wants to talk to a counselor or if she would like another doctor, but she says no. It was one of the reasons I came by today. I want to check if Maggie has any idea what's going on with Jasmine."

The door to the attic slammed as Jared pushed it shut with more force than was necessary. This was the closest she had ever seen Jared to losing his temper. He really was worried about the girl.

"How about I talk to her?" Sky asked.

Jared looked down at her, his body close to hers in the small hallway. For a moment she forgot what they'd been talking about. Those rogue hands of hers wanted to reach out and walk down all those hard muscles clearly outlined by his shirt. It was a normal reaction by a woman attracted to a man, this need to touch that she was experiencing. With another man she might have expressed her interest.

But this was Jared. The only games she was allowed to play with him had to be silent and mostly platonic since they'd always been in the workplace. And most of the time he didn't even seem to enjoy those.

So why was she standing there ogling the man? It had to be this new relationship outside of the clinic that was causing all this confusion inside her. Yes, she'd admit, at least to herself, that she was attracted to Jared.

And though she had always told herself that she just liked to tease him, there was a part of her that wanted him to notice her. To look at her, the woman, not the midwife. She'd been thinking about him ever since they'd visited the Carters. She'd told him almost all of her life story, something that had probably surprised her more than him. She didn't share her past with many people. She'd been judged for being abandoned and coming from almost nothing for most of her life, so now she refused to have people look at her with pity or judgment.

But Jared had done neither of those things. He'd even taken up for her, letting her know that her ex, Daniel, had been wrong, and expressing his belief that she was someone to be proud of.

She realized that she'd been staring at him for too long when his head tilted to the side, studying her deeply. "I mean… I'd like to help her and she might talk to me since I'm not involved with her care. How old is she? She looks so young. Well, everything but her eyes looked young. Her eyes are sad. Empty."

"She's seventeen. You see it too?" Jared asked, as if surprised that she could see that the girl was hurting.

"Yeah. Something is bothering her. She's due in what, three months?"

"She's almost thirty-two weeks. The baby has some intrauterine growth restriction. Another reason I'm worried about her," Jared said.

"I'm going to help Maggie today with some of the heavy cleaning. I'll try to talk to Jasmine. It's a lot to be pregnant and seventeen. I assume that she doesn't have a lot of support from her parents if she's living here." Sky tried not to judge Jasmine's parents. She remembered when her own sister had become pregnant at seventeen. It had been Sky that had been the most upset with Jill.

The last thing Sky had wanted for her sister was to be in a situation where she was responsible for a child she was unable to care for. But their grandmother, even after spending the last ten years of her life raising them, had supported Sky's sister.

"Her mother came to the first few appointments with her. They seemed close. But then Jasmine asked me about moving into Legacy House. She's never told me what happened. And I haven't asked Maggie if she knew. I didn't want to make Jasmine feel like she couldn't trust her."

Sky was surprised by just how intuitive Jared was being. He'd always appeared so disconnected. Not uncaring—she'd seen him worry over his patients just like the rest of them did—he just didn't let very many people into his life. Or at least that was how it seemed to her. It could be he had a legion of girlfriends he left every morning when he headed to work.

Okay, that was ridiculous and it might have come from a bit of jealousy that she would prefer to ignore. Besides, whether or not he had women in his life wasn't the point. It was the fact that he seemed to hold himself back from being involved with the people he saw every day. People like her.

Maybe he just didn't find regular people interesting. Maybe that was why he tended to keep to himself. Or maybe he was actually studying them all. Maybe that was why he'd questioned her about her attitude toward her life.

She shook her head and tried to concentrate on the issues Jasmine might be having. That was what was important now. Not Sky's own insecurities. "I'll see what

I can find out. And if there's some way for me to help her, I will. She might just need some reassurance that Legacy House will be here for her. If it's an issue with her parents… Well, I might not be the person to talk to but I'll find someone to help her. If nothing else, I can be a friend to her. Someone she can reach out to if she needs someone."

"Right now the most important thing is to keep her blood pressure under control. If the medication doesn't help I'm going to put her on bed rest."

They started down the hall to the kitchen, where Sky knew she would find Maggie and some of the other staff preparing lunch. They'd been lucky to find someone like Maggie to run the home after the original manager, Mrs. Hudson, had retired. Maggie had spent most of her nursing career working in the office with the elder Dr. Warner. The fact that Maggie was her best friend Lori's mom made it even better.

Sky's phone pinged with a message and she pulled it from her pocket. She read the message twice, making sure she understood what Mindy was asking before she let out a squeal. "You are not going to believe this," she said to Jared, her hand coming out and grabbing his arm to stop him. "Mindy and Trey want us to come to the party they are having tomorrow night. The one Marjorie said all the country music stars were coming to."

She looked at Jared and saw none of the excitement she was feeling. "You have to come. The invitation is for the two of us. Together."

Still, he just stood there and looked at her.

"Please?"

His shoulders slumped and she knew she'd won. She squealed again and threw her arms around his neck. His body tensed under hers, but she didn't care.

She, Sky Benton, from so far back in the hills of Tennessee that they had to pipe in sunshine, was going to an A-list party with all the music stars of Nashville. And she wasn't going to let Jared Warner ruin it.

CHAPTER FIVE

SKY WAS SPEECHLESS. After not being able to stop herself from talking nonstop on her first trip with Jared to Mindy and Trey's home, now she didn't know what to say. Her speechlessness surprised even her. She always knew what to say—or at least knew how to fake it. But this? This was too amazing. It was a dream come true for a little girl whose grandmother had listened to the *Grand Ole Opry* on the radio on Saturday nights.

The welcoming but overly large room she'd sat in just days earlier was filled with people. Some were people she'd seen on countless music award shows and others she recognized from the Carters' reality show. Some of the men were dressed in fancy suits while others wore jeans and cowboy hats. The women were dressed both casually and formally too.

And while Jared was dressed in an appropriate, if somewhat subdued, black suit, Sky had decided to go all out. With Lori's help, she'd found the perfect dress at a downtown boutique. Navy blue with a fitted bodice and a short flared skirt, the dress had enough glitter on it to make her feel glamorous and ready to party. It was a standout dress. One she had thought would give her the confidence she needed tonight.

Except now that she was here, seeing all of these beautiful, talented people, her confidence had disappeared as her memories of the past kept telling her that she didn't belong here. She did her best to shake them off.

"So, where do we start?" she asked Jared, glad to have him at her back. She'd been alone when she'd arrived in town after leaving her small hometown hospital. She'd never been to a city as big as Nashville before. But she hadn't run home then and she wasn't about to run home now. She'd decided that life was for living, not holding yourself back because you didn't believe you deserved something. This was a once-in-a-lifetime opportunity for her. She would not look back later with regret.

Before Jared could answer, she saw Mindy headed their way and Sky took a step toward her. After the first step, it seemed the next came easier. She could do this.

"I'm so glad you could come," Mindy said. Dressed in a flowing silver dress that accentuated her rounded abdomen, she was the most beautiful woman in the room.

"We're glad to be here," Sky said, taking hold of Jared's arm as that "I definitely don't belong here" feeling returned.

"Come in," Trey said as he joined his wife, wrapping his arm around her waist before holding out a hand to Jared. "Our producer was just asking about you. I promised to introduce the two of you."

"You're beginning to act like Marjorie. They just arrived. Can't they have a few minutes before you and Joe start talking business?" Mindy asked her husband.

"It's fine," Jared said. "I have some questions about the show and the interview they want to do that I wanted to talk to you about."

Mindy let out a heavy sigh, then linked her arm in Sky's. "Let me get you a drink and show you around. Don't get me wrong, I love Joe, but you'll get to meet him later. There are a lot more interesting people here that you need to meet."

Sky let go of Jared's arm and let Mindy pull her into the middle of the room. She looked back at Jared, who was already deep in conversation with Trey. She'd thought it would be Jared feeling out of place here, not her, but she'd been wrong. Of course, Jared had been raised in Nashville. Maybe that was why he wasn't showing signs of being starstruck like she was.

Just when she thought she'd gotten control of her nervousness about being around so many talented people, she was swallowed up into a crowd of the who's who of Nashville. There were singers and famous band members. There was even a Tennessee senator. Everywhere Sky looked, she saw another person she recognized from a video she'd enjoyed or a song she'd just been singing along with on the radio. By the time Mindy pulled her into the kitchen area, Sky was in celebrity overload.

"Would you like a drink?" Mindy asked her. "The bar is open in the family room, but I've got water and Cokes here."

"A water is fine," Sky said, taking a seat at the island, relieved to get away from the noise for a moment. "I'm sorry to pull you away from your guests."

"I need the break," Mindy said, taking the seat beside hers. "It's our first party to host in Nashville and I love it, but I don't think I was truly prepared for it."

"I can't imagine what the last year has been like for you. You have your first number one album. Your move to a new city. And then all the touring with the pregnancy. How do you do it all?"

"It's been wild, but it's the kind of crazy that we both love. And Trey has done everything he can to make it easier on me. Especially since the pregnancy. After the miscarriage he was very supportive, insisting that we decrease our tours for the next couple of months. But then everything took off. We had our first number one hit and we had to run with it. It was what we both had been working for and there wasn't a guarantee we'd get another chance."

Sky couldn't help but be a little envious of the relationship Mindy and Trey shared. What would it be like to have someone looking out for you? Someone who would be there when you got home? Someone you could count on? Someone you could share a dream with? But most importantly, someone you could trust not to break your heart? Sky had trusted her heart to someone before and she wasn't sure if she would ever have the courage to do that again.

Not that she had any right to complain. She dated often enough. She just made sure the other person always knew that she was only looking to have fun.

"We'd planned to wait a while before getting pregnant again after the miscarriage," Mindy said, rubbing her abdomen, "but this little one was meant to be. They're our special rainbow baby. The best surprise we could ever have hoped for. That's why we don't want to know the sex of the baby. We feel it should be a surprise until they're here."

Sky believed that all babies were special, but there was something so bittersweet about the babies that followed the loss of another child. "I love that. And you can trust that neither Jared nor I will share that information."

"I know. Jenny told me what a great experience she had with you as her midwife, but I was still nervous about meeting you."

"Why?" Sky asked. It had been only natural for her to be nervous about meeting someone like Mindy and Trey. They were stars. But her? She was just a simple midwife from nowhere Tennessee.

Mindy sighed and leaned back in her chair. "I knew that things were going to change if we ever made it to the top of the charts. And then there was the reality show. We'd just started to have a small amount of success when we agreed to the show. We were prepared to lose some of our privacy, but I wasn't prepared for the way the people around us changed."

Sky remembered how her friends and even some of her family acted when she'd made the decision to leave her hometown and head to the big city. She'd never understood why they couldn't see that there was nothing for her there. She'd been made to feel like she was letting them down even though they knew how hard it was to watch her ex walk around with the woman whom he'd decided fit his needs for a wife better than her.

"When a friend of mine let it out that I was pregnant, the media went crazy. We were so happy about the pregnancy, but we didn't want to share it yet. We'd just got over the media attention that my miscarriage received, and I'd made it plain to everyone who we told that I didn't want to share the pregnancy. Not yet, at least. We knew it would have to come out with the reality show and everything, but we wanted to wait. I guess I just didn't feel I could trust someone after that. But when I met you and Jared, you made me feel better. You were interested in me, Mindy, not Mindy Carter of the Carters. Does that make sense?"

"It makes perfect sense, and I'm sorry someone you thought you could trust let you down that way. I hope you know now that you can trust me. My goal is always to put mother and baby first. That's why I have a frank talk with all my patients as far as their birth plan. Your health and that of the baby will come first for me and Jared. Where they come from, their background, that's not a priority." Sky stopped to take a sip of her water.

"About Jared," Mindy said, "I hope it doesn't bother you that we asked to have the two of you work together. I really want a midwife to care for me, but Trey wanted to go the traditional route."

"It doesn't bother me. Jared and I are both happy to work with the two of you," Sky said. This was pretty much what Jack had told her and Jared the day he'd first spoken to them about Mindy and Trey. While Sky knew that some midwives would have been insulted by the request, she hadn't been. She knew that she could provide the care that Mindy and her baby would need. She'd reviewed Mindy's records closely and there were no risk factors that would keep Mindy from having a midwifery delivery. But if Trey needed the reassurance of Jared being involved, that was okay too.

"About you and Jared," Mindy said, her eyes lighting up with humor, "am I imagining that there's something there besides work going on between the two of you?"

For the second time that night, she was speechless. She took a big gulp of water, paying close attention to swallow it without choking, then set the bottle down. She liked Mindy but she didn't know her well enough to admit her secret attraction to Jared. She wouldn't even admit that to Lori. "We're colleagues. That's all."

It was the truth, yet she felt a small amount of guilt for not admitting to her unexpected interest in Jared. Mindy had been open with her about her fears and how someone had let her down. It had been more than just the normal patient-and-provider sharing of information. This had been more personal.

There was something about Mindy that put Sky at ease. And it had helped put all the absurdity of the crowd in the other rooms into perspective for her. Not too long ago, Mindy was just a normal person working to make her dream come true, just like Sky had been when she'd worked to become a midwife. How many of the people out there surrounded now by fame and fortune had started just like the two of them? Like Jared had said, they put their cowboy boots on just like she did.

"Thank you for helping me get over my nervousness tonight." Sky set her bottle down again and turned to Mindy. "I'm not usually like this. It's just…my world is so much different than this. This is…"

"Extreme?" Mindy asked, standing and taking Sky's arm again.

"Yes!" Sky said as they headed back into the crowd, this time feeling more confident. "So, let's go get crazy too."

Jared looked over the crowd, trying to find Sky. He'd had a good talk with the producer of the Carters' reality show. While Sky didn't seem to have any problem being on the show, he didn't like the idea of opening up his personal life to the public. He knew it wasn't like he or Sky were going to be featured except for the small part of being health care providers for Mindy. Still, he'd made the producer promise that there would be no unnecessary information given out about the two of them. With the handsome donation the producer had agreed to for Legacy House, Jared knew he'd made the best of the situation that he could. They'd do an interview or two and it would be over with. Now he just needed to find Sky so they could leave.

Sometime since he'd left the party to join the producer Joe and Trey in his office, a band had set up. The music was good, of course—he wouldn't expect anything less with the caliber of musicians in the room. When a man he recognized as a Hall of Fame singer joined in with his own guitar, Jared stopped to listen for a moment. His own hands itched to feel those guitar strings under his fingers. To feel the vibration of the music flow into him along with the emotions it brought him.

When the song ended and the applause started, he made his way back through the crowd to the other side of the room, where a dance floor had been set up. The band started back with a line dance favorite from the 1990s and it only took him a minute to spot Sky among the dancers. Then he recognized the man she was smiling at beside her. Nick Thomas was a local boy who'd formed one of the top bands in the city. He hadn't gained the fame that most of the people in the room had, but from the local media reviews it was only time before his band hit it big.

But it wasn't Nick that held Jared's attention. It was Sky. And it wasn't the way her short skirt twirled around her shapely legs as she danced or the way her head of blond curls bounced with her movements. It was her smile. That happy, wide-mouthed smile that made him want to join her in the dance. That made him want to pull her to him and swing her around and around with the rhythm of the music until they both were breathless.

The song ended and she said something to Nick, then turned toward him. He knew the moment she saw him as their eyes locked and her smile changed to that mischievous one she loved to tempt him with. His body tensed with an edginess he'd never felt before as she walked slowly toward him. The crowd faded away as she took his hand and began pulling him toward the dance floor.

The band started to play a slow, sad song filled with the sweet strains of a fiddle.

"Dance with me," Sky said, her blue eyes sparkling with a fevered excitement that flowed over onto him.

He knew he shouldn't. This wasn't a date. They were there purely as professional colleagues. Nothing more.

But as her arms wrapped around his neck, his own arms found their way around her waist, pulling her closer. And when she laid her head against him, he let himself relax against her. What could it hurt to share one dance?

It only took a minute for his body to answer that question. It was as if a fire had been lit inside him as his body reacted to the feel of Sky against him. His muscles tightened and he went stone hard. He tried to keep his breathing as even as possible as they swayed to the music, her body rubbing against him with each movement. He glanced down and their eyes met. As she drew in a breath that appeared as labored as his, his eyes went to her lips, the same lips that had teased him for months. For a moment he considered tasting them. Would they be soft and supple? Or would they be firm and needy? He had just started to lean down when the couple next to them bumped into him, breaking whatever spell he'd been under.

What could one dance hurt? It could destroy his whole reputation if he let himself lose control on the dance floor.

With a willpower he hadn't known he possessed, he pulled himself back from the brink of doing something that would scandalize the whole room. But when the song ended and she stepped away from him, his arms felt empty. It had only been one dance. The fact that her body had molded so perfectly to his didn't mean a thing. But he'd danced with many women before Sky and he'd never felt anything like this before.

"We should go," he said, though his traitorous feet refused to move.

"Why? Do we have plans?" she asked, her voice soft and breathy. His body responded as once more she stepped toward him.

He wanted to pull her back into his arms, to kiss that mouth that had teased him for the last six months. Only he couldn't kiss her now any more than he could have kissed her all those other times. He had to restrain himself just like he'd done over and over when she had tempted him. He needed to put things back to the way they'd been before that dance. Before he'd felt how right her body felt against his.

It should be simple. One step. Just take one step and walk away. But this was Sky. Nothing about the woman was simple. They constantly butted heads at work. She'd teased and tortured him for months with her sexy smile and sassy winks.

Someone tapped him on the shoulder and broke the spell that had held him captive. Turning, he saw that it was Nick standing behind him.

"If you aren't going to dance with the lady, I'd like to," Nick said, his oh-so perfect smile making Jared's teeth clench on the words he wanted to say.

"No. We were just leaving," Jared said, managing to

get the words out before taking Sky's hand and pulling her behind him.

It wasn't until they were at the door that he was reminded of where they were and why they'd come. None of this was supposed to be about him and Sky. Nor was the possessive way he'd just acted professional.

It sobered him to know how close he'd come to making a scene by telling Nick right where to shove his invitation. They were there to represent his father's practice and to help gain more donations for Legacy House. He remembered how beaten down his dad had looked when he'd shared that Legacy House could be in trouble financially. And Jared had almost blown everything, nearly embarrassed his dad in front of the very people whose help they needed. His father deserved a better son than that.

He let go of Sky's hand and took a physical step away as his brain took a figurative step back from the line his body had been prepared to cross.

"I'm sorry," he said. "I shouldn't have spoken for you. If you want to go back to Nick I understand."

Emotions bounced around inside of Sky like she was a pinball machine. Shock with a small amount of pleasure from the way Jared had reacted to Nick's interest in her. Anger at the way he'd spoken for her without giving her a chance to tell the other man she wasn't interested. And finally, the worst part, pain from the way he was now prepared to let her return to Nick after the intimate dance the two of them had just shared.

She looked across the room to see that Mindy was

involved in a conversation with one of last year's CMA winners. It felt rude to leave without thanking her for the invitation.

She looked over at the ramrod-straight statue that Jared had become and her anger pushed all of the other emotions out of its way. Stomping her high heeled feet through the crowd, she left Jared behind. She didn't care if he followed her or not.

She'd made it outside the house and halfway across the drive by the time Jared caught up with her. When he walked around to her side of the truck to open her door, she was already opening it. Changing her mind, she slammed it shut and turned on him.

"I don't understand you," she said, the truth of the statement hitting her hard. She didn't understand him because he had never let her get close enough. She'd been teasing this man for over six months now, trying to get a response out of him. Yes, she wanted to make him smile, but now she wondered if it had been more than that. The more time they spent together, the more she wondered if she'd been secretly wanting him to seek her out. To return her interest.

And for a few moments tonight, she'd thought he had been interested. Then the old Jared who she'd watched turn away from her over and over found that control he was famous for, leaving Sky now confused and hurt. Why couldn't the man just relax and enjoy the moment? Had he not felt that all-consuming need for her that she had felt for him? Had she been the only one who had experienced that magical moment on the dance floor?

"I was having so much fun." She wouldn't cry, not in front of him. She'd promised herself that she would never cry again when someone walked away from her, yet the tears felt so close now. "And then you ruined it. Why? Why couldn't you have just enjoyed the moment? Was it me? Was it something I did?"

"We didn't come here to dance," Jared said, his eyes emotionless and his body rigid as he ignored her questions.

How could this be the same man who had held her just minutes before? How could this be the same man whose body had reacted so eagerly to hers? Did he think she hadn't noticed the way his body had hardened against hers? Hadn't he felt the way she'd melted against the heat of him?

"Well, maybe you didn't, but I did."

"We were supposed to represent the practice and try to get donations," he said, his stern jaw turning up in challenge.

"We were supposed to blend in with the crowd while representing the practice and earning some goodwill for Legacy House. That was what I was doing with Nick. He's a good friend of Mindy and Trey's. They'd told him about what the home does to help local women. He's from Nashville. He was interested in helping."

"It wasn't Legacy House he was interested in on the dance floor. That wasn't why he wanted to dance with you."

"He wasn't the person I was dancing with. I was dancing with *you*. So maybe you should explain to me why it was that you agreed to dance with me? It certainly wasn't because you wanted to *represent the practice*." She filled the last three words with as much sarcasm as was possible.

They faced each other, both of them breathless from the emotions that swirled around them. Along with the anger, she felt a certain thrill running through her because she'd been able to make Jared show at least some sort of emotion for her. He might deny how he'd responded to her on that dance floor, but she knew better. He'd felt something for her when he'd held her. He'd wanted her. And she'd wanted him.

Unfortunately, it was just as plain to her that he wasn't going to admit it. That for a few minutes she'd made him drop that facade of detachment he wore. And if it truly wasn't something he wanted, it didn't matter. He wasn't the first man that hadn't wanted her. Her ex had made that plain when after years together he'd walked away from her without a second thought.

"I'm sorry if I embarrassed you and the practice," Sky said. "That wasn't my intention."

"You didn't embarrass me."

All the emotions that she had been feeling drained out of her as suddenly as they had come. She felt empty and so very tired. She opened the door and climbed into the truck. She turned away from Jared when he climbed in beside her and started the engine.

She'd assumed she'd leave the party tonight floating on air after meeting all the famous people of Nashville.

Instead, she wanted to dig a hole and climb into it to escape this familiar feeling of being unwanted.

Had she really thought she could blend in with people like those she'd met tonight? Jared had made it plain that she was only there because of the practice. She'd just been the hired help, at least that was what he thought. It had been stupid of her to think it was anything more than that.

Just like it had been stupid for her to think that sharing her secrets with Jared might have made a difference in how he saw her.

"Look, I just think it would be better if we remember that we are here to do a job. This isn't about us and all this…" he said, turning toward her and waving a hand between the two of them.

"This?" she asked, copying his waving hand gesture. "You mean the two of us acting human?"

Jared's eyes met hers and she saw a vulnerability there that surprised her. "What are you afraid of? Is it disappointing your father? Or is it me?"

She didn't want to think that there was something about her that scared him off from becoming involved with her. She had been over-the-top flirty with him, and sometimes she did push too hard when there was something that she wanted, but she'd only wanted him to notice her. "I'm sorry if I've been too pushy. I just thought…"

What had she thought? That he would jump at the chance of spending time with her on the dance floor? That he'd welcome her into his arms? That he'd secretly been harboring a crush on her just like she'd been harboring one on him?

"I just thought we could have a good time while we were here," she murmured, turning her head away from him so he wouldn't see the tears that she couldn't explain.

"It's not you, Sky. I just don't think the two of us getting involved would be a good thing. I'm sure you'll agree that the two of us are just too different. Things would get complicated."

He looked over at her as he started his truck, then sat there as if waiting for her to agree with him. Not that she did. All she knew was that when she'd been in Jared's arms, it had felt right. Finally, when she didn't speak, he put the truck in gear and started down the drive.

CHAPTER SIX

JARED WAS HAVING a bad day. From the time his alarm had gone off, nothing had gone right. He'd even growled at Tanya this morning when she'd reminded him that he had a lunch meeting with his dad and Sky at noon, though the office manager had only been doing her job He tried to tell himself it was just because it was a Monday and even he didn't like the first day of the work-week. But he knew it was more than that. He'd been in a foul mood ever since Friday night when he'd dropped Sky off at her home.

He knew he owed her an apology. He'd overstepped his place and in the process he'd ruined the night for her. He'd known she was excited about meeting all the famous people that had been sure to attend the Carters' party. He'd even overheard Lori talking to Tanya about helping Sky pick out a dress for the event. She'd wanted something to make her blend in with all those famous people.

Not that it had worked. She would never blend in with any crowd. She was too beautiful, too spirited for that. It was what drew Jared to her while at the same time making him want to be as far away as possible. He knew danger when he saw it and Sky was the most dangerous woman he'd ever met. She was like an atomic bomb that could blow the life he'd worked so hard to make right out of the Tennessee mountains. That was why he'd felt the need to remind Sky that nothing could happen between the two of them. But if he really believed that, why had he spent the rest of his weekend thinking about the dance the two of them had shared?

"Hey, Dr. Warner, can I speak to you for a moment?"

Jared looked up from his desk to see Lori's mom standing outside his door. "Sure, Maggie, and call me Jared, please."

"I don't want to disturb you, but they just took Jasmine back to the examination room and I wanted to talk to you before you see her," Maggie said as she stepped into the office. "You asked me to let you know if there were any changes with her blood pressure or her behavior."

Jared pushed the laptop he had been using out of the way. "How is she doing?"

"Her blood pressure is about the same with the medications you've given her and she is taking them without any trouble. It's her behavior that has me worried. She just seems so detached from the rest of the women in the household. She spends most of her time sleeping or at least in her bed."

"She told me the medication for her blood pressure was making her tired, but I don't think that's all there is to this. She's made too much of a change since she first came to see me with her mother. I'm wondering if she's homesick. Have her parents visited her?" He didn't know a lot about Jasmine and her parents' relationship. They'd seemed to be close on that first visit. Jasmine's mother had asked all the appropriate questions as a caring parent of a pregnant teenager. But something had happened between them, something big, and whatever it was, it had affected Jasmine badly. Sky had followed through on her offer to talk to Jasmine, but she'd told Jared that the girl had seemed very low energy and had no luck in getting her to open up.

"Her mother calls her I know, but the conversations I've heard were very short. From what I can tell, there was some type of disagreement between the two of them before Jasmine came to Legacy House. And as far as the medication is concerned, I don't think we can blame it for all of the changes. She's showing too many signs of a new onset of depression. I can't say she's not looking out for the baby. She's doing everything we ask as far as that is concerned. She's just not taking care of herself. There were times last week when she'd go days without bathing or dressing properly."

Jared sighed, then rose. They couldn't have found anyone to manage the home as well as Maggie did. With her medical background and her caring nature, she was the perfect stand-in mom for the women there. "Thanks for letting me know. I'll talk to her and try to get her to agree to see a counselor. Whatever is going on with her psychologically, it's not a good combination with her hypertension."

Maggie thanked him before returning to the waiting room, and Jared headed into the exam room to see Jasmine. Knocking and then opening the door, he saw immediately why Maggie had been concerned. The young girl lay on the examination table, not even opening her eyes when he entered. The last couple months with Jasmine had been like watching a thriving flower slowly wilt in front of him. There had to be something he could do to help this girl.

Pulling out his phone, he sent a message to Sky asking her to meet him in the examination room. He needed a second opinion along with any help he could give her. He hadn't seen Sky come into the office but he knew she normally had patient exams scheduled on Mondays.

"Good morning, Jasmine," he said, taking a seat and opening the room's computer where the patient's weight and vital signs had been recorded. Her blood pressure hadn't increased but neither had it decreased. He hated to add a second blood pressure medication but it looked like he was going to have to do it.

There was a knock on the door before Sky entered. She'd pulled her hair back into a ponytail today and he found himself missing those curls of hers that spiraled all around her face. When her eyes met his, they were all business. Yeah, she was still mad at him. It was something they'd have to deal with but it would have to wait till later. Right now his priority was his patient.

"Jasmine, Sky is one of the midwives here. You met her the other day."

Jasmine opened her eyes for the first time, then sat up at the end of the exam table. He noted the dark circles around the girl's eyes, but it was the increased puffiness in her face that truly bothered him. What had started out as a concern for hypertension was now looking more and more like preeclampsia.

"Hi, Jasmine. We talked the other day when I was helping Ms. Maggie."

"I'm not stupid just because I got myself pregnant," Jasmine said, the first sign of life showing in her defiant eyes. "I thought you were my doctor. Why do I need a midwife?"

"Sky and I work together on some cases. And neither one of us thinks you're stupid. If I remember correctly, your mother said you had earned a scholarship for college next year. What are you planning on studying?" He had her talking to him now and he didn't want her to stop.

"I was going to do pre-law, but that's messed up now. Everything is messed up now." Jasmine's shoulders lowered along with her head, that small spark of defiance gone.

"My sister is a lawyer. She practices family law in our hometown. What type of practice are you planning on going into?" Sky asked, taking a seat in the chair beside Jasmine as the girl looked up at her.

There was pain and disappointment in the girl's eyes now. Was that what was bothering her? Did she think that because she was having a baby she couldn't go to college? Couldn't have a future? She definitely wasn't like most of the teenagers she dealt with that were more concerned about the here and now. Jasmine had planned a future that hadn't included raising a child.

"I told you. It's all messed up now. My parents... It's just messed up and I don't want to talk about it. Ms. Maggie said you wanted me to come in so that you could check my blood pressure and adjust my medication. That's why I'm here." And there was that spark of anger again. He didn't like the fact that making her angry could increase her already too high blood pressure. Still, at least he had an idea what the problem was now.

"I'm going to change your blood pressure medicine and I want to do some more tests," Jared said. "And I'd still like you to consider going to see a counselor."

"I don't need a counselor. I don't need anything except to have this baby," Jasmine said before falling back against the table.

"You still have a few weeks until it will be safe for the baby to be born. I'm going to step out and get someone to come in and draw some blood. If you're okay with it, Sky can do a fast exam of your heart and lungs for me and check you for swelling while I'm gone."

Jasmine sat back up and looked Sky over from head to toe. "You still haven't told me why she's here."

"Like I said, we work together sometimes. It's good to get a second opinion, don't you think? We're working together right now with a famous country star." Jared saw the interest in Jasmine's eyes before it disappeared. "I'll send someone right in to draw that lab work."

He left the room, hoping that with some privacy Jasmine might open up further to Sky. A few minutes later Sky appeared at his office doorway. "They're drawing Jasmine's labs now. I was going to let her go after that, but I wanted to check with you first."

"Did she say anything else to you?" Jared asked.

"I mainly talked to her about where my sister went to school and some of the courses she took. She seemed interested at first. Then she went back to the same line she used before. Everything is messed up because of the pregnancy. I don't know what happened between her and her parents, but I'm pretty sure that's at least part of the source of the depression she's having now. I'm supposed to help Maggie again Wednesday. I'll talk to her again then."

"At this point her blood pressure has got to be my main concern. And now that she's starting to have more swelling, I'm beginning to suspect she's becoming preeclamptic." Like the poor girl didn't have enough going wrong for her. "She could really use her parents' support right now, but I can't contact them without her okay. Maybe you can mention that?"

"I'll try to bring it up to her. She's seventeen. Whatever it is going on in that head of hers seems insurmountable right now. Hopefully, she'll let one of us help her." She started to turn away.

"We're supposed to have lunch with my father today," Jared said. He had to find a way to apologize for his actions Friday night but now didn't seem like the right time.

"Tanya reminded me. I'll meet you there." With that, Sky turned and hurried down the hall toward her own set of examination rooms. He probably owed her another apology for taking her away from her own patients. Not that she would be interested in one. She was just as worried as he was about Jasmine.

It seemed like the two of them would be working together even more now. And Jared found, even though he was well aware of the dangers after their dance, that he didn't mind that at all.

Jared and his father were waiting for Sky when she arrived at the Barbecue Shack down from the office. Unlike its name, the place was more modern barn chic than a shack. A large brisket turned in the rotisserie pit at the front entrance and the sweet smell of roasting meat pulled a nice crowd inside throughout the day.

She spotted both of the Warner men at a corner table, their heads together as they studied the menu. She still didn't understand why they couldn't have met in Jack's office, but when Tanya told you to be somewhere you just followed instructions.

"Sorry I'm running late," she said as she took a chair across from them. "I had a heavy load of patients this morning."

"I meant to thank you for helping me with Jasmine. I know you had your own patients to see," Jared said, his distant politeness setting her teeth on edge, though she shouldn't have been surprised by it. He'd made it clear that he didn't want anything to do with her except professionally.

"I didn't mind. I just don't know if I did any good. I'm going to talk to my sister tonight and see if she has any advice for someone with a child wanting to go to law school. I'm sure there are resources out there to help single moms like Jasmine." Sky kept her voice just as polite as his.

Dr. Warner followed their conversation, his head ping-ponging back and forth between them, without commenting. As always though, his eyes showed a merriment that Sky herself wasn't feeling.

"Again, thank you," Jared said. His words were sincere. They shouldn't have hurt.

"It's nice to see the two of you working together so well. I knew the two of you would find a way to make this work," Jack said as the waitress appeared to take their order.

After she left, Jack pulled out his phone and held it out to them. "I received this from our accountant this morning. It seems that you two and the Carters have been talking up Legacy House to a lot of people in their circle. We received four significant donations over the weekend. I don't know the last time we've received donations like this, so keep up the good work. You're making a difference in a lot of women's lives."

Sky skimmed down the email till she got to the names listed and the amounts that had been donated. She recognized two of the names, one being Nick and the other the producer of the Carters' reality show.

"Joe promised another twenty-five thousand for allowing him an interview for the show. Also, he is going to let us put a plug in for Legacy House in the interview."

"Why would they want to interview us? There's nothing exciting about the two of us." It would be good to get Legacy House on the show though. Maggie had been talking about needing to update some of the kitchen with large appliances. And she'd said that the electrician had recommended an electrical upgrade too.

"I think it's just to get more interest in the show. The audience seems to be obsessed with Mindy's pregnancy," Jared said, acting like it didn't bother him that people could be asking them personal questions when she knew it would be the last thing he wanted.

"And how are things going with Mindy and Trey? It sounds like they are satisfied with their care so far," Jack said.

"Mindy's coming in Friday for her first visit. I'm going to let her in through the employee entrance so she won't have to come through the waiting room. I'm not expecting any problems as far as the pregnancy. She's done well so far. I do want to get an ultrasound to measure the baby's growth while she's there. What about you, Jared? Anything I'm forgetting?"

"It sounds fine. Except for her miscarriage she doesn't have any risk factors. Trey did specify that they didn't want to know the sex of the baby. It is really important to them to find out at the delivery."

"Well, that all sounds good," Jack said as their food arrived.

The rest of the meal they spent discussing what Jack wanted them to stress in the interview as far as the practice was concerned and Legacy House. It was like prepping for an examination and Sky wanted to make sure she was ready for any questions that might be directed at her.

She launched herself into her afternoon patients' exams feeling better than she had that morning when she'd come in. She and Jared had managed to share a lunch without either of them referring to the party they'd attended together. And if he wanted to pretend that the dance they had shared had never happened she could do that too. It had only been one dance, she told herself.

So why did it feel like it had changed everything?

CHAPTER SEVEN

WITH THE OFFICE closed and most of the staff gone for the day, Sky sat back in her chair and perched her bare feet on the desk. She'd gotten a blister on her foot while dancing Friday night and being on her feet all day had just aggravated it.

When the knock came on the door, she assumed that it was one of the techs saying good-night. As Jared stuck his head into her office door, she started to put her legs down, then stopped. It was her office after all. If she wanted to put her feet up after hours, she could do it.

"Sorry, I don't mean to disturb you. I just wanted a minute of your time," he said. He was still being overly polite and she still didn't like it. He'd made it clear that he wasn't interested in her except professionally, But he didn't have to act so cold to her.

"Is there something we didn't cover at lunch concerning the Carters?"

"That's not what I wanted to talk about. I just wanted to tell you that I'm sorry for what happened. I know you were excited about the party and I'm sorry I ruined that for you."

Sky didn't know what to say. She *had* been excited

about the party. And it had been amazing. She'd had a great time dancing with some of country music's biggest stars. She had enjoyed getting to know Mindy better too. But the thing she had enjoyed the most was the one thing Jared was apologizing for.

And why did they have to go over this again? Oh, he said he was sorry for ruining the party, but she knew what he meant. He was embarrassed that he had responded to her on the dance floor. The point being, *he had responded to her.* They both knew that. She just didn't understand why he was determined to ignore it. The two of them were single adults. And it wasn't like workplace relationships didn't take place there. As long as they were discreet, no one would care. There was something else keeping him tangled up that he couldn't seem to break free of. Something stronger than his desire to explore what the two of them had felt that night. If only she could understand what it was.

But that wasn't something she was going to solve tonight. "I enjoyed the party. You didn't ruin it for me."

Her phone rang and she almost groaned when she saw it was the women's unit of the hospital. "This is Sky."

She listened as the nurse on the labor floor gave her report on one of her patients who was thirty-six weeks and expecting twins. Sky had been her midwife for her other two deliveries and they had hoped that she would be able to deliver both of them vaginally. Now it didn't look like that would happen.

"I'll be over to talk to her," she said before ending the call. "Are you on call tonight for surgery?" she asked him.

"I am. Why? What's wrong?"

"Nothing's wrong. I have a patient that is expecting twins. They were both head down on her ultrasound last week, but it looks like baby B decided he didn't want to follow his sister's direction. He's complete breech now." Sky put her feet down and toed her shoes back on. "Sarah's water is broken but she's only two centimeters and not having regular contractions yet. I delivered her other two babies without any difficulty, but she has a small outlet. We planned to try for a vaginal delivery with the twins if they were both cephalic, but I don't feel good about trying to turn baby B."

"I'll call over and tell them to get her ready for a C-section," Jared said. "Have you discussed with her the possibility of surgery with twins?"

"Of course I have. It was one of the first things we discussed. I know how to do my job, Jared." Why did he always make her feel like he thought she was incompetent? "When are you going to accept that midwives are as competent as doctors? What is it you have against us?"

"I know you are competent. I didn't mean anything by my question," Jared said. "I don't know this patient. I'm just asking for information."

"It isn't just this time. You said you don't have a problem with midwives, but you do it all the time. Is it something I've done?" She knew this wasn't the time to get into this, but she needed to know. She was tired of feeling like she wasn't good enough for him. Like she was lacking something. She knew that no matter how much she denied it, some of her insecurity came from the way her ex had treated her. Still, she wanted to know that Jared trusted her to take care of her patients. "What do I have to do to convince you that I'm a good midwife?"

The sincerity in Sky's blue eyes cut through his need to keep his most painful history private. "It's not you. It's just…"

He took the seat at the desk across from her. How was it that this woman had the power to make him bare his soul to her? "My mother died after childbirth."

"I'm so sorry, Jared," Sky said. "Do you want to tell me what happened?"

This was something that he didn't speak of to anyone, but he found himself now wanting to explain it all to her. Maybe then she'd understand that it wasn't that he doubted her capability. He just wanted to make sure what had happened to his mother didn't happen again.

"After I was born, my grandmother told the midwife taking care of my mother that something was wrong. My mother had begun complaining of feeling bad, feeling 'funny.' My grandmother had no medical training, but she told me she felt it in her soul that something was wrong. But before she could insist that the midwife do something my mother had a seizure. She aspirated and coded while the midwife was repairing her episiotomy. She had an anoxic brain injury and a week later she was declared brain dead and removed from life support. My grandmother discovered later that my mother's blood pressure had been rising during her pregnancy but the midwife hadn't followed up and ordered any of the diagnostic lab work she should have." He didn't tell her that his grandmother had blamed that midwife for the loss of her only child from that day until her death, while he'd grown up blaming himself. It had only been when he'd been older and had learned more about childbirth that he had understood the things his grandmother had told him.

"I'm so sorry that happened to your family," Sky said. "You didn't become a doctor because of Jack, did you? You became an obstetrician because of what happened to your mother."

"Jack was a part of it." He'd come to believe that having Jack, one of the most sought out obstetricians in Nashville, as his father had been more than fate. "But yes, most of it was because of my mother. I don't want another woman to die unnecessarily."

"That's what I want too. What we all want. But even with all the medical gains in our field, maternal deaths still happen," Sky said.

"That's why we have to work harder to find ways to stop it from happening." Jared leaned forward, his hand reaching out to her in his need for her understanding. "Don't you see, Sky. That's why I double-check everything. I know I can be a bit intense, but I only want what's best for the patient."

"That's what we all want. Maybe working together, respecting the role each of us play in our patients' care is the best thing for our patients," Sky said, taking his hand and giving it a comforting squeeze. "Thank you for telling me about your mother."

Jared looked down to where their hands were joined.

He felt as if a burden had been lifted from his shoulders. As if telling Sky had opened up something inside him. Maybe she was right? Maybe instead of working at cross-purposes, they could work together to ensure their patients' safety.

"Speaking of patients," Jared said as he let go of Sky's hand, "we need to go take care of those twins of yours."

"I'd like to assist you in surgery, if that's okay with you?" Sky asked as she stood and stretched. Jared knew that her day had been just as long as his.

"I think that would be a great idea," Jared said, rising and following her to the door.

"Okay, then. Let's go deliver these twins. I can't wait to meet the little troublemaker who decided he wanted to take his own path instead of following his sister." Sky took her jacket from the stand where she'd hung it.

"I think that sounds like a plan we can both agree on," Jared said, excited about the delivery. He told himself he was just looking forward to the birth of the twins, but he knew that having Sky right there beside him would make it even better.

"Hey, let me help with that," Sky said to Lori, grabbing one of the bags of groceries that her best friend was juggling as she tried to open the kitchen door to Legacy House.

"Thanks." Lori moved back so Sky could open the door. "Mom told me you would be here today. She appreciates all the help you've been with the spring cleaning. Though I don't know how you have the time with everything going on right now."

"I love helping out. I can't donate a lot of money so I give the time I have available instead."

"So how did the party go? I heard you and Jared got some significant donations," Lori said as they began putting away the groceries.

With everything going on in the office, Sky hadn't had a chance to tell her about that night. "It was amazing. It was like attending one of those parties you see pictures of after the CMA show. And Mindy was the perfect hostess."

"What about Jared? Did he have any fun?" Lori asked.

Sky grabbed a couple sodas from the fridge and sat them on the table. "I'm not sure. It's complicated."

"What do you mean?" Lori joined her at the table. "He didn't talk to you?"

It wasn't the talking that Sky was thinking about. She still couldn't get over how Jared had gone from hot to cold so fast. She hadn't planned to discuss any of what had happened between them with anyone, but maybe she needed to. Maybe talking with Lori would help her understand how he could change from one moment to the next. Or maybe it was her. Maybe she had just imagined the red-hot need that had flowed between the two of them.

"We talked. It wasn't the talking that was the problem. Well, at least it wasn't a problem until after the dance we shared."

"Really? What happened? Is he a bad dancer? Did he step on your feet?" Lori smiled, her eyes filled with amusement.

Was he a good dancer? She really couldn't remember much about the dancing or the music that was playing. She only remembered how perfect it felt to be in Jared's arms and how much she had wanted to stay there. And his eyes. She remembered the heat that had filled them. He'd wanted to kiss her, she was sure of that. "I think it was more like he stepped on my heart."

The amusement in Lori's eyes died. "Tell me what happened. Then give me a good reason I shouldn't kick his butt."

"You can't kick his butt. He's our boss's son. Besides, he didn't do anything wrong. At least, not intentionally."

"Tell me everything," Lori said.

So Sky told her. She told her about the people she met. How she had felt out of place amongst all the famous and talented people, though they'd all been kind and welcoming. She told her how Mindy had been especially sweet. Then she told her about dancing with Nick Thomas.

"What is he like? Is he going to call you?"

"I don't think he'll be calling me. Jared was pretty rude to him." She wondered if Jared would be calling Nick to apologize. She didn't think so.

"Jared? Our Jared? I've never heard him raise his voice before. It's like human emotions are something too menial for him."

"He's not like that, not really," she said, not liking the way Lori made him sound.

"Has anyone seen Ms. Maggie?" a voice asked from the doorway.

Sky turned to find Jasmine, still dressed in her pajamas. The circles under her eyes were even puffier than the last time she had seen her.

"I'll go get her," Lori murmured, giving the young girl a worried look.

"Come, sit down," Sky said. At first she thought the girl was going to refuse. But after glancing behind her, Jasmine took a seat across from her. "How are you feeling today?"

"I'm okay. Just still tired. Dr. Warner changed the medication but I'm still tired all the time. I'm getting behind in my classes."

That was the most Sky had heard the girl volunteer in any conversation. "I'm sorry. I'd be glad to help. Or Ms. Maggie knows several tutors that help with the students here. You're doing online courses, right?"

"I had to change when I got here. I was ahead of the class at my school." The words lacked the teenage sarcasm she'd been filled with earlier in the week. "And now I'm falling behind because of this stupid medicine."

"You're right. The medicine can make you feel bad. But I don't think that your being behind in your classes is all that is bothering you. Talk to me, Jasmine. Tell me what is wrong so I can help you."

"You can't help me. No one can now." Then the girl broke.

Sobs wracked Jasmine's body and Sky moved to put her arm around her. Over the girl's shoulders, she saw Maggie and Lori come into the room. Sky shook her head at them and they stepped back out.

"I can't promise to have the answer but I'm here to

help if I can. You can't keep all of this bottled up inside of you. It's not good for you or the baby."

"It's the baby that's the problem," Jasmine said, looking up at her with eyes filled with tears she'd clearly been holding in for months. "I don't want to keep the baby. I know I'm being selfish. But I had my life planned. I've wanted to go to college for as long as I can remember."

"You can still go to college. You know that, right?" Sky didn't think that was the real problem but she wanted to make sure that Jasmine knew she had options.

"I know, but it won't be the same. I love this baby. I do." The girl's eyes begged Sky to believe her. "But I'm not ready to raise him. He needs someone that can do a better job than me. He deserves that."

Sky agreed with her that every baby deserved to be loved and cared for. If Jasmine didn't think it was something she could do, they needed to respect that.

"And there are a lot of people that would love him if that is what you want. Allowing someone to adopt your baby isn't something to be ashamed of. It's not selfish. It's one of the bravest things someone can do." Sky had been through that struggle before. "You know my sister, the one who's a lawyer?"

"You said she practices family law," Jasmine said as she wiped her eyes with the sleeve of her pajama top.

"She had a baby when she was just a little younger than you. She decided she wasn't ready to raise a child too. Her doctor put her in touch with an adoption agency and she found the perfect couple for her baby. They're very open about the adoption and my sister gets pictures and cards from them."

"My parents would never agree to that. They want me to keep the baby. They keep promising they'll help, but that isn't the problem. I'm just not ready to be someone's mom. I know that makes me a bad person."

"You're not a bad person. It takes a lot of courage to admit that you can't do something. And you're thinking about what is best for your baby." Sky hugged the young girl to her. Jasmine was being forced to make an adult decision about her baby when she was not much more than a child herself. She wanted to offer to speak to Jasmine's parents herself, but she knew it wouldn't help. Whether it was fair or not, Jasmine had to make that move herself.

"How about I get my sister to call you? She won't try to push you either way. It's a personal decision, not hers or your parents. She'll be honest with you about the process and how it has affected her life."

"That would be good. Did your parents try to talk her out of the adoption?"

"No. They weren't in our lives then. They left us with our grandmother when we were young. But my grandmother was ready to support her no matter what decision she made. Your parents might not agree with you, but I have the feeling that they will support your decision once you explain how you feel. They love you and want you to be happy. Just talk to them. Be honest with them."

Jasmine sighed and had just begun to stand when Maggie and Lori came back into the room. Sky had figured they were outside the door listening.

Maggie started fixing lunch. Jasmine volunteered to help, then Sky and Lori got up to join them. The girl still looked worn to the bone. It would take more than a talk with Sky to help her get back on track, however moving around and working instead of staying in bed and worrying was a first step.

CHAPTER EIGHT

SKY OPENED THE back office door and let Mindy inside. Dressed in a plain black hoodie that covered her hair, the country music star had none of the glamour that she was known for. In a worn pair of jeans and a pair of sneakers, she could have been any other patient in the practice. As Sky led her down the hall to her exam room, members of the staff walked by them without anyone looking twice.

She shut the door as Mindy pulled off the hoodie. "That's a pretty good disguise."

"Trey agreed to let me come by myself if I wore one of his old sweatshirts," Mindy said. "It actually was kind of fun sneaking in the back. Not that I want my life to always be like this."

Sky had a feeling Mindy hadn't accepted all the changes stardom was going to make for the rest of her life.

"Speaking of sneaking around, I didn't see you leave the party," Mindy said.

"I'm so sorry I didn't tell you we were leaving. It was kind of sudden."

"That wasn't a complaint. After watching you and Jared on the dance floor, I understand why you'd want to leave so fast. Though I'm confused about why you told me there wasn't anything happening between the two of you. That dance made it pretty plain that there's something between you."

"There wasn't. I mean, there *isn't* anything. We're just colleagues." Sky felt the flush of embarrassment flood her face. Now she definitely would look like she was lying. "Seriously, Mindy, we aren't dating."

"Honey, I know what I saw. The two of you were into each other. Even Trey said something about it after you left." Mindy's smile turned mischievous. "Though apparently Nick Thomas had his head in a barrel—either that or he needs glasses. He asked me for your phone number after you left."

Sky didn't know what to say to that bit of news. "We talked about Legacy House. He probably just wants some more information."

Nick seemed like a nice enough guy. There just hadn't been that connection she felt with Jared. That attraction that drew her to him whenever he entered the room. Of course, that same attraction made him push her away every time they got close.

"I'm going to let Jared know you're here, then I want to get your vital signs and measurements," Sky said as she pulled out her phone to text Jared. "Have you had any new issues this week? Any cramping? Swelling?"

She was hoping to change the subject from her and Jared quickly. The last thing she wanted was for Mindy to say something in front of him.

"No. I feel perfectly healthy. I just wish Trey wasn't

such a worrier. By the time I have this baby he'll have me swaddled in bubble wrap," Mindy complained as Sky helped her up onto the examination table.

Glad that Mindy was willing to let the subject go, Sky went through the exam quickly. When Jared knocked on the door, she already had Mindy draped and the ultra-sound machine positioned.

"Okay, let's see how this little one is growing," Jared said as he moved the ultrasound wand over Mindy's abdomen. Within minutes he had all the measurements. And when the baby decided to give them that perfect view that would let them know its sex, Sky quickly changed the screen's direction.

"Everything looks perfect. The baby measures right at thirty weeks, which almost perfectly matches your due date," Jared said. "Would you like me to get a picture to send home for Trey?"

"I'd love that. He had planned to come, but there was some problem with the production of this week's show that he wanted to clear up. He and Joe get along well, don't get me wrong, but Trey knows Joe's job is to hype up the show with as much drama as possible. Sometimes he has to reel him in."

Jared handed Mindy a towel so she could wipe off all the ultrasound goo. "Joe's coming in Monday to interview the two of us here in the office after hours."

Sky looked over at him. She'd known that the interview was coming up. But Monday? She just hoped that Joe wouldn't ask any personal questions. The show was named *Carters' Way*, so she assumed they'd just be asked a couple questions in general about the care they gave their patients and maybe a question concerning the way the two of them were working together.

She was still thinking about the interview as she walked Mindy to the office's back entrance.

"I feel I should give you a heads-up about the interview," Mindy said as she adjusted the hood over her head. "Trey and I weren't the only ones who saw what was happening between you and Jared at the party. Trey was with Marjorie when you were dancing together."

"It was just a dance," Sky said as she opened the back door for her.

"You better keep practicing that line. Maybe Marjorie will believe it." Mindy grinned, then sprinted out the door toward her car.

As Sky stood and watched the country star get in her car, she repeated the words over and over, practicing putting emphasis on different words. "It *was* just a dance. It was *just* a dance. It was just a *dance*."

By the time she'd gotten back to her office, she had even almost convinced herself.

When Jared had agreed to a one-on-one interview, this wasn't what he was expecting. He'd assumed that the producer had meant to interview them himself. Instead it was Marjorie, wearing another red suit, sitting across from them. Her first couple of questions concerning their education and qualifications he had been prepared for. They each talked about the colleges they'd attended and where they had done residency. Sky managed to get in a few comments about Legacy House and the work they did there, but then something about Marjorie changed. There was a gleam in her eyes that put him on guard. This must be what a poor mouse felt like right before a snake went in for the killing strike.

"I can't tell you how happy Mindy and Trey are to have you and Sky taking care of Mindy and the baby. They've made several comments about how well the two of you get along." Marjorie's eyes took on a predatory look as her hands with their metallic red finger nails clasped together and she leaned in toward him. "And after seeing the way you were together at the party, I can see why. The two of you on a dance floor can really heat up a room."

He was stunned. This wasn't the type of question he had been expecting.

"Jared does look good on a dance floor, doesn't he? And we did enjoy the party." Sky's smile was perfect and there was sincerity in every word she said. "I can't thank Mindy and Trey enough for inviting us."

For a moment he thought Sky had shut down Marjorie on the subject of the party. Then the woman turned back to him and he suddenly felt like the weakest link.

"Jared, what about you? Sky seems to think you look good on the dance floor. How about her? What was it like to dance with this beautiful woman? It was plain to see that she was the hit of the party. Nick Thomas sure seemed to think so."

Why did the mention of that man's name bother him so much? It was time to get this interview back on track.

"Sky is a beautiful woman inside and out. Her patients love her."

"I'm sure they do." Marjorie's eyes bounced between the two of them.

She was looking for another angle to go at him. He had to cut her off. "I just want to assure the audience that Mindy is in the best of hands with Sky. Working together, I know that we will be able to give the Carter family the best care in the country."

"I'm sure you will," Marjorie said, her eyes narrowing in warning that she'd come after them if they didn't take care of Mindy and her baby. Then she smiled. "You know, right now the two of you are almost the only people who know the sex of Mindy and Trey's baby. It seems that all of Nashville is wondering whether it will be a girl or a boy. Someone has even started an online betting pool. How does it feel to have such exclusive information?"

The woman seemed determined to find some kind of drama for this interview. "Actually, it's something we are very familiar with handling. Some of our patients want to wait till their baby is born to discover the sex."

"But I have to tell you, Marjorie, it *is* exciting having a secret that big," Sky said. Then leaning in to Marjorie, she whispered just loud enough for the camera to hear her, "But I'm still not telling."

The cameraman stopped filming. Marjorie clapped her hands together. "That was perfect, Sky. The sponsors will love it."

Jared had no idea why Marjorie was so excited, but if it kept her away from trying to hype up some type of romantic connection between him and Sky he was glad to go along with it.

As soon as he'd shown Marjorie and her cameraman out the door, he hunted down Sky in her office.

"Please explain to me what just happened," Jared muttered.

Sky gave him a smile then slung a bag over her shoulder as she headed for the door. "Marjorie wasn't going to let us go without getting something more exciting than the name of what colleges we attended. I watched this season's opener this weekend. It's a nice enough show, but there isn't a lot of drama because they are basically a happy couple. Happy couples don't draw ratings. I could tell that Marjorie and Joe wanted us to hype up the pregnancy. I just added a dramatic flair to the truth. We might know the sex of Mindy and Trey's baby, but we aren't going to tell anyone."

"So the questions about the party weren't just because Marjorie was being nosy? She was looking for some dirt to spread around?" Sky nodded, but it still didn't make sense to him. No one cared about two unimportant health care providers. It wasn't a glamorous job like being a country music star.

Which reminded him of Nick. "And I guess she was just trying to tie you and Nick together for ratings too?"

"Maybe," she said as he followed her down the hallway.

"I'll have to tell him about it the next time I talk to him." Sky opened the back door and when she turned to face him, he recognized that impish smile of hers.

Then after a wink that made his heart skip a beat, she walked away, leaving him wanting to follow her. And not for the first time that week, he regretted that he couldn't do just that.

CHAPTER NINE

SKY HAD PLANNED a nice quiet Saturday. Instead she found herself sitting next to Jared on the Carters' band bus on the way to a concert in Knoxville.

"You didn't have to come," Sky said, before she spun herself around in the swivel chair set up at one of the tables in the bus.

"You're going to make yourself sick if you keep doing that," Jared pointed out. "And I did have to come. We're in this together. Remember?"

When Sky had received the phone call from Mindy asking if she could tag along for the tour stop, she'd been too excited to go to ask many questions. But after seeing Jared there and finding out that Trey's worry had caused Mindy to call Sky because she hadn't been feeling good, the trip had changed from fun to one of professional concern. Still, if you had to work on a Saturday night, you might as well enjoy yourself. And with a bus designed for comfort, this wasn't a bad trip.

"Of course, I remember," Sky answered. "But Mindy is fine now. I checked her blood pressure and she denied having any contractions. You could have stayed at home."

Not that she really minded him being there. He'd dressed

the part tonight in jeans and a chambray buttoned-up shirt. His black boots had been shined to perfection. If she gave him a cowboy hat, he would have looked like another member of the band. With her own short, denim skirt and her brown, knee high boots, they both looked like part of the band, which worked out well since Mindy was adamant that no one suspect there were any worries about her health.

A couple of the band members came out of a back area, carrying their instruments. In minutes they were playing one of their new hits that had just come out. Sky smiled and tapped her bootheel to the rhythm. This was so much better than sitting around her house and doing her laundry.

She looked over at Jared and was surprised to see that he was enjoying the music just as much as she had. When she smiled at him and he smiled back at her, she thought her chest would burst open. Was this the real Jared? The one she'd caught a glimpse of while dancing with him, the one who'd opened up to her about his birth mom? She'd always known that he was holding back something. Hiding some part of him away from everyone. Was he so afraid of letting someone in that he hid that smile, those emotions of happiness and the joy of living, from everyone?

Then to her surprise, he picked up a guitar that had been lying on the table and began to play along with the band members.

Sky didn't move, afraid she'd break the spell that the music had wrapped around Jared. She listened with awe as the band changed the song, flowing into another one, an older song about loss and pain. It was a drinking song that had been redone by many music stars and it only took a few seconds for Jared to catch up with the rest of the group. They played for half an hour before the musicians set down their instruments and, after shaking Jared's hand and inviting him to play with them again, they disappeared into the back of the bus to change for the concert.

"That was amazing," she said when they were once more alone. "Why didn't I know that you could play?"

"I have my secrets," He said. His face was flushed with color. Embarrassment? He'd always had a confidence that Sky had admired, but she'd really only spent time with him at work until the last two weeks.

"Tell me one?" She loved seeing this side of him. Maybe if she kept him talking he wouldn't notice how much of himself he was allowing her to see.

"Like what?" he asked, his hands still strumming over the strings of the guitar.

"I don't know, just something you don't share. Like the fact that you can hold your own with a professional country band. It doesn't have to be something big. I'll even tell you some of my own secrets."

Jared looked up from the guitar he'd been studying. "Okay, but you go first. Tell me some more of those deep, dark secrets you are hiding behind that smile you always wear."

"First, I didn't say it would be that kind of secret. You already know most of my story anyhow. I mean more like something we don't know about each other. Like…" She searched for something insignificant to share. "I know. I hide chocolate bars around my house so that I have to look for them."

"Okay, that's just weird," Jared said. "Why don't you put them in the kitchen like everyone else?"

"Because then I'd eat them. If I hide them I have to make a point of looking for them. It gives me a few moments to decide if it's really worth the trouble."

"So it keeps you from eating chocolate?" The corners of his lips rose in a small, knowing smirk.

"That's a secret for another time," she said, returning his smirk. "Now it's your turn."

He leaned in, copying the way she'd leaned in to Marjorie when they'd taped their interview for the reality show. "Every week, even though I know I shouldn't…"

Sky leaned in closer, his lips so close she could feel his breath against her own. For a moment she forgot what he was saying, and then his eyes met hers and something flashed between the two of them. Her breath caught and her lips parted. She wanted him to move closer. She wanted him to kiss her. It wouldn't take much. Their lips were only a few inches apart.

Jared pushed back from the table, leaving her straining toward him. "I make a really big homemade pizza and I eat the whole thing by myself."

Sky leaned back and glared at him. Was he playing her? Didn't he know he'd just made her stomach flip inside out with the anticipation of feeling his lips on hers? "Why do you do that?"

"What? I like pizza," he said, beginning to strum the

guitar again. She saw his body relax, just like it had when he'd been playing it earlier. She wanted to push him and discover why he kept pulling back from her, but at the same time she didn't want to have him shut her out again.

"Where did you learn to play?" she asked. Surely this was a safe subject. "Self-taught or lessons?"

"Mom made me take lessons when I was ten. I hated them at first. But she played herself and believed if you live in Music City you should at least give it a try. At least that's what she told me. I think she thought it would help me make friends."

"And did it?" She'd heard that Jared had been close to his mom. She could picture him as a young boy playing the guitar with her. Sharing something creative like music had to build a strong bond between them. It had to have been a hard blow on him to lose a second mother. Everything she'd heard about Katie Warner had been good, even the way she'd dealt with the cancer that had taken her away from her family too early.

"I made a few. Once I started playing though, I kind of forgot the people around me."

Sky could believe that. She could see how the music had affected him. He was more relaxed. More open. "I'm glad she made you take the lessons. You clearly enjoy it."

He looked at her, that deep groove between his eyebrows telling her that he had something more on his mind than music lessons. "So, you asked me a question and now I have one for you."

"Okay," Sky said, something about the intensity of his

gaze making her stomach twist into knots with apprehension. "What do you want to know?"

She'd left her whole life open with that question. What had started as a way for her to find out more about Jared had taken an unexpected turn somewhere. She just hoped that it was a detour she was prepared to take.

"You told me about your life with your grandmother and your parents, but I still don't understand how or why you would fake feeling happy if you don't. It seems a lot like lying."

"I think we all lie about how we feel at some time. Don't you? I can't say I know all of your story, but you told me about losing your mother. I know you were hurt by that, anyone would be. And I know the Warners adopted you, so I take it you lost your grandmother or she couldn't take care of you."

"She died of cancer when I was six," Jared said, his voice a solemn whisper as if he didn't want to hear the words.

Sky could see that the memory of losing her still caused him pain after all these years. "I'm lucky that I still have mine. She's a tough woman. Strong and stubborn. I'll never forget the way she just accepted us when our parents left us. She might have been faking it, but if she was, I'm sure glad that she did. I guess that's where I learned you don't have a choice about what other people in your life do. But you do have a choice about how you deal with it. I dealt with my anger at my parents by accepting my grandmother's love even though my parents had convinced me that I didn't deserve it. I guess that means I owe my attitude toward life to her."

A door slammed in the back of the bus and Sky remembered where she was.

As members of the band started appearing, Jared leaned toward her and whispered, "I'm glad she was there for you. You deserve to be happy."

There was a sadness to that statement that she didn't understand. Did he think he didn't deserve to be happy? But why? Unfortunately, it was a question that would have to wait.

As the band started to assemble around them and they pulled into the parking lot of their venue, Sky reached out for the hand that was still strumming the strings of the guitar and covered it with her own. "We all deserve to be happy, Jared. Some of us just have to work harder than others to see that."

If the concert had been amazing, the after-party thrown by the Carters' reality show at the hotel where they were all staying was even better. They'd been treated to front row seats by Mindy and Trey for the concert, but as Sky wandered through the crowd of performers and invited guests in the hotel's ballroom, she found herself blown away once more by how far her country bumpkin self had come in the world.

Both she and Jared had checked on Mindy after the concert when some of the private security had ushered them into her and Trey's dressing room. Mindy had looked tired physically but invigorated with an emotional energy at the same time. It was plain to see how much she enjoyed performing.

"Sky, come over here," someone from the band called out to her. She recognized the woman as a backup singer she'd met earlier in the evening. "I want to introduce you to my husband."

"Sky," another voice shouted over the noise of the room as she was pulled into a hug by the band member whose recommendation had gotten her there.

"Hey, Jenny, it was a great concert," Sky said, hugging her back. The woman was becoming one of the most sought out fiddle players in Nashville and after the performance tonight, Sky understood why. "I haven't gotten a chance to thank you for recommending me to Mindy."

"You are an amazing midwife. I knew she would get the best of care with you," she said.

"Jenny does say you are the best," the young woman who'd called her over earlier said. "I'm Carly and this is my husband, Zack. We just found out we're pregnant."

The whole group let out a scream of excitement mixed with congratulations. "We were hoping you would be our midwife."

Sky agreed and once again congratulated the couple. A few of the performers had picked up guitars and started to play and she turned and smiled when she saw that they'd invited Jared to join them.

As the crowd gathered around them, Sky moved to the front. She eased her phone out of her pocket and snapped a quick picture of Jared. His head was bent over the borrowed guitar as his hands changed chords and strummed the strings. Jenny joined them with her fiddle and the music changed to an upbeat song that had the crowd clapping along with the melody. An older man, white haired with spindle-thin legs, offered her his hand and the next thing Sky knew she was being swung around in a dance that took her breath away.

When the music stopped, the man bowed to her and moved back into the crowd. Laughing, she looked around the stage to see Jared walking her way. She laughed and did a twirl. This must have been what Cinderella would have felt when she'd made it to the prince's ball.

Before she could stop herself, her arms flew around his neck and she pulled him into her dance, twirling him around with her. They stopped spinning and she looked up at him, laughing as she tried to catch her breath, surprised to see him smiling. That smile. Every time she saw it her heart seemed to explode with happiness.

Pushing up on her toes, she went to press a kiss on his cheek, surprising him as he turned toward her. His lips brushed against hers and the world around them disappeared. She kissed him with an abandonment that came from too much excitement, not enough sleep and a whole lot of happiness.

Then she lost control of the kiss, giving it all up to him when his lips parted hers and the kiss went deeper. Her hands dug into his shoulders, needing to hold on to something as her legs went weak when his tongue swept across hers and her lips opened up to him.

Gone was the music that had woven itself through her

just moments before. Her whole world was Jared and the feel of his lips on hers. It wasn't a sweet kiss. No, this kiss was primitive, hard and hot. When he let her go, she stumbled back, her lips feeling bruised and tender.

"What was that?" she asked as he stared at her. Looking around the room, she saw that, while they might have caught some of the crowd's attention, most everyone was gathered around where a new group of guitar players formed at the other end of the room.

"You kissed me," Jared said, his voice rough with an irritation she wasn't going to stand for.

"I let myself get a little too excited, I guess." Yes, she had instigated the kiss, but she'd planned on a quick smack on the cheek. Something fun. He'd been the one to deepen it.

"Well, I wasn't expecting it. I don't do things like this. You know that. I'm not like you," Jared said as he started to turn back to the impromptu stage set up by the group.

He was brushing her off again, just like he had the night they'd shared that dance. He was making her feel like she was unimportant, like she was the only one feeling this connection, like it was easy to walk away from her. It was the same thing her parents had done. The same thing her ex had done to her.

But she wasn't that little girl or that insecure woman anymore. She would never put up with someone ignoring her or not taking her seriously again.

"Go ahead, walk away. If you can ignore what we just shared, so can I. I'm sorry I kissed you. I won't bother you again."

She turned and walked toward the door leading out of the hotel's ballroom, glad that everyone was busy enjoying the music instead of watching her humiliate herself. If anyone had noticed the two of them kissing, they didn't seem to think there was anything unusual about it. It wasn't like the two of them were well-known among the people here.

Only she knew better. That kiss could have been the start of something special. Instead it had opened her eyes to the fact that Jared didn't want her. Oh, his body might respond to hers. That kiss, that dance they'd shared, had been proof of that. But if he couldn't admit that he wanted her, if he couldn't let go of that stubborn need for control that locked others out, she would have to be the one to let him go. And she wouldn't cry. Not now. Not ever. She'd wasted too many tears on people who didn't want her in their life when she was younger. That wasn't who she was now.

So, with her head held high, she walked out of the room and headed for the elevator that would take her to her room.

CHAPTER TEN

JARED STOOD OUTSIDE of Sky's door and knew this wasn't a good idea. She was mad at him. And though he'd like to deny it, he understood why. She had been right. There had been more to that kiss than he was willing to admit, just like there had been more to their dance.

Leave it to Sky to call him on his bull right in the middle of a ballroom. He was in awe of the way she was willing to just put herself out there. She was so open about her feelings, while he instinctively wanted to deny that he might want something more with her.

It wasn't something new. He'd struggled with admitting he needed anyone, or anything for that matter, since he was a child. It had taken him years to believe that Katie and Jack Warner really wanted him to be their son. Looking back, he knew that had hurt them, especially his mom. But after his grandmother's death when he was only six, then being sent from one foster home to another for the next two years, he'd learned that the only person he could rely on was himself and the best way to stay safe was not to draw attention to himself.

But Sky Benton had put a dent in the armor he'd always wrapped himself in, with every flirty smile and every sassy wink she'd given him over the last few months. Now the kiss they'd just shared had blown a hole straight through that armor, right over his heart. A hole that he had no idea how to patch.

Instead of going to his own room, which would have been the safe thing to do, all he wanted to do was find Sky. Maybe if he saw her, he'd find that he'd just imagined the attraction that somehow had grown from an irritating buzz of electricity when she was around him into the scorching heat of a lightning strike during that kiss.

"What are you doing out here?" Sky's voice came from the crack in her doorway.

He'd been so busy trying to make up his mind about what to do that he hadn't noticed when her door had opened.

"I'm sorry. I didn't mean to disturb you," he said as she opened the door a little more.

"I'm a woman on her own in a hotel. The sound of someone pacing outside my door is going to disturb me." She leaned against the doorframe with her arms crossed over her chest. There was no way the cartoon character pajamas she wore should be nearly as sexy as Jared was finding them.

"I wanted to…" he started.

"Whatever it is that you are about to say had better not be another criticism. I've had it with those." Her chin went up, her eyes challenging him like a defiant child.

The truth was he didn't know what he wanted to say. Sky was everything that scared him. She threw herself into life with an abandonment he didn't feel comfortable with. He'd seen her do it the night of the party at the Carters'. While he had been happy to stay on the sidelines, she'd quickly thrown herself into the center of all those famous people and fit right in. Then she'd pulled him in with her, with that dance they'd shared. She lived without any restraints—something he didn't understand. She'd been through as much as he had in her life, yet she saw no danger in opening herself up to people.

Tonight when she'd kissed him, he felt like someone had kicked him in the chest. Part of him wanted to believe her when she said they had something special. But another part of him worried that she was throwing herself into one more thing without thinking it through. She lived for the moment while he was a planner. He liked to know what the next step would be. He needed to have control of everything around him and with Sky he had no control. That need for her took it all away and it scared him.

"I'm not going to apologize," he said, though he did owe her one. He'd been brutal in his denial of how that kiss had affected him. "I know I handled everything wrong. It's just that we are such opposites."

"What does that have to do with anything? Because we have different personalities, we can't enjoy a kiss? I've never asked you for anything more than a dance or a kiss. We're two adults who are attracted to each other. It's that simple. What is wrong with the two of us enjoying ourselves for one night?"

"What we're doing here, working with the Carters, it's important for the practice and for Legacy House. We have to be professional."

And this was why Sky scared him. Any other woman could have said those words and he would have agreed with her. He'd had relationships with women through college and med school that had been short and uncomplicated. He'd always made it plain that his priority was his education. Even the women in his life since he'd gone into practice with his dad, he'd made sure they had careers of their own that left no more room for anything more serious than an occasional date. It had been a good arrangement. And if a woman started to act like they might want more from him, he backed off. What Sky was offering him was no different from what he had offered those women.

He wasn't even surprised by that. Sky lived her life to the fullest. She made it plain by her actions that she was there for a good time. He just didn't know if being another one of her good times would be enough for him.

Yeah, Sky's way of living scared him, but what choice did he have when all he could think of with her standing there in front of him was that he'd be a fool to walk away from her.

"Nothing," he said, his mind reeling from the realization that this had been inevitable all along. Somewhere in the back of his mind, when he'd made his way to Sky's room, he'd known that kiss had changed things between the two of them forever. There was no going back to ignoring how Sky affected him. He could no longer deny that his body went on alert every time she was near him. He could continue telling her that it had been just a kiss they'd shared, but he would be lying to them both. "Maybe we should try that kiss one more time and see what happens?"

Without thinking it through or trying to figure out how this would fit into his plans, he stepped toward her. One of his hands cupped that defiant chin she'd challenged him with just moments before, while his other hand reached behind her head and pulled her toward him. Their lips met and this time, there was no mistaking the magnetic energy that drew the two of them together until he didn't know which affected him the most: his desire or hers.

Her lips parted, welcoming him inside, and the sweet taste of her filled him. His hand slid lower and he pulled her closer to him.

"Well?" she asked him when he let her go. Her smile was back and as always, it made his heart beat a little faster. Knowing that somehow he put that smile on her face made it race even more.

"Why don't you invite me inside so we can try it again?" he said.

Sky wasn't sure what had changed in Jared in the last few minutes, but she wasn't going to complain. She had no doubt that he had shownd up at her door with just another of his apologies on his mind. She'd wanted to break through Jared's hard outer shell for months, her interest going from curiosity to caring when he'd started opening up to her, to full-blown desire once she'd seen that he had the same response to her as she had to him.

They'd played a game of cat and mouse, her being the

cat for the most part. Some women wouldn't be comfortable with that, but with Jared it had been fun. But after the way he'd reacted to their first kiss, she'd been ready to walk away. With him now asking for an invitation inside her room, things had suddenly taken an unexpected turn.

"Come inside," she said. She turned away from him, not reaching for his hand. This had to be a decision he made by himself. She needed to know that he wanted to take this step on his own. She didn't want to wonder later if she had led him in there. Jared valued control of his own life more than anything else. And if he took that step inside her room, if he laid her on that bed, she would give him all the control he needed.

She felt his hand on her back as he joined her before closing the door behind them. The room wasn't large and the king-size bed took up most of it. Turning, she waited for him to make the first move. When his arms came around her waist, she wrapped her own around his neck, settling into his embrace. His lips touched hers, hesitant at first. Was he having second thoughts?

But when he deepened the kiss, she let all her doubts go. They stood there kissing for several minutes, his hands exploring her body with a thoroughness that was just a part of who Jared was. They moved up her body, skimming the sides of her breasts before running down her sides to cup her bottom, pulling her against the hard length of him. She arched her body until her most intimate parts slid against him.

Her nipples puckered from the cold air in the room and she realized she had somehow lost her top. When he lifted her against him, she wrapped her legs around his waist. She started to protest when he laid her on the bed and untangled her legs from him, then stopped herself.

"I want to see all of you," he said, rising back from the bed and pulling her pajama pants from her body.

Her panties came next and she felt exposed to him as he stood there in front of her, still wearing the clothes he'd worn to the concert. Then she looked at his eyes and saw the heat there. She had never had a man look at her that way, with so much desire and need. She let herself relax into the bed as he began to remove his shirt. When his pants followed, she found it harder to keep from squirming. He was a beautiful man and the anticipation of touching all of him made it hard not to reach up and pull him down to her.

But she'd promised herself that she'd let him have control tonight. So she waited for him, all the while her body becoming more aroused by the sight of him. When he finally moved toward her, her breaths were coming quicker. She wanted to touch him. To kiss him. She wanted to take him inside of her and find the release her body craved.

"You are so beautiful," he said as he placed one knee between her legs and began to climb onto the bed. When he stopped and kissed her calf, then skimmed his tongue up to the top of that thigh, she couldn't help but squirm against him. When he parted her legs and moved between them her hips bucked up to greet him. She needed him inside her now. How could he still have so much control? Couldn't he see that he was driving her wild?

"Jared, I need…" Her voice broke off as his lips grazed one of her nipples.

"Tell me what you need," Jared murmured before his lips moved up her collarbone and behind her ear. "Tell me and I'll give it to you."

He knew what she wanted. He knew yet he held himself back from her. She started to protest but then she saw his hand tremble as it came up and pushed her hair from her face. No matter how strong his control, he was close to breaking. She could wait him out, knowing that he was reaching his limit, but why? She didn't want to play games anymore.

"I need you inside me," Sky said, the words barely out of her mouth before he was parting her legs and guiding himself inside her. Her body welcomed him as he filled her with his first thrust, but he still held himself back.

"Let go for me, Jared. Give me everything you have." As if her words had broken through all his restraints, his lips took hers in a kiss that left no doubt all his control had been abandoned. His hips thrust against her, filling her with every stroke. She wrapped her arms around his shoulders and held on as she rode out a storm of desire like she had never known.

He placed one of her legs around his waist and she arched her body as the pleasure of this new position started to build.

Her release came over her with no notice, her body shuddering as she felt Jared's body stiffen against her before he thrust inside of her one more time.

She lay there, her body spent and empty while at

the same time her heart was filled with something she couldn't recognize. Satisfaction? Oh, yes, she was definitely satisfied. She'd never felt so satisfied in her life. But that wasn't it. It was something more, something that she wasn't ready to admit. Not now. Not yet. Right then, all she wanted to do was enjoy the moment. Tomorrow would take care of itself. Didn't it always?

CHAPTER ELEVEN

SKY'S PHONE RANG and she blindly reached over to the nightstand. Pushing up in the bed, she realized two things. One, it had to be very early as the sky was just beginning to lighten. And two, Jared was gone.

"Hello," Sky said, disappointed that instead of Jared it was Mindy on the phone. She'd made plans to meet her for breakfast, but not this early.

"Hey, Sky, it's Trey. Mindy's not feeling good. I've already called Jared and he's on his way up to our room. He wanted me to call you too."

"What exactly is she feeling?" Sky asked as she hurried to slip on the clothes she'd laid out the night before.

"She was up several times last night with her stomach. She says it's only a stomach bug, but I'm not sure." The concern in the man's voice was enough to have Mindy walk out of her room while still trying to get her shoes on.

"What's the room number?" she asked as she hopped on one foot into the elevator, pulling the last shoe on.

She pushed the button to take her up. The elevator stopped on the next floor and Jared joined her.

She didn't say anything about the fact that he had left her room during the night. Had he regretted their night together? She refused to believe that. Jared had wanted her last night. Unlike the kiss she had initiated, he had been the one to come to her room. But now wasn't the time to discuss what had happened between the two of them.

"Thanks for having Trey call me," Sky said, feeling an awkwardness she wasn't familiar with. "He said she'd been sick during the night, but not much else."

"It could only be a stomach bug like she thinks or it could be something more serious. She might have to cut back on performing until after the baby is born." The elevator stopped at the penthouse floor and Jared waited for Sky to exit before following.

Trey met them at the door and took them to the bedroom, where Mindy sat in bed. Her face was pale and there were dark circles under her normally bright eyes.

"I'm feeling better," Mindy said. "I'm sure it's just a bug."

"Let Jared and Sky check you out," Trey said as he kneeled beside her.

"Okay, but I don't need both of y'all. Why don't you and Jared go get a cup of coffee?"

Sky waited for Jared to protest, but instead he handed her a satchel she hadn't seen him carrying. Opening it, she saw that there were several pairs of sterile gloves inside along with scissors, a clamp and a suction bulb. Leave it to Jared to have a bag readied in case he had to deliver an unexpected baby.

"So why don't you tell me exactly what you're feeling?" Sky asked Mindy once the men had left the room.

"It's just some cramping. My stomach is a little upset I guess. I don't think it's the baby."

"When is the last time you did a kick count?" Sky asked, as she casually placed her hand on Mindy's stomach. Sky didn't have anything to monitor contractions so she would have to do it the old-fashioned way.

"I just did one. The baby is very active. Do you think there's something wrong with them?" Mindy placed her own hand on her abdomen, whether to soothe herself or the baby inside her, Sky wasn't sure.

"I don't think so," she said, her hand remaining on Mindy's abdomen as it tightened, then after a few seconds relaxed. She hadn't grabbed her watch on her way out of her hotel room so she began to count manually in her head.

"Tell me about the pain you're feeling. Does it come and go?" Sky asked. The contraction she'd felt had only lasted a few seconds, but Mindy was only around thirty-one weeks now. She didn't need to be having any contractions.

"Just some stomach cramping, like period cramps. It's not too bad. It started last night after we went to bed."

"Any bleeding?" Sky moved her hand off Mindy's stomach.

"No. I would have called you if I'd had any bleeding," Mindy said. "Should I be worried about this?"

"Sometimes that period cramping can be short, weak contractions. It's not unusual to have them during the last trimester of your pregnancy. They're usually Braxton-Hicks. Some people call them false labor, but they actually tone your uterus and help it get ready for when you do go into labor."

"So is that what I'm having?" Mindy asked. "Is that the cramping feeling?"

"Probably. I did feel a couple contractions, but they weren't strong. But with your history of having an earlier miscarriage I'd like to have you monitored. Unfortunately, I don't have one here so we'll need to go to a local hospital."

"Can we do that? Will they let you use their equipment?" Mindy's apprehension seemed to grow with each word.

"Not like you're meaning, but you can be seen at any hospital when you are pregnant. No hospital can turn you down. But let's talk to Jared. Knoxville is a big city. He can probably contact a local obstetrician who will be willing to cover you in one of the local labor and delivery wards." Sky knew that neither Mindy nor Trey would like that idea.

"Trey's going to be upset. He'll probably cancel the rest of the tour. We only have two more concerts and they are both local."

"Let's see what's going on before y'all decide anything. If it's Braxton-Hicks and your cervix hasn't made any changes, you might manage two more concerts, though that is between you and Trey. I do think it would probably be best to rest more. Maybe cancel the after-parties?"

Mindy nodded her head in agreement. "The party last night was fun, but I shouldn't have done all that dancing."

As if in afterthought, Mindy added, "I didn't see you or Jared on the dance floor."

"I headed to bed early while the party was still going. I'm not used to all that partying like you." It was a true statement if maybe not the whole story. Why she left and what happened afterward wasn't something she was prepared to tell anyone. She'd have to talk about it with Jared at some point. It wasn't like the two of them could ignore what happened, though, by the way he was acting, it wouldn't surprise her if Jared planned to do just that. And the fact that he had left during the night without saying anything to her still bothered her even though she knew it was probably just her insecurity that had her feeling as if he regretted the night. She'd been left one too many times for it not to bother her, even though she knew she was being oversensitive due to her history.

A knock came on the door before Trey entered the room, followed by Jared. When Sky explained that she was concerned that Mindy was having some mild contractions and wanted to have her transported to a hospital for further monitoring, Jared pulled out his phone and started calling the nearby hospitals.

It was only a few minutes before he returned. "Okay. I talked to Dr. Ward at Knoxville Medical. She knows my father and she agreed to let the hospital staff know you are coming in. She's aware of the circumstances of wanting privacy and she notified the labor and delivery staff. She speaks highly of them and assures me that they'll guard your privacy."

"Do we need to call 911? Or an ambulance?" Trey

asked. He'd been pacing the whole time Jared had been on the phone.

Sky removed her hand from Mindy's abdomen. "I think if you can get us a car, it would be fine. The contractions she is having are weak and irregular right now."

Jared gave her a questioning look and she answered him with a smile. "I think Jared will agree with me that we are just doing this as a precaution."

"A car should be fine," he said. "I'll call downstairs and see if they can take care of that. I saw that they had shuttle vans available if needed."

Jared headed out the door to make the call and minutes later there was a knock on the door. Mindy scowled when she saw the wheelchair, but Jared assured her it was just another precaution.

Four hours later, the four of them were on their way back to Nashville with the assurance of Dr. Ward, as well as that of Jared and Sky, that Mindy and the baby were fine. Mindy had received a liter of IV fluid as it appeared that dehydration had been the reason for the early contractions. An exam showed she hadn't begun to dilate, and the baby's fetal heart tracing had been perfect. Once the contractions had stopped and after promising everyone that she would increase her fluid intake, Mindy had been discharged and cleared to travel.

When Trey had cornered him questioning if he should cancel the two concerts that were planned over the next two weeks, Jared had done the smart thing and recommended that he discuss it with his wife, as he had assured the man again that neither his wife nor his baby were in any danger at that time.

Jared had been in this situation before, with overprotective husbands worrying that something out of their control could happen to their wife or child. After the way Jared had lost his first mother, he understood their concerns. He knew that if it was him in that position, he would have wanted reassurances too. But he knew there were never any guarantees in life. His mother had been in perfect health before the pregnancy and even then her pregnancy had been without complications. It wasn't until after she had delivered that things had gone bad.

"Thank you again for being here," Trey said after coming out of the large bedroom in the back of the bus, where Mindy had lain down to rest.

"I'm glad I was here, though you would have been fine with just Sky." His father had been right about it being a good thing for the two of them to work together. Sky was a good midwife and had handled everything with Mindy the same as he would have himself.

It was the change in their personal relationship that he wasn't sure about now. Last night had changed everything. Becoming involved with a coworker wasn't something that he had ever considered before. He knew it was always safer to keep your personal life separate from your professional life. He'd crossed that line last night.

Yet still, he didn't regret it. What he'd experienced with Sky was different than anything he'd ever experienced before. And if he was honest, at least to himself, he had to admit that it had been much more than just a night of sex.

Holding Sky while she slept in his arms had given him a feeling of possessiveness so strong that it scared him.

"So Mindy keeps reminding me. I know my overprotectiveness drives her up the wall, but I can't help it. I keep telling her that it's my responsibility to keep them safe." Trey scratched his head before looking back up at Jared. "You would be the same way, right? If you were married and expecting a baby?"

Thoughts of Sky pregnant with his child sprang into his mind with no warning. His imagination flared with visions of a pregnant Sky, her abdomen round with his baby. Another wave of possessiveness washed over him. Sky pregnant with his baby?

Somehow, having a wife and a baby had never seemed to fit inside his plans. He worked too much. He didn't have time for a family. He wouldn't be a good husband. There were a thousand reasons for why he didn't think he was husband or father material.

But the biggest obstacle was that he had never met anyone he wanted to share his life with. There had never been anyone that he could feel safe enough to trust his heart to. No one who he trusted enough to give up the control that ensured his life was orderly and secure. And if he had met that person, that one person who he was willing to risk his heart for, would he even have enough courage to love them knowing they could be taken away from him at any time?

"I'm sure I'd be just as protective." And that protectiveness would annoy Sky no end.

He had to stop this. He couldn't think of Sky that

way. This was exactly what he'd been worried about happening just moments before. He was letting what they'd shared the night before trick his mind into thinking that they had some type of future. It had only been the two of them sharing a night together. They'd both agreed to that. Hadn't they?

And even if they hadn't, the two of them couldn't be more incompatible. Sky with her live-life-in-the-moment lifestyle and his obsessive need to make decisions in a practical manner would never work together.

He thought about the night before, how she'd given up all her control to him. He would have thought that would be hard for her, but she'd seemed to enjoy it. It made him wonder how it would feel to switch roles and let Sky take control. Thinking about her being in control of him in the bedroom sparked an interest he didn't need to explore. It had taken all his strength to leave her bed the night before, he couldn't allow himself to think of picking up where they had left off. Like she had said, they were adults and it had been only for the one night.

"She's asleep," Sky said, joining the two of them at the gathering room on the bus.

The rest of their group had been sent home earlier along with the reality show's production crew. Only a couple of the Carters' trusted bandmates had been informed of why Jared and Sky were staying behind and traveling back to Nashville with Mindy and Trey. And the people who had been informed knew that Trey did not want any of this shared with any of the production crew.

"She's worried that Joe and Marjorie are going to be

mad when they hear she went to the hospital without informing them," Sky said as she took a chair beside him.

"She's right, but if we'd told them they probably would have wanted to have a crew there in the hospital recording it all for the show. I wish I'd never let Marjorie talk me into doing the show," Trey said as he pulled his phone out and headed to the front of the bus to place his call.

"I think Mindy is regretting it too, but what are they supposed to do? They signed the contract. According to Mindy they're stuck in it for another two years." Sky yawned and closed her eyes. "Hopefully something more interesting will happen to take all the show's concentration off of the pregnancy. I don't understand why Marjorie is pushing the focus on the pregnancy so much. She obviously cares about them."

"We still have an hour and a half till we get home. Go take a nap in one of the bunks. Maybe if we all get lucky, Marjorie will find something else to concentrate all her attention on."

"I hope so too," she said as she headed to the back of the bus to one of the curtained bunks, "just as long as it isn't us."

CHAPTER TWELVE

SKY HAD TO drag herself into the office Monday morning. She didn't know how Mindy did it with the late-night parties and all the traveling. After getting home Sunday afternoon, she'd barely finished the laundry she'd left for the weekend, before she was crawling into bed. She guessed the glamorous life of musicians came with a cost. Just like being a midwife came with her being on call the next twenty-four hours.

"Good morning," she called to the receptionist, stopping to see if there were any messages from any of her patients.

"Good morning. I see you had a good weekend," Leo said, handing her a couple notes. "Lori said for me to have you call her as soon as you came in."

Lori had been on for the weekend midwifery coverage at the hospital and would want to give a report on any of Sky's patients she had seen. "I'll give her a call. Anything else I need to know?"

"Nope. What about you? Anything you'd like to share?" Leo moved in closer over his desk. "You know I can keep a secret."

Leo could keep a secret about as well as she could give up chocolate. "Nope. No secrets today."

Besides, the only secret that anyone at the office would be interested in concerned her and Jared, and that wasn't anything she planned on sharing with anyone...well, except maybe Lori.

She put her bag away and put on the white lab coat she wore around the office before glancing down at the messages Leo had taken for her. One was the message to call Lori. The other was a message from Jasmine asking her to call.

The call had been left with their answering service before the office had opened, which meant that the girl had been up early, probably getting ready for her classes. Sky put in the call but didn't get an answer. Jasmine had probably already started her classes for the day and couldn't answer.

Next she returned Lori's call. "Hey, what's up?"

"Where are you?" Lori asked, her words fast and breathless.

"I just got to the office. Why didn't you call my cell?" Sky asked, taking a seat at her desk. By the sound of Lori's voice, she knew something was wrong.

"I did call your cell. It goes straight to voicemail." Now Lori's words were clipped and sharp. Her best friend wasn't happy with her.

Sky pulled the phone out of her pocket and realized it was turned off. "Sorry. Just tell me what's up."

"Me? Why don't you tell me what's up? I wasn't off

in Knoxville partying and I definitely wasn't making
out with Jared."

Sky's stomach did a bounce, a twist, and then dove
down to her toes as her heart rate did its own dangerous
dip. "How do you know about that?"

Sky was sure Jared hadn't told anyone and she would
have sworn no one had been paying attention to them at
the party. But unless Lori had developed some new psy-
chic abilities, someone had talked. She held her phone
up and waited as it powered up then signaled that she
had three missed calls and six text messages, most of
them from Lori.

"Because ever since the office found out that Mindy
has become one of our patients, the staff has been following the Carters' reality show on social media. Check
your phone. I sent you the picture someone sent me."

Sky scrolled past a message from Mindy to the first
message she had received from Lori this morning. A
picture appeared on her screen and she recognized the
room. It was the ballroom at the hotel. Trey Carter stood
over to the side facing the camera with his arm around
Mindy's waist. In front of him with their backs turned
to the camera, some of the band members were playing.
Sky could recognize Jenny from this view, but not the
other players. But it wasn't the famous music stars who
had been circled in red marker on the picture. From the
angle of the camera, you could see two people in the
background. It was unmistakably her and Jared tangled
together in a kiss. That was what had been circled. That
was what most of the staff had seen?

"Can we talk about it later? Maybe lunch?" Sky needed to make a call to Jared to warn him before his father saw the picture. And then she needed to have a talk with a certain receptionist who she was sure had sent the picture out to the staff.

Her phone beeped with a call from Jared. Someone must have already shown him the picture. While normally she'd be able to look at it as a reminder of a magical night she'd always treasure, she knew that this would upset him. He'd kept his life so private until they'd started working for the Carters.

And his father? He'd trusted them to represent the practice.

"I have to take another call. I'll call you back to get a report on the weekend."

She clicked over to Jared's call. "Hey. I'm sorry. I'll explain to your father that it's all my fault."

"Sky, I'm glad I got you. I'm over at the hospital. One of your patients, Khiana Johnson, just came in and it looks like she is having a placental abruption. They're taking her back to the operating room now, but I thought you might want to come over. I've got to go. I need to scrub up now." He hung up the phone and for a moment she just stared at it before she realized what he had been saying.

Khiana Johnson was a single mom and a nurse who worked at the hospital on the surgical floor. Jared hadn't said how the baby was doing but if they had been in distress she was sure he wouldn't have stopped to make a phone call.

The hospital was just across from the office, no more than a five-minute walk. If she hurried she'd be able to slip into the OR by the time the baby was delivered. She pulled off her lab jacket, threw it on the desk and headed for the back door.

Because she was starting her call rotation she was already dressed in scrubs, which meant she didn't have to change her clothes once she'd made it up to the L & D unit. She covered her shoes and hair, then after washing her hands donned her mask. Opening the door to the OB operating room, she heard the weak cry of a baby. Jared looked over at her as he handed the baby to the nursery nurse waiting with a blanket to receive the little one. The baby looked to be around five pounds, a good weight for being at only thirty-five weeks gestation, but the little boy was pale and cyanotic. Not good.

The anesthesiologist recognized her and offered her his stool beside Khiana, but she shook her head. The young mother appeared to be sleeping after receiving a dose of general anesthesia. She was in good hands. It was the baby that Khiana would want her to watch over.

"How are we doing?" she asked the pediatrician as she watched monitors being applied to the baby.

"Not bad. Usually we see this in preemies. I'm thinking his Dubowitz score will put him around thirty-five weeks gestation so he has that going for him. He's requiring some oxygen and we're getting stat labs. Just looking at his color, I suspect he's going to need a transfusion. Do you know if there was anyone here with his mom? I'll need to get consent."

"I don't. She's a floor nurse on one of the adult floors. She might have been at work. I've met her sister at one of Khiana's visits though, and I'm sure her number is in our paperwork. I'll call the office and get the number." Sky left the room feeling better now that she could at least do something to help Khiana. She wracked her brain for some missed sign that this could happen but there wasn't anything—Khiana had been in perfect health the last time she'd seen her. They'd both been happy with her weight gain and there had been no concerns for hypertension.

After calling the office, she called Khiana's sister and found out that she was already on her way to the hospital after receiving a call from Khiana's nursing manager. As soon as she hung up, her phone chimed with another call and she saw that it was Jasmine.

"Hey, Jasmine, I'm glad you called me back. What's up?"

"I'm going to tell my parents that I'm giving the baby up for adoption today. I can't do it, Sky. I want to, for my parents, but every time I think of trying to raise the baby on my own it doesn't feel right. Maybe there's something wrong with me." The girl was becoming upset again, just like she had the day they'd talked at Legacy House.

"Take a deep breath, Jasmine. It's going to be okay. Jared told me that he could tell your mother cares about you when she came into your visits. You might disagree on what is best for you and the baby, but if you tell them what you've told me I'm sure they will support you. Give them a chance to see that you've thought this through.

In the end, this is your decision, not theirs. Even if they don't understand it now, I'm sure they will come around. And until then you have a place to stay at Legacy House as long as you need it."

"Okay," Jasmine said, her voice calmer now. "Thanks for everything. I talked with your sister. She gave me the name of a local adoption agency where I can meet the people who would want to adopt the baby."

Sky gave Jasmine some more reassurance and asked her to call back after she talked to her parents. A few minutes later Jared joined her in the physician's consultation room.

"There wasn't anything I missed. Her blood pressure has been in the normal range her whole pregnancy. She doesn't smoke or do drugs. This shouldn't have happened." She'd had Leo pull up the vital signs from Khiana's last three visits and had been reassured that just like she'd remembered, there had been no issues.

"I thought I told you when I called. We know the cause of the abruption. She fell on the floor after someone spilt something and didn't clean it up. Her manager was livid."

Sky's body relaxed and she realized she'd been dreading this from the moment she'd gotten the call. She'd assumed that Jared would think it was something that she had missed. She'd hoped they were past that—working together so closely the last few weeks, he had to see that she took her patients' care as seriously as every other provider—but clearly she hadn't quite shaken off the fear that he would always view her, and possibly all midwives, as in some way less qualified, because of the circumstances of his birth mother's death.

There was nothing she could do to change that. A part of her would have even understood—an error had been made and his life had been changed forever. And still, she was surprised at the depth of her relief at hearing that he hadn't assumed she'd done something wrong with Khiana's care. His professional trust meant a lot to her.

"I'm glad you were here to take care of her. I'll go check on her before I go back to the office." She looked over to see Jared busy working on his operating report. She hated to interrupt him when he was busy. Waiting to talk to him at the office would probably be the best. Except there was no guarantee that someone wouldn't mention seeing the picture of them together before she could warn him... This might be the only chance she had.

"So, about this weekend..." Her voice trailed off. Why did this have to feel so awkward? The man had seen her naked. She should be able to talk about this without feeling so self-conscious.

"It's okay, Sky. It was one night. Like you said, we're both adults. And now that we're back to the real world, there's no reason to let it affect our professional association."

Professional association? Was he serious in thinking that nothing had changed between them?

"Look, I just need to know if anyone has asked you about the two of us being in Knoxville with Mindy and Trey?"

"Who would know we went to Knoxville? I haven't

even told my father yet," Jared said, his head still bent over the computer.

"Oh, I'd say most everyone at the office and even some of the nurses here in L & D know we were in Knoxville." There was no telling how many people had seen the picture posted on the *Carters' Way* socials. Fortunately, most would be concentrated on the stars of the show, not two lowly health care workers.

"What are you talking about?" His fingers went still on the computer and he turned in his chair so that he could see her.

"Apparently ever since it was announced that we would be taking care of Mindy during her pregnancy, most of the office has been following the reality show."

"You said you watched some of the shows. It's not surprising that some of the staff might be curious about it too. What does that have to do with us?" His shoulders shrugged and he turned back to the computer. "If they posted something about us going with them to Knoxville, it's not a big deal, though I doubt they said anything about their preterm contractions scare."

She could only beat around the bush about this for so long. It might have been easier on her if someone else had made a comment about that picture so she didn't have to be the one with news that she knew he wasn't going to like. "I don't think that was mentioned. Well, at least no one said anything about it. It's one of the pictures they posted of the two of us that's circulating through the office that has everyone's attention."

"Why? Everyone knew we would be working closely

with Mindy. My father made it clear that good public relations with their reality show would be necessary. I don't see why a photo of us would be cause for much interest."

"Maybe you should see the photo. Then you'll understand." She waited for him to stop typing before she handed him her phone, where she'd pulled up the picture Lori had sent her.

He stared at the photo, not saying a word, for several moments before he handed her back the phone and turned once again to the computer without saying a word. For a second she thought about stealing the keyboard from him so he would be forced to talk to her. Then she thought of hitting him over the head with it to see if maybe that would be enough to get a human reaction out of him.

"How can you sit there and ignore this so calmly? If your father doesn't know about this already, he will soon."

"My father is not into reality shows, nor is anyone likely to have the nerve to send him the picture."

"I think we should tell him. I'll explain that it was all my fault. He knows how spontaneous I get sometimes. It might not be the kind of attention the practice needs, but except for our staff no one is going to recognize us in the background of that picture." She realized that she wasn't really worried about what other people's reaction would be to seeing her and Jared kissing. Why would she be? It wasn't like it was something she was ashamed of. It was only Jared's reaction that had worried her.

Everything between them was new and fragile. She'd convinced Jared, and almost herself, that she just wanted to have a casual relationship with him. Nothing serious. Just two adults enjoying a night together.

But after what they'd shared in Knoxville, she didn't know how that would really be enough for her now. Now she wanted time with Jared to discover if this thing between them was real. Because no matter how much she wanted to deny it, she'd fallen in love with him, something that he most definitely wasn't ready to hear. Jared was a planner and he always liked to play it safe and keep a low profile. The last thing she needed was for the two of them to come to everyone's attention, something that would be sure to have Jared running for cover. But it looked like it was too late to stop that now. All she could do was damage control.

"Telling my father isn't necessary. Like I said, it's not likely that he'll hear about this. The best thing we can do is ignore all this and not give them anything else to talk about. In a week everyone will have forgotten all about it," Jared said, his words calmly destroying all her hopes as he made it plain that was exactly what he planned to do.

So he was just going to ignore what they'd shared? Was it really possible that what had seemed so special to her had only been what she had claimed to want? Just one night for them to enjoy each other? She knew this was all her fault. She'd asked for just that one night without thinking it through. And now that she knew she wanted a chance for more, it was too late.

Without saying another word, she walked out of the room. Maybe he'd only meant they would let everyone *think* there was nothing going on between them, but she didn't think that was the case. He'd never felt comfortable getting involved with her. He saw her as someone who liked to rush into things without thinking them through.

And in this case he'd been right. She believed life was too short to measure out all the moves you made in advance. But that wasn't what this was between the two of them, she was sure of that now, because it had been building for a long time. She just hoped that Jared would see that.

She took her time getting back to the office from the hospital. The walk was mostly sidewalks and parking lots, but the spring air was soft and sweet. Spring had always been her favorite time of year. It held the promise that the cold, dark winter was over and the future held only sunshine and warmth. She used to love helping her grandmother with the planting of their garden. Then there was the waiting for those seeds to grow into the plants they would harvest. But sometimes, a late cold snap would come and freeze all the fragile ones. It always made her feel like everything she had worked for had been for nothing. Why put so much of yourself into something when you weren't going to get anything back?

That was how she felt about her relationship with Jared now. She'd tried everything to show him who she was, and to get him to let her see who he really was and what they could have together. She'd put herself out there and bared herself to him in a way she'd never done before. And for what?

She opened the back door of the office and glanced

down the empty hallway, glad that everyone was busy with their patients. The last thing she wanted right now was to be questioned about her and Jared.

She'd almost made it when one of the exam rooms opened and Lori walked out followed by a very pregnant young woman with a baby on each hip.

"Megan, I promise you it won't be much longer," Lori said as she opened a door leading out to the waiting room. "I'll have the receptionist make you an appointment for next week just in case, but I suspect you'll be delivered before the weekend."

Sky had started back down the hallway when Lori caught up with her and, taking her arm, pulled her into the supply room.

"Don't think you're going to get away that easily. Spill it, bestie. I want to know what happened in Knoxville. Don't leave out any of the details and maybe I'll forgive you for not telling me before everyone else in the office found out."

"I was going to tell you," she said, studying her hands before looking up to see one of Lori's eyebrows lift and her smile turn into a smirk that said she knew Sky wasn't telling the truth. "Okay, I don't know if I was going to tell you. I don't even know if there is anything to tell."

"I saw the picture. Why don't we start there?" Lori moved farther into the room until she came to an old exam table that had been stored in the room. Sky followed her and took a seat beside her.

"That was all my fault. The concert had been great and we were having so much fun at the party. Jared was playing with some of the band members and I was danc-ing with this cute old man."

"Wait. Jared was playing?" Lori asked. "Our Jared?"

"He's really good. His mom made him take lessons. He said it was so he would make friends, but I think she knew he had talent." Or maybe she was trying to give him a way to escape all the trauma he'd experienced as a child. "Anyway, it was just a spontaneous thing. He was having fun. I was having fun. I wrapped my arms around him and somehow we ended up kissing."

"And that's all it was? Just a once-and-done kiss?" Lori asked.

"Well, that was all it was supposed to be." And it would have been, except Jared had surprised her when he'd kissed her back and now there was no forgetting that kiss and the lovemaking that had followed that night. "We might have gotten a little carried away. You know how adrenaline works."

"I do. So did you tell Jared that your first kiss has now been captured for the world to see?" Lori had a wicked grin on her face. Her friend knew, just as she had, that it would be the last thing Jared would want to happen.

"I did. He seems to think as long as we ignore it, it will go away." She tried to keep the hurt from her voice.

"The attention from the kiss, or whatever it is that's happening between the two of you?" Lori asked.

Leave it to her friend to get right to the point. "I think he meant both."

They sat in silence for a moment. Sky knew she had

to get to work. Her patients had been waiting too long already and she knew Lori had patients of her own to see.

She stood and stretched before heading for the door. "I wish you could see him play the guitar. It's like the music brings him out of his shell."

"I think he needs someone like you to do that. He might not know it, or at least he might not be ready to admit it, but you're good for him. He needs some fun in his life," Lori said as the two of them walked out of the supply room.

Sky went over Lori's words as she grabbed her jacket and made her way to see her first patient. She'd started out just wanting to put some fun in Jared's life with her teasing, but now she knew he deserved more. He deserved someone who would love and accept him, just the way he was. For a moment she'd thought that person might be her, but now she knew better. Because no matter what her brain tried to tell her, her heart knew she deserved to have someone accept her just the way she was just as much as Jared.

CHAPTER THIRTEEN

THERE WAS NOTHING Jared wanted more than to head home. With his day starting out with an unexpected surgery, his schedule had been thrown off from then on. The advantage of his running late was that he hadn't had time to think about Sky or the picture she'd showed him. If any of the staff were curious about it, they hadn't said anything to him. Like he'd told her, it was best just to ignore the whole thing and not give anyone else a reason to speculate about the two of them. She hadn't been happy about it, but she had to accept that he was right. He'd learned early in life that it was better to keep your head down and let people forget about you. It was safer that way when you were a foster kid who was easy prey for the bullies in the world. Without a mother or father to take up for you or protect you, becoming invisible was the only way to stay out of their way.

He'd almost made it out of the office when he heard his father's voice calling his name. He stopped and retraced his steps to his father's office.

"I thought you had gone home," he said, taking a seat in front of Jack's desk. "What are you doing here?"

"I was waiting for you to finish. I heard you started

your day with an emergent C-section this morning. An abruption, Sky said." Jared's dad took off his glasses and laid them on his desk. He looked more tired than Jared felt, and that was saying a lot as Jared had barely slept since he'd come home from Knoxville.

"One of the nurses at the hospital had a fall. I just checked on the baby. He's received a transfusion and is doing well now. They expect him to get out of the NICU tomorrow if he continues without any setbacks."

"That's good," Jack said, his eyes studying his son a little too hard. "Sky told me the two of you traveled to Knoxville Saturday with the Carters and that Mindy had to be seen at the hospital there."

And what else had Sky told his father? He was afraid he knew the answer to that question. "She was a little dehydrated. She received some fluids. Nothing major."

His father's eyes still bore into him and it reminded him of the time when he was about eight and his father had questioned him about the dent in his mother's car. Jared had known that he was about to be sent back to the foster home when he'd admitted that he'd been riding his bicycle too fast on the driveway and had turned into the car to stop himself. After his dad had been assured that Jared wasn't injured, he'd sat him down and told him that he didn't need to hide things from them. If Jared messed up, his father wanted to know so he could help him make it right. It had been a turning point in their relationship. For the first time he'd felt safe in the knowledge that his parents had no intentions of sending him back into the foster system. He was their son. Forever.

"I guess Sky told you about that picture of us," Jared said. "I can explain."

"You mean the picture that I saw this morning on the *Carters' Way* show's socials?" his father asked. "No, Sky didn't say anything about it, though I gave her plenty of opportunities."

So she hadn't gone behind his back and told his father. Not that he'd had any right to ask her not to. She was involved in this as much as he was. "I asked her not to mention it. I didn't think you'd see it."

"I might not have if I hadn't overheard one of the techs chatting this morning. Do you want to talk about it?" his father asked.

Did he? It wasn't like the picture didn't explain itself. He and Sky had shared a kiss. Except it hadn't been just a kiss they'd shared. Not that he would be telling his father anything else about the night.

"I don't think so," Jared said. "I know it was very unprofessional and I'm sorry if we embarrassed you and the practice."

He started to promise his dad that it wouldn't happen again, but something held him back. No matter what he'd told Sky about the two of them, he knew there was still something between them and he didn't want to lie to his father.

"Who's embarrassed? In my day, you could kiss a girl without worrying about all the cameras people have these days. If anything, I owe you an apology for putting you in the situation. I know you value your privacy and I'm afraid you've lost some of that because of me."

"It's okay. I think you were right about me and Sky needing to work together with the Carters. You know I've had a problem with working with the midwives since they started here."

"Because of what happened with your mother. I know. It was a terrible thing to have had happen, Jared. But doctors make mistakes too. You can't hold what happened to your mother against every midwife you ever work with." They'd had this conversation a hundred times, yet it was like Jared was only now ready to hear it.

"I know. I was biased and wrong. Sky is as credible as any doctor I've worked with. We work differently, but I'm beginning to see that it doesn't have to be one or the other. Like I said, it's been good for me. I hope it's helped me grow as a doctor."

"And what about as a man?" Jack asked. "Sky's not only a competent practitioner. She's also a beautiful, strong woman."

She was all those things and more, yet still he held some part of himself back from her and he didn't even understand why. Would he ever get over being that little boy who was always too afraid to trust anyone?

"It's complicated," he said, hoping his father would let it go.

"Love's always complicated. And don't try to deny that you're in love with her. I saw the picture. That wasn't just any kiss. I'm not so old that I don't recognize the signs."

Jared started to argue with his father, then just shook his head. Once Jack decided that he was right about something, you couldn't change his mind. Besides, Jared wasn't even sure that his father wasn't right.

For the past six months he'd told himself that he was doing his best to ignore Sky, when really he couldn't wait each day to see what outrageous thing she'd do next. He'd enjoyed every wink and every ridiculous flirty smile that she'd sent his way. Now he got up each morning looking forward not only to her smiles, but also to the time they spent working together.

"I think I'll leave now, before you get any more ideas about my love life," he said, noticing how tired his dad looked tonight. "You going to be long?"

"No, I'll be right behind you. I just want to finish this last chart of the day. Go on home."

As his dad waved him away, Jared resolved to talk to him the next day. His father had to start cutting back his time at the office. He'd worked hard building the practice and Jared knew it meant a lot to him, but it was starting to take a toll. Jared had lost too many people in his life sooner than he should have. He didn't want to lose his father too.

Sky jumped as a knock came against the door of the providers' sleep room. She couldn't complain about the interruption to her sleep. She'd only been called for one patient so far. She reached for her phone, then realized she had left it in her jacket that hung on the back of the door.

"I'm coming," she called as she rolled out of bed. The clock on the side of the bed said it was just past midnight. She couldn't have been asleep for more than an hour.

She grabbed her phone from her jacket before she opened the door. The night-shift charge nurse stood waiting for her. "What's up?"

"The emergency room just called. There's a patient on their way in by ambulance," Kelly said. "They want you down there."

"Why can't they just send the patient up here?" Sky asked as she badged herself into the unit. All obstetric patients were immediately taken up to the L & D floor unless they had a life-endangering injury.

"They didn't say, just that the emergency room doctor wanted you there when she rolled in. The report they got was the patient is pregnant and had a seizure," Kelly said as they both headed to the elevators that would take them down. "They said they weren't expecting a delivery, but I thought I'd come check out the situation."

"Thanks," Sky said as they stepped onto the elevator. The charge nurse had years more experience than Sky and more than once she'd asked the older woman for her advice with a patient.

The elevator doors opened up right in the middle of the busy emergency room. "Did they say which room they wanted me in?"

Before Kelly could answer, she recognized one of the pediatricians headed toward her as the one that had taken care of Khiana's baby.

"They called you too?" she asked, not sure why he would have been called unless they had expected a delivery.

"I was down here seeing another patient and they told

me they had a pregnant seventeen-year-old coming in after having a seizure so I decided I'd stick around in case I was needed," the man said. They followed him when he turned toward the resuscitation rooms that were near the ambulance entrance.

Sky wished she had more information. She was going into this blind. If this was a real emergency then they should have called the doctor on call instead of the midwife on duty. Her phone dinged with an incoming message and she pulled it out of her pocket. Her screen showed she'd missed three calls from the same number. And she recognized the number. Legacy House. The incoming message was from Maggie, asking her to call.

Then it hit her. Seventeen years old. Missed calls from Legacy House. And finally, a seizure that in pregnancy was usually brought on when a patient had high blood pressure and proteinuria.

She started to make a call as they reached the room only to be pushed back into the hall as a couple of EMTs came through the door with a stretcher, where Jasmine lay unresponsive and intubated.

Instead of following the stretcher into the room, Sky moved farther back from the crowd of people waiting for the patient to arrive. The phone rang twice before she heard Jared's voice. "Sky, what's up?"

She realized then that she should have waited until she had the ambulance crew's report before calling him. She needed more information to make a true diagnosis. "They just brought Jasmine into the hospital. She's had a seizure."

"I'll be right there," Jared said, before hanging up.

She knew he would be upset that he hadn't been called instead of her. Jasmine's condition was much too critical for a midwife's care, but until Jared made it there she could at least help as best she could by giving the emergency room staff the girl's background.

As the ambulance crew rolled out their empty stretcher, Sky made it inside the room. It was busy in that orderly chaotic way of emergency rooms everywhere. One nurse was applying the monitors that would give them the necessary vital signs and heart tracings while another nurse was starting an IV.

"Where's that midwife?" a young doctor called from the head of the stretcher. Sky waited as he applied his stethoscope to Jasmine's chest to check her lung sounds to make sure the ET tube was properly placed before calling out to him.

"The patient is one of my colleague Dr. Warner's patients. Jared Warner. I've called and he's on his way. I do know the patient and I can tell you that she's seventeen years old and a Gravida One, around thirty-five weeks. She's been treated for high blood pressure for the last few weeks and I know Jared was concerned about pre-eclampsia."

A nurse called out a blood pressure and heart rate. Both were too high.

"You need to give her a four-gram magnesium sulfate bolus, then a continual infusion of two grams per hour. Otherwise she's going to seize again." Sky turned to Kelly, who had come to stand beside her. "Find a Doppler and get fetal heart tones, then call upstairs and tell them to set up the OR for a C-section."

Kelly looked at her for a moment, then headed out of the room. Sky knew that it wasn't usual for a midwife to be the one initiating a cesarean section, but she also knew Jared wouldn't want to wait any longer than necessary to deliver the baby. Sky just prayed that the baby was okay.

She spotted a small ultrasound machine across the room. Instead of waiting for Kelly, she rolled the ultrasound over to Jasmine's side and after coating the wand with jelly, placed it on her abdomen. Taking a deep breath to prepare herself for the worst possible outcome, Sky maneuvered it till she could see Jasmine's little boy's heart. She let out her breath and her body relaxed for the first time since she'd arrived in the emergency room. She took a few screenshots for Jared, then turned to the ER doctor, who had been watching her.

"The baby's fine. Fetal heart tones look good on the ultrasound, but I want to get her on a continuous monitor." One of the baby's feet kicked out at the ultrasound wand and she laughed with relief. "I think he's ready to get out of there though."

Kelly appeared back in the doorway, the Doppler in her hand. "Sky, the patient's parents just showed up in L & D. I didn't know what you would want me to tell them."

"I wasn't sure where to send them when we picked up the patient. I guess they assumed she'd be taken up there since she's pregnant," said one of the EMTs that Sky recognized from Jasmine's arrival.

"Were her parents at Legacy House?" Sky asked. She

remembered the conversation she'd had with Jasmine earlier that day. Had her parents come to the house to talk her out of going through with the adoption?

"No. She was brought in from home," the EMT said before leaving the room.

Sky needed to talk to Jasmine's parents to see what had happened and to let them know her condition, but she didn't want to leave her till Jared arrived.

"Okay, start the mag sulfate and then get her over to CT. We need to make sure her head is cleared. I want to rule out anything else going on," the ER doctor said, then nodded to Sky before leaving the room.

Though she'd seen a nurse check Jasmine for responsiveness, Sky went through the motions herself, checking Jasmine's pupils and response to pain. The minimum amount of sedation the EMTs had reported giving her to intubate could be part of the reason the girl was less responsive, or it could be that she was still postictal from the seizure.

"What happened?" Jared asked as he rushed into the room, an ER nurse behind him with the bag of magnesium sulfate Sky had requested.

"I don't know all the details, but it looks like she had a seizure. Her blood pressure when she arrived was two-twenty over one-seventeen. They're treating that, and with her history I asked them to bolus her with four grams of magnesium sulfate and then start her on two grams an hour."

Sky and Jared moved back as the nurse, having started the medication, began to roll Jasmine out of the room with the respiratory tech at her bedside assisting with the ventilator and other equipment. "They're taking her to CT now and I asked Kelly to have L & D set up for a cesarean section."

When Jared didn't say anything, Sky looked over at him to find his eyes glued to his patient. "I shouldn't have listened to her. I knew I should have admitted her last week but she got upset about being in the hospital because of her classes. She agreed to being on strict bed rest and her blood pressure reports from Maggie had been improving."

"I didn't know you'd put her on bed rest," Sky said. If Jasmine had been put on bed rest how had she been at her parents' house? Was that why the girl had called her earlier? Was she so determined to see her parents that she'd ignored Jared's orders?

"I don't understand what happened. I called Maggie on the way here and she said that when she went to give Jasmine her medications, she was gone."

None of this made sense. The last time Sky had talked to Jasmine she'd been determined to get her parents to agree with her about putting her baby up for adoption. Even though she hadn't known about the bed rest, Sky had assumed that Jasmine would call her parents on the phone or that she'd have them come see her at Legacy House.

Jared was quiet as they followed Jasmine's stretcher over to the CT department. She didn't have to ask to know that he was thinking about his mom. "This isn't your fault, Jared. I don't know everything that happened, but I do know that Jasmine left Legacy House to go see her parents."

"Why would she do that? I know she's been upset about whatever happened between her and them, but they could have come to see her."

"I don't know why she went there, but I do know..."

"Dr. Warner, the radiologist wants to see you," the charge nurse said, rushing over to them.

Sky waited while Jared and the radiologist reviewed the CT screens. Sky needed to tell him about the conversation she'd had with Jasmine and her suspicion that the young girl had gone to see her parents, hoping to get their support for her plan to find a couple to adopt her baby. But that would have to wait.

"The CT is clear. Call the ER and let them know that we are going straight up to the OB floor. I want to get her on a fetal monitor and talk to her parents," Jared said, before walking out of the room.

Unsure of what she could do to help him, Sky stayed back with Jasmine and called Kelly to see what room the charge nurse planned for them to use. Once Jasmine was taken to the pre-op area, where they were met by an anesthesiologist, Sky went to find Jared.

Jared had no problem picking Jasmine's mom out from the rest of the visitors in the waiting room, though he'd only met her a couple times. Even if he hadn't met her before he would have known Jasmine's parents anyway, because they were the only two huddled in a corner of the waiting room looking anything but excited as they waited for news of their daughter.

"Mr. and Mrs. Jameson?" he asked as he approached the couple. He'd been aware that Jasmine's parents were older than most parents of a seventeen-year-old, but the woman whose eyes met his seemed to have aged a decade since the last time he'd seen her. "Can we step out for a minute to talk?"

"Is she…is our Jasmine gone?" the woman asked him, her voice breaking with the last word.

"No. She's very sick but she's stable right now," Jared said. "What has Jasmine told you about her pregnancy?"

"Nothing, until today. She's barely talked to us since she left home. I call her every day, but she barely talks to me. She used to tell me everything…well, maybe not everything. The pregnancy was a surprise and maybe we didn't handle it as well as we should have." Jasmine's mom stopped and took a breath.

"It wasn't that we didn't support her. You know that, Lily. We told her from the first that we would help with the baby any way we could," Jasmine's father huffed, placing his arm around his wife's shoulders. "It doesn't make sense to me."

"Can you tell me what happened tonight?" Jared asked. Right now the only thing that mattered to him was the welfare of Jasmine and her baby. Everything else could be sorted out between this family later.

"Jasmine called and asked if she could come talk to us," Jasmine's mother said. "Of course I said yes. I thought she wanted to talk about coming back home. I was so excited. I offered to come pick her up but she insisted that she would take the bus."

"I thought that was why she looked so tired when she got there," the father said. "Remember, Lily? I told you that our girl didn't look good. That bus stop is three blocks from the house. She didn't have any business walking all that way."

"Actually, you are right, Mr. Jameson. I had put Jasmine on strict bed rest due to her blood pressure being too high. She didn't tell you?"

"No, she didn't say anything about that. All she wanted to talk about was this idea that she didn't want to keep her baby. She said that she's been talking to someone in your office and she was going to help her with an adoption. We tried to make her see that she didn't need to do that. We're her parents, that baby's grandparents. She should be talking to us, not some stranger."

Why was Jared not surprised that Sky had gotten tangled up in this family's affairs?

"She said that was why she came to see us. That this woman, this midwife, told her that Jasmine had to tell us what she planned to do." Mrs. Jameson's grief had turned to anger now, something that Jared was all too familiar with.

"Like I was saying, I had put Jasmine on strict bed rest because of her blood pressure and because she was beginning to show signs of preeclampsia. From what I've been told, she had a seizure while she was at your house."

"That's right. One moment she was arguing with us and then she said she felt funny and sat down on the floor.

That's when she started shaking. I didn't know what to do. Her eyes were open but it was like she wasn't there," Lily said.

"I called 911 the moment I realized what was happening. By the time they got there she wasn't shaking, but she couldn't talk to us. The EMTs said something about her airway being bad so they put a tube down her and brought her here," Jasmine's father said. "But none of this matters. What we want to know is how is she now?"

"And the baby. How is the baby?"

"Like I said, Jasmine is stable for now and the baby looks good. We've got Jasmine on some medicine to keep her from having more seizures for now and she does have a tube down her throat—more to protect her airway if she has another seizure than because she needs help breathing. Unfortunately, the only way Jasmine is going to get better is for us to take her to the operating room and deliver the baby."

He had just finished explaining to the Jamesons about the procedure and the risks to both Jasmine and the baby when he saw Sky coming toward them.

"Excuse me. I'll be back in just a moment," he said, then stepped in front of them to intercept her before she could say anything that would upset the couple. The last thing he needed was for Jasmine's parents to discover that it had been Sky who had been speaking to their daughter about giving up the baby.

"Can I talk to you?" he asked her, taking her arm and leading her farther down the hall.

"Anesthesia is here and the OR is ready," she said. "Are those Jasmine's parents?"

"Yes, and you are not to go anywhere near them," he said, keeping his voice low so he wouldn't be overheard. "They said someone told their daughter that she had to tell them that she didn't want to keep the baby, and they know it was someone from our office. They're going to blame this on you. They said that she went to see them because of what you told her to do."

For a moment Sky didn't say anything. When she finally spoke, her own voice was low and her face was expressionless. "Do *you* blame me for this?"

"I know you didn't make Jasmine have a seizure," he answered, brushing his hand across his face as if he could scrub away the night. Unfortunately, it didn't work. "I just think you should have talked to me before you began advising my patient about her baby."

"You asked me to talk to her," Sky said, her voice louder now.

"If you had talked to me maybe we could have found a way to help her without her having a fight with her parents. You knew I was concerned about her blood pressure. If you'd talked to me first you would have known that Jasmine had been put on bed rest and didn't need anyone upsetting her. Didn't you know that her facing off with her parents could make her blood pressure spike?" Jared found himself getting upset and he didn't know why. "I can't even disagree with her parents—it might be that argument that caused the seizure."

"Let me talk to them. I'll explain that I was just trying to help their daughter."

"No. The last thing they need right now is for you to get them more upset. You've done enough for now." Jared wanted to take the words back as soon as he saw the hurt in Sky's eyes. He wanted to tell her that he didn't blame her for any of this, but deep inside, a part of him—the part that still hadn't found a way to forgive the midwife he blamed for his mother's death—wasn't sure. He knew that she never would have intentionally done anything to hurt Jasmine. Of course she wouldn't.

But Sky did have a tendency to do things without thinking them through. That was part of the reason he hadn't trusted this thing between the two of them. He didn't want to be yet another thing she got involved with without thinking it through.

Sky looked past him to Jasmine's parents before turning her gaze back to him. "I'm sorry."

With those two words, she turned and walked away, leaving him wondering what she was apologizing for. For getting too involved with Jasmine and her parents? Or for getting involved with him?

CHAPTER FOURTEEN

SKY WANDERED IN and out of the room as the nurses prepared Jasmine to be taken to the OR. She felt helpless in
doing anything for Jasmine, and just as helpless in dealing with Jared. Could he really be blaming her for what
had happened to Jasmine?

Was he right?

She wasn't sure why she hadn't talked to him about
Jasmine and her problem with her parents. And while she
hadn't thought to tell him about her advising Jasmine to
contact her parents and being honest with them about
the reasons she didn't want to keep the baby, he hadn't
shared with her that Jasmine had been put on bed rest
either. Had they both been so tied up in their personal
drama that they'd forgotten what was really important?

"We're taking her back now," Kelly said to Sky just as
she was about to step into the room. The team started to
push past her as they rolled Jasmine out toward the OR.
"Are you coming with us?"

Sky started to say yes, then remembered the look
Jared had given her and his warning for her to stay out
of things. He'd made it clear that he didn't want her in

his OR. She was pretty sure he didn't want her anywhere near him.

"No," she said, turning and walking away from Jasmine before she could give in to the need to stay with her.

That wasn't her place. Jared had also made that clear. Sky needed to take care of her own patients and stay away from his. She made one more pass through the unit to make sure a patient from their practice hadn't come in while she'd been dealing with Jasmine, then decided that instead of going back to the doctors' sleep room, she'd go back to the office and get some work done. She had to do something to keep her mind busy while she waited to see if Jasmine was going to be okay.

She found herself becoming angry now, and she didn't like the feeling at all. She didn't do angry. She believed in the power of positivity, but there was nothing about any of this that was positive. How could Jared expect her to just walk away from a young girl that she had come to care for? Just because he could walk away from people didn't mean that she could do the same thing.

Because that was exactly what he had done. Hadn't he made that clear when he'd left her bed after making love to her? She'd wanted to talk to him about their relationship, but he'd seemed happy to pretend the whole night had never happened.

No matter how it hurt, it was time for her to face the fact that no matter how much Jared might have wanted her that night, he regretted becoming involved with her. Once more, she hadn't measured up to be the person that someone she cared about wanted.

And once more, she would get up, dust herself off and start living her life again. Next time she'd be more careful. Next time she'd protect her heart better.

Jared stood over Jasmine with the scalpel in his hand and forced his mind to forget how hurt Sky had looked when he'd refused to let her talk to Jasmine's parents. He had no doubt that she only meant to help the girl. It wasn't her fault that Jasmine's parents weren't listening to their daughter.

He had to put his thoughts of Sky away now. She'd been all he had thought of since the night they'd spent together. No, it went farther back than that night. He'd fought against thinking about Sky for months now, ever since that first time she'd looked at him across that crowded conference room and given him a smile that was as sexy as it was sweet. When she'd followed it up with that flirty wink of hers, part of him had known his life would never be the same. He'd been defeated even before he'd begun the fight. Only he'd never told Sky that. He'd been too afraid to let her know just how defenseless he was where she was concerned. And now he'd hurt her when she'd only tried to help him. He had to make that up to her, though he didn't know how.

But for now, he'd have to put all of that aside. Right now, all that mattered was his patient.

Jared took a breath and looked around the room, taking in the NICU team that had gathered to take Jasmine's baby as soon as it was born. Then he turned to look at the anesthesiologist, who nodded his head that he was ready. With his hand steady and his mind cleared, Jared made his first incision.

Thirty minutes later, there was a screaming baby boy being taken care of by the NICU team and the anesthesiologist was discussing whether to extubate Jasmine then, as she was showing signs of becoming more responsive, or wait until her blood pressure was more controlled and she was out of danger of having another seizure. Agreeing to err on the side of caution, the two of them decided that for now Jasmine would be left intubated and transferred to the critical care department, where she could be watched more closely.

By the time Jared had met with the Jamesons and shown them to the unit where Jasmine would stay for the next few days, it was past two in the morning. He knew he needed to head home and get what sleep he could before he had to start his day, but he wanted to let Sky know that Jasmine was improving and that her baby was perfect.

He expected to find her waiting for him on the unit, but when he couldn't find her one of the nurses informed him that she'd said she was going to the office to work on some charting. He knew immediately that she had left because of him. He'd hurt her and she'd chosen to leave instead of facing him. He had to fix this. Besides, he didn't like the thought of her over in the office alone in the middle of the night.

Checking on Jasmine once more, he made the walk across the parking lot to the clinic. When he opened the back door, the motion light above him came on, illuminating the entryway. Passing the exam rooms, he called out to Sky, not wanting to startle her. He started to take the hallway that led to her office when he heard a sound farther down the entry hallway.

His heart sped up and he looked around to see if there was something close he could use for a weapon.

"Jared? What are you doing here?" Sky asked as she came down the hall, stopping when he put his finger against his lips and listened.

He heard the sound again, this time recognizing it as a groan. Realizing that the only room left down that hallway was his father's office, he motioned Sky behind him and made his way there.

The pair of motionless legs sticking out from behind his father's desk was the first thing he saw when the lights came on in the room. "Dad?" he called as he and Sky rushed around the desk to find his father lying on the floor, his eyes closed but his chest rising irregularly.

"Dad?" he whispered, his voice sounding more like the little scared boy he'd once been than the grown man he was now. He barely registered Sky's urgent voice speaking behind him. When his father's eyes blinked open, his own eyes filled with tears.

"I had to wait. I had to tell you," his father began, his voice weak as he grimaced with pain.

"I've called 911," Sky said, before dropping down beside him. Jared watched as she applied a stethoscope to his father's chest. "Jack, just rest. There's help on the way."

"Just want to tell you, I love you, son. From that first day…" His father's voice gave out and his eyes closed.

"His pulse is irregular and weak. There are no signs of trauma. I don't think it was a fall," Sky said as she ran her hands down Jack's legs and then up his arms before turning her attention to his head, then standing and running out of the room.

"Can you hear me, Dad?" Jared asked as he took his father's hand and squeezed. He knew he should be doing something, anything, to help him, but he was frozen by the fear of losing him.

Sky rushed back into the room with the office AED. After turning on the monitor, she didn't take the time to unbutton his father's shirt, instead she just ripped it open and began applying pads. As the cardiac rhythm began to scroll across the machine and the AED machine told them that a shock wasn't advised. Sky squatted down in front of it and studied the rhythm. "It looks like a STEMI. See how the ST segment is higher here." Jared looked at where she pointed but found he couldn't take in the information. "Stay here with him. I'm going to open the door for the EMTs. If anything changes call out for me." With that she jumped back up and was gone down the hall.

"She's something, isn't she?" his father whispered, then cleared his throat. "She reminds me of my Katie. So full of life. You'll be a lucky man if you don't mess things up with her."

His father's face became pale and his lips tightened.

Jared was a doctor. Surely there should be something

that he could do for his father besides sitting there and holding his hand, but nothing came to mind.

Minutes later, Jared heard Sky's voice directing the EMT crew to the office. Jared started to move back but his father's hand tightened on his with a strength that surprised him. "You're going to be okay, son."

His father's hand let go of his as the ambulance crew moved him over to their stretcher. Moments later they were gone, leaving packaging from the IV they'd started and debris strewn across the floor.

"I just talked to the ER doctor. He's calling in the interventional team now. We can probably meet the ambulance in the ER if we cut across the parking lot."

Jared stared at her. The last few minutes had been a nightmare for him, but Sky had remained calm and had taken care of his father while Jared had been unable to form a complete thought. All he could do was think about the other losses he'd suffered, and how he wasn't ready to lose his father too.

"Thank you," Jared said as he closed his arms around her. From the moment he'd seen his father lying helplessly on the ground, Jared had felt cold and alone. The warmth of Sky's body against his took all those feelings away. He hadn't been alone. Sky had been there for him the whole time. "I don't know what I would have done without you."

Sky sat next to Jared as they waited for the interventional cardiologist. Jack had been taken straight from the ER to the cath lab as soon as the emergency room doctor had confirmed that he was indeed having an ST-elevation myocardial infarction. The fact that Jack had lain in his office, unable to call for help for all those hours, had her worried about what damage had been done to his heart.

"How's Jasmine?" she asked Jared. He'd said very little since they'd found his father.

"I forgot to tell you. That's why I came over to the office. I wanted to let you know she's stable. They'll probably extubate her today, once they decrease her sedation medication."

"Thanks. I appreciate you letting me know." At least he was still keeping her updated on the young girl.

They stood as the doctor came into the room. The man looked almost as tired as she did, and she knew that she and Jared weren't the only ones who had been up most of the night.

"How is he?" Jared asked. He surprised her when he reached out and took her hand in his. "Can I see him?"

"He's going to be sleeping for a while. We had to keep him sedated for longer than usual, but we were able to place two stents. I'm going to have him watched in the ICU overnight, but I think he'll move out to the floor tomorrow. I know he has a busy practice, but he's going to have to slow down. I don't want him working at all for the next few weeks."

Jared assured him that he'd make sure his father abided by his orders. Once the doctor left, Sky quickly removed her hand from Jared's. Now that she knew Jack would be okay, there wasn't really a reason for her to stay with him. Still, she waited until one of the cardiac intensive care nurses came to take him back to see his father.

"We need to talk," Jared said, looking over to where the nurse waited for him. "About everything."

There had been so many things that she wanted to tell him, but in reality none of them would make a difference. Jared's actions had made it clear that it was better the two of them forget their night together. He hadn't even wanted to tell his father about the picture that had captured their kiss. He believed that if they ignored it, it would all go away. At first she had thought he'd meant the attention from the picture, but now she knew he meant whatever it was that had been happening between the two of them. And the truth was he was probably right. If he ignored it, eventually she would have to give up on him. Looking back she could see that it had always been her that wanted more from him. Even though he'd come to her room the night they were in Knoxville, it had been her kiss that had compelled him.

Not once had he ever been the one to make the first move. In fact, if she hadn't started flirting with him all those months ago, they'd still be nothing more than colleagues who passed in the hallway. That wasn't saying that she regretted anything they'd shared recently. She was just realistic enough to know that no matter what she thought the two of them could have together, it wasn't going to happen.

So instead of responding, she gave him the best smile she could muster. The moment he disappeared down the hallway, she headed for the closest elevator. She wanted to get out of the hospital and away from the man that she had almost let break her heart. But there was one more stop she needed to make, no matter how mad it would make Jared.

She took the elevator to the surgical ICU waiting room on the next floor, where she spotted Jasmine's parents.

"Mr. and Mrs. Jameson, my name is Sky. I'm a midwife at Legacy Clinic," Sky said. "I just wanted to check and see how you are doing."

"You're the woman Jasmine was talking about. You're the one that told her she could give her baby up," Mrs. Jameson said.

Sky noticed that the poor woman was probably too tired to be angry at this point. "Jasmine told me that she didn't want to be a mother right now. She didn't feel that she was ready for the responsibility of a baby and she didn't think she could give her son everything that he deserves. I think your daughter was very brave and selfless in making that decision, but I assure you that it was *her* decision. I only encouraged her to speak openly with you about it. She just wants to do the right thing for her child. She might change her mind about what she wants tomorrow when she sees her son, but I hope if she still wants to go ahead with the adoption you will listen to her and respect her wishes. As a child who had parents that never wanted her, I wish my parents would have considered what was best for me instead of themselves. I'm sure you have always done what was best for Jasmine even over your own desires. That's all she's asking for you to do now."

Sky waited for Jasmine's parents to yell at her, or at the very least to tell her that she needed to mind her own business, but they just stood there staring at Sky like she had been speaking a foreign language.

Without saying another word, Sky left the waiting room. She didn't know if the Jamesons would even consider what she had to say, but for their daughter's and grandson's sakes, she hoped they would.

Jared paused at the door of the waiting room to look back at Sky before he let the nurse lead him to his father's room, where he found his father asleep, his respirations deep and even. He sat down beside him and waited for him to wake.

He found himself questioning the look Sky had given him before he'd left her. There was something about the way she'd looked at him before he left that made his chest hurt. The smile she'd given him had been nothing like the smile that always took his breath away. Instead this smile had been a little sad and her eyes had been empty, with none of the happiness they usually shone with. It reminded him of the smiles from his time in the foster system when he had to leave a new friend, because he knew they'd never be together again. A goodbye smile. A smile that said, *So long, it's been great while it lasted.*

Jared shook his head to clear it. His mind was just playing tricks on him. Sky wasn't leaving. As soon as his father woke up he'd go get her. And tomorrow when he came into the office she would be there waiting to torture him with one of her usual sassy smiles. Right now, he had to take care of his dad. Then he'd make time to talk to Sky. She had been right, they needed to talk about what was happening between the two of them.

"Why the face? Am I dying?"

Jared had been so tangled up in his thoughts that he hadn't noticed when his father had awakened. "No. You're going to be fine, though we are definitely going to have a talk about your work schedule."

"So if I'm not dying, what's wrong?" his father asked, clearly hoping to avoid the necessary conversation about the amount of hours he'd been working. "Is it Sky?"

"Do you just want me to say you were right again? Our working together has been good. Seeing her in action when we found you has given me even more of a reason to appreciate her work."

"I didn't put the two of you together so that you could learn to work together, son. I wanted to force you to open your eyes and see that there was a woman who's perfect for you." His father's voice held a hint of irritation and Jared saw that his heart rate had jumped up into the one-twenties.

"Calm down before the nurse comes in here and throws me out," he told his dad. "And what do you mean you didn't put us together because of work? You said that the Carters asked for the two of us."

"Mindy did ask for Sky, and her husband requested that there be a doctor following his wife closely, but they had asked for it to be me. But I knew that you would never make a move past that flirting game the two of you have been playing for the last few months if I didn't step in and force you to acknowledge your feelings for her." His father sighed, then closed his eyes. "I hoped you'd have the good sense to make a move, especially after I saw that picture of you two kissing. What is it going to take to make you see what's right there in front of you? You're a smart man. You can't believe that a woman like Sky is going to wait around forever."

Jared thought of that smile she'd given him earlier. He might have tried to deny it, but he'd known that something was off with Sky. His father was right. He'd pushed her away every time she got close. She'd come into his life and shattered that old, dirt-streaked window he'd always used to look out into the world and she'd pulled him into a world of laughter and joy where she chose to spend her own life. And now, no matter how hard he tried to board up that old window, he knew what it felt like to live outside it now. Oh, there was still a part of him that wanted to play it safe, that wanted to hide back behind that window. Looking out at the world instead of living in it was where he was comfortable. But that part had been getting smaller every minute he spent with Sky. His father had seen a future for him that he'd always denied wanting. But with Sky, that future looked possible. Or at least it could be if he hadn't messed it up beyond repair.

"Sir," the nurse began as she walked into his father's room, "I'm sorry, but I'm going to have to ask you to go. Your father needs his rest."

Jared reached over and grasped his father's hand in his. He remembered the first time his dad had shaken his hand. Jared had been so scared when his foster mother had told him that a couple was coming over to meet him. That they were looking for a little boy just like him to be their own little boy. His father's grip wasn't nearly as strong as it had been that day when he'd dropped down on his knee in front of Jared and offered the scared little boy he'd been a handshake. He had thought his father was the strongest man he'd ever met then. Now, after all those years, he still believed that.

"I'll be back later to see you," Jared said, repeating the words his father had said that day, all those years ago. And even though young Jared had not believed the man's words as he watched the strong man and the beautiful woman walk away from him, he'd hoped with everything inside of him that he was wrong. Just like he hoped now that he'd been wrong about that sad smile Sky had given him.

But when he returned to the waiting room and found it empty, he knew he'd been right. He'd hesitated too long, making excuses for why he and Sky shouldn't be together. He'd let her be the one that made every move, unable to admit that he'd wanted her from the first time she'd given him that priceless smile and that outrageous wink. He felt the same as the little boy he'd been as he'd watched his future father and mother walk away. There hadn't been anything he could have done that day. He'd had to wait there, helpless to control his own future.

But he wasn't helpless anymore. He wasn't going to wait and hope that Sky would seek him out to give him another chance. He was going to take control. He would get her back. And he would show her just how much she meant to him. He was tired of fighting against the love he felt for her. Instead, he was ready to fight *for* that love. Fight for Sky. Now he just had to figure out how.

CHAPTER FIFTEEN

AS SKY DROVE up to Mindy and Trey's house, she felt none of the excitement that she had felt the first time she'd seen it. Maybe she was already becoming jaded by all the glitz and glamour of the country music stars' life. Maybe she was just tired. Or maybe it was the fact that Jared wasn't beside her today.

Well, at least this time Marjorie wasn't running toward her waving a mile-high stack of papers for her to sign. To be honest, the place almost looked deserted. When Mindy had called and asked her if she could do her a really big favor and come to the taping of her reality show today, Sky had wanted to say no. But who could refuse Mindy? The woman was as sweet as Sky's grandmother's cane syrup. Still, she wasn't up to smiling for any cameras today. Right now she wasn't sure if she would ever smile again.

As soon as she'd left Jared at the hospital, she'd gone home and slept the day away. She'd hoped that after finally making the decision to walk away from him she'd wake up ready to move on. She'd even thought of maybe leaving Nashville. There were so many places she'd never seen. Now might be the perfect time to go exploring the rest of the world.

She didn't know how long she'd sat there in the driveway before a man she hadn't met before knocked on her car window. "Ma'am, are you Skylar Benton?"

The man backed up as Sky opened the door and climbed out of the car. "That's me." She didn't know what she was expected to wear today so she'd settled on a blue flowered maxi dress and a pair of strappy sandals. Sky wasn't sure whether Mindy wanted her to actually be on the show or be there only for moral support as she explained to the show's viewers the reason for her hospital visit.

"They're waiting for you down at the barn," the man said before tipping his cowboy hat at her, turning and walking down a path along the side of the house.

"Mindy's in the barn?" Sky asked, confused. Where was everybody? Something about this didn't feel right. She felt like the heroine in one of those horror flicks being led to her demise.

"She's around there somewhere," the man said without turning around.

Sky had never been in Mindy's backyard and upon following him along the side of the house she was surprised to see that what the man was calling "a barn" wasn't the horse barn she had been expecting. Instead, it was a pretty cedar building half the size of the house, with old-fashioned Dutch doors. She could smell fresh cut hay before she made it to the opened half door, but there were none of the usual smells of horses. A huge chandelier suspended off a thick cedar beam that ran the length of the building. Other, smaller chandeliers had been hung throughout the space, bathing it in a golden light.

Then she saw him in the middle of the large open room sitting on a stack of hay. He'd traded his spotless white lab coat for a pair of faded jeans and a chambray buttoned-up shirt. He looked like a ranch hand who'd come in from work and decided to sit awhile. Sky's heart stuttered and her breath caught in her chest when he looked up at her and began to play the guitar in his hands.

She didn't see the man who'd led her there pull open the barn door. She'd made it halfway across the room before she'd even realized it. What was she doing? She'd made the decision to walk away from this man. He'd made it plain that he didn't want her. Not like she wanted him. He hadn't been willing to give the two of them a real chance, though time after time she'd all but thrown herself at him.

She started to turn around, to leave before he could see the tears in her eyes. She didn't cry. Not anymore. She shed enough tears when her parents had left her and when the man she'd thought had loved her deserted her. The only tears she ever allowed herself nowadays were happy tears. So why was she crying now?

Then she recognized the song he played. It was an old Alabama song. A love song about falling in love. Then Jared began to sing, "How do you fall in love? When do you say 'I do'?"

His voice wasn't trained and he'd never be a country music star, but to her it was the most beautiful song she had ever heard. By the time he got to the end, she'd given up holding back the tears. Still, when he laid the guitar down and walked toward her, his arms held out, she couldn't move. She'd gone to him over and over. She'd flirted. She'd teased. She'd opened up to him and worked so hard to get his attention and still he'd fought against what she knew they could have together. If he wanted her, he had to say the words.

As if he'd heard her prayer to heaven, he stopped in front of her and took her hands in his. "I love you, Sky. I know I've been saying that the two of us are too different, but I think those differences are what make us perfect for each other. I need the sunshine and happiness that you've brought to my life and sometimes you need me to bring you down to earth. And no matter our differences, I can promise you that for the rest of my life, I'll always love you. Will you marry me?"

"Yes," she whispered, afraid to break the spell from Jared's song.

Then he brushed her tears from her face and with his hands on her cheeks, he kissed her. It was a sweet kiss, full of a love she had feared she'd never have. But when Jared's hands slid down to her waist, pulling her closer and deepening the kiss, the barn suddenly echoed with applause.

Pulling away, Sky turned to see the whole camera crew from Mindy and Trey's reality show. Beside them stood Mindy, looking as guilty as sin, and Marjorie looking as happy as if she'd won a CMA Award.

For a moment she was afraid this had all been just a

performance for the show, but when Jared's arms slid around her, she relaxed. He would never do something as callous as that. "I think you have some explaining to do, Dr. Warner."

"Well, we had cameras for our first dance and first kiss. It just seemed right that there should be cameras for the first time I tell you I love you," Jared said. He moved his lips down to her ear and whispered, "I had to sign a form saying that even if you walked away from me, I'd let them air the footage on the show."

"And what if I had refused to agree to this being on the show?" Sky asked, still stunned by all the trouble Jared had gone through to do this for her.

"Actually, one of those forms Marjorie had us signed covered it. They just wanted me to sign for backup since this was all my idea," Jared said before taking one of her hands in his and leading her over to the camera crew.

As he began to thank Joe and the crew, Mindy walked over to stand beside her. "Are you mad?"

"I can't believe any of this. Was this really Jared's idea?" Sky had a hard time believing that he would have ever wanted to take part in something like this, let alone that he had planned this.

"Oh, yeah, I even tried to talk him out of it. He'd have been the talk of the town if you'd walked away from him. Marjorie was hoping you'd do something dramatic like slap him across the face. Not that I thought you would do anything like that. Still, there was that chance... But he said he had to do something big to make you see he was serious."

"I guess you don't get much more serious than declaring your love on national TV," Sky said.

Once the camera crew was packed up, Jared asked Mindy and Trey if they could take a walk down to the pasture to see the horses. Holding hands as they made their way to the back of the property, Sky enjoyed the quiet of the farm after all the noise of the crowd in the barn. But there was still something they needed to clear up.

"I spoke to Jasmine's parents. They know I was the one who helped her get the information on giving her baby up for adoption."

"I know. I spoke with them too and explained that you were working with me. I also told them that you did the right think providing their daughter with information on all the options available to her."

"Thank you," she said. Having Jared's support meant everything to her.

"They assured me that they love their daughter and they only want what is best for her. And, most importantly, they're willing now to support her, no matter what choice she makes about her baby."

"I'm glad. Both Jasmine and her child deserve a chance at a good life," she said.

She knew she'd never been as happy as she was in that moment.

"I'm not sure you understand what you've done," Sky said. "Even though we're nobodies next to Mindy and Trey, we're bound to get some media attention."

"I know."

"We're really getting married," she said, stopping on the path as it all suddenly hit her now that they were alone. She could hear the note of panic in her voice. "I don't care what Marjorie offers us, they are *not* going to film any part of our wedding."

"Of course not," he said, his voice a little too calm. "I've already talked to her. She has no interest in filming the wedding."

"Oh, good," Sky said, starting back down the path.

"All she wants is to film the bachelor party. I declined that one also."

She looked over at Jared, who was smiling. "What that woman needs is a man of her own."

"Don't look at me, I'm taken," he said, squeezing her hand before raising it to his lips. He stopped as they came to the fence where they could see three horses galloping across a field. Still holding her hand, he held up a beautiful gold ring with a trio of diamonds, the one in the middle larger than the other two. He'd planned everything out so perfectly for her.

"Yes, you are," Sky said, as he slid the ring on her finger. "For now and forever. You're mine."

EPILOGUE

"JUST ONE MORE big push, Mindy. The baby's crowning. Just one more and you'll finally get to hold your baby," Sky said as Jared reached over her and wiped the sweat that had formed on her forehead.

"You can do it," Trey said, helping his wife get into position for that last push.

As Mindy took in a breath and began to push, Jared handed Sky a surgical towel to use to wrap around the baby. Carefully, she helped guide the baby out, first its head and then one shoulder after the other, until she held the new little baby who would soon be the talk of Music City.

"It's a boy!" Trey yelled as he hugged his wife, who had begun to cry the moment the baby began to cry.

"With a voice like that, I bet he'll be following in his parents' footsteps," Jared said as he handed Sky the instruments to clamp the baby's cord, then handed Trey the scissors to cut the cord.

"Here's your baby boy," Sky said, reaching across Mindy and handing her the baby.

While the nursery nurse began to help the new mother,

Sky stood and turned to Jared. "I'm really going to miss us working together like this."

"Who knows? Maybe Mindy and Trey will have another one," he said, smiling down at her. "What I think you're going to miss is all the media attention."

"Speaking of which," Trey said as he moved to stand beside them. "I'm supposed to tell you that Marjorie has a camera ready to record all of us together so that we can announce the birth."

A few hours later, Sky found herself straightening the collar of Jared's lab coat. As always it was spotless and pressed to perfection. While he might have become a little more relaxed in his life since she had moved in with him, there were some things that would never change.

She'd been surprised about how well he'd taken the attention his proposal had gotten. As soon as it had aired, there'd been comments on the show's media accounts ranging from kind and sweet to some suggesting that her fiancé shouldn't quit his day job. He'd taken them all with good humor, along with the ribbing by the staff at the hospital.

But today would finally be their last time in front of the cameras. Something, no matter what Jared thought, Sky was glad of. Living a life of privacy with him was much more fun than being the center of attention. Not that the two of them would be the center of attention today. Today all the attention would be on Mindy and Trey.

"You ready?" Jared asked her as they made their way to Mindy's hospital room. "You know, if you find yourself missing the limelight, Marjorie might let you come back as a special guest on the show."

"The only person that's going to be recording me after today is the wedding photographer," Sky said as they made their way through the crowd in the hallway that had gathered to see the taping of the season finale of *Carters' Way.*

Sky and Jared followed Joe's direction as he placed the two of them behind the chair where Mindy sat holding her new baby boy. Trey sat beside her, his smile just as big as it had been the moment Sky had first shown him his son.

When Jared reached for her hand, Sky smiled and looked over at him. His eyes caught hers and to her amazement, and right in front of the cameras for all the viewers to see, he winked.

* * * * *

A BABY TO CHANGE THEIR LIVES

RACHEL DOVE

MILLS & BOON

In honour of the late, great and much-loved Eric Bell.

CHAPTER ONE

THE IRONY OF meeting her work nemesis on an NHS 'team-building' day was not lost on Lucy Bakewell. She didn't want to be here in the first place and, given what she had just endured, she knew her gut, as ever, had been right on the money. She didn't 'do' people at the best of times, and enforced bonding such as this set her teeth on edge. The last hour had been particularly abysmal: mud, testosterone, stupid, cumbersome apparel and bullets pinging past her ears. It was her worst nightmare.

Well, it was right up there, anyway. Definitely top three, and she was no shrinking violet either. Lucy was used to high pressure situations—at work she thrived in them—but this? This was her idea of pure unadulterated torture, all in the great outdoors. What was even worse than the last hour was her current situation. She was doing something that she'd never thought she would in a million years. Instead of being at work, doing what she loved, she was here, *hiding*, sheepishly hanging out in the huts that masqueraded as toilets, praying for a miracle to get her out of there.

Just as she was wiping the last bit of thick mud off her face, there was a loud barrage of knocking at the door.

'Are you still in there, or did you fall down the pan?' *No way.* She knew that voice. She'd just listened to it howl in pain.

'Er…yeah! Still here.'

Worst luck.

She eyed the toilet bowl. If she'd thought she could crawl her way out Andy Dufresne style, she'd already have been long gone. 'I'll be right out!'

She used the last bit of toilet roll in the stall at least to try to look clean before reluctantly sliding back the lock and facing her aggressor. He didn't look amused.

'I wondered if you were in there trying to fake some kind of emergency.'

'Of course not,' she lied. 'Just…freshening up. What is it that you want, exactly?'

He frowned, leaning closer and plucking a glob of mud from her pinned-back light-blonde hair. The masked helmet thing they'd made them wear had destroyed her usual neat and functional look—another reason to detest the day. The guy in front of her looked right at home. He didn't look ruffled, which made her feel even worse.

'Yeah?' His voice was deep, masculine. The kind of voice that you took notice of. 'No mirror in there, I'm guessing?' He looked amused. She could tell he was suppressing a grin. His twitching lips gave him away. 'I just wanted to see if you were coming. They're waiting to start the next game.'

Dear Lord in heaven, I'd rather deal with an outbreak of diarrhoea and vomiting on my ward than play again.

She focused on keeping the look of pure revulsion from breaking out across her rather sweaty face. 'Oh, that's fine. I can sit it out.'

He was already moving her away from the hut back to the paint-balling area.

'Not a chance. All participation is compulsory, remember?' She did remember.

All department heads are to attend. Cover has already been arranged.

It was so annoying. Also, it wasn't true. Her future brother-in-law Ronnie wasn't here as Head of A&E! She was still salty about that too. Sure, he was only Acting Head, but he was a sure thing for the job. He'd been filling in for two months since the department head had left. He should have been here, if only to endure this so-called morale booster with her.

She didn't need a morale boost, she needed real funding for her department. She needed her nurses and support staff to get paid a decent wage so she could keep them on her team and not lose them to better paid private sector positions. What was running around in a muddy field in the middle of a chilly February going to achieve?

'Anyway,' her adversary continued, unaware of her snarky inner monologue, 'After the last game, I have a score to settle, Lucky Shot.' He pointed to his long, camo-clad legs where a very noticeable and brightly coloured paintball splat was glaring up from his crotch area. Lucy winced; he had her there, not that she'd ever let him know it.

She puffed up her indignation instead. 'I did apologise for that.' She huffed. 'And you didn't have to be such a baby about it. It's not like we're using live ammo, and I've never done this before. I'm not exactly the gun-toting type.'

'Yeah, more Calamity Jane than GI Jane, eh?' he scoffed, making her scowl deepen.

Having her flaws pointed out by anyone was not something she relished, never mind from a stranger who she'd almost maimed.

'You hit that neurosurgeon guy pretty hard in the coccyx,' he banged on, frog-marching her back to her fate. 'He's been icing his backside for the last ten minutes.'

They were almost back at the starting point, and Lucy's anxiety was growing with every step. She could see the other medical professionals all looking around, some brandishing paint guns as though they were extras in an action movie. A couple of them were eyeing her warily. Normally, she would have revelled in the fear she had produced. Today, she felt as if she might end up on the evening news for shooting an ear off a consultant or something. It did nothing to soothe her frazzled nerves, and if there was one thing on this planet Lucy hated it was the feeling of not being in total control.

'Well,' she retorted sulkily, tutting when her jailer jumped away from the business end of the weapon she was waving. 'Why did we need to do this anyway? I barely get time off from the hospital as it is, and now I have to spend an entire day off shooting at other stressed out department heads? I mean, who's running the hospitals while we're all here playing "shoot them up"?'

He chuckled at the side of her, pushing her gun down to aim at the floor as they walked. When she glanced his way, she could see he was almost…smiling. His groin and pride were obviously recovering. He looked as if he belonged here, dressed like a soldier in the woods. He was tall, dark, handsome and rugged with a five o'clock shadow that made him look as if he'd slept rough under the stars after a day wrangling wild horses.

He was different from the other, weedier men on the field today—almost too alpha male to be some department head in some hospital somewhere. Most of the doctors she'd encountered over the years were like Ronnie—softer; geeky, almost—less Bear Grylls and more teddy bear. Most of them considered golfing a serious sport. This guy, in comparison, looked gruffer than that. He was wood-chopping burly. He probably loved these activities or even did them for fun.

He was kind of cute, she noticed reluctantly. If she ever decided to have a dating life other than a few scattered first dates, he would probably be her type. Not that she'd taken the time to consider what her type was beyond the odd passing thought.

'I mean, look at them all. Hardly the A-Team, are we?'

'Why don't you say what you really think?' he joked, his laugh deep, rich. Stopping short of meeting the others, he came to stand in front of her. 'I'm Jackson, by the way.'

He flashed her a smile that on impact disarmed any remaining snarkiness she felt. Sure, he'd not reacted in the best way to her assault, calling her a 'ridiculous woman', but she'd never been shot in the crown jewels. She decided to let it pass. Maybe her day would be tolerable after all.

'Lucy—Head of Paediatrics at Leeds General.' She shook the huge hand he held out, feeling it dwarf hers entirely.

He shot her one of those smiles again. It made the dimples in his cheeks stand out. Lucy had to look at her feet to stop herself from fawning over him. If her work colleagues back home saw her like this, she would never live it down. Being a ballbuster was something she prided herself on. 'Well, hello, Lucy! It's so weird I met you today, I'm actually—'

'Come on, you two!' The over-enthusiastic paintball instructor, who was ironically named Tag, came and shuffled them both over to the waiting teams. Lucy was on the red team, Jackson on the blue. 'Game two commences in two minutes! Get your masks back on, make sure your guns are reloaded.' He stared pointedly at Lucy. 'And remember, it's the torso you are aiming for. No below the belt shots. Team building, remember?'

Lucy shot him a sarcastic grin, thrusting her mask over her face to stop her from biting back with a retort. She was pretty sure she heard a rumbling laugh from Jackson's direction.

'Positions, people! Let's have some fun!'

Lucy's groan was drowned out by the others' loud whoops.

The second game was even worse. Released from their usual whitewashed, walled workplaces, and possibly hungry for lunch, the medical professionals were unrecognisable from their usual polished and pedantic selves. The second the whistle went, it was all out war between the reds and the blues.

'Let's do this!' one of the red women bellowed. 'For the win!'

'Come on, now!' Lucy tried to placate the baying masses. 'It's just a game!'

'I am not going back labelled a loser! Reds, we win this—we win or die!'

'Slightly dramatic,' Lucy countered, but someone shoved past her and she ended up knee-deep in the mud. 'Hey!' she yelled, her surprise turning to anger when she saw who'd pushed her.

'Blue team, with me!' Jackson growled, taking off for the tree line like some kind of Viking warrior. He turned to look at her when she shouted his name, and she was waiting for him to say sorry when he kept running and raised his gun, pointing it at her breast plate. 'Take the red scum down! Death to the reds!'

Lucy heard the pings and splats of his paintballs sail past as she rolled away. Jumping to her feet, she grappled for the gun slung from her waist.

Okay, now it's on, jerk.

'Reds!' she yelled. 'Get it together!'

A short bloke with a red sash ran to her side. 'We're out-numbered! We're never going to make it!'

Lucy grabbed his jacket as he babbled about targets and something about not being made for violence. 'Shut up and fire at something!' she chided, half-dragging him to the tree line further down. Their flag was in the hut near where Jackson had run, and she just knew he was going to try to get the win. Which would not only mean he would equal-ise, with her scrotum shot having secured their first win by slowing him down, but even worse than defeat it would go to best out of three. Which would mean another game with these hungry, half-crazed knuckleheads. It was getting very *Lord of the Flies*, and she wasn't about to endure this a third time. 'We can't lose this one!'

The man, an ENT specialist from somewhere in Scot-land, whimpered as they made the trees and sank to the floor, out of sight. 'We only won the last one because you took out the sasquatch! We have no hope now; he'll be at the hut by now! Emmett won't be able to hold him off; he's only an orthopaedic surgeon, not Rambo!'

Lucy bit her lip. 'Seriously, this is the NHS's finest? We faced Covid, and the government dropping us right in it, and one big dude with a cheeky smile and a gung-ho atti-tude is enough to terrify you all?'

The woman who'd hollered earlier crawled across from the nearest crop of trees commando-style. 'Basically, yes. I told management that this would suck. I suggested a spa day...'

She suddenly stood up, firing off a volley of shots and punching the air when she heard a satisfying yelp from a distance.

'Yes! Got one!'

'Nice!' Lucy cheered, picking up on the woman's Scottish

accent. Pointing at her quivering tree mate, she motioned to the woman. 'I'm Lucy. He one of yours?'

'John? Yeah. I'm Annie. Do you think he breached the hut yet? That Emmett dude is on his own up there. Bigfoot will snap him like a twig.'

Hmm; it seemed Jackson had made an impression on everyone, not just her. She rather liked his height...

What? Concentrate! He's the enemy.

If he got that flag, lunch would be even further away, which would mean more of this torture. Looking at John, who was now hugging the tree and reciting anatomically correct body parts like a mantra as the blues hollered in the distance, she knew they were never going to make it.

'I'll try to take him out before he gets to the flag,' she whispered, pointing to the break in the line of trees where their hut stood. 'Make sure our team goes for theirs. Cover me, okay?'

'God speed,' John urged, releasing the tree to hug her and take up position, gun aimed. 'Annie, watch my six!'

Annie was already picking off another blue player who'd popped up at the wrong time.

'Go, Lucy, now! I'll go for the blue flag!'

Lucy closed her eyes, took a deep breath and ran as fast as she could for the hut. 'Thank God I love the treadmill,' she huffed to herself, ducking as a blue player popped up from behind a bush and nearly took off her head. Springing back up, she popped a shot at his leg.

'Ow! I'm out!' he yelped, before slinking off towards the refreshments tent, his gun trailing along behind. Lucy didn't wait to see who he was talking to, nor to see what had happened to make John scream behind her like a banshee behind her. She had one goal: to take Jackson out. Annie was right: he was the real enemy on that team; the others were just following his lead. They would be no match for Annie. Lucy had a feeling she worked in microsurgery or radiology or something, judging by her crack shot. She'd ask her over lunch, she decided, spying the hut with a grin, when they were enjoying their winning feast.

She stopped by the closest barrier, a wooden fence covered in burlap and curved around the edge of the red hut. It was quiet—a little too quiet.

'Emmett?' she called out. Nothing. 'Emmett?'

Still nothing. He wasn't there yet! If Jackson had taken Emmett out, the game would be over. The blue team would be crowing over the rest of them for sure.

The background shots sped up. Annie was going for it, by the sounds of it. Lucy could hear the blues shouting to each other, 'Take her out!' When she heard a string of profanity in a thick Scottish accent, she knew that her number two was holding her own. She saw another barrier nearer the red hut and decided to move position. The lack of blues heading for their red flag told her that they had a plan, and Jackson was no doubt near, waiting to pounce.

Before her foot hit the floor, she heard it—the snap of a tree root a few metres away. Ducking down, her eyes narrowing beneath the mask, she saw him. Even bent over at the other side of the opposite barrier, he was bigger than her, more noticeable. She waited for him to turn the gun on her, but his aim stayed focused on the hut. He hadn't seen her. She reached for her gun, aware of every little movement of her clothing, the placement of her feet on the forest floor. Even her breath, which was coming out in shallow, excited bursts of adrenaline, filled air.

'Lucy.' She jumped at the sound of her name being called out. 'You got some explaining to do! Where are you? You know the aim of the game is to get the opponent's flag, right?'

She had to bite down hard on her lip to avoid the retort she wanted to throw back at him. *Smug git.* He knew she was there and was trying to get into her head.

Nice try...wrong woman.

'Lucy!' he sang out again. The competitor in her was well and truly fired up by this Neanderthal. He'd really got under her skin for some reason. She wasn't used to it, and the fact he was good-looking was a distraction.

Behind them, a volley of shots rang out, raised voices bouncing off the trees around them. Lucy couldn't make out the voices. She hoped it wasn't Annie getting taken down.

'Sounds like your team to me,' Jackson teased. 'Best of three, eh, Lucky Shot?'

Not on your life, she fumed inwardly.

She focused back on him, just in time to see him move from behind his cover. *Now or never*, she realised. *This is for lunch. For the red team. For women doctors everywhere.*

Holding in a jagged breath, she closed one eye, focused on the trigger and squeezed.

Pop-pop-pop!

'What the...? Son of a— Ow!'

She scrunched down tight as he came into the clearing with a jump, holding his backside. He pulled off his mask, his head scanning the terrain, and she could see the anger in his expression. 'Lucy! Where are you?'

She stood up, waggling her gloved fingers in his direction.

'Right here, my favourite yeti. I win again, it seems.'

'You didn't win! You shot me in the butt—what do you mean, "yeti"?'

The siren rang out in the distance. Lucy saw Jackson's

scowl deepen, and she saw why when she followed his gaze. A huge plume of red smoke was floating above the trees. Turning back to him, pulling off her own mask and letting her blonde hair fly free, she grinned triumphantly. He was glaring at her, rubbing at a spot on his rump.

'Like I said, we win.'

She could hear the others laughing and celebrating a short distance away, and she turned to join them. She was already looking forward to her spoils—a good lunch and an early shower after this enforced activity day.

She was almost out of ear shot when Jackson's words stopped her in her tracks.

'I was telling you something earlier when we got interrupted.'

'Yeah,' she called out, not bothering to turn around.

'Yeah,' he half-growled back. 'I was telling you that I'm the new A&E department head.'

Turning on her heel, she looked him dead in the eye. It was intoxicating, all this winning. She felt as if she could take on the world right then. He was still rubbing at his backside, and she pushed away the pang of remorse she felt at shooting the man yet again—the first cute man she'd seen in a long time too, worse luck. Good job she didn't have time for all that romance anyway. Somehow, work always got in the way somehow or the other. Even winning today had become a bit of an obsession, she realised.

'Congratulations on the job,' she told him earnestly. 'Perhaps your new staff can patch you up when you get back. Just don't tell them a little bitty woman did it, eh?' She bit at her lip, realising she could be a little nicer in victory; Harriet, her sister, was always telling her that. 'Listen, it's just a game. I got carried away, you were being smug… Let's go get some—'

'Smug? You shot me—twice—in two very painful places! I know your type; you have to win, don't you, have to come on top? Seriously, you didn't even want to play the game!'

'Says you! You were acting like the SAS, all testosterone and macho pecs.'

'Macho pecs? Who do you think you are?'

'I think I know your type. Your fragile male ego can't take being outsmarted, with your big old manly chin, and your growly voice. It's paintballing, not war.'

'Oh, yeah, it is.' He snorted. 'You taking a shot at my posterior saw to that. We'll be seeing each other again, so it looks like you'll be seeing my *manly pecs* on a regular basis.'

Lucy rolled her eyes. 'I'm sure we can survive lunch without killing each other.'

'I don't mean that.' He laughed softly. 'A&E at your hospital, Lucy.' He half-limped over to her. 'I'm starting at Leeds General on Monday.'

She felt her jaw drop. 'My hospital?'

This time, it was Jackson doing the grinning. 'Yep. You're looking at the new Head of A&E.'

'I didn't know,' she admitted, her eyes wide with realisation.

'Yeah, well, that was obvious.'

'I thought Ronnie would get the job.' She said this half to herself, thinking about her sister's husband. She knew he'd gone for the job.

Another reason to hate this dude.

'So I don't deserve the job?'

'Well, no, but Ronnie is already there—part of the team.'

'I interviewed fair and square. Take it up with HR if you don't like it.' He folded his thick arms against his chest, still bristling with anger. 'It was Ronnie who told me about the job in the first place, if you must know.'

'You know Ronnie?'

He laughed. 'You could say that, yeah. I thought he was joking about you, but I can see now he underplayed his description.'

What? Ronnie had told this jackass about her? Why was he telling people about her?

Her defences were well and truly up now. She'd been up for flirting with this guy, and he'd already known who she was. She didn't like it. 'Yeah,' she countered. 'Well, Ronnie said nothing about you, and my world was better for it.'

She couldn't help but smirk, seeing him pout. He raised a dark brow when he saw her mocking expression. His eyes flashed bright, which made her smirk all the more. It was quite fun, sparring with him. At work, people tended to just do as she asked. She wasn't mean, but her need for perfection and absorption in her job often made her come across as curt, aloof. It was kind of nice to butt heads with someone. 'Don't pout, Jackie boy. With shoulders as big as those, I would have thought you could carry an insult a little better.'

He huffed out a laugh. 'Yeah, well, with little sparrow legs like yours, I would have thought you would be used to running to keep up with the crowd.' They both stood there, lips twitching with the need to suppress their laughter. She was enjoying this, but so was he, she realised when he grinned back at her wolfishly.

What is going on here? Why hadn't Ronnie told her about this guy, about him being here today? Was her sister matchmaking again?

'Yeah, well, good things come in small packages. I could run rings around you any day of the week. Don't think that I'll give you an easy ride when you come to General.' She fixed him with her sternest gaze. 'We don't play games at work, and if you got the job over Ronnie, well, you had better earn it.' Family was important to her, something to be protected. They didn't need a fox in their hen house, disturbing things, ruffling feathers. When was change ever good, other than in medicine?

'Earn it, eh?' His playful look was long gone now. He was closed off. She might have mourned it if she hadn't been so guarded. 'Well, time will tell, little lady.' He side-stepped her on his way to meet the others. 'I'm Ronnie's brother, by the way—Jackson Denning. I'm sure he mentioned me.'

Lucy almost fainted on the spot.

His brother? Oh, my God.

It clicked. Ronnie's older brother, Jackson, was a doctor, working overseas. Harriet had babbled on about him moving back to the UK. As usual, Lucy hadn't listened. 'You're...' She was stumbling over her own tongue now. 'You're his brother, Jackson.'

It was his turn to smirk now. He'd turned around and she could see it now—the Denning jawline, the chocolate hue of his eyes. 'Didn't I just say that?' The fact he was still nursing his bottom while pinning her with his gaze made her face flush for more reasons than one. 'See you at work. Enjoy the rest of your weekend, Trigger.'

He waggled his fingers behind him as if he was pressing a gun trigger, and for the first time in her life Lucy understood what people meant when they said their blood was boiling. Something about the big idiot currently walking away from her made her want to grind her teeth down to stumps.

'You're being childish,' she called after him. 'I didn't know who you were!'

'"You're being childish",' he mocked back in a squeaky voice. 'Be seeing ya, Lucy. Real soon.'

He disappeared out of sight, and she stood alone in the forest.

'Hell,' she muttered to herself. 'Well, you've done it now, Bakewell.'

She started her slow trudge towards camp. Ronnie and Harriet were going to have a field day when they heard.

CHAPTER TWO

Five years later

'HARRIET, YOU KNOW I'll try.'

Lucy allowed her forehead to rest against the large glass window for a moment, listening to her little sister's trademark slow sigh. The one that told Lucy in no uncertain terms that her sister was disappointed. She'd been doing it since they'd been fresh-faced teenagers, taking very different paths despite there only being a couple of years between the pair.

'I know,' Harriet said down the line. 'I get it. I just wanted you there. You know it's just us.'

Lucy lifted her head when a nurse came to check a patient history with her. 'Just a sec, Harry.

'Yes,' she agreed with the nurse. 'Monitor her every hour and call the parents to update them. I sent them down to get something to eat while the tests were being done.' The nurse nodded, leaving Lucy alone again in front of the viewing window of the SCBU—Lucy's little haven, where she came to remind herself why she did the job in the first place. Why she was probably going to miss her niece's second birthday, and why she was currently getting the sigh from her younger sibling. To remind herself why she annoyed her family with the sacrifices she made again and again.

'I'm back, Harriet, but I have to get back to the ward. And

you are not allowed to play the "dead parents" card—no other family guilt trip for another month at least. I promise, I will try my best to get there. I already changed my shift, but you know what it's like.'

But Harriet didn't, not really. She'd been a teaching assistant before having Zoe; now she was a full-time mum. She'd never been one for all-consuming careers and motherhood together. She was happy to have taken a few years off to raise Zoe full-time. She'd wanted family more than anything else, and now she was a mother herself—a great mum; the kind who used Pinterest and made handmade gifts and elaborate cupcakes every Christmas. The polar opposite of Lucy, who was a workaholic with half a cucumber and a bottle of vodka in her fridge as opposed to real food.

When their parents had passed away when they'd been younger, Lucy only just an adult, they'd both veered off in different directions. Lucy had devoted herself to medicine and looking after her teenage sister, and Harriet had grown up wanting family life more than ever. The one thing they had in common though, was their fierce love for each other. Trauma was a pretty strong glue, and it held people together.

'Well, Jackson's coming; he took the day off.'

Lucy turned to look back at the special care babies, feeling her irritation grow tenfold at the mention of Dr Perfect. She scowled at the floor, wishing he could feel her scorn through the layers of brick. Being an A&E doctor was hard—and, sure, running a department was hardly a doddle; she could attest to that herself. But still, did he have to make her feel like an idiot in front of her sister?

His Mr Wonderful routine over the last few years had really got on her nerves, if she was honest. He still insisted on calling her Trigger, which made her want to peel off her own skin. He pulled faces at her like a petulant toddler whenever she alone was looking, and he seemed to revel in the fact that he irritated the ever-living hell out of her just by existing in the same proximity. Sure, she did the same to him, but still—he was the jerk in this situation. Sometimes she even wished for a paintball gun, just so she could pop one off again. That day had set the tempo of their working relationship. They were like stagnant embers around each other, fired into life by the other's presence. Every time she crossed paths with him at the hospital, she had to consciously work on not strangling him with her stethoscope.

To make matters worse, he was liked by everyone else. Of all the people to be her sister's brother-in-law, of course it had to be the flashy doc who loved to wind her up at every opportunity. The one guy she secretly fancied even while he was the biggest pain in her butt.

They'd become family after that day. She'd been maid of honour at Ronnie's and Harriet's wedding and he'd been the best man. He was there every time they did something as a family. Family holidays were quite often torture, with Jackson in his bathing shorts, tanned and beautiful, being ogled by women around the pool, while Lucy stuck her head in a book and slathered herself in suntan lotion.

She knew he at her looked too; she could see him run his eyes over her sometimes. He'd make little comments about a new dress. He always seemed to notice when she had her hair cut or did something new with it. It had been five years of tension between them, sexual and otherwise, and it showed no sign of stopping. But he was family, her sister's brother-in-law, uncle to her niece, so she did what she usually did—she buried it. Focused on the fact that, despite the fact he made her pulse quicken, he also well and truly got on her wick.

'Yeah, well, he would.'

Of course Jackson was going. He never put a foot wrong, did he? *Jackass*. Whenever he worked late and missed a family occasion, he was given a free pass by her own sister.

'What was that?' Harriet said down the phone line.

'Nothing,' Lucy half-sang back. 'Listen, I have to go, but I'll see you there, okay?'

'Fine.' Harriet breathed. 'Love you, sis.'

'Love you too.' Lucy smiled back. 'Give Zoe a big hug from her favourite aunt.'

'You're her only aunt.' Harriet laughed. 'I will. See you soon.'

Lucy glanced at the time on her phone before going back to paediatrics. If she was going to try and get to that birthday party, she had to get going.

'Cute, aren't they?'

Jackson took in the little sleeping bundle in the back of his brother's car. Her hair was stuck up in little tufts, and she was sweaty from the afternoon's exertions. She was adorable.

'Yeah, but I couldn't eat a whole one.'

Ronnie chuckled, wiping a stray blob of chocolate off his daughter's cheek. She stirred, her eyelashes fluttering, before her head dropped again.

'You're the worst, you know that, right?'

'Of course. That's why I don't procreate like you.' Jackson leaned in, brushing Zoe's little warm hand. 'She is all your wife, though, right down to those baby blues.'

Ronnie wasn't offended in the slightest. 'I know. Good genes.' Jackson watched his little brother's contented grin turn devilish. The pair of them were standing by Ronnie's car in the car park of the local soft play area where they'd just partied. Well, if he could call ten very enthusiastic toddlers screeching and whooping for two hours on a sugar high partying.

'Speaking of genes, here comes Auntie Lucy!'

Jackson's lip curled into a smile before he could stop himself, seeing Lucy turn into the car park. She practically screeched to a stop a few spaces away. Seconds later, the door was flung open to a chorus of, 'Sorry, sorry! I had an emergency at the last minute I couldn't hand off!'

Jackson watched her face fall when she took in the scene, Zoe tuckered out and sound asleep.

'Oh, no! I missed the whole thing? Really?'

She scooped a huge cellophane-trimmed basket from the back seat and huffed her way over. Jackson saw the tension in her shoulders; she was wrapped up tighter than the over-the-top birthday gift.

'Sis, I told you not to go mad!' Ronnie, as ever, was thrilled to see his sister-in-law, who looked like his pretty blonde wife. They had the same hair colour and cute little brows sitting over bright blue-green eyes.

That was where the similarities ended, however. Harriet was always calm, collected. The twisted-up pretzel stomping over to them was someone who played a whole different ball game. Even at a kid's party, her face looked pinched. Her eyes roved over the party goers leaving with their progeny, who were all either half-asleep in their parents' arms or still bouncing up and down from their cake and fun overload. Jackson watched her watching them and wondered what was going on in that pretty head of hers. It was kind of a hobby of his, working her out.

Ronnie took the gift basket from her, his eyes boggling at the array of clothes and toys stuffed into the gift. 'This is ridiculous. She's only two, you know, not leaving for uni with the need for a capsule wardrobe. Did you leave anything in the shop?'

She rolled her eyes with a good-natured smirk, and Jackson watched silently as her shoulders started to dip.

'Well, I don't see her as much as I'd like. I have to spoil my only niece, right?' The furrow between her brows returned with a vengeance when she spotted her in the back seat. 'She's asleep.' She looked...disappointed. Jackson could see it written all over her face, just before she hid it behind the expression he was most accustomed to seeing—that of the closed-up professional. The expression that had given her the nickname Medusa at work. Not that anyone dared say it in her proximity; that would be professional suicide. If her glare didn't turn them to stone first, her tongue lashings were strong enough to strip the hide from a rhino.

Personally, he preferred his pet name for her, Trigger. It suited her better. She even answered to it sometimes, when she wasn't thinking, which made it all the sweeter to Jackson. The fact it raised brows from the other terrified staff members cheered him up on the bad days. The irony of him watching her, figuring her out, while the rest of the hospital watched them never lost its sparkle. After working overseas in some of the hottest climates, their banter kept him warm. He couldn't help it. She got under her skin as much as he did hers. In different ways, he thought with a familiar pang that he brushed aside. She was family, and that was that.

'Yeah, sorry.' Ronnie winced. 'She wore herself out in there. She'll love waking up to this, though.' He dipped his head towards the huge gift.

'Yeah,' his sister-in-law murmured, the sadness weighing down her words. 'Sure. I'll just have to come and see her at the weekend—take her to the park or something. Where's my sister?'

Ronnie thumbed behind him. 'She's saying goodbye to the other nursery mums; you know what they are like when they get together.'

Jackson thought he saw another wince cross Lucy's features before she locked it back down under that prickly persona. She looked at him then, as though she'd only just realised he was there. Or, more likely, was only just deigning to acknowledge his presence.

'And I suppose you were here on time.'

Jackson held down the sarcastic smile he almost threw at her and kept it hidden. It would only inflame the fiery woman in front of him. Whilst he normally got a thrill out of it, especially at work, something about her expression made him hold back. He knew she was genuinely upset to have missed Zoe's party. Even he couldn't mock her for that; they both adored Zoe.

'I was. Day off.' He added unnecessarily, 'I'm not on call today either. Good result at work?'

'Tricky, but yeah.'

Jackson nodded back. 'I'm glad. Worth it, then.'

Her gaze slid back to Zoe, still tuckered out in the back seat. Her little blonde curls were ruffled from the breeze coming through the open door. Lucy didn't look too convinced. She was already chewing the inside of her cheek, a tell that she was working something out. He looked away when her eyes locked onto his. She stopped biting.

'Yeah, I guess. Well, I might as well go.' She didn't wait for her sister. She'd be mad, and they all silently acknowledged it. To Harriet, family was first over work, everything else in the world. That was one of the many ways the two women differed. Even being a doctor's wife hadn't softened Harriet on that. Work was the only thing that ever came between them. Jackson thought Harriet harsh at times, but of course he kept that to himself. Lucy wouldn't thank him for voicing it anyway, and he knew that Ronnie had never managed to get through to her on the topic. What Harriet didn't realise was, when they weren't home with Harriet and Zoe, they were saving other people's families. Allowing them to have more time together that otherwise they might never have had.

Ronnie put the gift away to give Lucy a goodbye hug. Jackson didn't step forward; they didn't hug. They clashed when she came down from her department in paediatric care and entered his realm in A&E. The nurses usually went running the second they started to lock horns.

Ronnie had even joked once that Jackson was Perseus. After witnessing one rather heated exchange in the stairwell, Ronnie had sent him a plastic sword and shield. He still had it above his desk at home. It made him laugh every time he saw it. Ronnie was definitely the referee between the two of them at work, and the glue that held the four of them together. He and Zoe, who'd been adored by all of them from the second they'd laid eyes on her.

'Well, thanks for coming. Harriet will understand. You know she just likes the family thing.'

Lucy's brows rose in line with the scepticism Jackson saw across her strained features.

'No, she won't.' Lucy smiled. It didn't meet her eyes, and Jackson busied himself with his phone as Lucy said goodbye to Ronnie, and said nothing as she pulled her car back onto the main road in the direction of her flat.

'Will Harriet really be that annoyed? I miss stuff; she never says anything to me.'

Ronnie shrugged. 'She tries to understand. She takes it different when Lucy's not there. She gets the job; I work enough hours myself. She just thinks differently. Losing their parents hardened one and softened the other.' Jackson had no need to ask which. 'They might be sisters, but DNA is about all they share. You know Harriet—she loves all this.' He waved a hand in the direction of the venue in which they'd just spent two eardrum-shattering hours. 'Lucy just wants different things. Harriet will be fine. I've got a babysitter for tomorrow night so I can take her out. You know, to celebrate the incoming terrible twos.'

Both men's eyes fell back on the sleeping baby nearby.

'I can't believe she's two already,' Jackson commented, marvelling as he always did at the tiny little person his brother had created. 'It doesn't seem like two minutes since you brought her home from the hospital.'

'I remember.' Ronnie laughed. 'It was the last day I got any sleep.'

'Ronnie!' Harriet appeared at the doorway, a bundle of gift bags hanging from her arms. 'Can I have a hand, love?'

Jackson took his leave. He was looking forward to the rest of his day off, away from the bustle of A&E. 'I'll let you get on. Have a good night tomorrow, okay? Send Harriet my love.'

Ronnie was already heading over to his wife, who was waddling towards him with the weight in her arms.

'Will do, bro. Pool next week?' he called out.

Jackson nodded with a grin. 'To take your money again? Try and stop me.'

He waited till the pair of them were heading back to their car before heading to his own, making sure Zoe wasn't alone. As he drove away, he saw Ronnie take the bags from his wife, encircling her in his arms. He looked away, focusing on the road ahead.

It would be nice to have that one day.

He pushed the thought away, not for the first time. He

wasn't at that stage yet. He wasn't even dating, really. He hadn't met anyone he'd wanted to see beyond a couple of dates. He liked his easy life, working in a job he adored. He had the house, the car, financial stability. Sure, someone to sit on the couch with him would be great, but he couldn't really see what that would look like in real life. He didn't even have time for a pet, so how would he fit his life around a family? His thoughts turned to Lucy—her face when she'd realised she'd missed the party.

Maybe people just weren't meant to have everything they wanted.

He was doing fine on his own. The big life plan could wait, for now. There was no rush. He'd come home to put down roots after years of doctoring abroad, and he had plenty of time. In the past five years, he'd adjusted his expectations, that was all.

He headed home, looking forward to an afternoon of gym and rest. There was plenty of time for toddler parties and date nights, he told himself for the millionth time. He had family and friends; the rest could wait. Perhaps the pieces of his life didn't fit as he would like them to. But maybe it was enough that he had them in the first place.

CHAPTER THREE

The next day

JACKSON COULDN'T HELP but smirk as he heard the curtain swish back.

'You called for a consultation?'

'Yeah, I did.'

Lucy looked at the empty bed, her eyes narrowing as she looked at him standing there.

'Well, where's the patient? Triage One, you paged.'

'I put them in bed five—but Trig, wait!'

She'd already turned on her heel, but his hand whipped out to still her. He felt a zap of electricity pulse through him.

Huh; static of the uniform. Well, we are like repelling magnets.

Her aqua eyes widened, as though she'd felt it too, before they fell to see where his fingers had wrapped around the flesh of her forearm.

'Don't call me Trig,' she chided as his hand pulled away. 'What's wrong?'

'I needed to talk to you first. I think the child has pica.'

'Okay.' She nodded. 'What was the reason for attending today?'

'The little fella, Tom, aged five—he was helping his grandmother in the garden. Ate a bulb they were planting, or part of it.'

'Did you check whether it was toxic?'

Jackson nodded. 'Dahlia bulb; his grandmother acted pretty quickly. She got most of the bulb out of his mouth, and gave him water. No treatment needed this time, but it's his fourth admission in three months. The last time it was a Lego brick. He passed it without surgery, but I think he needs checking over—there could be more than pica at play here. He presents with some rigid behaviours, sensitivity to some sensory input… He doesn't speak very much, gives minimal eye contact. His mother's on the way; she was at work. The grandmother's pretty upset.'

He pursed his lips, remembering how the little guy's grandparent had wrung her hands together, her eyes never leaving the boy in the bed. Kids had that effect on people. He saw it time and time again. It was also one of the reasons he wasn't in the quickest rush to join the parenting brigade himself. Having that much worry and responsibility on top of running A&E seemed like a step too far—something he was reminded of by his patients from time to time.

'I bet she is, but from what you said she shouldn't blame herself. I remember a kid in my primary school class who used to eat sand. Children do the oddest things; they have no sense of danger. If pica is the diagnosis, it's a compulsion. Sounds like we might need to refer on to the neurodiversity pathway. I can speak to my team.' Lucy took the clipboard from him, her eyes scanning the paperwork. 'Thanks for the heads up. I'll go speak to the family. Have you mentioned your suspicions to them yet?'

Jackson stretched out his aching back with a wince. He'd been in resus before this case, working on a patient who'd had a heart attack in his front garden. He'd been one of the lucky ones, his next-door neighbour being a nurse who'd administered help quickly. The ambulance had blue-lighted him to the A&E doors, but he'd flatlined on the way in and the CPR had been tough. Jackson's back had started to sing during his stint, but he'd ignored it until the man was breathing and safe from the circling drain.

'Jackson? Earth to Dr Denning!'

'Sorry,' he apologised, shaking his head to wake himself up. 'And no, I figured I'd leave that to the Goddess of Paediatrics.' She rolled her eyes, but the usual fire and snark didn't come. He felt a little cheated. She'd been almost genial. Her game was off. Usually when he was feeling a little tired, or off *his* game, sparring with her fired him up and gave him an energy boost better than anything he could get from the vending machines around here. 'Come on, Trig— nothing? No comment back?'

She held the clipboard tight to her chest.

'Nope, I've got to get on. Busy day.'

He came to stand in front of her. 'Every day around here is a busy day. Really, what's up? You weren't right yesterday.'

'You noticed that, eh?'

He raised a brow. 'Spill. Patients are waiting.'

The sigh that rattled through her rib cage ruffled the papers she clutched to her chest.

'Fine, if it will shut you up. I feel like Harriet's mad at me. I rang her last night, and she was okay with me, but…'

'She judged you for not getting to the party?'

Her mouth lifted on one side, making her look oddly vulnerable.

'Yeah, I think so. She bites her tongue most of the time, but…' She bit her lip, and his eyes tracked the movement.

This is really getting to her.

'I didn't tell her the full truth, but we did have an emergency. I couldn't tell her how bad it was, of course, I never do. Perhaps if I had, she'd understand finally. I couldn't just leave to get to Zoe's party. Zoe was happy, healthy, eating cake with her friends. Sure, her auntie wasn't there, but would she have noticed really? She's two. She won't even remember the party, but if I said that to Harriet she'd explode!'

She was pacing around the cubicle, Jackson tracking her rant around the small curtained space, letting her get it out before they both went back to work. He rather liked these moments. When it was just the two of them, she was different, less guarded. She let him in. Not for the first time, he wondered what their working relationship might have been like if they'd met in different circumstances. If the dye of his character hadn't been set so firmly in her mind that day. If their families weren't entwined together.

'I...' She trailed off. 'Never mind.'

Jackson didn't want her to stop. 'Go on,' he said, his voice soft, low. 'Tell me.'

She pinned him to the spot with her baby blues, nibbling at her lip. He waited.

'Sometimes I wish she'd trained in medicine, like us, like Ronnie. I wish I could show her some of the horrors we see. The tiny coffins we work hard to avoid for our patients. You get it, and Ron does. Hell, A&E isn't all cuts and scrapes. She doesn't get it. I mean, our parents died in a horrific accident.'

She stopped walking, her free hand covering her heart as though saying the words had produced an ache. 'She remembers that; I mean, it's not something you'd ever forget, right? You'd think she'd be proud of us all, saving people. It's why I...'

The words fell away when her eyes met his again. He could see the mental shields click back up into place in her mind. Huffing out a breath, she straightened the already collated papers in her hands. 'Anyway, I just feel a bit off today. I hate feeling at odds with her. She's my—'

'Family,' he finished for her. 'I get it.'

The pair stood across from each other, the hospital continuing on behind the curtain, noisy and full of life.

'Yeah.' She shrugged. 'Nothing will mess you up quite like blood relatives, eh?'

He laughed, and she looked surprised.

'Been a while since I made you laugh, eh?'

'Intentionally, yeah,' he agreed. 'I laugh *at* you all the time.'

'And we're back to normal. I'm glad. Heart to hearts aren't our thing, frenemy.' She tapped the board. 'I'll go see the patient now. See you later, Denning.'

Jackson was pretty sure that, before she left, Lucy had a smile on her face.

Hours later, he was still thinking about their talk. The emergency alert on his pager went off, jolting him from his thoughts. The second he got there, took in the scene. He wanted nothing but her—Lucy. He needed her here. She didn't know it yet, but their lives had just changed for ever. Even when the chaos had died down, he thought of that time in the cubicle. He wished that they could go back there. Wished he had said more. They could never go back to being those people, not now. The people they'e been in that moment were gone for ever.

CHAPTER FOUR

HOW IS THIS HAPPENING? How did we get here?

The voice in Lucy's head wasn't as clear as normal. Her usual sharp mind felt as if it had been dipped in treacle, the cogs gummed up with the slush and debris of the last week and a half.

A week and a half. Ten measly days since she'd last been at work. Since her world had collapsed for the second time.

This was all she had now: a treacly brain, regrets and the welcoming, numbing feeling of shock and disbelief. It had taken all she'd had to dress this morning and to put make-up on. She'd not trusted herself to drive and, given she didn't remember the taxi ride here, that was a good decision. Better than some of the others, which had been haunting her this past week. Since before the funerals, the two coffins, side by side. She willed the image out of her head, concentrating on something else, anything else. She picked up a magazine from the table next to her and pretended to flip through it.

I should have been at the party. I never even said good-bye. If I'd known that was the last time, I would have done better—been a better sister, a more attentive aunt. I thought there was more time. Stupid, stupid, stupid.

'Did the solicitor say what this was about?'

Giving up the pretence of magazine skimming, she turned to look at her companion. He'd already been waiting outside when she'd pulled up. The waiting room of the law firm was roomy, but he'd still taken the seat next to hers. Which was why his deep brown eyes were so close, leaving her feeling exposed under his scrutiny.

She'd caught him watching her a few times since…that day…a look of concern and wariness in his big dopey eyes. Those eyes almost seemed to see right through her, as if he could see the core of her, when no one else did. It had irked her immensely. Now, after this, it was torture. She wanted to tell him to leave, to go back to work and deal with his own grief. The one person in the world she had that knew both Ronnie and Harriet had to be him.

Ronnie and Harriet.

Her heart stopped working for a second. She felt the stutter in her chest when she thought of them. Of her sister, bloodied and broken on that gurney. RTA: three little letters that had taken their brother and sister away. They'd been going on a date and had ended up dead. The only saving grace was the fact that Zoe hadn't been with them in the car. She hadn't been lost too. She hadn't seen any of the horror of the aftermath, unlike Jackson and her.

Now they were both here, sitting in this waiting room, once again linked by family…only this time that family was gone for ever.

'Lucy,' he pressed. 'You with me?'

She had to look at the floor to get the answer out.

'He has the will. He said he needed to get things rolling. Are your parents not coming?'

Jackson shook his head. 'No. I spoke to Mum this morning. She didn't know about the meeting.'

'That's weird, isn't it?'

He shrugged. 'This whole thing's weird.'

'Was Zoe okay?'

His face brightened at the mention of their niece. 'Yeah, she's good. Mum said she's been a bit fussy but she's good.' His expression sobered. 'To be honest I think her being there is helping them hold it together.'

Lucy managed a nod. Anything else was blocked by the lump in her throat.

Jackson went to stand by the window, and she took him in for the first time. He looked dishevelled in the early afternoon light. She could make out minute wisps of grey in his longer than usual stubble and dark circles under his everseeing eyes.

'What? I know you want to say something.' He didn't move an inch, aside from moving his lips. 'Out with it, Trigger.'

'Lucy,' she corrected automatically, irritated that he'd caught her studying him. 'You always say things like that. You don't know me, Jackson. You think you do because we were forced to spend so much time together. The only good thing to come out of this will be getting rid of you, actually. We won't have to pretend to get on any longer.'

'Nice. "Forced" was right. You are the prickliest pear I have ever met.'

'Prickly pear? What are you, five?'

'Yep, that's right.' His tone changed. 'I'll be six soon. Gonna buy me a cake?'

'You can shove your cake up your— What the hell are you doing?'

He strode across the room and knelt at her feet in one angry motion. When she went to get up from her seat, he stopped her.

'No, Lucy. What are you doing? Do you see anyone else helping you? We're waiting to see Harriet and Ronnie's solicitor. Harriet and Ronnie are dead!' The flicker of pain across his taut features was hard to miss. 'I know you've decided to just power through this in your usual way, but I'm a human! My little brother died. Your little sister died, and their little girl is here in this world all alone. Why do you not get that? Do you really not see anyone else? The whole hospital is devastated. We lost one of our own. My team is crying in the locker room between patients. Do you not see that?'

His eyes were wide, even darker than normal. 'Do you really not see me? I stood by your side at the funeral. Did you even realise I was there, Luce?' He sprang up, pacing to the window and back. 'I can't take this!'

There you go, you did it again—pushed too hard. He's right, who else have you got? You've chased everyone away. He has his parents. You have no one.

She took a steadying breath, willing her heart to stop racing. Her cheeks were flushed with shame and embarrassment.

'I'm sorry. I forget you lost someone too. I do care. I care about the people at work, about Zoe. I care that Harriet and Ronnie are…gone. I just deal with things my way. Grief is different for everyone.'

His sigh rattled the windowpane. 'Your way is to bottle it up. It's not healthy.' Lucy's eye-roll produced an irritated growl. 'See? There you go again, being all snarky when I am trying to get through to you.'

'I didn't say a word!'

'You don't have to! Your poker face doesn't work on everyone. It doesn't work on me. I just want to help, to make sure you face this properly.'

'I don't need your help, Jackson. I never did.' She jabbed a finger at her chest.

'Fine,' he snapped back, sitting at the farthest corner of the room. 'But this is not over, Luce.'

'Don't call me Luce,' was all she could spit back. No one called her Luce. It was Lucy or Dr Bakewell. Trigger was bad enough; he knew it wound her up. 'I don't need help. I'm fine. I just want to get this over with. Get back to normal. Get back to work.' The fact her manager had insisted on her taking a leave of absence didn't help. She needed to work. Rattling around her place, alone with her thoughts, was making her climb the walls.

'Right,' he scoffed. 'Whatever you say, Dr Bakewell.'

She busied herself with the contents of her handbag for a while, Jackson flicking through old magazines so hard she thought she heard some of the pages rip beneath his fingertips. After the longest twenty minutes in recorded history, a secretary came through a set of imposing double doors, inviting them in.

The solicitor's office was just as she remembered it from when her parents had died. A bookcase wall stuffed with weighty tomes provided the backdrop for Mr Cohen's huge walnut desk. The air smelled the same—a mixture of old books, paper and peppermint.

He greeted them at the door, his hair a little greyer, his stature a little shorter, but still the same comforting presence.

'Miss Bakewell, you're all grown up!'

Lucy couldn't help but laugh. 'I am. How are you?'

She could feel Jackson at her shoulder, hear his awkward cough.

Mr Cohen didn't miss a beat. 'I'm well, thank you. This is Mr Denning, I presume?'

'Jackson, please,' he replied, the smile on his face as broad as it was genuine. Lucy had to look away. Behind that

easy welcoming grin, she could see the taut expression as
he exchanged pleasantries, see the hollows under his usually annoyingly sparkly eyes.

*Stop it. You can't hold anyone else together. You are fall-
ing apart as it is.*

'Please, take a seat,' Mr Cohen instructed.

Jackson took the chair next to hers, flexing his hands on
the plaid leather arms.

'So,' Mr Cohen started, tiny little glasses perched at the
end of his nose. 'As we discussed on the telephone, Harriet
and Ronald left a will.' He eyed them both above the rims,
pausing at the delicate nature of the conversation. 'It's pretty
simple.' He eyed Jackson. 'Your parents were well aware
of the contents of the will when it was written, and I have
their agreement.'

Lucy sneaked a glance at Jackson, who looked as surprised as she felt. Harriet had never mentioned a will to *her*.
Mr Cohen focused back on the papers in his grasp.

'Now, as to the financial aspects… It is instructed that
the house be sold and any monies made as a result of said
sale are to be put into a trust for Zoe.'

Lucy nodded along, barely listening as he spoke about
jewellery and some other items of Ronnie's that were left
to Jackson. The wedding rings were to be kept for Zoe. The
pieces of Harriet's jewellery were to be shared between Lucy
and Zoe. The ring from her mother was to go to Lucy, to be
passed down to Zoe or any daughter Lucy had. Lucy sniffed
at this, thinking of how Harriet had thought of her daughter and her, wanting things to be right and passed down to
the future generations.

She willed her tears to stay away, blinking hard to clear
her field of vision. A movement at her side caught her eye.
Jackson was gripping the chair arms so tightly, she could

practically hear his nails scratch against the leather. Her own hands flexed, and she held them together on her lap to stop herself from reaching out to him.

Stay strong.

Mr Cohen's professional tones pierced through her rampant thoughts a second later.

'As for the care of Zoe, Lucy Bakewell and Jackson Denning are named as her guardians, and are to raise said child together in a home to be determined by the beneficiaries. This will be subject to an initial six-month review to ascertain that this arrangement is working for all parties and benefits all parties. Any monies left in the deceaseds' accounts after all debts are paid are to be used for the purposes of raising said child, and the trust can be accessed through myself if further financial assistance is required.'

The money stuff didn't even enter Lucy's head. She was still baulking at the first part. Jackson looked like a clenched-jawed waxwork.

'I'm sorry,' she spluttered eventually when the sentence that had just rocked the very axis of her world had absorbed into her already addled brain. 'What was that? Joint custody? Me?' She jabbed a finger to her right. 'With him? Not Ronnie's parents—us?'

Joint custody? Is this a joke?

Zoe had been with the Dennings since the night of the crash. They were parents already. She'd just assumed... Well, she hadn't thought about it. Ronnie's parents had had Zoe that night, as they'd been babysitting. It had made sense for her to stay there until things were sorted. Until after the funerals were over and until Lucy was back at work. She'd just assumed that was what would happen and what they would want. She'd thought she and Jackson would just be there, Zoe's aunt and uncle, like always.

'Mr Cohen, I might be being dumb here, but I don't get it. There must be a mistake.'

Mr Cohen didn't look surprised at her reaction. In fact, he almost looked as if he found it rather comical.

'There's no mistake, Miss Bakewell. The instructions are clear. They were made when Zoe was born.'

Two years. Two years and no one had said a word.

Rounding on Jackson, she poked him hard in the arm. 'I'm supposed to raise Zoe? Me? With him?' He didn't even flinch. Her finger almost snapped as it hit a solid wall of tensed muscle.

'Yes, Miss Bakewell.'

'Lucy, please. This can't be right.' She looked at Jackson again. 'Did you know about this?'

He shook his head, leaning forward and putting it into his hands. 'No, of course not. Mum was being weird, but—'

'But what?'

'But she's just lost her son.' His tone was sober, flat.

'Right.' Lucy nodded. 'Right, okay. Sorry.'

Mr Cohen shuffled some papers in his file. 'I assure you, both Harriet and Ronald—'

'Ronnie,' Jackson corrected.

Mr Cohen pressed his lips tightly together. 'Of course. Harriet and Ronnie were very clear in their instructions. We discussed it at some length.'

'Yeah, well, they didn't tell me!' She was spewing her thoughts out loud now. 'I mean, I thought I might be named. It crossed my mind: I'm Harriet's only family. But why Jackson?'

'Why not?' Jackson pressed back. 'He was my brother. I know Zoe.' His eyes were darting all over the room. Lucy realised he was processing the news too. She was watching his freak-out in real time, as he was hers. She was wringing her hands, still waiting for him to erupt when he let out a surprised little chuckle. 'Ronnie, man.' He kept laughing. 'Well played, man.'

Lucy was apoplectic. 'This is funny to you? Are you freaking kidding me? Mr Cohen, why are the grandparents not named?'

Mr Cohen steepled his fingers together. 'Mr and Mrs Denning are well into their retirement. It was felt that the best chance of long-term stability for Zoe was for her to be raised by the pair of you.'

Lucy took it in, remembering times she'd dealt with patients in situations like this, with injured children orphaned by catastrophe. She'd dealt with enough social workers to see the logic. She and Jackson were both young, financially secure. They owned property. It made sense, if one didn't know their relationship. They bickered and taunted each other. HR had made them sign a waiver due to their legendary spats. They were so sick of hearing about complaints one made about the other they'd drafted a 'friendship agreement', as if Lucy and Jackson were toddlers fighting over the same toy at playgroup. Now they were supposed to sign up for a child together?

No. Not happening.

'Fine.' She sighed, finding her shields and barracking herself behind them. She would do what she did when her parents had died. She'd be the mother figure. She'd raise Zoe. She'd helped raise her little sister; she could do this, but she wasn't a team player. 'I am Harriet's only living relative. Zoe's aunt by blood. I don't need a co-parent in this.'

'Oh, really?' Jackson's voice was a gravelly hum. 'I didn't even know you were thinking about taking Zoe on.'

'Taking her on? She's not some project, Jack!'

'And you can't do this alone, Luce!'

Her fist slammed down on the desk before them and made a loud thump.

'Don't call me Luce! You know that drives me crazy!'

Mr Cohen made a loud, 'Ahem,' silencing them both.

'Sorry,' they both mumbled in unison. They were toe to toe, in each other's faces. Slowly, they sheepishly returned to their seats.

Mr Cohen's sigh ruffled the papers in front of him.

'I know that this has been awful. For both of you. I did try to insist that the pair of you were informed beforehand, in case this event did occur, but Harriet was...reluctant.' His lips thinned. 'I suppose they never thought this day would come. I wish it hadn't myself, but the instructions were clear. Ronnie and Harriet wanted the best for little Zoe, and they chose you—together.

'Now...' He turned over the paper, pushing his glasses back up his nose. 'If one or both of you wish to object to this, or relinquish your guardianship, then there are contingencies in place.'

Zoe went to open her mouth to yell, *hell, yes*. She couldn't live and raise a child with her work nemesis, but Mr Cohen beat her to the chase.

'Lucy,' he addressed her. 'I have seen you and your sister navigate hard times before, and make no mistake, Harriet was the driving force behind this. Ronnie was on board, of course, but your sister, as you know, was a very determined planner. Even in death, she wanted the best. To that end, she left you this.' He opened the file and Lucy's eyes took in her sister's neat script across the surface of a crisp, cream envelope. 'I'll give you a moment. Jackson, would you like to follow me? We have refreshments waiting.'

Lucy didn't take her eyes from the envelope as the two men shuffled out of the room and didn't take in their muted voices or their back and forth. As soon as the door clicked closed, she reached and tore open the thick paper, her eyes brimming as she saw her sister's final words laid bare before her.

Dear Big Sis,

If you're reading this, then the worst has happened. I'm gone, and my Ronnie too. I'm sorry I had to leave you, dear Lucy, but I want you to know that I love you. Fiercely. Always have, despite our differences. When we lost our parents, you barely into adulthood yourself, it bonded us for ever, but divided us too. I might have been the little sister, but you were always much more than an annoying older sibling to me. When Mum and Dad died, you became my parent too. My role model.

When I fell apart, you were the one who told me to buck up. To get up and get on with it. To be strong, to face things head on. To never give up. To stop being stubborn.

So that's what I am asking...telling...you to do now. Buck up, big sister. Get up and get on with life. I mean this with the greatest affection, but you're not doing the best job of that now. I know you love your career, but somewhere along the way—between holding me together and sticking families back together—you lost a piece of yourself. That little girl who danced with me to the radio in our mother's kitchen knew that life was fun. I miss that girl, miss that part of you. I see it in Zoe already, in her tiny, joyful little face. I hope she keeps it.

I know we didn't always see things the same way, but I know you love us. Love Zoe. She's a beautiful baby and, writing this, I just know that you will be there to watch her grow. To give her strength and gumption. You taught her mother the same things.

I also realise that right about now, you're feeling pretty mad too. The control freak in you will be fuming with me. Don't be mad at Ronnie's parents. We asked them not to say anything. They deserve to enjoy their retirement. To be grandparents and not parents again. It's too much for them. This is the right thing and, one day, you'll see it too.

You're probably giving poor Jackson hell. You two are more alike than you think. I'm laughing from heaven right now at the rage I know you're feeling at me too. Our solicitor wigged out when I told him this was to be our little secret, but I knew, if I told you, you would have gone mad—not see the plan I have in my head. Be nice to Mr Cohen, he was always good to us. He steered us through our parents' deaths, and he'll see you all through mine too.

Back to Jackson. While you are my ride or die, don't forget that Jackson just lost his too. Try not to torture him so much. Ronnie was worried not telling you both would make it harder, like some cruel final trick played on the two of you, but I have never been more sure of anything since meeting Ronnie that this is the right thing. I had you, and only you. I don't want that for Zoe, or you. Putting the burden of raising our child solely on your shoulders wouldn't be right. Jackson and you will need each other, like it or not.

Zoe will need people. She's already lost too much. I know you can guide our daughter to be fierce and brave. Braver and fiercer than I ever was. Jackson can tell her stories about her dad, help his memory stay alive for Zoe, like your memory of me will. He can be the dad that we had for that short time. The man she'll compare all those after against—someone to fix her bike, tell her to drive safely. Check the tyres on her car before she drives to college. And yes, you did that for me, but we missed Dad more than ever in those moments.

Jackson will be the one to protect her, to look after you both. You deserve someone to take care of you, even though I know you'll struggle to let him. Ronnie knows he won't leave, but try not to break him or send him away. I don't want you to struggle in this world alone, like we had to.

So, darling sister, my rock, my heart, my best friend— for once in your life, listen to your little sister and do what I wish. Don't shut people out, don't lose the softer parts of you. Be kind to Jackson and, if he wants to help, let him. You can shout at me later. I hope it's much later, dear sis. No more wishing life away, or letting it pass you by. Look after Zoe for us, and each other.

Ronnie and I love you all so much. I'll say hi to our parents for you. I'll see you when you get here.

Be brave, Lucy. I love you for ever.

Harry

Lucy jerked the letter away before her tears marred it. She read it twice more, the tears multiplying each time her eyes ran over the words.

'Oh, Harriet,' she said between shuddery breaths. She looked up to the ceiling, till the tears had dried on her cheeks. 'Way to play the sister card. You always, always knew how to pull a good guilt trip.' A sob escaped her. 'I can't even argue with you! Kind of hard to hash it out with you now.' She wiped at her face, wanting to pull herself back together. To get out of this room, this funk, and get back to doing.

I'm better moving forward. If I wallow in this, stay still, I'll be done.

She drew a deep, shuddery breath into her lungs. 'One more minute,' she said to her sister. 'One more minute, and then I'll get up.' Looking at the clock, she sobbed quietly as she watched the seconds on the clock tick down.

When she emerged from the room, the letter tucked into her bag, the two men were standing there. Jackson searched her face, as if he was looking for clues, and she scanned his.

Can I do this? Can we really live together? Can I raise a child, with a man who irritates the hell out of me?

All she could hear was her sister's voice in her head. The words from the letter were embedded in her brain for eternity. She thought back to when it had just been the two of them, parentless and alone, so much older, more aware, than poor Zoe. They had memories Zoe would never have, as painful sometimes as they were to recall.

The moment we knew we were alone.

She recalled vividly drying her sister's tears that day, telling her she would look after her, that everything was going to be okay. She knew just what to do then. She'd lived through this before. She could do it again and, as before, she would look after her niece. Her family. No matter what the personal cost.

'I don't want to contest the will,' she said, her voice a ghost of its usual self. 'Jackson?'

It suddenly occurred to her that *he* might want to. All this was new to him too. It didn't help that, for once, his usually very expressive face was like stone, immovable and impenetrable.

'Jackson what?' He also seemed to be playing dumb.

Was he playing for time?

She felt her heart thud in her chest.

Do I want him to say yes?

It was watching his stone-cold face that begged another question, one that she hadn't asked before.

What if he doesn't, and I am going to be alone in this anyway? I've hardly been nice to him.

She remembered what he'd said, about being by her side. He had been. He'd held her up at the funeral. He'd sorted out both their work leaves, though she'd chewed his ear off, even though he'd been right about them both needing the time off. He'd been there, every day, looking after Zoe, his parents and her. He'd rung her daily, offering to bring over food. She'd never said yes, but he'd tried.

As confused as he made her feel sometimes, he was always there—whether she wanted him to be or not. This was a big shock to both of them and, right now, he was so angry with her she couldn't tell which way the storm was blowing his sails.

His deep-brown eyes grabbed her the instant she dared look him in the face. 'So, do you want to? Contest the will, I mean?'

She felt her face flush.

'No,' he said, his voice even, soft. 'I don't want to contest.' The bite of his lip gave his worry away. 'Unless you want me to.'

She thought back to her panic seconds earlier: the prospect of doing this on her own; the letter from her sister that felt like a burning hot poker in her bag. Whether she liked it or not, they were in this together. Zoe needed people who loved her, who understood her. A mother's last wish couldn't be ignored over her own barriers.

Six months. Give it six months.

'We'll have a lot to organise.'

A slight nod was all she got at first. The tension in the room was so palpable she could have cut it with a scalpel.

'We've got time,' he added with a sad little smile. 'We'll figure it out, right?'

CHAPTER FIVE

AFTER SIGNING AWAY what felt like their whole lives, an hour later the pair of them stumbled out into the daylight. When Lucy reached for her phone, Jackson put his hand over the screen.

'Don't get a taxi. I'll drive you.' Before she could tell him to move his hand, he cut her off. 'Get in the car, Lucy.'

They headed towards Jackson's car in silence, her head full of all the things they had to consider. Mr Cohen had explained that a date would be set for six months' time to confirm that the arrangement was working. If both parties agreed, and everyone was satisfied that Zoe was well cared for, the arrangement would continue. Six months to figure out how to co-parent with the Head of A&E, a man who was the subject of her tongue lashings and was now going to play 'Mummy and Daddy' with her.

'Whoa!' She felt Jackson's hand around her waist, yanking her back, just as the honk of a car in front startled her. 'What the hell are you doing?'

She'd walked out into the road. The driver wound his window down and shouted an obscenity in their direction.

'Get lost!' Jackson countered, his fist banging on the roof of the car. He spun her round, holding the tops of her arms tight. 'You okay?'

'Yeah. No. Not at all.' His concerned features softened;

his gaze was fixed on hers as if he was checking her for injuries. He wouldn't find them. They were on the inside, buried so deep, no surgeon would be able to cut them away from the healthy flesh. 'This is not normal, right?'

His laugh surprised her, jolted her out of her melancholy.

'No, Luce, this is far from normal.' He put her arm through his and guided her to the car park. 'Come on; let's get out of here before you try to stop the traffic again.'

Lucy stared out of the window when the car came to a stop. She'd barely registered the car ride and, staring at the neat house in front of her, she wondered how long they'd been driving.

'Come on.' Jackson nudged her, coming to open her car door before she got a chance to object.

'Where are we? Shouldn't we get back?' Over the last ten days, the pair of them had spent most of their time at his parents' house or dealing with the funeral arrangements.

'Zoe's fine. I want to show you something.'

She shrank back into the passenger seat.

'You have to get out of the car for me to do that.' He held out his hand and she gave in.

'Fine.' She huffed, getting out on her own and following him up the neat stone path. 'Whose house is this?'

He answered her with a key, which fit neatly into the front door.

'My house. I realised you've never actually been here.' He bent to pick up the post, stopping when he saw she was frozen on the doorstep. 'You can cross the threshold, you know. I disabled the booby traps and removed the garlic cloves, Elvira.'

She stepped over the threshold into a large, well-decorated hallway. He put the pile of post down on an end table near the door, rolling his eyes and pulling her in far enough to shut the door behind them both.

'And why are we here?'

His head snapped back at the question. 'Well, Zoe can't stay with my parents for ever. Now we know what's going on, we need to start making some decisions. Since you live in a one-bedroom flat, I thought we'd make this place our base.'

Our base. Our...base...

'What makes you think I'd want to live here?'

'The one bedroomed flat was the first clue. I have three bedrooms, a garden, space for all your and Zoe's stuff. It's not too far from work and...you're bugging out.'

Lucy closed the jaw she didn't know had been gaping open, wrapping her arms tightly around herself as if she could shield herself from the lair of Jackson Denning.

'I'm not bugging out.'

'Did you tell your face that? You look like you're about to be sent to war.'

'Well...'

He headed down the hallway, pushing open a door at the end. She followed him into the kitchen which looked like a stainless-steel fortress. Jackson stuck his head in the fridge, pulling out various items, then moving over and lighting the stove.

'I thought we should eat, then I can show you around the place. The smallest bedroom is currently my office, but I can move things around. I can set up in the corner of the dining room or something.'

He cracked some eggs into a bowl, motioning for her to sit down at one of the stools set under the island. She looked around, trying to reconcile the man she knew with the one standing in front of her. 'Omelette okay?'

Her stomach grumbled. Sheila Denning was always try-ing to feed her, but she couldn't remember the last time she'd actually eaten anything substantial. 'Sure. Thanks.'

He shrugged his shoulders, getting to work cutting ham into little slices and grating cheese. She watched him work. For once, the silence wasn't entirely uncomfortable. The knives that usually cut through the air between them seemed to be resting in the drawer.

'I don't know why I've never been here before.'

He chuckled, mixing the ingredients in a large glass bowl.

'I know. I did invite you to the house warming, and a few barbecues, but you always said you were washing your hair.' He flashed her a sarcastic grin. 'You seem to wash your hair a lot. Remember when Arron from the fracture clinic kept asking you out? I'm pretty sure you gave him that same ex-cuse for two months before he gave up.'

How did he know that? She thought she'd been discreet in turning him down.

'I remember,' she muttered, still distracted by the sight of Jackson doing something domestic. She was used to seeing him on the A&E floor, in scrubs or covered in blood. Today he looked different with his sleeves rolled up, his corded forearms flexing as he spooned the mixture into a frying pan. 'So, you own this? It's pretty big.'

'I bought it as a long-term investment.' He shrugged. 'I thought I might have a family one day, you know? I hate flats. I spent too much time in temporary digs whilst work-ing away to live like that again—no gardens, thin walls. A buddy of mine's a builder, and he updated it for me. I like having the space. When I had a flat, I felt like I was on top of people, you know? Being so busy at work all day, the chaos, the noise; it batters the senses after a while.'

He pushed a plate holding a folded-up omelette over to

her, together with cutlery. 'It's quiet here. I sit in the garden sometimes and have a beer, or fire up the grill. It's nice.'

He spoke about living here as if it was a foregone conclusion, and that got her hackles up.

'So you want us to live here just like that?'

He took a seat next to her with his own food, tucking in. 'It makes sense. It's near to work, there's room for two cars. You can have your own room. Space for us all.'

He noticed she wasn't eating, gently nudging her arm with his. Cutting off a piece, she popped it into her mouth. 'Wow.' It was quite possibly the best omelette she'd ever had, fluffy and filling. 'This is good.'

His bashful grin told her he didn't do this a lot. 'I like to cook too.' He waved his fork around the kitchen. 'State of the art.'

'Bragger. Bet you tell that to all the conquests you bring here too.'

He almost choked on his omelette. 'Conquests?'

'Yeah; Ronnie told Harriet things.' His brows shot up into his hairline. 'Sisters talk too.'

'Nice!' He huffed. 'Cheers for that, brother.' He saluted the ceiling, and they both went quiet, reminded of their loss.

'That's a point, though—dating.'

She felt him stiffen at her side.

'I didn't realise you were seeing someone.'

'I'm not.' She laughed at the absurdity, snorting by accident. 'All right, Miss Piggy.'

'Shut up!' She jabbed him with an elbow. 'I didn't mean to!'

His shoulders were shaking with mirth. 'Oh, I know, but that was funny. I intend to make you snort more often.'

'Jerk,' she said, but she was laughing along with him.

'You're really not dating, at all?'

She shook her head, finishing off the last morsels of food on her plate. 'Nope. No time for all that.' She thought of Zoe. 'Guess that won't be changing any time soon either, but if you date anyone we'll have to come up with some kind of plan.'

Jackson stood, collecting their empty plates and stacking them neatly into the dishwasher.

'I won't,' he said simply, leaning back against one of the tall, shiny, steel cupboards. 'I didn't do it much anyway, and never here.'

Wait, what?

'Never?'

'Nope.' He chuckled as he came over and pulled her to her feet. 'You'll be the first woman to sleep over, believe it or not.' He yanked her up so fast that she wobbled on her feet. Steadying herself against his chest with her hands, she looked up at him and heard his surprised gasp before she stepped back a little. He licked his lips and withdrew. 'Er... I'll show you around, then we'd better get back.'

He strode away, and she saw his fists clench together at his sides.

That was... They'd been...close.

'You coming?' he asked from the doorway.

'Yep.' She shrugged herself out of...whatever that had been. The last couple of weeks were giving her whiplash. She thought of her sister's letter, looking around at Jackson's house. Could she really live here, give up her life? Taking a deep, galvanising breath, she went to find Jackson.

'I think it's only fair if you see my place,' she said when she found him in the living room. 'Before we make any firm decisions.'

To his credit, he readily agreed. 'Fine; we have time. I've shown you mine,' he said with a wink. 'Let's see what you've got.'

* * *

'You can't be serious.'

There was no mistaking his mocking tone and, now she was here, she couldn't blame him. Compared to his place, her flat was a little on the small side. She'd never needed a big home, and had never wanted the expense or felt the need to rattle around in some huge, posh abode. She didn't have the time for decorating, and she didn't entertain. She was barely at home—she usually took extra shifts, ended up at the gym or went out with friends or with her sister. Her days off at home were usually spent sleeping or doing laundry so she didn't have to wear the grungy undies at the back of her drawer on the next shift at work. Having Jackson standing in her kitchen, rooting through her fridge, she almost felt silly at feeling so stubborn.

'Smells like something died in here.' He pulled out an old pizza box, opening it and retching.

Oh, yeah, I forgot about that tuna and sweetcorn pizza I had in there. When did I order that—last week?

He looked around the neat, little unused kitchen. 'Bin?'

She shrugged, taking the box from him. 'I usually just use plastic bags and take them out daily.'

He raised a brow but said nothing. 'I'm not here a lot. I don't really eat here.'

'Zoe will, though.' He motioned around him. 'This place is nice, but my place is a house, with a garden—like she's used to. I know that you want to keep your life, but maybe… Oh, I don't know.' He seemed to shrink into himself. Even then she had to look up to meet his eye line. 'It's only been a couple of hours. I can't tell you what to do; I don't know myself.'

'I don't know either, that's the problem. It's a lot to take in.' She joined him in peering at the fridge innards. 'Wow, it does stink.' Leaning forward, she pulled out a takeaway box that was pretty much mush. She couldn't even remember what it *had* been, let alone when she'd ordered it. 'Oh, my Lord, it smells like medical waste.'

'Told ya,' he muttered and, when she caught his eye, she couldn't help but laugh. He dissolved into laughter along with her, and the two of them were laughing hysterically in seconds. 'I knew you usually ate at work. Now I know why. It's not like the canteen food is that good.'

She wanted to bite back at him but couldn't stop laughing long enough to get any words out. She laughed till her sides hurt, Jackson laughing along with her. He leaned against the counter when their laughter subsided, looking around him at her home. He was here, in her space. The fact it wasn't the weirdest thing that had happened that day didn't make it any less...odd.

'I can't believe you're standing in my kitchen and we were laughing again. Us laughing in kitchens is becoming a habit.' She pulled her hair back into a bun and fastened it with a couple of chopsticks she pulled from her cutlery drawer—her very spartan cutlery drawer. 'It's been a weird day.'

'A weird time,' he said with a rueful smile. 'It's not a bad place. I hope you don't think I was—'

'I don't.' Lucy pulled a large disposable bag from a stack in the drawer, getting to work on emptying the fridge. 'I'm kind of a slob, I get it.' She looked around at the barely used utensils in the pot on the side. 'Harriet bought that for me. She said it would encourage me to cook more.' Her voice cracked, and she fell silent. Yesterday she'd had a different life, now she was barrelling blindly into a new one. Still, there was no time to stop. Stopping meant dwelling.

She threw more things into the bag, not even caring what the food was now, whether it was in date or spoiled. It didn't matter any more. She'd known the second she'd walked back into her flat that she wouldn't be bringing Zoe back here Her home was for her old life. She dumped the bag on the floor and walked over to Jackson. 'You knew what you were doing, didn't you, bringing me here after your place?'

Jackson folded his arms, watching her as if he was waiting for her to say more before he reacted. He had a tendency to do that, she noticed. She noticed more things about him these days. Probably because she couldn't exactly walk away from him, or pretend he was on the outskirts of her life any more, a bug to be swatted. She felt his hurt as keenly as her own.

'I'm not judging how you live, Lucy. I know how hard you work. Harriet told me you always looked after her. Living alone, it's different. Working long hours, those things are not as important.'

'I know, but you're right. Your house…well…it's a house, for a start. Zoe is used to having a garden to play in. She has that swing set at her house. I can't exactly hang it off the balcony, can I? I don't have a bedroom for her. I have one allocated car parking space; you have a driveway.' She picked up the bag of spoiled food, reaching for her handbag. 'Let's go see Zoe, okay? We have the six-month review to prepare for.' She lifted the food bag and waggled it at him. 'I think we might need to get a plan together.' As she walked to the door, his voice stilled her.

'Grab some clothes too.'

Her head snapped to look at him. 'Why?'

'I have a bottle of Scotch I've been saving.' His lips curled into a smile. 'I think our life-merging plans might need a two-drink minimum.'

She didn't argue with him on that one. Leaving the food bag by the front door, she headed to the bedroom to grab her overnight bag.

* * *

The sun was barely up in the sky when Lucy looked out of the large, decaled window. She'd sneaked out early from Jackson's, intending to go to her place and pick up some more of her stuff. After seeing Zoe and Sheila and Walt, Jackson's parents, they'd been too drained to talk much. His parents had been so apologetic about keeping the contents of the will a secret from them. The relief on both their faces was obvious, and Lucy hated that they'd had to shoulder that on top of burying their son and daughter-in-law.

When they'd got back to Jackson's house after putting Zoe to bed at his parents' house, the events of the day had felt enough. Instead of making plans, they'd opened the Scotch, put on some dumb action movie and ordered a takeaway. They'd talked about work, their patients; they'd swapped stories each had never heard before.

She'd headed to bed early, feeling awkward going up to the spare room. She'd spent half the night staring at the ceiling. In the end she'd tiptoed back downstairs, taking another full tumbler of the good stuff to bed to try and knock herself out for a few hours.

Instead of heading home, she got the cab to stop at the coffee shop near work. She needed something familiar, something that hadn't changed. Before work, she often met her colleague Amy for coffee. When she pushed through the steamed-up glass doors, seeing her friend there gave her a jolt of sorely needed comfort and she spilled her story.

'So that's it, you're a parent now?'

Amy, who worked with Lucy in Paediatrics, pushed her coffee closer to her. Lucy didn't reply for a moment, focusing on the pretty little leaf art on the surface. Picking up her spoon, she stirred the liquid, erasing the image, turning pretty perfection to swirling chaos.

'Not a parent, still an auntie. Just more…hands on.'

'Mmm-hmm.' When she finally met Amy's eye, she could tell she wasn't buying it. 'That simple, eh? Any other person would be curled in a ball somewhere. I know you're tough, Lucy, but still; you must have so much to think about. It's been, what, two weeks? And Jackson—Daddy Denning? Mate, that's a lot.'

Lucy bit at her lip, buying time with a slow sip of her coffee. 'I know. I haven't even told work. The hospital gave us both time off, and we have to adjust to this new normal, I guess. Curling into a ball isn't going to get things sorted. Harriet left instructions for everything, but I still don't really know where to start.'

'And you have six months to get sorted before you make a final decision?' Amy was always a good listener, one of the few people Lucy trusted, other than Harriet. Seeing her confusion and shock brought home just how gargantuan her situation was. Perhaps she was still numb. Maybe curling into a sodden mess would come later. It hadn't with her parents' passing; she'd had to get on with things.

She ran her hands down her cheeks, realising that this time wouldn't be any different. She was glad that her autopilot button hadn't let her down again. She hadn't cried since being at the hospital. 'Seems like a short space of time for the rest of your life.'

'Yeah, but it's not like I'm going to walk away from Zoe.'

Amy sat listening with that look she always had: attentive, helpful. Ever since they'd started working together throughout early mornings, late nights and coffee shop breakfasts, Amy had been a good sounding board. Whenever they got to talking, she always got that look on her face, as if she was digesting everything and judging nothing. Lucy made a mental note to tell her one day how grateful she was for her friendship. She never really had, and the reminder that life was short had made her more aware of the few relationships she had and how important they were.

'I never said you would. Still, it's not like it's just for the six months. A kid takes eighteen years—minimum. My little brother Ben is twenty and still bringing his washing home from university for my mum to sort out. I swear, how that boy still doesn't know how to use a washing machine…'

Lucy laughed under her breath. 'I think it will be a while before we have to think about that.'

'Exactly!' Amy seized on her point. 'She's what, two? It's a long time to share your life with someone you don't even like, and what if you meet someone, or Jackson does?'

A couple of customers walked in, stopping their conversation. Lucy's phone buzzed in her pocket. Thinking it was work, she fished it out: *Jackson*. She'd left a note letting him know she'd gone out. It had felt weird, skulking out of a man's house. It was not something she usually did, not that any of this was usual.

Got your note. Everything okay?

It was weird to see him asking her that on a text. Normally they texted about work, the odd time about Harriet or Ron, but mostly they sent each other sarcastic memes or snippy comments. He was listed in her phone as 'Satan', for goodness' sake. She tried to remember her sister's letter, but still, the day to day was hard. How the hell were they going to navigate the next six months, let alone life beyond that?

Yeah. Is Zoe okay?

She's fine. My folks would have called us. Not why I was texting.

She texted back.

I went for a walk.

He knew Amy. Why hadn't she told him the truth? She'd slept over, not done the walk of shame! Looking around her, she envied the other customers, enjoying their morning pastries and coffees without the side of drama.

'Everything okay?' Amy asked, tapping her nails on the table top. 'You look guilty.'

Amy struck again, knowing how to read Lucy's usual poker face in an instant. She remembered Jackson's comment about how he could read her. Perhaps she trusted him more than she thought. She must do, for him to see through her defences.

'Jackson.' She waved the phone at Amy. 'He messaged me to see where I was.'

Amy's tattooed brows knitted together with the force of her frown.

'You didn't tell him? I thought you stayed over?'

Lucy's defences sprang up, along with her shoulder blades.

'I left a note!'

'Saying what?'

'Gone out?' Hearing it out loud made her wince. 'It's barely past seven; I didn't think he'd be up yet. I did nothing wrong.'

Amy checked her watch and began gathering her things. 'You did nothing wrong, but you can't just leave a note and go out early in the morning. You might have worried him, going off like that. You're going to be living together.'

Lucy opened her mouth to object, but Amy shut her down with a pointed finger. 'Before you say you have your own place, you're an independent woman, blah-blah-blah, the man opened his home to you. You live on salads, smoothies, caffeine and three hours' sleep. I've seen how you live and work, Lucy: laser-focused. You are more than capable of looking after yourself, but it's not about just you any more! Imagine if you were Jackson, just for a minute. You've hardly been yourself lately. Who would be?'

Amy got up to leave, pulling Lucy onto her feet for a hug. 'Take back some drinks and pastries with you and sort it out.' She winked. 'Go home, Lucy. For once, let someone in. Having someone to take care of you might not be so bad. That person being Jackson? It could be a lot worse.'

'I'm not sure about that,' Lucy whined. 'Take me to work with you instead!'

Amy laughed. 'No chance, Bakewell. Now, be the tough nut I know you are and face him. I think you might find things will work out better than you think.'

'You think?'

Amy grinned. 'I'd bet money on it.'

Jackson's front door was unlocked when she got back. It felt weird, just walking in without knocking, but she was laden down with the bribes Amy had suggested so she pushed through her nerves. He met her at the door, taking the coffee cups from her full hands.

'Thanks,' she muttered. 'I brought us some goodies. I thought I was going to drop the lot.' He walked off into the kitchen and she followed him sheepishly.

'You didn't need to go out for coffee.' He looked as if he'd just woken up, his usually perfect hair looking messed up. He was wearing a pair of grey tracksuit bottoms, his T-shirt one of some old band from their youth she'd never liked. She'd never had time for music growing up, other than to shut out her university cohorts in the library when she was studying. Even then it had been more emo-grunge-type stuff, rather than the hard rock Ronnie and Jackson had preferred to blast out. 'I have a pretty good coffee maker here.'

'I prefer the coffee shop.'

'Okay.' She put the box on the counter, and he opened it. 'Wow. I can see why.' He pulled an almond croissant out of the box and sank his teeth into it. 'Dear Lord of medicine, that's good.' He finished the whole thing in three bites.

'The coffee's decent too. I've been going there for years.' She side-eyed him. 'I'm sorry I slipped out.'

His cup was halfway to his lips but he paused. 'You don't have to answer to me; I'm not your parole officer. You left a note.'

'So why did you text me, then?'

'Because of the note.' He nodded to the fridge where her words sat, glaring at her like a beacon.

Gone out. Lucy

'Not exactly *War and Peace*, is it? I just wondered if you were okay, if you were somewhere safe.'

Lucy took a donut and ripped it in half. 'What did you want, GPS coordinates?'

'No, but we just lost… It would have been nice if you'd said where you'd gone, that's all.'

'Would you have done the same?'

He didn't hesitate. 'I will, yes. I know yesterday was a lot, but I do think that before we do this and go back to work we should make a few ground rules together, don't you? I know Zoe has a nursery to go to, but we should talk about when we are both on the same shifts, nights off…'

Thinking about the nursery reminded her of Harriet and a memory of when she'd first started there. On a rare day off, Lucy had been at the dry cleaner's in town when Harriet had called her, distraught. She'd managed to sob out a plea to meet her for coffee and Lucy had abandoned her pressed clothes on the counter and run the whole way.

'Thanks for coming.' Harriet had sniffed when Lucy got to her table, panting. 'I ordered for you.' She'd pointed to a large coffee, but Lucy didn't register it.

'What's wrong?' She'd been alone. 'Where's Zoe?'

'She's gone,' Harriet had croaked out.

'What?' Lucy had been about to have a full-blown panic attack when her sister had spoken again. 'She didn't even look back this morning. The nursery staff just took her and she went off, happy as a clam.'

Lucy sagged into her seat. 'Harriet, I thought something was wrong!'

'Something is wrong!' Harriet sniffed again. 'I wanted Zoe to go to nursery a couple of days a week to let her play with other kids, you know? I don't want her to feel different when she starts school, but...'

'She still very much needs you. You're her mother. Just because she goes to nursery doesn't mean that she's gone.'

'I know.' Harriet had glugged at her green tea. 'I just... didn't expect it to feel like that.' She'd wiped at her eyes, flashing a smile that told Lucy that she'd pulled herself together. Harriet had known how to do that. Lucy had always been a little jealous of that ability. Lucy did the opposite: she just pushed everything down. 'They grow so fast.'

'I know.' Lucy had taken her sister's hand in hers. 'You did the right thing. Zoe will make friends, learn new things. It's only two days a week. You have Zoe for the rest of your life. Years of holding her little hand.'

Harriet's returning smile had been dazzling that day.

'Thanks, sis, you always know the right thing to say to calm me down.'

'That's my job.'

Lucy remembered the warm feeling she'd felt from those words…

The memory faded, and she realised Jackson was looking at her expectantly.

'Yeah, we can do that—make a schedule. I really want to keep her at that nursery. Harriet would want that.'

'Then we keep it going,' Jackson agreed. 'I agree. Mum and Dad will help too. We can do it. Other people do, don't they?'

They were looking at each other just a little bit too intently when the silence was broken. Jackson's phone rang: *Mum* flashed up on the caller ID.

'I'll just grab a shower and let you get that.' She jumped off the stool and half-ran up the stairs, anything to avoid the domestic scene she'd just left.

'To be continued, Lucy!' he called up the stairs. She was pretty sure he heard her groan of anguish. *She* was pretty sure she heard him chuckling.

'This is going to be a nightmare,' she muttered under her breath.

CHAPTER SIX

WHEN LUCY CAME down from her shower, Jackson was ready and waiting with an invitation from his mother for dinner.

'Sure, that sounds nice, actually. Has she said anything about us taking Zoe?'

Jackson shook his head. 'She just said she'd give us time. You know, to sort things out here. I don't know what you were thinking, but I get the feeling my folks are pretty tired. They've had her since—'

'Yeah.' Lucy shuffled her feet. 'I know. They need time to grieve too, to rest.'

'Yeah,' Jackson echoed. The silence hung around them at the bottom of the stairs. 'We need to get on with it, I guess.'

Heaving out a sigh, Lucy rolled up the sleeves of her long T-shirt. 'Right—so we bring her here tonight after dinner.'

Jackson's brows raised, but he said nothing to contradict her. 'Okay, I have some boxes in the garage. We'd better get the office cleaned out. I read somewhere that kids need to be settled in their own room, so…'

'Yeah,' Lucy agreed. 'It's best if she has her own room from the start. Gets a routine.' She narrowed her eyes. 'You read that where, exactly?'

The blush on his face was unmissable. 'Er…a parenting blog.'

She didn't want to laugh at that moment—it wasn't a happy moment—but she couldn't stop the smirk on her face from erupting. 'Right.' An odd kind of burble sprang up from her chest. 'Read many of those lately?'

'Laughing.' He smirked. 'Nice.'

She'd reached out to pat his arm before she realised. 'No, no. It's cute.' She laughed again, not bothering to supress it. 'Are you planning to breastfeed too?'

He grabbed her arm as she pulled back, as if he missed the contact. 'Ha! Funny!'

'I think so.' She cackled. They both noticed how close they were at the same time, and their arms dropped to their sides. 'So, you want to get the boxes?'

He cleared his throat. 'Er...yeah. I'll...er...see you up there.'

She heard the garage door open just as she was pushing open the wooden office door.

'Wow.' She breathed, and it wasn't seeing his office that took her aback. She knew that they'd been in the same space, but the contact, his hand on her bare skin, was still something alien.

Weird: that was the word for all of this.

Keep moving. Suck it up.

The office was pure Jackson. His desk was super-neat, like the rest of the house. Running her hand along the wooden surface, she picked things up, taking it in: little pots of rubber bands, paperclips and staples. The files on the shelves were all colour-co-ordinated, the same as his files at the hospital. His writing was a perfect set of uniformed letters, bold and confident, unlike her scribbly scrawl. *Everything in its place*, she mused. *So organised*. On the back wall above the desk, the pin board was full of photos, all neatly placed. There were photos of work nights out, a picture of Zoe wearing her Elsa dress, back when she'd been obsessed about being a cute little ice queen. Lucy laughed when she saw it, tears brimming in her eyes.

'I remember that outfit,' Jackson said from the doorway. She hadn't even heard him come up the stairs. Putting the flat-packed boxes to one side, he came to stand beside her. 'Harriet had to prise that dress off her every night for weeks.'

Lucy smiled. 'Yeah?' Jackson's aftershave was nice. It matched the room, she thought—light, but woodsy, strong but gentle somehow. 'She definitely knows her own mind.'

His head dipped closer as he took the board off the wall. 'I'll put this in my room for now.'

She reached for it, seeing something. 'Is that...us?' Jackson's gaze followed her finger to the photo in the centre. 'From the paintballing day?'

It was a group photo, a crowd of blues and reds, paint-and mud-splattered.

'I don't know.' He went to leave but she stopped him.

'It is!' She took the board from his grasp, leaning in to peer at the sea of faces. Jackson was laughing, head tilted to another player. When she found her own face in the crowd, she knew why—there she was, bright-red cheeks and mud smeared face, flipping him off. 'How do you even have this? That's so funny.'

When she turned to look at him, he looked as if he wanted the ground to swallow him up. 'Jackson?'

'I asked for it.' He shrugged, but the action was too forced to be real. 'No biggie.'

She passed it back, watching as he left the room.

What was that? He kept a photo of her where he could see it all the time?

She was still looking at the door when he came back,

busying himself with making up boxes. He didn't meet her eye as he started to pack away the coloured files. Taking a box, she got to work, not sure what, if anything, she'd done wrong.

'It's a nice photo,' she muttered when she couldn't stand the awkward pause in their conversation any longer. He side-eyed her, and she witnessed the sag in his tight shoulders.

'I like it.'

It didn't take long to clear everything away. Putting the boxes in a neat stack in the corner, they got to work on the furniture.

'Careful,' Jackson warned as they navigated the stairs. 'Don't drop this desk and flatten me.' She pretended to consider it, a playful look on her face that made him shake his head.

'And raise a kid on my own? Death by desk would be the easier option.'

She felt his deep laugh through the desk, and the tension slid away. They managed not to maim each other getting the rest of the furniture down, which surprised them both.

They had just brought the last of the boxes down to the corner of the dining room that was now an office nook when she noticed the time.

'We need to go. We're going to be late for your mother.'

Looking around the now empty third bedroom, Jackson sighed. 'I forgot about dinner. Least we got this done. The blinds will do for now, till we can decorate at least. What does she have in her room again?'

Lucy tried to remember what Zoe's room looked like. It felt as if she'd not been there for ever.

'I think it was still decorated as a nursery. Yellow,

maybe?' She rubbed her forehead. 'I know she has a cot bed, a dresser and a toy chest.'

Jackson was looking around the room as if he could picture it all in place.

'Cool. It should all fit, I think.'

The longer they were in there, staring at the furniture marks in the carpet, the closer the air felt. Lucy pulled at her T-shirt, feeling as if the collar was tightening around her neck somehow.

'Is it hot in here? I feel hot.' She went to the window, opening it and gulping at the air. 'I can't get my breath.'

'Lucy? Are you okay?'

Her chest was so tight, she felt she couldn't breathe. 'I... No... I...'

She felt Jackson's arms around her. 'It's okay. You're okay.'

'How is this okay?' she managed to push out. 'This was your office, and now it's a kid's room! How are you just okay with this?'

'Breathe,' he kept saying over and over in an even voice. 'It's okay. We'll be okay.'

When the panic released her long enough to cry, she bawled, gut-wrenching, stomach-hurting sobs. 'It's not my house. It's not Zoe's house. It shouldn't be like this, and we're just playing house and pretending that the world's not on fire.'

'I know,' he mumbled, his arms holding her tight, which for once she didn't even think to object to. They were necessary to hold her up, hold her together. 'We can do this. I promise, Luce. Rent your place out, move in here and we'll bring Zoe home. Do this one day at a time, okay? Breathe. You're okay.'

Listening to his voice, she looked around the bare room.

'I'm rubbish at painting,' she muttered when her breathing was even. She felt his laughter jolt her as they stood squished together. 'Don't laugh.'

His hand rubbed circles along her back. She felt her skin warm from his heat, her muscles unclench.

'I'll get you a paint gun.' His deep voice was full of warmth too. 'I seem to remember you could handle that.' She huffed, squeezing him to her like a reflex, before stepping away. This touching thing was getting out of hand.

Wiping her tears, she widened the gap between them. 'Come on; your mother will be worried if we're late.'

She didn't see the expression on Jackson's face when she left the room but the deep, throaty 'I'll drive' sent an oddly familiar shiver down her spine.

Keep it together, she told herself for most of the car ride over. *Grief does strange things to us all.*

Sheila and Walt were happy to see them both, but the fatigue on their faces was evident. When Jackson said they'd like to take Zoe home, they didn't object. They had dinner, and before they knew it, the pair of them were driving away with Zoe in the back seat, a load of toddler paraphernalia and enough food in containers to feed them for a week.

A couple of hours later, Zoe was well and truly making her presence known. Sheila and Walt had packed a travel cot and some supplies for them but they'd barely had a chance to set it all up before Zoe started to scream the place down.

'I wonder if she's just unsettled,' Jackson tried to say over the noise of her ear-splitting screams. 'I read that kids pick up on things, even when really young. Emotions, changes, you know.'

'You think?' Lucy snapped back, panic overruling every

sane thought in her body. 'I'm not stupid, Sasquatch. My medical speciality trumps your parenting blogs.'

'Never said you were stupid, Trigger.' His jaw tensed, making his whole cheek judder from the sudden tightening. 'I hate my nickname too, shorty!'

Zoe started to cry louder the second he raised his voice, and both of them stilled. She could see the tension in Jackson's jaw as he lifted her higher up in his arms. 'Hey, Zo-Zo, it's okay! You hungry?'

'We tried that.' She pointed to the spaghetti hoop stain on her hoodie. 'We've tried changing her, she won't go to sleep...' The wailing intensified the second Jackson tried to put her down on the floor.

'She had a nap earlier but Mum said it was barely twenty minutes.'

Jackson lifted Zoe onto the kitchen counter. 'Does she feel warm to you? She's not warm, is she?'

Lucy placed a cool palm on the little girl's forehead. 'A little. No fever, though, I already checked her temperature earlier and it's normal.'

Zoe was sobbing now, tears spilling down her cheeks as her whole face went beetroot-red.

'Is she thirsty? What about a drink?'

'She'd a beaker of milk at dinner, and she had—what?— sips of juice half an hour ago.'

'What?' Zoe's wails had drowned out her words.

'Sips of juice!' she repeated, retrieving the beaker of cold apple juice from the fridge and showing him the measuring scale. 'See? It was at the top before.'

Jackson frowned. 'Maybe we should take her into work.'

'For crying? I'm not going into work for that. We'd get laughed out of the place!' Lucy scoffed, picking a now screaming Zoe up and passing her the beaker. Zoe screeched

harder and knocked the cup away. 'Have a drink, come on.'
She tried again, and this time Zoe pelted the beaker across
the kitchen. The ear-splitting decibels she emitted make
them both jump. 'We don't need to take her in.'

'Well, I don't know what's wrong. It could be a stomach-
ache.'

Lucy didn't answer. She was too busy running irratio-
nal scenarios in her head. Her training was lost to her as
she ran through every possible condition from hand, foot
and mouth to meningitis…and the screaming thought that
Zoe knew she had been left to her aunt and uncle and was
just distraught at their lack of parenting skills. Trying to
stop her inner panicked monologue from giving her another panic attack with her niece in her arms, she took her
through to the lounge and tried to lay her down on the sofa.
Zoe's whole body went as rigid as an ironing board so she
gave in and changed tack.

You can do this, she told herself. *You save babies on a
daily basis. Heck, figure it out!*

'Will you just hold her a second? I'll check her tummy,
but I don't think it's to do with her digestion.'

She tried to lift Zoe up to pass her off to Jackson, but she
was screaming blue murder and rigid everywhere but her
legs. Her legs were not stiff; they were quite the opposite,
in fact. She was windmilling them, kicking both of them
as she bellowed at the top of her lungs.

'Let me, just… Zo-Zo! You're okay, darling. Let Auntie
Lucy have a look at you.'

Jackson finally managed to get a grip on her, holding her
up and out as if she was a bomb and he was a rookie dis-
posal expert. 'She's like an eel! Hurry up, Trig!'

Lucy was trying to lift up Zoe's little top, but it was like
wrestling an anaconda in the midst of an air raid siren.

'Don't call me that! I'm trying; I don't want to hurt her!'

'Hurt her?' Jackson half-shouted over the ear-splitting wails. 'She's got more kick than a striker! I've treated easier drunks in A&E! Just pull her top up!'

'I'm trying!' She managed to do a quick examination, trying to remember her years of training and experience—and not get kicked in the face. 'Her stomach's normal, no blockage. She had a bowel movement earlier—that was normal too.'

Jackson went to put her down on the floor, but she lifted her legs away, clinging to his clothing.

'Well, what's left? Exorcism?'

'That's not funny,' she half-yelled back. 'And, for the record, you're a doctor too!'

'Yeah, well, I'm just waiting for her head to spin round.' He tried to soothe her in his embrace, his hand over one cheek. 'She's not hot, but her cheeks are.'

The pair of them looked at each other at the exact same time. 'Teething,' they said in unison.

Jackson pulled his car keys out of his pocket.

'The supermarket—they have a pharmacy that is open late.'

Lucy was already grabbing her bag.

'Good thinking.' She rubbed at her head where a bitter headache was beginning to form. 'I'll get her coat.'

The coat didn't get closer to Zoe than the back seat. She turned purple when Lucy came near her with it, and Jackson turned a ghostly shade of white and muttered something about her throwing up in his back seat. It took them ten minutes to get Zoe to bend enough to fasten her into the car seat, and by then they were both so frazzled they just wanted to get to the local supermarket without driving the car into the nearest brick wall.

Jackson backed out of the driveway at a slow crawl.

'Jackson, the supermarket closes in three hours. Any chance you could drive faster?'

He pulled onto the main road, Zoe's wails now receding into shuddering sobs with the movement of the car. She loved the motion, Lucy remembered. Harriet and Ronnie used to drive her round together when she wouldn't sleep.

He made a throaty huffing noise. 'Last time I was in a car with you driving, I got whiplash. We have a kid on board.'

'Yeah, well, a toddler on a trike would beat you in a race. She's not a new-born.'

'Yeah, thanks for that, Mrs Paediatrician.'

'That's Ms Paediatrician, actually, and you're welcome.'

A car pipped its horn behind them. When they both looked, they were greeted by a pensioner behind the wheel who promptly mouthed, 'Put your foot down!' at Jackson.

Turning to face the front, Zoe now quiet in the back, cheeks aflame, Lucy pressed her lips together.

'Don't say it,' Jackson droned, putting his foot down. Lucy laughed all the way to the supermarket car park.

Zoe was like a different child the second they sat her in the trolley seat. Her cheeks were still flushed postbox-red, but she was happily looking around her as they strode down the aisles.

They both stopped dead when they came to the baby section the pharmacist had directed them to—very quickly, they noted, which probably had something to do with the people in the queue and the ear-splitting wails Zoe had produced in Lucy's arms. They reached two long rows of shelves filled with toys, equipment, toiletries and pregnancy gear.

'All this stuff? Really?' Jackson was clinging to the shopping trolley with white knuckles. Lucy arched a brow and charged forward. In that moment she had never been more grateful that she'd gone into paediatric medicine and not the cardiology specialism she'd once considered. Affairs of the heart she didn't know, but this, she knew. From watching Harriet and the parents of the patients she cared for, she'd picked up a few things along the way. For some reason, the fact that Jackson wasn't the polished A&E doctor he normally was helped too.

'Yep. It's a multi-million-pound industry, Jackson. You been living under a rock?'

'Nope, but that doesn't sound so bad about now. Ronnie didn't talk much about this side of things.'

Lucy headed straight for the teething gel, picking up a couple of boxes and chucking them into the trolley. Zoe was starting to grizzle again, the distraction of the bright lights and people wearing off in favour of her irritable gums. Sanitising her hands, Lucy ripped open one of the boxes and squeezed some of the gel out onto a finger.

'Er, shoplift much?' he teased.

Lucy jabbed him with her elbow and started to rub some of the gel onto Zoe's gums. The little girl pulled a face at first, but then settled down. The relief was evident, and Lucy felt a small frisson of achievement.

'Well, that worked,' Jackson said, a touch of wonder in his words. He went over to the shelf and picked up another five boxes. 'We need to stock up on that. What else can we get? I'm guessing that they don't have holy water in their range.'

He was looking up and down the products, and Lucy couldn't help but smile as she pushed the trolley and watched him taking everything in. He was quite funny as an uncle. She'd always known that he loved Zoe, but seeing him take such an interest made her think that perhaps Harriet and Ronnie had not been so far off the mark. If she'd been alone with Zoe screaming the place down in her little unkempt flat, would she have been here now, so calm, getting supplies? She knew the answer to that—*heck no*. She'd either have driven to work in a panic to get help or been online, desperately looking for same-day-delivery miracle purchases to help her out.

'Hey.' Jackson shook her out of her thoughts, waggling a teething ring at her. 'These things go in the fridge; the cold is supposed to help soothe the gums. What do you think?'

Lucy pushed the trolley closer. 'I think we should get some.' She pulled a pack of pull-ups off another shelf. 'Let's get stocked up.'

Jackson's dark-brown eyes locked onto hers for a moment longer than she was used to.

'Deal.' The corner of his mouth turned into that smile she secretly liked, the one he'd flashed the day they'd met all that time ago. 'I say we get some alcohol too.' He grinned. 'For the adults—we deserve a treat too.'

'Double deal!' She laughed, pulling another pack of pull-ups off the shelf. 'Fifty-fifty, though, right? Anything we spend has to be fifty-fifty.'

She could swear his eyes sparkled. Supermarket lighting, she told herself, blinking hard.

'Fifty-fifty all the way.'

CHAPTER SEVEN

'ARE YOU SURE your parents didn't mind having her again? I feel like we're putting a lot on them. They've just had her for over two weeks solid.'

They were sitting in Jackson's car the next day, parked at the front of Harriet's and Ronnie's house. They were both exhausted after Zoe's first night in her new home. Her bedroom was a priority, now it was emptied. The travel cot looked sad in there all on its own. The poor little love had been unsettled, meaning that they'd each slept in fitful shifts. Over one of Sheila's lasagnes and a bottle of red, they'd also managed to sort out a rota system for who did what, and Lucy had ordered a wall calendar online for when they went back to work. They'd been so tired and distracted from Zoe that they hadn't even fought about any of it—progress.

'She can start back at nursery soon, help give them a break. Mum offered—she'll take Zoe to nursery when we're at work, and pick her up when we need her to. She has a key for my—*our*—place already. Trust me, they want to help. When I dropped Zoe off, Dad practically ripped her from my arms. I think they've missed her, but at least they got some sleep.' He sounded almost jealous and, given the fog of fatigue currently swirling around them, Lucy understood his tone. In her early days in the job, studying and working all hours, she'd thought she could never be so tired. Turned out, having a toddler thrust upon her was just as exhausting.

'I'm glad they were happy to have her. They're still grieving too. Zoe's their one and only grandchild, so no wonder. Especially after losing…' She cut herself off from forming the words she could never quite vocalise. 'I guess they'll want to cherish every minute.'

She felt him tense at her side.

'What makes you think Zoe's going to be an only grandchild? I've dated. I didn't buy the house to live alone in for ever.'

Lucy thought of her flat. She hadn't bought it to live alone for ever either. When their family home had been sold, and she and her sister had split the money, a flat had just seemed logical. Not quite a 'for ever' home, she realised now. She'd already played house, though, far before her time. 'When have you dated?' she asked, glossing over the house comment entirely. 'I never see you with anyone past the fortnight mark.'

'Well, yeah, not lately.' He fixed his dark eyes on her, making her feel silly, on show. 'I'm not a monk, Luce.'

'Lucy,' she corrected automatically. 'And I didn't think you were, I just…'

'Since when have you followed my love life, anyway?'

'Since never. I don't care. Anyway, you can talk; I didn't know you knew about Aaron asking me out.'

His jaw clenched. 'You know what hospitals are like. Staff never have time to date; you hear things.'

'Yeah, well, I was just saying, it's good Zoe has your parents. I think it's nice your mum is able to help. She has someone that's maternal.'

Jackson's face fell. 'She has you.'

Fiddling with the strap of the handbag on her knee, Lucy looked away. 'Yeah, sure.'

'She does. You're her auntie, her mother figure, now. She'll be fine. You turned out all right, didn't you, without a mum around?'

'Oh, yeah, I'm a totally well-adjusted human being.'

His chest rumbled with a deep, free kind of laughter she'd never heard from anyone else. It always made her laugh but, as now, she'd always tried to suppress the laughter of her own that it caused. Usually, the rumble came after she'd mocked him, or been zinged by her with a clever one liner. Today was no different.

'You never thought about having a family one day?'

Until his question dropped. She didn't know how to answer—families to her meant pain, loss.

Perhaps buying my place wasn't such an impulse purchase.

'Hello!' The rapping on the car window startled them both. There was a man peering through the glass at them. 'You lost?'

'Saved by the bell,' Lucy muttered under her breath as she went to get out.

'Hey, Luce, wait!' Jackson tried to stop her, but she was already out.

'Hi,' she addressed her saviour stranger. 'No, we're not lost. My sister lives here.'

Jackson appeared at her shoulder, bumping it from coming in so hot. She looked up to give her clumsy giant companion a quick glare before addressing the man again. '*Lived* here, I mean. Can I help?'

The bloke was smartly dressed in a suit and tie. He fitted in well with the upmarket suburban backdrop. In comparison beside her, dressed like a swarthy lumberjack in his checked shirt and jeans, Jackson looked as if he'd just stepped off his country ranch. The fact the suited man had to look up at Jackson wasn't lost on her either.

'Oh, no, I actually live a couple of doors down. I'm sorry for ambushing you. I didn't realise who you were. New car?'

'No,' Jackson butted in. 'It's mine, actually.'

'Ah, right. I knew Harriet had a sister; I didn't realise you had a partner.'

'We're not together,' they replied in unison. Jackson moved a little closer. So close, in fact, he blocked her line of sight. Lucy stepped closer to the man.

'You sound like you knew Harriet.'

The neighbour thumbed towards his house. 'My wife did. We have a son the same age as Zoe. We were really sorry to hear about what happened.'

'Thanks.' Lucy's eyes flicked back to her sister's house. 'Me too.' Jackson stepped forward, putting an arm around her shoulder. She shrugged him off, flashing her best professionally honed smile at the man. 'That's very kind of you. We'll be coming back and forth for a while, so...'

'No problem; well, nice to meet you.' He put out his hand to shake Jackson's, but Jackson folded his arms in response. The man's smile dipped. 'Right, well, better go see the wife.' He patted Lucy's arm. For a second, she thought she heard Jackson growl, but when she flicked her gaze to him she saw him looking at the neighbour as if he was stuck in a boring business meeting. 'If you need anything, you know where we are.'

Lucy turned to walk towards the house when the man left. 'That was rude.'

'I know. Who is he? Neighbourhood watch?'

'No,' Lucy spat back, fumbling for the keys in her bag. 'You jackass. You were rude then. He was only checking on the house.'

'No, he wasn't, he was being nosy.'

They got to the front porch at the same time. Lucy tried to sidestep him to get to the lock but she was met by a wall of muscle.

'Do you have to stand so close, you big oaf? I felt like you were my bodyguard back there. What did you think he was going to do—throttle me with his tie in broad daylight?'

He tutted, stepping to one side. 'No, but that's another thing.' He followed her into the house, shutting the door behind them both and looking out through the side window as if he was expecting a sniper assault. 'He knows my car; it's been parked outside enough times. The guy was just fishing. What kind of man do you know wears a suit and is home in the daytime?'

Lucy reached for the scattered letters on the mat, shuffling them into some kind of order as she rolled her eyes. Jackson was muttering to himself, his eyes glued to the window.

'I don't know, do I? We're not at work, are we? I've seen him around before, but usually I'm alone and in my own car. I don't know. I don't really care. The house is empty now. We could do worse than have a vigilant looky-loo watching over the place.'

Dumping the pile of post into her bag, she put it on a side table and turned to face him. He was still glued to the window. 'Why are you so squirrelly today? It was a neighbour. Can we please just get on with getting some stuff done here? We need to empty Zoe's room first.'

She was halfway up the carpeted stairs before he spoke again.

'I'll get the boxes from the car. Sorry, Luce. I guess I don't like being questioned.'

'Funny. You don't seem to mind asking them.'

She gripped the banister when her eyes met his. He looked so…confused, out of his depth. Something deep within her stirred, but she didn't poke at the feeling. His fear sparked hers. That surprised her more than anything that had happened in the last few days.

'You see why I am so guarded now?' she offered. The curl of his lip encouraged her to say more. 'Sometimes, the more pieces of yourself you give to people, the harder it is to keep them together yourself. You don't always get those pieces back, Jackie boy.'

He didn't reply at first, just pressed his lips together. She was at the top of the staircase when she heard him say, 'I understand. Sometimes, though, the right people keep those pieces safe because they know just how precious they are.'

She spun round, but he'd already left the house.

What did he mean by that?

She stared at the closed front door for a long moment, before turning back and walking across the landing towards Zoe's room.

Six hours and three car trips later, they were done. Everything of Zoe's had been moved from the house, and they'd made a huge dent on the other rooms. The sight of Jackson taking apart furniture with a set of tools she hadn't even known he owned had been an event. Not entirely an unwelcome one, either. It was the first time in her life Lucy had understood the attraction women could have to a muscly man brandishing a drill. She'd had to go and get a glass of water to cool down at one point and remind herself of the reason they were there in the first place. Looking around her late sister's house had soon refocused her attention.

The kitchen had been easy enough: anything that she or Jackson didn't have went to the car. They would sell everything else with the rest of the stuff…eventually. The 'For Sale' sign would soon go up, and they'd hired a company that morning to put the rest of the stuff into a storage unit. Jackson had sorted that; he had a mate who worked there, so it had been a lot less painful than she'd first thought. They could go through the stuff later, when they were both stronger. They'd keep everything they could for Zoe, when she was older.

Lucy had taken some of the photos that were framed, and she'd packed one that she'd seen Jackson linger over in the dining room: one of the three of them together at work. They were all looking pretty tired in wrinkled, stained scrubs. They'd worked together on a particularly hard case involving a teenager who'd come off his brand-new motorbike.

She still remembered it: the smells and sounds in the room; Jackson frantically pumping the lad's heart while she and Ronnie had raced to stop the bleeding, stabilising him enough to get him to the operating room. Hours later, when the patient was in the clear, his parents had asked them for a photo, to remember the people who had saved his life on that dark day. They'd sent the photo of the three of them standing there, by his bedside, smiling, to the hospital later. Ronnie had asked for a copy. She'd not looked at it properly in years. She reckoned Jackson might want it, and it would be good for Zoe to see her dad in action, see how close they'd all been. The thought of it being in storage gave her a pain in the pit of her stomach.

'You ready?' Jackson called from the front door. 'I thought we could ring Mum on the way, see if she wanted some dinner picking up as a thank you.'

She grabbed her bag and went over to him. Balancing the photo in one hand and her bag in the other, she fumbled around, coming up empty. 'You got the keys? I can't seem to find them.'

He waggled them at her. 'You left them in the door, Little Miss Organised. You hungry?'

'Starving,' she admitted. The sandwiches they'd had at lunch were a distant memory. Reaching for the keys, she almost dropped the photo frame. Jackson caught it. 'Jeez, thanks. I'm all fingers and thumbs.' Jackson laughed.

'I know. You're a mess.' He tucked the frame under his arm and leaned in close...so close. Lucy tensed until his hand came up and pulled something out of her tied back hair.

'Spider web,' he muttered, but when his eyes locked onto hers she could see his pupils up close. They were dilated. 'You still don't trust me, eh, Trig?'

He was close enough to reach out and touch, but the look in his eyes made her wish she were an ocean away. It was all too familiar a feeling. She'd felt it the day they'd met. Before the snarking had started.

'I trust you. I just thought you were going to pull my hair or something, our usual playground games.'

She felt his fingers brush a lock of hair back from her face, his touch along the shell of her ear.

'I was thinking about that, actually.' His voice had dipped lower, more a rumble than a voice. A sound that a woman could get addicted to if she wasn't quite so dead inside.

'You were.' She breathed, suddenly feeling as though the pair of them were in some kind of weird bubble. 'And?'

'And I think we're a little old for the playground now, Luce. Given that we now have a kid of our own who will soon be in an actual playground, I think we should try to get along better.' He reached for another lock of hair. 'For example, it would be nice to be able to get a cobweb out of your hair without you freaking out.'

'I didn't freak out.'

'Your muscles tensed up so fast you almost snapped a tendon.'

'That's not a thing!' She laughed.

'Sure is; seen it. We have to share a house for the next sixteen years at least, Lucy. I'm probably going to see you naked at some point.'

Jackson naked? What an intriguing thought.

'Yeah! Probably… I mean, probably not. You do have doors at your place.'

'*Our* place. My point is that, if you flinch every time I come anywhere near you, it's going to get weird. Zoe will pick up on it too.' She was trying to concentrate on what he was saying, but he was still playing with her hair between his fingers. When he'd reached for it the first time, she'd seen the look on his face—as if he'd been wanting to do it the whole time. As if he was answering an old question when he touched it. She'd wondered things about him too over the years. Now, the grief was playing tricks on her mind. Yeah, that was definitely it. Close proximity broke down barriers—totally explicable.

It wasn't the only thing his words made click in her head. Zoe was probably going to pick up on a lot of things, if she wasn't careful, and their new charge wouldn't be the only one either. She'd have given the game away for sure if her colleagues could have seen her now.

His voice washed over her. 'Can we just…drop the fighting?'

That almost sounded like a plea from his lips.

'Try the whole "being nice" thing?'

Her hair was coiled around his index finger. She couldn't pull back if she tried, not that she really wanted to. Not if she was honest with herself. It felt too nice to be near him. To be close to someone like this, feel that connection.

Well, this is it, Lucy-Lu. You're going mad, acting like some kind of rescue puppy, starved for affection. If you're not careful, you'll start humping his leg.

His hand stopped moving, slowly shifting back so the hair corkscrewed free. Her silence had been too long; he'd taken it as an answer.

'Okay,' she said a little too quickly. 'I'll really try this time.'

His brows raised; he studied her face.

Why do his eyes have to be so piercing? One of life's little twists, she told herself, to make something she avoided looking at most of the time so ruddy entrancing.

'Good.' There it was, that crooked smile of his. 'You got everything?'

'Er, yeah. I thought you might like this, too.'

He studied the photo behind the glass, giving her the excuse to keep watching him, as if she could work out the path forward in the few seconds he was distracted. 'I remember this. The motorbike kid—Danny something.'

'Kirk,' she supplied. 'Danny Kirk.'

Jackson's lip curled. 'Yeah, that's him. He's actually studying medicine now. He wrote to Ronnie a few months ago.'

'That's…crazy!' Lucy breathed, looking again at the boy in the hospital bed. 'I bet Ronnie was thrilled.'

'He was.' Jackson was staring intently at the three of them all smiling in the photo. 'He said that we all inspired him that day. Ronnie was really proud of that.'

He met her eye, and the two of them looked around the hallway at the marks on the walls where the photos had once hung.

'It's weird, being here with things in boxes again. I always thought that Zoe would be driving to college from this house, you know? Taking photos in this hallway.' She pointed to the white front door. 'Harriet would have taken one of those annoying pictures, with Zoe in her school uniform—all hashtags and crying emojis.'

Jackson laughed. 'Yeah, she would.' His smile faded. 'Guess that's down to us now, eh?'

Lucy groaned and he laughed again. Tucking the photo under one arm, he took her bag with the other and headed to the door.

'Come on; I'm starved.'

Jackson's mother wouldn't hear of them bringing dinner. When they got to her house, Lucy realised why.

'Come in!' Sheila practically dragged them both through to the kitchen. Zoe was sitting in a high chair tucking into a bowl of chicken and rice. Well, she was flicking more rice on the floor than getting it into her mouth, but Sheila didn't seem to care a jot. 'I made you some dinner. Not much, just chicken and a bit of rice, some fresh bread… The fruit pies are not ready yet; I'll pack them up for you to take home next time.'

Two place settings were set side by side on the island next to Zoe. The smell of cherries and pastry filled the air. It looked as if Sheila had been cooking the whole day. There were containers stacked up on the counter, with a pile of labels on the side. Lucy was taking in the scene of domestic bliss when Sheila grabbed her, pulling her in for a hug.

Lucy had seen her quite a lot over the years at birthday dinners she'd been dragged along to, and other family events for Zoe, or Harriet and Ronnie. She'd cried at their wedding and fussed over Jackson in his best man suit. Lucy always felt a warmth from her, an 'earth mother' vibe she'd normally baulk at. From Sheila, it hit differently.

Jackson's mother was something that she never teased him about. The love both men had for their parents had been tangible. The way the whole family spoke about each other made Lucy miss her parents all the more. Her mother and father had never seen their children as adults. Had never seen what they had become in life. Every event and rite of passage was celebrated with the usual Denning joy; she and Harriet had never really talked about it, but she knew her sister had felt it too. She had cherished being part of their clan. Their love for each other was easy even now, tinged with loss. She could see the way Sheila and Walt were caring for Zoe and Jackson—and Lucy, for that matter.

She'd never divulged it to Jackson, but Lucy always thought it was sort of cool that he cared so much about them, enjoying the time they spent together. She loved the way he hugged his mum when she reached for him next. After all, who said a man couldn't spend time with the woman who'd given him life? Daughters did it all the time and no one thought anything of it. She watched him chatting away as he grabbed a baby wipe from the pack on the island. This father thing looked natural to him, easy.

Uncle, she reminded herself. *He's always been involved with Zoe. He made more time for her than I ever seemed to be able to do.*

He was talking to his mother about the packing they'd got done, the arrangements for the movers and the storage. All while making funny faces at Zoe and picking the worst mushed bits of rice off her clothes and floor.

She didn't even realise she'd been gawping like an idiot until Sheila spoke to her.

'Sorry, what?'

Sheila shot her a knowing look. 'I was just going to say it's lovely to see you two getting along so well. Sit down—eat!'

Lucy obediently took a seat next to Jackson, her stomach gurgling as a plate piled up with food was placed in front of her. Jackson was busy tucking into his, and the pair of them sat in a comfortable silence. Sheila put even more food into various containers, checking the oven from time to time. She chatted away to Zoe, who was now de-riced and de-molishing a yoghurt and some fruit.

'She's been as good as gold today; she helped me in the garden earlier. She liked baking, although some of the buns she helped with might not be fit for the bake sale at church. The flour made her sneeze on one of the batches.' She turned to Jackson. 'I saved that batch for you.'

Lucy suppressed a laugh; Jackson gave her a side-eye. 'Thanks, Mum. Glad you enjoyed it. We're back at work next week, so I'll expect more sneeze buns in my future.'

Sheila giggled. 'You do that, love. Are you sure it's not too soon for you both?'

Jackson did one of his trademark shrugs. 'We'll manage. We both have departments to run, and they're already stretched as it is.' He didn't need to mention the hole that Ronnie had left in A & E. Sheila nodded at them both and turned her attention to Lucy. 'I will look after her. I know Jackson said you were a little worried.'

Lucy wanted the ground to swallow her up. 'I never—'

'Yes, you did.' Jackson sold her out before she could finish. She kicked him under the breakfast bar. He jumped but acted as if nothing had happened. 'I told you, Mum will pick her up from nursery. She'll bring her to ours too, so that she can be in bed on time.'

Ours. Still sounds weird.

Sheila didn't show a flicker of awkwardness. It was as though everyone was just okay with it, as if they were just doing this.

We are doing this, you fool.

'If you're sure it's not too much.' Lucy tried to get back into the conversation. 'I… We…' Jackson turned his head to her, but she didn't dare look at him. 'We do appreciate all this, really.'

Sheila waved her off with a flick of her floral-patterned tea towel. 'Give over. It's what grandparents are for. Retirement is boring at times, I can tell you. Zoe and the three of us will have some adventures.'

Lucy couldn't help but smile at the thought of that. If her grandparents had been around, her adolescence might have been easier to cope with. It was one of the reasons Harriet hadn't waited to have kids. Her parents having them later in life had meant that their own two sets of grandparents had already passed. Harriet had talked about it before she'd got pregnant. She hadn't wanted to wait.

'Family is not something to wait for,' she used to say.

Zoe would be with family she knew when Lucy and Jackson were at the hospital. Thinking about work next week was stressing her out enough—worrying about what Zoe would be doing, whether she would be happy…how the heck she would juggle work with her new life and responsibilities. 'I bet you will,' she told her earnestly. 'Zoe will love that.'

By the time Jackson's mother let them go, laden with yet more food, Zoe was tired out. Jackson could see her head lolling in the car seat on the way home, and he drove at the speed limit for once. When they pulled up at the house, Lucy lifted her out. 'I'll go put her to bed.'

Jackson put the food away, glancing at the boxes stacked

in the dining room with a tired sigh. Decorating could wait, Lucy had said. The office walls were cream, the glossed paintwork unchipped. They'd taken most of Zoe's stuff straight to her room and added the rest of the boxes to the piles in the dining room. They'd deal with putting the furniture together tomorrow, which would make a huge difference to the rooms. They'd clear the clutter and help Zoe feel more at home.

There was still a fair bit of stuff to sort before their shifts started again. Work had been great about the time off, but he knew without Ronnie *and* him A&E would be stretched. Lucy's department was strong, but he knew both the staff and Lucy would be glad to be reunited. Never mind with her patients, who Lucy loved dearly. Children never saw her snakes; they got the softer side every time. He'd seen it, and he witnessed it now, watching her with Zoe.

Once everything was in order in the kitchen, he went upstairs to take a shower and wash off the day. After throwing his things into the hamper in the bathroom, he stood under the shower until he felt the hot water knead out all the kinks in his muscles. He felt it wake him up after the last few days of rubbish sleep. He felt like a medical student again, with that hazy, adrenaline fuelled way of moving through the day. When he turned off the shower, he felt human again. Wrapping a towel around his waist, he walked out to his bedroom and crashed straight into Lucy.

'What the—?'

'Oh, my God!'

His wet chest smacked straight into her face as she collided against him. Without thinking, he brought his arms up to catch her, which made things ten times worse. The towel tucked into itself around his hips fell away, just as he wrapped her tightly into his strong hold. For a second, neither said anything. Zoe let out a little cry from his former office, and they didn't move a muscle. At some point during the tussle, Lucy grappled for purchase with her flailing legs and arms and grabbed for something to steady her.

'Shh!' they said together. Listening, they both heaved a sigh of relief when they heard nothing more but silence.

Under his chin, he felt her head move up to look at him and he lowered his. Her marble-like blue-green eyes were right there, up close, wide beneath her impossibly dark lashes. His bare arms were wrapped around her tight, but he didn't move an inch.

'Jackson,' she whispered. 'My hands are on your bottom.'

'I noticed that, yeah.'

It's one of the reasons I didn't move.

She nibbled her lip, a cute little movement that did nothing to help his current situation.

'You're naked.'

'I know. I did have a towel,' he said, his voice low. 'I think you ripped it off.'

'I did *not*!' she squeaked, and Zoe made a loud snuffling noise. He gripped her tighter, just as she tightened her grip on him. 'I did not,' she said again, whispering. 'Be quiet.'

'You were the one that squealed.' He paused. 'Luce, you can take your hands off my bare bum now, if you want. I got you.'

'Oh, my God, sorry!' She gasped, pulling back. He went to grab the towel, but not before she saw...well, everything. She'd never call him Yeti again, that was for sure. He was hairless, aside from a line of thick, dark hair that ran down to his...parts...which she definitely saw a flash of before he whipped the towel back around himself. He noticed with a frisson of a thrill that her voice was breathy, almost panting—

the shock, obviously. The panic of waking the toddler in the next room, who seemingly hated sleep at the best of times.

Still, a man can dream...

'I was trying to stop myself falling.'

He smirked, his chest heaving too. His breath was as ragged as the fast little puffs of air from her luscious lips. A rivulet of water dripped down his chest, running down his abs like a raindrop down a window pane. She tracked its movement as he stole a long look at her.

'You grabbed me like a squirrel does a tree.' Her jaw dropped, but when she met his eye he could see he was flushed.

This woman. She'd been in his head for five years, one way or another, a swirling tornado in his logical brain. She was addictive, maddening, enchanting, challenging.

He wondered how much he could fluster her right now. He was tempted to push it, just to see. 'It's fine, Trig. I told you we'd see each other naked eventually.'

His lopsided smile was the last thing she saw as he walked past her to his room.

'So, we could unpack some more, if you want. My vote is for a movie and a drink, what do you think?'

Those choices were not the thing on her mind at this minute. Either way, both meant being close to him for the evening.

I need a minute to recover.

'Whatever you want,' she said, trying to shrug nonchalantly. 'I'll just get changed.'

She shut the bathroom door and sagged against it. On the opposite wall, she caught her reflection in the steamed-up mirror. She saw her flushed red cheeks, the sparkle of attraction in her eyes. On her top, she had an imprint of where his wet body had touched hers. She could almost make out the ab imprints. Pulling the damp hoodie over her head, she stuffed it into the hamper.

Looking up at the ceiling, she closed her eyes. 'Harriet, if this is part of your plan, girl—it's not happening.' Taking off the rest of her clothes, she turned the shower temperature to cold.

She had work to think about, boxes to unpack, her place to sort and Zoe to look after. As the cold water hit her, she resolved to stick to the plan, like she always did. Teeny moments of attraction had peppered their involvement for so long, she was surprised she still felt them so acutely. Of course, it was easier when she hadn't been up close and personal with his butt cheeks. Wondering what was under his scrubs when she was bored at work had paled into insignificance the second that towel had hit the deck.

It wasn't the only thing hitting it, either. Breakfast was going to be awkward with a capital A. A for abs—washboard ones. She was surprised the drop of water she'd tracked hadn't sizzled to nothing.

'No, Lucy. Focus!'

'You say something?' She froze under the spray when Jackson's voice came from the other side of the door.

'No, no! Be out in a minute!'

'Okay. Meet you downstairs?'

'Yeah!' she squealed, her voice sounding strangled. 'Coming!'

She waited until she heard him downstairs and scrambled to get out. 'Coming?' She chided her reflection after she wiped the steam off the glass. 'Coming, seriously?' She jabbed a finger at her mirror image. 'That's one thing you won't be doing. Get it together!'

She needed to get back to work. She had a lot to sort out and, last time she checked, a hot, glistening wet Jackson Denning was not on her to-do list. It would stay that way.

CHAPTER EIGHT

'Do you think we should go in separately? I could hang back.' Jackson's incredulous look told her his answer. 'Okay, stupid question.'

'Yeah, pretty dumb.'

Since the naked body-bumping incident, they'd fallen into a pattern of sorts. By the time she'd settled her nerves enough to go downstairs, he'd poured out wine for them both and was sitting on the sofa, flicking through the streaming options as though nothing had happened, and that was good enough for her.

The cold shower and verbal telling off she'd given herself upstairs had strengthened her resolve a little. Her sister had just died, and her brother-in-law. She'd inherited a baby and had had to move house, one huge event after the other. He'd gone through it too, and had to watch his parents grieve for his brother to boot. Whatever tingle his touch produced was one-sided. Those long looks he'd thrown her were nothing, built up in her head, or by her surprisingly awakened libido. Whatever she'd felt in that moment, it was nothing on the scale of 'whoa' moments she'd endured. Although seeing Jackson naked, feeling his hard body up against hers, wasn't exactly something she'd 'endured' and it was not so much 'whoa' as 'wow'.

She'd been ever more aware of his presence since, in the

proximity of him when they were cooking together. Passing on the landing when taking turns to settle Zoe back down to sleep. The smell of his aftershave in the bathroom, seeing his clothes in the washing machine along with hers and Zoe's.

He had looked after both Zoe and her. She'd watched them together. She'd never really bought into the whole 'man holding a child being sexy' thing. In her line of work, she saw it often, but seeing Zoe in Jackson's huge arms hit differently, put it that way.

No matter what she tried to tell herself to the contrary, she was seeing him in a new light. The trouble was, she couldn't find the switch to turn it off. She'd had a moment of what she could consider to be jealousy too, if she hadn't known better.

Over the years, she'd never cared about someone enough to feel the green-eyed monster's breath on her back. When it had happened, she hadn't cottoned on to what the sudden rush of emotion was at first, but it would have been pretty hard *not* to notice the way the nursery staff fawned over him. She was pretty sure they wouldn't be able to pick her out of a line up. They all but ignored her. Either that or they were fluttering their lashes so fast, they missed her in their line of sight.

Making the most of being with Zoe before they went back to work had been kind of nice. She felt more at home in his house. The boxes were slowly getting sorted. The to-do list didn't feel so overwhelming. Zoe was settling down. They'd been to drop off Zoe at nursery together. They both agreed it was better to settle her back in before work schedules came into play, make things as normal as possible for her, or what was the new normal of her life now.

They'd planned to use the time she was at nursery to tackle another day of clearing Harriet's and her places out ready for the respective sale and rental ahead. She was keeping her mortgage on. She felt absurdly better with an escape plan, not that she could ever realistically use it. Still, that place was the first home she'd bought on her own. The inheritance from her parents was tied up in it. Something made her want to keep hold of it and cover the mortgage with a long-term tenant. It would even provide a little income.

Jackson had agreed it made sense and insisted that he would cover his own mortgage. She'd played the fifty-fifty card on him on that one. She didn't want to take half his house, and she wasn't going to live there without fully paying her way. He'd reluctantly given in, eventually. The compromises were getting easier as each day went by. The easiest decision they'd come to was to take another two weeks off work together, to get things done and be there for Zoe.

Lucy found she didn't even mind that. Work was a huge part of her life, but for once she wasn't in such a hurry. The FOMO wasn't as sharp as it had been in the past. The hospital had agreed without issue, so that was that. Their time in their little bubble had been extended. Each day, the grief and feelings of being overwhelmed fell away, tiny pieces at a time.

Zoe was a source of joy for them both. Being so young, after a few weeks the calls for Mummy and Daddy had lessened, which gave them a lot of relief, but also broke their heart at the same time. Jackson's walls now held the photos from Harriet's and Ronnie's house, and he'd even come back from shopping one day with a few of the three of them together.

Lucy had barely managed to hold her poker face at seeing those. She wondered how many of them he had, how many more snaps she'd not been aware of. The paintball photo was one of them, now enlarged and framed. One was of Harriet and her on the day of their wedding, and she knew it wasn't one from the official wedding photographer. Harriet had made her look at those for weeks after the wedding, to the point where Lucy had begged her to stop.

It was a strange photo to put up, really. Harriet wasn't even fully in the shot. Her face was hidden from view, hugging Lucy to her, and Lucy's eyes were shut tight. A tear glistened on her cheek. Why Jackson had taken that shot at that moment, she didn't understand.

She remembered the moment well. It had been after the first dance, and Lucy had stood on the sidelines and cried— not full on sobbing or ugly crying, of course, just silent little tears as she'd watched her little sister dance with her new husband. She remembered the emotions she'd had swirling through her. She could see them on her features in the photo, even with her eyes hidden behind tear-soaked lashes.

She'd felt like a proud parent, as if her child was being married off, that her job was done. She'd been beyond sad that her parents weren't there to see it. She'd wished she truly believed that they were watching from somewhere, happy that their children had turned out so well. She remembered Jackson had come to her side as she'd watched the newlyweds dance. She'd brushed her tears away quickly, folding her arms. The DJ had just called for the other couples to join the couple on the dance floor.

'Dance with me?' he'd asked, but she'd shaken her head the second the words had come out of his mouth. 'I'd rather stick pins in my eyeballs, thanks, Denning.'

'Yeah, I figured as much.' He'd laughed, passing her a handkerchief from his pocket and moving away. She'd seen a few of the guests cast admiring glances his way. She was pretty sure his dance card would get filled.

When the dance had finished, Harriet had come straight over, beauty radiating from her. She'd been a stunning bride, and when she'd hugged Lucy to her she'd whispered, 'Thank you', and Lucy had cried again.

Jackson must have taken the photo then, she realised. When he'd hung it up in the lounge, she'd lingered over it.

'Jackson, why this one?' she'd asked him. 'You can't even see Harriet's face.'

He'd just shrugged, muttering something vague and getting back to his hammering. It still hung on the wall, and she had to admit she did love it. She quite liked the house, too. They'd brought the swing set over from Zoe's old house. The more they moved around each other, cooking together, looking after Zoe, the more she felt at home—if she ignored the sizzling sexual tension she'd felt ever since Showergate.

Zoe was calmer, sleeping better than she ever had. It was nice, their little bubble. She didn't want to strangle Jackson nearly as much as she used to, and he called her Trig less and less—although Luce seemed to have stuck. She'd stopped bothering to correct him any more.

She'd started calling him Jack. Zoe's 'Jack-Jack' was seemingly not so bad to share a life with. It was tolerable. When she caught a flash of his muscles, it was more than tolerable, in fact. She'd had a few more cold showers recently, that was for sure. She'd even taken them both to her special coffee shop after one very early morning wake-up call from Zoe.

Amy had just been leaving when they'd arrived. She'd texted, rapid-fire, seconds after leaving:

Call me! You look so cute together! OMG! It's so weird to see you getting on. We need to talk, boss!

Lucy had fobbed her off.

Whatever...see you at work!

That was going to be a conversation and a half when she got back on the ward. She still didn't know how to shut it down, either. Their worlds were merging fast and work had seemed a far-off concept at the time. Until now, when they were about to walk through the doors.

As they sat in the car, staring at their workplace, Lucy knew that the woman she'd been the last time she'd been in that building wasn't the one setting foot in there today.

'So,' she ventured, pushing her mindset back into the here and now. 'How are we going to handle this? People will ask questions.'

'Sure.' He nodded. 'HR know your change of address, though, right?'

'It's not about HR. What do we say when people ask about Zoe?'

Jackson chuckled, leaving the car without answering her question.

'Rude,' she muttered, about to get out when she realised he was walking round to open her door. 'Thanks.' He held out the crook of his arm. She shouldered her handbag, an airbag between them as they fell into step.

'People are not going to be interrogating us about the ins and outs. They'll just be happy to see us back.' His steps slowed. 'Are you wanting to keep it a secret or something?'

'No, no.' She wouldn't have Zoe be some secret. 'I'm not sure people will understand it, though. Liz in HR choked on her bagel when I called to change my address to yours.'

'Ours,' he corrected. 'I bet she did. Remember that dumb agreement we had to sign?'

Lucy smirked up at him. 'I have it framed in my office. Scares the newbies into line.'

Jackson's laugh was a loud, hearty rumble that she enjoyed just a little too much.

When they reached the foyer, he shot her a wink. 'If people dare ask, you tell them what you need to. It's our business, Trig.' Her nickname sounded almost affectionate. 'I won't say anything till you're ready. Deal?'

'Deal.'

'Have a good day.' He smirked. 'Play nice with the other children.'

Rolling her eyes, she headed to the ward.

She didn't have time to answer any questions, as it happened. The second she'd turned her pager on, she was back in A&E.

'What happened?' she asked Jackson as she panted at the nurses' station. 'I'd barely got changed.'

Seeing Jackson in his uniform was a jolt too.

Had he looked that good in scrubs before?

She never got the chance to think about it; seeing his expression had her following him to one of the trauma rooms.

'Glad you got the page. I know it was quick.' He paused behind the curtain. 'Tom Jefferson, eight years old. Partly unrestrained passenger.' His lips were tight, words clipped. 'RTA. Mother's gone to surgery already. Fractured pelvis, open femur fracture.' His jaw clenched. 'Looks like he took the top half of his belt off without his mum realising. Dad's on his way from work.'

He paused, as if he needed a minute to process his own words. 'He has a fractured clavicle, head lacerations. He had his brain and spine cleared before we got here, but he's pretty shaken up. Nurse is still digging glass out of his right side—superficial cuts, luckily. Breathe, Luce.'

She gasped, air inflating her lungs in one shuddery breath. 'Thanks,' she muttered. 'Didn't realise I wasn't.'

They gave each other a tiny little nod, as if acknowledging the moment, before they pulled back the curtain.

'Hi, Tom, I'm Dr Denning, and this is Dr Bakewell.'

Harriet stared back at her from the hospital bed, her blonde hair matted with blood. When Lucy blinked, she was gone. A young boy stared back, hair the colour of Zoe's, with wide, scared eyes. His legs only came halfway down the long bed. He looked lost, tiny against his stark white surroundings.

'Where's my mum?' he asked. His bottom lip was trembling from the effort of trying not to cry. It was enough to break Lucy out of her stupor. 'Is she okay?'

'She's going to be, Tom. Your dad's on his way.' She offered him an encouraging smile as she stepped closer, scanning his body and itemising his injuries in her head as Jackson spoke to the nurse. She heard her telling him that the glass was all out now, him telling her they'd take it from here. 'In the meantime, your mum wants us to look after you. That okay?'

Once the nurse had brought back dressings and a sling, closing the curtain behind her, he gave a slow nod.

'Good work, pal.' Jackson pointed to the equipment. 'Now you've been checked out and cleaned up, I need to dress these little cuts. Your arm and shoulder are going to be pretty sore for a while.'

'It hurts.' Tom's voice was hoarse, pained. 'I'm not going to school today, am I?'

Jackson shook his head. 'No school for a few days, but that's okay.' He leaned in, giving Lucy a chance to blink her tears away as she prepared the suture kit for his head. 'Dr Bakewell here is my friend, and she runs the children's ward. We need to give you a little sleepover tonight, but the children's ward has all the good, fun stuff.' He looked around him, pretending to be bored. 'Not like down here.'

Lucy's heart warmed as the little boy smiled for the first time, colour returning to his cheeks.

'That's right,' she agreed. 'Tom, we have all the good stuff. So, while your mum has a little rest, you and your dad can come hang out with me.' She dropped her voice to a near whisper. 'I have so many video games, you won't believe it.'

His eyes lit up. When she looked at Jackson, he was watching her, that little crooked smile matching the sparkle in his deep-brown eyes.

'Me and Dad love video games!' His little nose scrunched up. 'Xbox or PlayStation?'

'Both,' she pretended to brag. 'Now, I'm going to put some little stitches just here.' Her gloved hands gently touched the skin near his head laceration. 'Dr Denning will put bandages on your other cuts, and then we will have to put a sling on your arm to support that pesky broken bone.' She pointed at his shoulder. 'Do you know what bone you broke?'

He gave a head-shake. 'Well, it's called your collarbone.' She pointed along her own, showing him the wing-like bone jutting from her shoulder. 'The medical name for it is a clavicle, so when your dad comes you can tell him you learned all about the human body, eh?'

Another little smile came, which felt like the best reward.

Jackson leaned in, meeting him at eye level. 'Now, we need to give you some medicine for your pain, buddy. We need you to be brave, because it's a little needle, and another one in your arm.'

The little boy gulped, but sat a tiny bit straighter. 'I'm brave. Dad said when I turn nine I'll get more brave too.' He went to shrug, but winced despite the pain relief he'd already been given. 'So it's okay. I'll get more.'

Jackson's laugh felt like a balm to Lucy's triggered grief.

'Exactly.' He thumbed a gloved hand at Lucy. 'And, once you get settled upstairs, Dr Bakewell has special treats for bravery.'

Tom flashed little white teeth, showing a gap where his two front teeth had been.

'Tom?' a frantic voice called, and the curtain swished back to show a man who looked just like the boy in the bed. His Hi Vis jacket loomed bright-orange, throwing colour into the room as he started to cry. 'Oh, buddy!' He didn't even glance at the doctors as he went to his boy and kissed his forehead. 'Oh, mate. I'm so sorry, I got here as fast as I could. Are you okay?'

Tom raised his good arm and cupped his dad's cheek. 'I'm being brave, Dad.' He eyed Lucy. 'She has Xbox and PlayStation, and she said we could play later.'

Tom's dad laughed and Lucy watched them, noting the relief on his dad's face as he laughed, kissing his boy and looking at his injuries. When she had pushed down her emotion enough to look Jackson in the eye, she couldn't help but see the tear he was wiping away with his sleeve. Clearing her throat, she got back to work.

'Mr Jefferson? I'm Dr Bakewell. Do you have a couple of minutes to have a little chat while Dr Denning stays with Tom? Tom?' She smiled. 'I'll be back soon. I just need to tell your dad how brave you are. Dr Denning will give you something to make your head feel a little bit numb, so we can get you sorted. Okay?'

The father followed her out, and she moved him away

from the cubicle far enough that she could no longer hear Jackson discuss video games with Tom as he dealt with his dressings.

'I can't believe this.' The father was drip-white. The adrenaline fading with the happy relaxed façade he'd put up for his son. 'The police called me, said he'd not had his belt on properly. He was on the way to school with his mum.' He leaned against the wall. 'I could have lost them both. They're everything. Is my wife going to be okay? Is Tom?' For a second, Lucy saw a flash of bloodied blonde hair.

It's never going to be okay. Not really.

'Doctor?'

She took a deep breath. 'Mr Jefferson, your wife and son are going to be fine. We are all here to look after you. I promise you; your family is in good hands.' She pointed to an unoccupied row of chairs along the corridor. 'Come, take a seat. I'll get the nurses to get an update on your wife.' She pointed to the foyer. 'In fact, I'll do that now for you. Go get a coffee and, when you get back, I'll update you on everything. Tom needs to stay here overnight for observations, but we can make up a bed for you.'

'Thank you.' Mr Jefferson finally drew breath. 'Coffee sounds good at the moment.'

She watched him head away on shaky legs and, calling over a nurse, wondered if Mr Jefferson would ever truly know just how lucky he was.

She was back at the funeral, standing alone by the flower-adorned coffins. There was no minister, no mourners. She was alone, and then Harriet was there. She saw her, standing at a distance. She was speaking, her lips moving fast, forming words that didn't reach Lucy's ears.

'I can't hear you, Harry! Come here! Please!'

She'd begged her to step closer to her side, past the wooden boxes. Her legs wouldn't move. She tried everything, but the grass held her feet fast to the ground.

'Harry!' she shouted, over and over, begging her sister to come closer, knowing she was saying something but not hearing it. 'Harriet, I can't hear you!' she yelled, crying with frustration. She longed to run to her sister and hold her, hear what she had to say. 'Tell me, please! What are you telling me?'

Harriet didn't come. She just kept smiling as she spoke her silent message. Lucy kept shouting, the coffins standing between them fixed points. 'Tell me!' she screamed, wishing she could rip her body away from the turf. 'Please?' she cried. 'Tell me!'

'Luce, it's ok! Stop, it's okay!'

'No! No! He doesn't know how lucky he is!' she screamed as something grabbed her. The coffins disappeared and she was in the dark, blinking the water from her eyes as she tried to focus. 'Jackson?'

'Yeah.' He soothed her. 'It's me. You're okay.'

'Harriet,' she gulped out between gasps. 'Harry was here.'

'It was a dream. Deep breaths.' Her eyes adjusted to the dim light from the landing. She was in her room, her bed, in her new home.

Home. Huh.

Her racing mind, focusing on five things at once, almost skipped over the relief she felt that she was here. The lack of shock that it wasn't her flat's bedroom walls she could see in the dim light. Jackson was stroking her arms, his bare chest rising and falling at a tempo matching hers. 'Everything's okay.'

'No,' she pushed out, unable to breathe. Her heart was pulsing in her ears, a thudding drum beat. 'I—'

'You can.' He stopped her. 'You can breathe. It's okay. I've got you. Control it. In through the nose, doctor, out through the mouth. Focus on me, Look at me.'

She pushed away the image of the flower-strewn coffins, replacing them with the dark pull of his concerned gaze. She did as he asked until the burning in her chest subsided.

He'd sensed it, the looming panic attack. Moving closer, he ran his hands down her arms one more time. He reached for the shaking hand in her lap. 'I'm here, Luce,' he'd said softly, the breath pushed out from his words whispering over her skin as he kissed the back of her hand. 'I'm not going anywhere, ever. Okay?'

She looked back at him, and the strength of conviction in his expression almost felled her. It was as though the swirling brown of his eyes was more intense, boring into her soul to bring the words home. 'You believe me, right, Luce?'

'Yes.' She nodded, squeezing his hand tight with her own. 'I know you'll stay with me.'

His face relaxed, his furrowed brow easing. 'For ever,' he mumbled, pulling their entwined hands to rest against his chest. 'For ever, Lucy. You'll never be alone again. Not while I'm here.'

The tears came soon after. He soothed her and shushed her. He brought her into his huge, unyielding embrace and lay down with her. She rested her head on his chest and fell asleep, listening to the beat of his heart.

The sun was up when Zoe woke them with her shouts, still wrapped together, her hand still caged by his, his fingers wrapped around hers. As she roused from sleep, from the feeling of waking with someone for the first time in, well, a long time, she stilled her body. She knew she had to move, but delayed it anyway. His heartbeat was steady against the shell of her ear. Neither had moved an inch the whole night.

Zoe yelled louder. 'Jack-Jack!'

When she felt him stir beneath her, the night before sprang into her head. His whispered words in the dark: *for ever.*

Oh, it was going to be another weird day.

'Morning,' he mumbled. He lifted their entwined hands, brushing a stubbly kiss onto her skin. 'You okay?'

'Yeah,' she bluffed, before she pulled away. Reality was rising faster than the sun through her window, sending her scrambling from their embrace like a startled vampire. 'I'll go get Zoe.'

'Luce?' he tried, his hold lingering before she untwined her fingers.

'I'm fine. Honestly. First day back was tough, that's all.' She sprang away from him and tucked her hand out of sight. He didn't reach for it again. His words were few after that, clipped. They went through the motions, their morning routine awkwardly stilted.

Now they were here again, back out of the bubble. Back to the normality of work. She didn't know quite how to feel about it yet. They'd dropped Zoe off at his mother's house that morning, both of his parents meeting them at the door with a tender smile. Sheila had pulled her in for a hug while the men had taken Zoe indoors with her stuff.

'Have a good day, love,' Sheila had said softly into her ear. 'You look tired. Take it easy on yourself, okay? Juggling family and work are hard enough at the best of times.'

Jackson appeared behind her, so she didn't get the chance to reply. She didn't know what she would have said anyway.

I had a nightmare? Your son is dreamy to wake up next

to, and now I'm freaked out about it happening again—or not happening again?

The way she'd woken in his arms wasn't normal; she knew that much. Even without Jackson's and her complicated relationship, and their arrangement, she'd never felt like that waking up with a man in her bed. She didn't have much to compare it to, sure, but she had the feeling waking up with Aaron from the fracture clinic would *not* have felt that good, that, safe, that good. She was running out of ways to categorise it, which frustrated her all the more. She was so turned around, she didn't know what to trust. Even her gut was an unreliable narrator around Jackson.

She pushed the scramble of thoughts away, focusing on the here and now, one foot in front of the other, allowing one of her other new emotions to push to the front. Parental guilt popped its head up first, begging to be acknowledged. It had felt strange, leaving Zoe there and going off to work again. She'd got pretty used to being home with Jackson and her. Was this what working parents experienced every day? She wasn't sure she liked it. Watching Jackson at home that morning, losing his keys, spilling his coffee down his shirt, she knew she wasn't the only one affected by things.

Does he feel what I do, or is that just him being his usual caring self?

Perhaps she should have chosen Neurology. Maybe then she'd know what was going in his head.

Oh, shut up, you daft fool. Not even science can help you on this one.

They'd spent the car ride in silence. Lucy had busied herself scrolling through her phone while Jackson had grumbled about pretty much every other driver in the morning traffic.

Now they were sitting in his car in the staff parking area,

drive-through coffees in hand, neither making a move to leave.

She felt his hand cover hers. They moved closer in the car, his hand still holding hers.

'You look a little tired,' she murmured. He looked away, focusing on their entwined hands. She followed his gaze and, despite herself, gave him a little squeeze with her fingers. 'I slept like a baby,' he eventually offered. His eyes found hers again, his brows furrowing a little. 'I was a little worried about you, though. I've never seen you like that. It was worse than the panic attack before. What was on your mind?'

'Just a bad dream—the Jeffersons yesterday...'

'Definitely a baptism by fire,' he replied softly. 'It got to me too.'

'I'm okay,' she assured him. 'After a bit of sleep and coffee. It's all good.'

She saw his face change, relax, and felt the relief flowing through him.

He's relieved it's not about him. He doesn't feel this tension, she thought.

The pang was unexpected. Her shields jolted to life. 'I'm not made of stone, Jackson. I know I'm difficult at times, I push things down, but I'm a wreck too.' She nudged her head towards the building before them. 'I've been looking forward to work, to getting back to some kind of reality. Moving, Zoe...everything's been so different, hasn't it? I thought it would feel easier, coming here—comfortable— but I feel sick about it.' If he wasn't going to talk about them spending the night together, then neither was she.

'I get it, more than you know. I love having you both at home. I know it's been tough, and sad, but I like having you two to come home to. You're not as prickly as you think, you know.'

Her smile was genuine then; she felt his words wash over her and her heart swelled. It was a strange feeling, but one that was happening more and more. The more she was around him at their house, looking after Zoe, fighting over the remote, it felt sort of…nice…and sexy.

Confusing! You mean confusing.

She'd fallen asleep listening to his heart beating; that had been more than sexy. It had been…more than a long-buried sexual frisson.

'I like it too.'

'You do?'

'Yeah,' she told him earnestly. 'I don't think I would have coped on my own. I like being home with you both. It feels…normal almost, or it's starting to feel that way.'

His thumb started to move up and down the skin on the back of her hand, slow circles that made her nerve endings sing.

'I'm not as bad as you thought, eh?'

His tone was teasing, but it didn't make her her blood boil as it usually did. In fact, it made her feel a heat she'd never expected to feel. *For ever*: those words in his gravelly voice kept playing on repeat in her head.

'No,' she admitted. 'Not at all.' He was closer now; their faces had gravitated together. She could smell his aftershave, the one she had grown accustomed to in the bathroom they shared, on his skin. Heck, on her sheets now. It was all around her.

'You're not so bad either.' He breathed, his eyes falling to her lips. She licked them, feeling the air change in the car and dry out around them. 'Luce, about last night. Do you want to…?'

Her mobile rang out and they both jumped. The spell broken, she went to get it and saw the time on the dashboard.

'We'd better get in,' she told him. 'I bet that's work.' She was desperate to hear what he was going to say but, either way he went, it felt as if pain wasn't far behind. If he felt it too, so what? He and Zoe were all she had left. If it failed, it would be unbearable.

Even less bearable than knowing what could be, and not having it.

'Listen, thanks for last night.' She licked her lips again, which had gone bone-dry. 'For being there…you know, for my panic attack. It…well, it won't happen again, I'm sure.' There it was—an out wrapped in an apologetic thank you.

When she looked at him again, he was running his hands through his hair, an odd expression on his face.

'Yeah, of course.' He huffed, picking up their coffees. 'If you're sure, let's go.'

CHAPTER NINE

JACKSON DIDN'T TAKE a full breath until he got to the locker room to change into his scrubs.

What the hell was that?

Lucy had been on the phone on the walk in, giving him a coy little wave before dashing off to her department. His heart was still beating hard in his chest. A bit like the night before, when he'd lain in her bed listening to her soft little breaths as she'd slept against his bare chest. He'd lain there in the dark, cradling her and wishing he knew what was going on in that feisty, stubborn head. He'd been torn between wanting to wake her to ask if she felt a fraction of what he did and willing the sun not to rise so they could stay like that for ever.

It was harder to brush off how he felt about someone when he were in close proximity all the time. His toothbrush sat next to hers in the bathroom but she still felt like a stranger sometimes. They'd held hands until she'd woken up and shut herself away from him again, behind the snakes that had slumbered soundly in his embrace hours earlier. If he didn't know better, he and Lucy Bakewell, tormentor and tormentee, had just had a moment—a big moment. On top of many moments they'd had over the last few weeks. If that phone hadn't rung, he'd have finished that sentence.

What the hell are you thinking?

He knew what he'd been thinking. What he'd been thinking was that he wanted to ask Lucy out to dinner. He wanted to crack open those shields of hers and have her willing to let him in.

If he was honest with himself, having her at his house, their house, had been good. Since Ronnie had passed, he'd had to stop himself from feeling like it was a gift. He'd liked having her around. He fancied her, big time. She was unlike any other woman he'd ever met before, or since. She'd shot him in the nether regions on their very first encounter, and when he'd tackled her about it she'd riled him up in more ways than one.

After that day, when his pride was hurt, when it became obvious that not only did she not see him as a love interest but a rival, he'd forgotten about it. He shouldn't have entertained the thought anyway. He'd expected to meet the sister of the woman Ronnie was dating. He'd never expected to see her any other way. He shouldn't have, but he was addicted. He enjoyed the banter, the feelings she evoked within him when they locked horns. Then he'd become part of her world, her family, and it hadn't been possible. He'd brushed it off as a passing fancy, something not meant to be. The way it was possible to fancy someone one minute, and then realise it wasn't attraction at all, or something that might turn into something that would last longer than an angry, sexy, frantic screw.

He'd dated, but no one seemed to measure up. He'd thought it just wasn't his time. There'd been no deadline to meet. Then Ronnie and Harriet had passed, and he'd thought *that* was why they'd met. It was part of a cosmic plan somehow. He was meant to be there to raise Zoe, stop her being alone in the world—his brother's last wish. Lucy had just been part of the deal, and he was okay with that.

Ronnie had known he could handle it, and Harriet too. He seemed to be the only one who wasn't terrified of her, who didn't step away when she pushed.

They pushed each other and made the other feel alive, passionate. The second he'd touched her hand, he'd known co-parenting wasn't the full story. This feeling wasn't a by-product of being so closely connected, or the grief. It was a primal need to have this woman. She was his. He was hooked, and he didn't even realise when his cravings had started. If her phone hadn't gone off, he'd have asked her out, told her he *wanted* to talk about last night.

Which couldn't happen, obviously. He thought he'd been more than a comfort blanket, but it was all in his addled head. They were raising a kid together, working together. If he stuffed this up, made things awkward when they were just starting to get on, when she was just starting to let him in, it would ruin everything. They had to solidify this arrangement in a few short months. Even acknowledging the logic of it all, he couldn't quite quell the irritation he felt. Maybe he should have got a clue when she'd been worried about people finding out about their new situation.

He was pulling on his scrub top when Dr Josh Fillion walked in, the doctor filling Ronnie's job. Jackson had exchanged a few emails with him, and had had an online meeting while he'd been off to get the guy up to speed on the way he ran his department. From what he'd been told by his staff, Josh was doing a pretty good job.

'Hey, man, first week back? Sorry I missed you yesterday—day off.'

'Yep.' He clipped his ID to his uniform. 'Everything still standing, that's a good start. Settling in okay?'

Josh immediately launched into what was going on and what patients they'd had in. Taking his wallet and keys from his pockets, stashing them in his locker, Jackson listened while he checked his phone. On the screensaver was a photo of Lucy and Zoe. He'd taken it when she hadn't been look- ing, at the local park near his house. Lucy had taken Zoe down the big slide. They were both laughing, faces happy, full of fun. He dashed off an action snap as they'd zoomed down the steel slope. It had been a good afternoon, carefree.

'That your daughter? She's cute.' Josh cut through his thoughts, bringing him back to reality. He thought of Lucy, and decided, for now, work was work. Perhaps the more separate they kept things, the less likely he'd be to lose his damn mind.

'Er…yeah.' Jackson click-locked the phone, turning the screen black. 'I'd better get out there.'

'Sure, see you in a minute,' Josh replied, turning to his locker—Ronnie's old locker. Jackson had cleaned Ronnie's stuff out himself and taken it home. He knew it wasn't his any more, but it still hit hard, as if Ronnie had never been there. He pushed his way out of the door, suddenly find- ing the air thin.

He could see some of his staff at the nurses' station; they all stopped when they saw him approaching. Steeling him- self, he shot them a strong smile he didn't feel.

I should have addressed this yesterday.

They didn't know how to act around him.

'Hey, everyone,' he addressed them together. 'I know you all probably have things you want to say. I spoke to some of you yesterday but, since most of us are here, I'd just like to say thanks for covering, and for all the cards and stuff for Zoe, but I'd like to concentrate on the work now.'

Their faces all had the same expressions: pity, sorrow, understanding. A few nodded, and he was grateful more than ever for the team he had under him. 'I know we all miss Ronnie, but he'd want us to carry on, kicking butt and saving lives.' He folded his arms, holding himself together when he felt as if he might come apart. The wave of grief crashed against his sand walls. 'That okay with everyone?'

One of the nurses spoke first. 'Hell, yeah.' He nodded. 'For Ronnie, guys.'

He could tell the rest of them were on board. A couple wiped at tears.

'For Ronnie,' he echoed. 'Let's save some lives, eh, people?'

As his team got back to work, and he headed to his first patient of the day, he wondered if Lucy was okay. He'd check on her later and see if she wanted to grab lunch. If this was all that being in her life was going to be, he'd just have to take what he could get.

'It's okay, Emma. Just a little scratch.' The flushed seven-year-old made a little whimper as the nurse inserted the cannula. Lucy was standing at the other side of her bed, holding her hand and keeping her steady. She had a pretty nasty infection. If her mother hadn't brought her in when she had, it could have been a lot worse. Sepsis worked fast, but it had been caught early, and getting fluids into her would help, alongside antibiotics.

Emma nodded from under her oxygen mask. Her breathing had been shallow when she'd arrived, a bad chest infection causing an asthma attack. Lucy had seen it a hundred times, but watching a child struggle for breath was tough.

'That's it, all done! It might just feel a little cold down your arm for a minute, and then you should feel a little better.'

'Thank you,' her mother said from the back of the cubicle. 'She couldn't breathe in the car; I was so scared we wouldn't get here in time.'

Lucy turned to her. 'You got her here, and she's going to be fine. We'll keep her overnight, monitor her, but she's doing great. Her oxygen levels have improved already. We'll keep her on high-flow O2 for now till they increase over ninety percent. The liquid steroids we gave her act fast, and the fluids on IV will help to hydrate her.

'Emma,' she said gently. 'I need you to be really careful with your hand here, okay? Be careful not to pull the wires.'

She read through her notes again. 'So, your GP diagnosed asthma at four?' Her mother nodded. 'How is she doing with the inhalers? Did he explain about using them with the spacer and mask?'

'I don't like my spacer,' Emma's muffled voice retorted from under the mask covering her nose and mouth. 'It smells funny.'

'She doesn't like doing it.' Her mother blushed. 'I try my best, but…'

Lucy nodded gently. 'I'll tell you what, Emma, I'll make you a deal. I'll give you a couple of new spacers with some masks attached and we'll see if they are any better. That medicine is boring, I know, having to do it every day, but it helps your lungs to work better. Especially when you get a nasty cold.'

'You've been great, the A&E doctor too. He came running over to us when we got to the main doors. He just picked her up and carried her to a bed. Will you be able to thank him for us?'

'Sure, did you get his name?'

The mother looked pained. 'Oh, gosh, you know—I didn't. He was very tall, though—huge, actually.'

Lucy continued marking up the patient file, but she felt the smirk creeping out.

'I know who you mean. I'll pass on your thanks.'

Leaving the cubicle, she pulled out her phone.

Heard you've been all heroic this morning, carrying damsels in distress.

It pinged seconds later.

Just an average Wednesday. You eaten lunch yet?

Nope. Thought I would just grab something quick later.

'K. I'll be in the canteen at one if you fancy it. Lunch, I mean.

Lucy's eyes bugged out when she saw his reply. They'd never eaten together without Ronnie…and with a side of innuendo? She began to type back.

Pretty busy… *delete*

No time…*delete*

Maybe… *delete*

Your chest makes the best pillow… *delete*

I like what your thumb did in the car…*delete*delete*

Do you feel anyt…? *delete*delete*delete*

What am I? Twelve?

She tapped the phone against her lip, wondering what the heck was going on. It was like a switch had flipped, and suddenly Jackson wasn't maddening, frustrating Dr Denning any more. Well, he was, but he was also the guy who'd held her tightly last night while she'd fallen asleep. The guy who always bought her favourite snacks from the supermarket without being asked. The huge, sexy guy who read to Zoe and make her laugh when he did the voices for all the characters. The guy who she shared a kitchen with, who whipped up more than omelettes in low-slung PJ bottoms and a bare chest she now preferred to any pillow she owned.

When they'd first started working together, she'd gone to bed particularly wound up about one of their little work disagreements and had eaten half a cheesecake before bed. She'd blamed the cheese, of course, but she'd woken up that night horny and sweaty, half-wishing it had been real. The next time it had happened, she hadn't been able to blame the dairy.

Now he was sleeping across the landing from her every night, looking all sexy in the morning in his PJ bottoms, that sexy line of dark hair disappearing under the waistband. How on earth was she supposed to bear the space across the landing now that she had the scent of him on her duvet? Something told her the cold showers and sex dreams were going to increase tenfold.

His chest. Man, his chest.

She got it now: the cliché of a body being sculpted from marble. Now she had to sit across the island from him with that chiselled temptation. All this craziness wasn't good for the environment.

How could she go for lunch with him, when little freaky moments like that popped into her head? Zoe needed two parents, no matter what. She had to focus on that, and work; nothing else.

That call this morning, breaking up their moment in the car, bothered her. She couldn't stop thinking about what he had been about to say. Whether, if she knew, she'd be glad of the knowledge. She'd shut it down anyway, but the look on his face… It couldn't all be in her head. Surely two people would *have* to feel the chemistry between them, whether they wanted to or not?

The screensaver on her phone had come on, and she saw Jackson smiling back at her. It was a candid shot she'd taken on the sofa one night. She'd gone to clean the kitchen after he'd made dinner and bathed Zoe. She'd put the dishwasher on for the fourth time that day and had taken a bottle of wine into the lounge. They'd got into the habit of watching a TV series together, a glass of red as a reward for a busy day toddler-wrangling and sorting out the properties and paperwork of their new life.

She'd found them both asleep on the couch, Zoe laid on his chest in her little bunny onesie. Her freshly washed curls were fluffed up, her little face content. He had his arms around her, his head back, mouth wide open. She'd snapped it to tease him later, but when she'd looked at the image she'd made it her lock-screen photo instead.

'Damn it.' She huffed, bringing up his message.

'Stick to the plan,' she muttered under her breath. 'Co-parenting—no cheese.' A shiver ran down her spine, remembering his body wrapped around hers in the dark. 'Cold showers. Lots and lots of cold showers.' She started to form a brush-off text in her head, when a deep voice stopped her.

'Talking to yourself is a sign of madness you know.'

Her heart sped up as she looked straight into a pair of teasing brown eyes.

'Jackson…' She breathed far too breathily. 'What are you doing here?'

She tried for a scowl but it didn't take. His eyes dropped to the phone in her hands, his finger tilting the screen. 'I came to check on my patient. I see your phone's working.' She locked the screen, regretting it the instant the photo popped up. 'Nice photo.'

'Thanks.' She blushed. 'I thought Zoe looked cute.'

He tilted his head and gave a slow, knowing nod. 'Right. So…'

'So…' she stalled, wondering when she'd turned into a simpering idiot and how to stop it. 'About lunch,' she started, just as he finished mumbling,

'About last night…'

'Oh.' She couldn't get a full breath. 'Um… I know. It was… I…'

'All good sentence starters.' He smirked, and she had to grip her phone tight to stop herself from kissing it off his face right there and then. 'You want to pick one?'

'I'm sorry.' She was rambling. 'I appreciate last night, but I'm fine. I… If Zoe had seen us, I think it might have been confusing for her.'

'Zoe was in her cot. Unless she learned backflips overnight, she wouldn't have.'

'I know, but she's growing fast. Soon she'll be in a bed, and running into our rooms, so I don't think…'

The clench of his jaw told her she'd made her point.

'Got it. No more sleepovers.' He straightened up and she felt lost in the shadowy distance. 'I just came to check on Emma.'

She reached for his arm as he turned to leave. 'Jackson,' she tried.

His voice was as sharp as flint. 'I get it. Zoe comes first.'

When she stared back at him, he raised his brows pointedly. 'The patient?'

Oh, yeah. He is annoyed. That sign is loud and clear.

Emma's mum was thrilled when Jackson walked in with her.

'Oh, it's you!' She rose, reaching for his hand to shake. 'Thanks for bringing him.' She grinned at Lucy before turning back to Jackson. 'I asked Dr Bakewell who you were, so I could thank you.'

Jackson shook her hand, putting his other on top to give her a doctorly pat. 'It's my job, honestly.' He leaned down, smiling at Emma. 'Glad you're feeling better. You gave your poor mum a scare.'

'Kids, eh?' she joked, the emotion belying her easy-natured chat. 'Such a worry, but you do everything you can to keep them happy and healthy. I am grateful, to you both.'

'It's no trouble. I get it.' He sounded almost sad. 'When you have children to worry about, you have to put them first, at any cost. I have to be going, but I'm glad you're okay.'

He took his leave and Lucy checked Emma's vitals.

'She's responding well,' she told the mother. 'The nurses will monitor her closely. Excuse me.'

Jackson was halfway down the corridor when she looked. Sighing, she pulled her phone out of her pocket. The photo lit up the screen, and she fired back a message, watching as his steps slowed to read what she'd written.

See you at one.

He didn't look back, pushing the door-release button and disappearing from sight. Just as she was kicking herself for being such a chump, her phone beeped.

One it is, roomie.

CHAPTER TEN

BY THEIR FOURTH week back, Lucy felt that things were getting back to normal at work. Sure, there had been questions. Her team had rallied smoothly, accustomed to her workaholic, 'say nothing' personal work style. Amy had been there for her; she went to the coffee shop before work when Jackson was on a late shift and had child duty. Jackson told her a few people had wondered about the pair of them getting along without HR intervention, but no one asked her. She secretly suspected that they didn't dare, and Jackson hadn't said much of anything that didn't involve patients and Zoe since that first awkward lunch.

The first week was hell. They were both so tired that they barely spoke. Other than work and Zoe, they slept, ordered in or lived on Sheila's cooking that she left stocked up in the fridge. Lucy had forgotten how knackering the job was, and now she had no gym time and couldn't sleep away her days off. Not that she needed a gym; she was on her feet all day at work, running around after Zoe the rest of the time. She and Jackson got into the habit of taking her places when they were both off: the zoo, walks in the park or soft play. All of this was a lot of fun, but none of it was exactly sedentary—no time for awkward chats or hand holding.

She had a newfound respect for new mothers. She realised just how naive she'd been, even as a paediatrician, about how hard it was, job or no job. How people had more than one kid, she would never know.

When lunch time came round, she headed to the canteen. They fell into a pattern of eating together when they could. She automatically scanned the tables for his face whenever she walked in. Even when she knew he wasn't at work, she found herself scanning the people for him.

Jackson was already there today, sitting with another doctor she'd seen in passing. They were deep in conversation; Jackson didn't even spot her walking past. Getting her lunch, she went to sit with a couple of the nurses from her ward, leaving them to talk. Since that night in her bed, she'd learned to judge his silences. Sometimes he would be right next to her but feel miles away. New people picking up on their weird tension wasn't something she relished.

'Lucy,' Jackson called to her. She smiled at her staff and headed over, lunch tray in hand. 'Come sit. This is Josh. Josh, this is Dr Bakewell, Head of Paediatrics.'

She took a seat next to Jackson, shaking the other man's hand across the table. 'Oh! Dr Fillion; new A&E doctor, right?'

He nodded, taking her hand in a cool palm and holding it for a second too long. He was younger than Lucy had expected. From Jackson's description, she'd imagined him as being over fifty. He was a good fit, Jackson had mentioned: reliable, old school and professional. None of that seemed to fit the rather handsome hazel-eyed man before her.

'Please, call me Josh.' His brows knitted together for a moment. 'Have we met before? I swear you look familiar.'

Lucy shook her head. 'No. Well, yes—I've seen you around.' She'd noticed him in the corridor a couple of times, mostly because Amy had shown her his picture on the hospital website. She'd had a bit of a crush since she'd picked up an extra shift in A&E. 'How are you liking it?' She flicked her head to Jackson. 'Boss is a piece of work, isn't he?'

Josh laughed, flashing white teeth against the olive tones of his skin. 'He's definitely got high standards.' Diplomacy laced his words. He suddenly clicked his fingers. 'Lucy Bakewell! Of course, I've heard a lot about you too. Apparently you're a bit of a stickler for being the best.' He looked between them. 'Probably why you get on, eh?' He ran a hand along his jaw. 'Still, I feel like I know you from somewhere. Where are you from?'

'Here,' she and Jackson said in unison.

'Where are you from?' she asked, tearing open the vinaigrette sachet in her hands and drizzling it over her chicken salad.

'Manchester, the last few years. Sussex growing up.'

'Interesting. I always thought I'd move around and work in different hospitals.'

He leaned forward across the table. Jackson moved his chair a little closer to hers. When she glanced at him, he was staring at Josh, an odd look on his face. When he saw her watching, he returned to stabbing at his food with his fork. 'Really?' Josh said, oblivious. 'Why didn't you?'

She thought of Harriet and shrugged. 'Oh, you know, it just never happened. Timing always seemed wrong.'

Josh smiled, a cute little dimple-punctuated grin. 'Well, I for one am glad you didn't.'

Jackson cleared his throat loudly. 'Josh, we need to hurry up.' He tapped his watch. 'It's busy on the floor.'

Josh looked down at his half-eaten meal. 'Er, yeah. Sure.' He winked at Lucy. 'No rest for the wicked, eh?' Jackson mumbled something under his breath, but Lucy couldn't make it out. Within seconds, the two of them were on their feet. 'It was nice to meet you, Dr Bakewell.'

She stood up from her chair, aware of Jackson watching the pair of them with an odd look on his face. 'Lucy, please. Nice to meet you too.'

'I'll see you later, Luce,' Jackson cut in sharply, before striding off. Josh started after him, but just as Lucy was finishing off her food he came back to stand in front of her.

'Er, I don't know if you are free, but...' He fished into his pocket and pulled out a business card. 'I'd love to take you to dinner one night, if you're available?'

Wait, what?

The grip on her fork tightened.

'Er...' The business card was still in his hand, in front of her nose.

'It's just that I don't know a lot of people. Jackson's nice, of course, but he's pretty busy with his family. I thought it might be nice to get to know you better—colleague to colleague.'

'Family?' she echoed.

Oh, he didn't know. How had the gossip missed the newbie?

'Yeah, wife and kid.' He smiled innocently. 'He's always going on about them. Even has a cute little nickname for his missus—Tigger or something. So, dinner?' When she didn't answer, his smile dipped. 'Or coffee?'

'Trigger?' she checked, his words ringing in her head.

'What?'

'Trigger. The nickname.'

'Yes.' He clicked his fingers again, pointing his index finger in her direction. 'That's the one.' He laughed. 'You think I'd get it right...he's told me enough times. I swear it's the only time he cracks a smile.'

He raised himself to his full height when Jackson half-bellowed, 'Dr Fillion?' from behind him, dropping his card onto the table.

'See?' He shrugged. 'Think about it,' he said. 'Give me a call.'

Staring at the card, Lucy realised that sometimes having snakes for hair was not half-bad. Except in situations like this, when she was asked out by Ronnie's unknowing replacement right in front of the man she secretly desired. It was getting harder and harder to keep a lid on everything when the lines kept blurring.

Jackson was waiting by her car when she finished her shift half an hour late. She walked up to him, pulling her jacket around her shoulders. He took her bags from her, as he always did, putting them on the back seat when she unlocked the car with a click of her key.

'Your car's a mess again,' he grumbled as they pulled their seat belts around them. 'Crumbs all over the footwell.'

'Yeah.' She laughed, pulling the car out of the space. 'Well, Zoe had some of those biscuits she loved the other day on the way back from the park.' He huffed in response. 'What's with you? Bad outcome?'

'No,' he snapped. 'I just think that, since you insisted on taking turns with the cars, you would have cleaned up.' He pointed to the reusable coffee mugs filling the cup holders. 'Pretty sure Zoe doesn't drink double-shot lattes.'

Lucy breathed as she turned the wheel. 'Okay, Grumpy, I'll get it cleaned out. We can take yours instead next time. What's with you?'

They were almost out of the staff car park when Dr Fillion walked towards his car. He didn't look up from his keys as they drove by.

'What did he want today at lunch?'

Awkward.

'Lunch?'

'Yeah, Luce. At lunch, when he came back to the table.' She saw his fist clench and unclench on his lap, and tried to focus on the road. 'He doesn't know about our…living arrangements. I kept your wish. Did he ask you out?'

'No. Well, kind of.'

'Kind of?'

She pulled out of the hospital grounds onto the main road, straight into heavy traffic.

'Hell. This is going to take a while; you might want to ring your parents; tell them we'll be late.'

'Fine. Will you answer the question?'

He pulled out his phone and tapped a few keys. A few seconds later, it pinged. 'Mum says it's fine, and do we want them to give her a bath? She's at ours, and said Zoe was getting sleepy.' The traffic lights turned to green and Lucy quickly took the next left.

'Tell her thanks, she just saved us about half an hour in that jam. I don't mind bathing her, though; I've missed her today.'

He tapped away, shoving the phone back into his jacket.

'Done. Did he then, or not?'

'Yes,' she relented, feeling more than a little weird about the conversation. It wasn't as if she'd expected it or flirted. Heck, she didn't know how to flirt. 'He mentioned coffee.' She bit at her lip. 'Or dinner, colleague to colleague. Do people really not know about us raising Zoe together?'

'No. You didn't want that, so I kept it quiet. Your terms, remember? So this dinner—just the two of you, I'm guessing, since he never gave me an invite.'

'Er, yeah, I think so.'

'Wow, he works fast.' The words came out like gravel. 'He only met you today.'

'Yeah, I think he's just a bit bored. You know, new town, new faces.'

'Not once has he asked me to go for a beer after work, or any of the other doctors. He can't be that lonely.'

'Why are you so mad? I didn't ask him to ask me out.' She looked across at him. He was already looking at her, his eyes dark pools in close quarters. 'I didn't say I'd go, either.'

They were pulling into their drive when he finally answered.

'You didn't say you wouldn't, either. If we're going to play this game at work, you could at least do me the courtesy of not dating my team members.'

'Games? He thinks you have a wife and kid!'

'I never told him that!'

'Well, why would he think it, then? He said you talk about us.'

'Oh, great.' He scowled. 'So I can't talk about any part of my life now? Not all of us are emotionally stunted, Lucy.'

'Oh, and I am, right, because I don't want Leeds General to know every detail of our lives? Answer me, Jackson!'

He didn't wait for a reply before getting out of the car.

'Jackson!'

He ignored her.

'Hi, love.' Sheila met them at the door, Zoe toddling along behind.

Lucy nodded to Grandad Walt, who was sitting on the sofa watching the football. He muted the TV.

'Evening, Lucy, good day at work?'

'Yes, thanks.' She scooped Zoe up. 'How's my girl been?'

Zoe babbled away, laughing when she tickled her.

'Good as gold,' Walt said, getting to his feet. 'Come on, Sheila love. Let's let them get on.'

Jackson shrugged his shoes off and headed straight to the drinks cabinet in the corner of the lounge. Clicking off the child lock, he pulled out a bottle of whiskey and a glass. Lucy saw his dad's eyebrows knit together when he noticed. 'You all right, son? Bad shift?'

He turned to see all of them watching, and he stopped pouring. 'No, Dad, all good.' He put it back, heading over to Lucy and Zoe and dropping a kiss on Zoe's little cheek.

'Jack-Jack,' she said to him, reaching out to touch his face. He kissed her pudgy hand. His gaze shifted to meet Lucy's eye and he shot her a rueful smile.

'Bath time, Zo-Zo,' he said softly, turning to his parents. 'Thanks for having her guys; you know we appreciate it. I'll see you out.'

Lucy stayed back as he waved them off. He didn't meet her eye when he passed Zoe to her. When their car pulled away, she was already upstairs. She needed the distance to cool her temper and give herself a second to process his cheap shot. She'd just put Zoe in the bubble bath when he appeared at the doorway.

She sensed his brooding presence before she saw him and kept busy, washing Zoe with her frog-shaped bath mitt.

'I'm sorry.'

'So you should be; you acted like a jerk. What's your problem?'

'I…don't think it's a good idea that you go out with Josh, that's all. I don't like it. You said we needed to keep work separate from home.'

Her hand paused as she took in what he said. Zoe lined up a duck to go down the slide.

'And I never said that I would go out with him, did I? I hardly have time to manage everything now.'

'Is that the only reason?'

'No. We work together too.'

'Hardly; he's been there weeks and you've not crossed paths till today.'

'Still, work is work. Dating a colleague never goes well.'

'Right,' he replied, but he didn't sound convinced. She could feel his pensive mood from across the room. Rinsing Zoe off, she wrapped a towel around the tot and started to dry her off. When he didn't say anything else, she looked over her shoulder, but he'd gone. A few minutes later, she heard the front door go. When she'd got Zoe off to sleep, she came down to a note on the kitchen island.

Gone out. Don't wait up. Phone is on if you need me. Jackson

'Nice.' She sighed. After showering off the day, she dragged her tired body under the covers. She'd found the business card in her trouser pocket when she'd undressed. It sat on her dresser next to Jackson's note. Picking both up, she scrutinised them. She could be stupid and play dumb. She could say that she had no idea why Jackson was mad, why he'd questioned her, but she had a feeling she knew exactly why. If someone asked Jackson out, she knew she wouldn't like it. He'd talked about them at work—his family.

His wife and kid.

It would be sweet if it wasn't so wrapped up in a big ball of messy emotional angst in the pit of her stomach. Her phone was on charge, sitting on the dresser. Pulling out the cord, she brought up the message screen and started typing.

It's me. Don't be mad... *delete*

I'm not going out with him... *delete*

Come home... *delete*

She picked up one of her pillows and threw it at the far wall.

'This is ridiculous,' she said out loud. 'What am I doing?' She looked at the photo of Harriet and Ronnie on her dresser. 'You two have a lot to answer for.'

Turning in for the night. I'll take Zoe to nursery tomorrow. Let you sleep in and enjoy your day off. Lucy

It read a bit cold. She added a letter to soften the words.

X *delete*

Should she?

X *delete*

She hit Send before she could debate the kiss any longer. Shoving the phone, the business card and the curt note in her top drawer, and turning off the lamp, she tried to fall asleep.

When she left the house the next morning, Zoe and her backpack in tow, Jackson's bedroom door was closed. He'd read her message but not replied.

Fine, she thought to herself. *Awkward it is.*

It wasn't as though they'd never played *that* game before. This morning, she found the whole thing silly. Yeah, they'd been getting closer, but it was just the bubble they'd been in. They'd both said as much: Zoe needed stability.

It was lust, that was all. Sure, there were feelings too, but *wife and kid* kept haunting her. She tried to tell herself it was just her libido talking for the millionth time. She hadn't been near a man in, oh…for ever…and now she was living with an extra tall version of a near-perfect specimen who was good with kids, saved lives while rocking a set of scrubs and wasn't a total player. Any woman would have looked, she reasoned, and it would pass. The hand-holding tingle would stop. She'd get over the loss of her perfect night, the one where he'd held her tight and told her 'for ever'. 'For ever' was a fantasy—nothing lasted; people didn't stay. Perhaps she should say yes to the date with Josh just to put paid to this nonsense. It was easier somehow when he hated her.

'Tell me what to do, Zoe love,' she said to her niece as they pulled up to the nursery. 'Auntie Lucy is floundering here.'

'Jack-Jack,' she said with a toothy smile, and Lucy laughed.

'Well, you're a big help. Another female totally under his spell, eh?' She turned off the engine, checking her phone again. She'd texted him again that morning—for a valid co-parenting reason, of course, telling him they were low on milk and she'd pick some up after her shift. A nothing message. Still, she was sad to see that he'd not read it. Perhaps he was still asleep. She'd told him to lie in. Or maybe he was ignoring his phone because he was still mad. She'd not heard him come in the night before. Stuffing the phone back into her bag, she tried to focus on her day.

'Morning, Zoe!' an exuberant redhead said the second Zoe toddled through the secure doors.

Maddison? Melanie? Something beginning with an M.

She looked to see Lucy at her heels and the disappointment was evident. 'Oh.' She smiled, recovering too slowly to make it look realistic. 'Hi, Lucy! I thought you were Jackson. He dropped her off last week.'

'Mmm-hmm.' Lucy passed her Zoe's backpack. 'Different shifts every week. Just me today, sorry; Jackson's got the day off.'

'Aww.' She simpered, taking the bag. 'He deserves it, working so hard.' Lucy bent to give Zoe a kiss.

'Bye, darling, have fun.'

The redhead opened the interior doors and Zoe sped off to join the other kids on the carpet. One of the newer nursery staff members was reading a story to the other kids, and Zoe was a sucker for being read to. Once the door was closed, Lucy turned to leave.

'So, what's he doing today with his day off? Out with his girlfriend or something, I bet.' Lucy met her eye. Her name tag said 'Maddy'.

One mystery solved—another person who didn't know their urgent situation either.

Perhaps she should correct that on Zoe's records. They were still listed as aunt and uncle, though the manager was aware.

'Er…no,' Lucy replied, reaching for the high door handle.

'Fiancée, then?' Maddy pressed.

'Nope, not that either.' She let go of the handle, turning back to face the woman who was seriously starting to tick her off. She was too…perky.

Was everyone in heat these days?

'Can I pass on a message or something?'

Maddy's sculpted brows raised in surprise. 'Er…well, it's not exactly professional, but…'

Lucy smiled, cutting her off. 'Of course—you're right, it's not. I'll let you get on, then, Mary.' Maddy nodded, dumbstruck. Reaching for the door, she pushed it open and felt the morning air hit her flustered face. 'Have a good day!'

'Er...you too, Lucy,' Maddy called out weakly.

'Always do,' she trilled, heading back to her car. By the time she got to work after enduring the thick morning traffic, her mood was murderous.

'Hi!'

The second she walked through the hospital doors, she came face to face with Josh.

'Oh, hi, what are you doing here?'

Idiot.

Josh laughed awkwardly, pointing to his scrubs. 'Well, I work here.'

Lucy's cheeks exploded. 'Sorry, sorry! Of course you do!' She slapped her forehead with a palm. 'I haven't had my coffee yet; it's been a bit of a morning.'

'No problem,' he said with a sparkle. 'Perhaps you should have that drink with me, tell me all about it.'

She bit her lip. She was still mad at perky Maddy, but it clicked when she saw Josh—now she understood Jackson's mood. She'd felt that way, knowing that someone was angling for a date with him. It was exactly how he'd felt at lunch the day before. She didn't like the feeling one bit.

'Listen...' She steeled herself for yet another awkward conversation. 'I'm flattered, but the reason why I'm frazzled this morning is because I had to take my...er...little girl to nursery. A little girl I share with Jackson.'

Josh's jaw dropped, his pallor at least two shades lighter. 'Oh, my God. I had no idea you were his wife.' He swore under his breath. 'Gosh, no wonder he was so moody yesterday. Why didn't he say something?'

Lucy put a hand on his shoulder. 'It's fine. You did nothing wrong. We're not married…or even together.' She took a deep breath. 'Jackson's brother, Ronnie—the other Dr Denning—he was married to my sister. She died when he did, and Zoe's their daughter.'

'Oh, my god.' Josh's face was a picture. 'I wondered why people were so weird about talking about him. Jackson's closed off, but I just thought he'd lost a brother…so it made sense. I reckoned the staff weren't talking about it out of respect for his grief, or because they were grieving too. I didn't know he even had a daughter. When I saw a photo of Zoe, he never corrected me.'

'Well, they were grieving,' she agreed. 'And it's my fault Jackson didn't say anything. He was trying to respect my wishes. But also, I'm…Trigger…and also Medusa, around here. Actually, only Jackson calls me Trigger, which annoys the ever-living hell out of me, but I'm a bit of a dragon here.' She laughed, realising that was no longer a hard fact. 'Well, I was. They call me Medusa because I'm a hard-faced tyrant—or I was.'

Josh shook his head, his cheeks reddening. 'So many things make sense now. I thought people just didn't like me or something.'

She waved him off. 'No. No, it's just a weird time. Jackson and I were sort of family, and very much work enemies. Then our siblings went and died and left their daughter for us to raise together.' She tried to wrap it up. 'So, in short—' she pointed at herself '—Medusa, Trigger. Not wife—co-carer. We live together and raise a kid.

'Listen, it's a long, very confusing story, but I'm just not dating anyone at the moment. I just needed to set the record straight. I don't want you to feel awkward at work because Jackson and I can't communicate. I'm really sorry for word-vomiting all over you, but I think it's about time people know the truth instead of skirting around me.'

'That's a lot,' he said when she'd finally stopped to draw breath. 'Well, thanks for telling me. I'm sorry for your loss, too.'

'Thanks. And sorry again for dragging you into our drama.' She went to leave, turning back to him when something occurred to her. 'Thanks, though,' she said, meaning it. 'You helped me realise a few things. I'll see you around.'

'Does he know?' he called after her.

'Does he know what?' she asked, frowning at him.

'That you're not together,' he said, his voice low to avoid attention. 'I don't know what the deal is with you two, but I'm not sure he has the same way of looking at things you do. The way he spoke about you, that didn't sound like just a co-carer to me.' He dipped his head by way of goodbye and strode away.

She watched him leave, but didn't feel a pang of regret. His words turned over and over in her head. Lucy thought of Jackson's mood, of him being at home, all huffy. Thought of her behaviour earlier, bristling at Maddy for daring to ask about her housemate. Pulling out her phone, she rang Sheila.

'Hi, Sheila, sorry for ringing early. I'm just going on shift. Yes, yes, everything's great. Zoe's at nursery. Listen, I hate to ask, but is there any chance you and Walt could possibly do me a favour and collect her for me tonight and let her sleep over?'

CHAPTER ELEVEN

LUCY FELT EVERY step her aching feet made towards her car. Her whole body was singing with both exhaustion and nervous energy. She didn't know whether to laugh, cry or vomit. Seeing Jackson leaning against the back of her car, she didn't get a chance to choose.

What is he doing here?

She'd planned to go home and ask him if they could talk. Tell him Zoe was away for the night to give them both time to hash this out once and for all. She'd banked on the extra time driving home to gather the bravery she needed to get her words out. Spewing words all over Josh earlier wasn't something she wanted to repeat, not when these next few hours would change their dynamic again, no matter what his reaction was when she finally managed to get her words into the order she needed them.

Her heart leapt even as her steps faltered. She had to make a conscious effort to put one foot in front of the other. He looked gorgeous, which made it worse. He was wearing the soft dove-grey sweater she loved on him, the one with the V-neck that showed off his chest. The muscles in his broad back flexed noticeably beneath the wool when he moved. She'd thought about that chest so many times that she could draw it from memory. His long, thick legs were encased in a pair of midnight-black jeans, the ones that showed off his tight behind. The first time she'd seen him leaning over the dishwasher in them, she'd had to leave the room before he clocked her ogling.

He was looking in the other direction, checking his watch, ruffling his thick, dark locks between the fingers of one hand. Seeing the tension in his gait, she braced herself for what was about to happen.

'Hey, you.'

He pushed off the car, levelling her with one look.

He's absolutely stunning. How the heck have I ever been around you and not been a gooey mess?

'Hey. Hi.' He stepped forward, making her feel smaller as he stood close.

Not smaller—dainty.

He reached for her work bag, and she gave him it to him readily. 'Good shift?'

'Not bad.' She breathed, willing her body to stop feeling as if it was on fire. Her heart was thudding in her chest cavity, so loud she felt he must hear it. 'What are you doing here?'

He pointed to his car a few spaces away. She'd not even noticed it.

'I thought we could take a drive. Talk.'

'What about my car?'

'Leave it here. I can bring you back after.'

Well, this is not my plan, she thought, but he obviously had things to say too. It wasn't as if she'd expected anything different.

'Luce,' he mumbled, so close to her now she could have reached out and touched that legendary chest. 'You trust me, right?'

She almost laughed at him. It was such a daft question

now. She trusted him more than anyone else in the world. 'Of course,' she said instead.

'Then come with me,' he urged, his voice deep, pleading. He held out a huge palm and she put her hand straight into its grasp.

He pulled out of the car park and headed away from the direction of Zoe's nursery.

'Where are we going?' she asked, looking at the buildings going past as he drove in the opposite direction from the city centre.

'That trust thing didn't last long.' He smirked. 'I spoke to my mum, by the way.'

'Oh, really?' she said nonchalantly. Her squeaky voice didn't get with the program. 'Is she okay?'

'Thrilled to have Zoe for the night, yeah, which is why I didn't drive to the nursery earlier to get her.' He turned to look at her as they hit the motorway turnoff. 'You didn't say why you wanted the night off, though.'

Zoe felt her cheeks get hot. 'Is that why you came to work—to check up on me?' Something else occurred to her. 'Did you think I might be going out with Josh?'

'It crossed my mind.' She didn't miss the clench of his jaw. 'But I spoke with Josh. He called me about a patient, mentioned he was going out with some of the team.' He cleared his throat. 'I might have suggested some of the work lads take him out for a drink—welcome him properly. You don't have any plans, do you.' It was a statement.

'No,' she replied.

'Thought so. I thought you might want to talk too, so I came to get you.'

'So you did all that and came to stalk me in the parking lot. Nice.' He laughed when he saw her knowing smirk.

'Well, I didn't want to risk the chance some other doctor asked you for a date before you got home. I didn't want to wait to see you.'

He took the next turnoff. They were on the outskirts of Leeds, she noticed, where a large retail park and some industrial units stood. 'And now you're taking me to the warehouse district. I know we sorted the joint life insurance, but I'm pretty sure murder voids the policy.'

'Hah-di-hah!' He headed to the bottom of the main industrial park, turning off just after a bathroom wholesaler. 'I just wanted to talk to you. We've not spoken since yesterday, I wanted to clear the air.'

'You weren't talking, actually. I sent you messages.'

'I got them.'

'I know.'

He pulled into the car park of a grey warehouse. Neon lights lit up signage on top of a large set of double doors. 'I was mad.'

'Yeah, and you're weren't the only one, Jack.' She looked at the name of the place: *Axe Me Another*. 'Where are we, anyway?'

He turned off the engine, pinning her with a grin so cheeky and so sexy she wanted to slap him, then pull him in and snog his face off.

'Well, since you bagged us a night off, I thought that we should do something about being mad with each other once and for all.'

'You've got to be kidding me.'

Jackson was positively gleeful as he passed her a set of overalls. She looked up into his eyes and they were bright with excitement.

'Nope.'

'You're an A&E doctor. You put people back together after dumb accidents like this.' They were in a side room, having just signed a bunch of disclaimers and been shown where to change. Jackson shrugged, pulling off his sweater without warning. Lucy squeaked, turning to face the lockers on the other wall. 'Jackson! What are you doing?'

'Getting changed! Come on, don't be a priss. It's nothing you haven't had hold of before, remember?'

Remember? Ha! It's etched onto my grey matter.

'How could I forget?' She sighed, looking again at the bright-orange jumpsuit and goggles in her hands. 'Fine. If we must dress up like hardened convicts, at least turn around.'

She heard him behind her, closer than before. 'I promise not to peek.' He half growled; his voice sounded strained. She looked over her shoulder; he was standing with his back to her and his stance was taut. She turned round and got changed as quickly as she could. Then she tapped him on the shoulder and he turned round, goggles on the top of his head like a pair of shades.

'I look ridiculous,' she told him. 'Orange is definitely not the new black.'

He laughed with that low rumble that did things to her insides.

'I like that laugh.'

His brows raised in surprise. 'Thanks.' His smile was genuine, bashful even. She went to push a lock of hair away from her face and he beat her to it, curling it round his finger before sweeping it behind her ear. 'You look cute in orange.' He paused, and she stood there, looking up at him and prompting herself to breathe. 'Come on,' he muttered, breaking the spell. 'Let's go get that rage out.'

Half an hour later, Lucy was throwing axes like a pro.

The whole place was a rage-relief experience. They had a rage room full of stuff such as china, bottles, old furniture and weapons like bats and golf clubs. She could hear people screaming and bellowing from the other rooms, and the smashes and crashes. Their space was like a shooting range with big targets on wooden walls, and axes laid out for throwing.

'There you go, Luce!' Jackson hollered as she sank another axe into the target, this time almost on the bull's-eye. 'You nailed it!' She turned to see his palm up, and high-fived him as he laughed. 'Feel better?'

'Well, I'm not mad any more.'

I might have imagined Maddy on a couple of the throws, though.

He chuckled. 'Good. We should come again.'

'We should join up to their loyalty scheme or it might get expensive.'

He laughed, that rumble giving her a tingle under her overalls. 'Hungry?' he asked.

'Starving,' she answered.

'Let's go get something to eat,' he said, putting his arm around her shoulder. They put down the axes and headed back to the changing room. They were the only ones there, and Jackson clicked the lock on the door. They stood behind the door for a moment, toes almost touching, suddenly feeling awkward after the chaos.

'Why did you come to meet me at work?' she asked him. 'Why didn't you just ring me?'

'I thought you might ignore me, after yesterday. When Mum said you'd asked her to have Zoe, I connected the dots. I found this place online a while ago and thought it would be good to have some fun for once.'

'It was.' She grinned. 'Especially after this morning.' Her eyes widened. She hadn't meant to say that.

He lowered his head closer to hers. 'This morning?'

'Er…yeah.' She shuffled from foot to foot. 'I spoke to Maddy.'

His expression was blank, which cheered her up to no end. 'Maddy who?'

'Maddy, from nursery?'

He shook his head, his lip curling into a 'so' motion. 'And?'

'And she wanted to know if you were spending the day with your girlfriend.'

She could have sworn on the medical textbooks she revered that his eyes lit up.

'Ah. Right.' He grinned, all lopsided smile and pearly white teeth. 'You were jealous.'

She flushed, the fear of being so close to him scaring her. She didn't just mean body to body either. 'No, of course I wasn't.'

'Liar.'

'Jackson, come on.'

'No, you come on, Luce.' He sighed, thumbing towards the door. 'We did the rage. I'm not doing the denial thing any more. I was jealous.'

'Of Josh?'

'Yeah.' He huffed, taking a step closer. 'I swear, I wanted to fire the guy on the spot. I saw him hand you his card.' He bit down on his bottom lip and she tracked the movement. 'I didn't like it. I don't want you to date him.'

'Yeah.' She raised her chin a little. 'Well, I saw Josh this morning.'

There it was again—that low, reverberating growl.

'I set him straight—told him the truth and that I won't be accepting any invitations from him.'

'You did?'

'Yep. I will not be dating Josh, so I don't want you dating Maddy.'

'Done. I don't want you dating anyone.'

'Done,' she shot back. 'Same goes for you. What else did you want to talk about?'

They were both breathing a little faster now, moving infinitesimally closer.

'Why you arranged for Zoe to sleep over at my folks'.'

'Because I wanted us to talk without distractions. Why did you really come to meet me in the car park?'

'Because I couldn't wait to see you a minute longer.' His lip twitched. 'I meant it. I didn't want someone else hitting on you before you got home and I got the chance to tell you that you drive me crazy.'

'You drive me crazy.'

'I know.' He growled. 'But you drive me crazy more than when we fight, Luce. I...'

He sighed, a bone-shattering, deep sigh as his arms came up around her. She put her hands on his chest and he stilled, as though she was going to push him away. When she didn't, he went on.

'I can't lie to myself any more. I won't. Fighting with you is the most alive I have ever felt. You get under my skin so badly, I want to unzip it and tuck you in. Since the paintballing day, you were it. But I knew Ronnie and Harriet were end game; it was too complicated to even try. I thought you hated me, too. So, I told myself it was fun, sparring with each other, picking fights, and it was—but I can't sleep across the hall from you for much longer without losing my mind.

'I spent the night in your bed, and now I can't stop wanting it again. I just lay there, holding you, smelling your hair and wishing I could wake you and chase those bad dreams away *for ever.* I started using your conditioner just so I can smell that coconut smell you had that night; I need it with me when I'm away from you and can't get my fix. I can't afford the damn water bill any more, with all the cold showers. That day, when we crashed into each other, I barely got out of that alive, Luce. I wanted to just pick you up and carry you to my bedroom.'

She heard her breath hitch in her throat.

'I want your hands on my bare ass *for ever.* I swear, it took everything I had in me not to wrap your sexy legs around me and take you to my bed.'

'Why didn't you?'

Lucy was so turned on, she couldn't stand it. His words were like caresses she'd wrap herself in. *For ever...* Every time he said it, she wanted more, wanted to tell him yes. To beg him to do all that, and more.

'Because you weren't where I was. Because you pretend to hate me. Sometimes, I think you really do.'

'I don't,' she rebutted. 'I've shampooed my hair so much since we moved in together, I think my hair might fall out. The other day you were taking the rubbish out and I wanted to wrap myself in a bin bag just so you'd lift *me* up and throw me over your shoulder. You wind me up so much, I can't stand it. I don't hate you Jackson, I have cold showers too, to stop myself from blurting out how freaking gorgeous I think you are. Then I think about you *in* the shower, and I forget I washed my hair already, so I do it again. Then I smell your shower gel on the shelf next to mine and the whole cycle starts again. Even when we're with Zoe, my mind wanders. I can't help but notice how sexy you are when you're being cute with her.'

At some point when she'd been talking, he'd tightened his grip on her; her feet were barely on the floor now as he held her to him. She could feel him breathing hard, almost panting beneath the orange jumpsuit.

'I'm not stupid, Jackson. I know I'm a mess, and stubborn and prickly, but I swear, when Maddy asked about you this morning, I got it. I know why you were angry about Josh.'

She bit her lip, afraid to say the final thing she had to tell him. She felt it would be too much, she'd be too exposed. And far too turned on to concentrate on the dull panic her rational brain was trying to convey down her frazzled nerve endings.

'Because...' Her voice gave out. 'Because it's not hate, or lust, it's...'

'Because you're mine,' he answered for her. When she nodded, he lifted her off the floor into his arms, and she wrapped herself around him as he leaned her against the door and pressed his lips to hers. 'Finally.'

Oh...this man is going to be the end of me, she thought as she tasted him for the first time.

His lips were soft at first, as if he was waiting for her to come to her senses. The second she moaned into his mouth, all doubts were gone. He kissed her like a starved man, as if he'd been waiting his whole life to caress her mouth. 'Lucy. You're...so...mine,' he rasped out, his voice all growly.

'Shh,' she said, threading her fingers through his hair and pulling his mouth back to meet hers. 'No more talking.'

She felt his little laugh and she wriggled closer to his body. The laughter stopped, replaced by a visceral rumble as he ground her against the door. Sexual tension years old was unleashed. She grabbed his zip, pulling it down. His torso was bare, and she pulled away from his mouth to marvel at it. 'I love your chest,' she murmured as his lips fell onto her neck, nipping and kissing along the length. She leaned down and took a nipple into her mouth, licking at it and feeling the sensations in her own groin.

'Are you trying to kill me?' he mumbled, lifting her higher as she reached for his zip.

'Yeah,' she panted. 'Death by sex.' The orange jumpsuits were getting hot; she felt her body roasting from the inside. 'Take it off,' she begged.

He met her eye, and she could see it was taking him everything to slow himself down. 'Are you sure? We haven't talked about…'

She was already pulling at her own zip. 'Jackson,' she begged. 'No talking.' If they started talking about this, what it meant, she'd sober up from her lust. She was drunk on him, and she didn't want to stop. 'Take off your clothes. Now.'

One minute she was pressed up against the door, the next she was on her feet, her breath ragged, loud, in the room. He undid his zip the rest of the way, leaving him standing there in black boxer shorts.

She shuffled out of her jumpsuit, leaving herself in her underwear. The dark hue of his eyes deepened as she looked back at him shyly.

'Oh, no, not the green…' she heard him mumble. Looking down at her matching jade underwear, she started to pull her clothes back up, but he stilled her with his hand, picking her up once more.

'Don't you dare,' he warned. 'I just meant I knew I'd be lost when I finally saw you in them.' His teeth found her nipple through the lace as his body covered hers once more, leaning against the wooden door, overalls discarded. 'Ever since I found them in the dryer, I've been obsessed with the colour green.' He sucked gently, and she gasped as her nipple hardened beneath the lace. Pulling his head back up to meet hers, she wrapped herself around him tighter. She was desperate for him to do more, touch her more, say more.

'Stop teasing me, Denning,' she begged. This time, when their lips met, neither of them spoke. The dam finally broke between them and they were all hot breath, fingers, pulling and pushing. She clawed at his back. He was everywhere all at once, tongues and teeth, skin on skin. He groaned when his fingers finally dipped below the lace, and then he shifted her in his arms.

'I'm about to get a condom…' He panted, his arms solid around her quivering body. 'Last chance to stop this, Luce. We need to…'

She pushed her finger to his lips. 'Get it,' she begged. 'Don't stop now.'

She ground against him. 'Sex now. Talk later.'

His eyes darkened and, when his lip curled up, she knew who the victor was. Not letting her loose, he grabbed a foil packet from his jeans and passed it to her, only releasing her to drop his pants. Hers followed suit. Rolling it on, she felt him stiffen in her grasp, and then she was back in his steel hold. He kissed her frantically, pinning her to the door and lifting her legs higher. He told her to hold on tight and then he was inside her, thrusting, teasing and hitting everything just right. She was flush against the wood, limbs clinging to him as he started kissing her.

Why the hell weren't we doing this the whole time? she thought as his hot length speared her harder, deeper, hitting the sweet spots she dimly remembered and some she'd never known she had.

She tried to be quiet, aware that she could hear shouts

of rage coming from behind the door, so at odds with the sounds of pleasure from within. He took every moan she had and muffled it against his jaw, against his mouth.

'Lucy...' He breathed. 'You feel so good. Lucy, my Luce...'

His movements were faster, more erratic, as she tightened around him. When he whispered her name again, she was done for, toppling over the edge as the white-hot orgasm ripped through her body, but still he drove on. Thrusting and cradling her to him as if he couldn't bear not to touch every inch of her, he growled and she felt him come hard. His arms came up under her bare bottom like a muscular shelf, holding her steady as she felt him shake on his own legs. He kissed her again and then touched his forehead to hers. Coming back down to reality, they both looked into each other's eyes, still wrapped around each other, sweaty and glistening.

'I guess that's what they mean by make-up sex.' She giggled. He huffed out a laugh, kissing her forehead and flashing her a smile she'd never seen before.

'A few years in the making,' he mumbled, before his expression turned serious. 'I meant what I said—you're mine, Lucy.' He kissed the corner of her mouth, and she felt him tighten himself around her protectively, as if he was afraid she'd bolt from his embrace. 'If you'll let me, I promise to make you happy—you and Zoe. I can't bear to go back now. Not now I've had this.' His look turned positively feral. 'Had you. There's no other woman on this planet who drives me insane. No other woman I'd rather be with.'

He kissed the opposite corner, turning her in his arms as he carried her away from the door. She wrapped her arms around his broad, sexy shoulders. 'What do you say?' He looked so nervous, so utterly gorgeous, her mouth went dry just looking at him. 'I'm pretty good at reading you, Luce, but I need a clue here.'

She leaned forward, brushing her lips against his. 'I say I'm ravenous.' His hopeful grin dipped, and she couldn't bear it. The bubble they had was thicker now, and she didn't want to pop it. 'Take me home, Jackson. Feed me, and then you can take me to bed and show me just how much you mean all that.'

His face split into a devilish, delirious smile and he twirled her round as he spun on the spot. 'Jackson!' she squealed as he bellowed out a whoop. 'People will hear you!'

He put her back on her feet, reaching for his clothes. 'Let them,' he said, slapping her on the butt cheek as they both scrambled to get dressed.

That was the last night they slept in separate rooms. He kept good on his word. He drove her home right away and fed her appetites until she was satiated. He showed her how much he meant every word, more times than she could count. Much, much later, he curled her into his arms, smelling her hair with a contented sigh as they cuddled in her bed. As she felt her heavy lids close, lulled by the sound of his heart under her, she smiled as he whispered more words to her.

'I want to sleep like this for ever, Luce. There's no getting rid of me now. I love you.'

Lifting her head, she saw the nervousness in his face as he stared back.

'I do. I love you.' His grip tightened, just a touch. 'Don't run. I haven't the energy to chase you right now.'

She laughed softly. 'Where would I run to?' she asked. 'I'm home.' She kissed him, wanting the little furrow in his brow banished as he waited to see her reaction. 'I love you too, Sasquatch.'

His returning grin was her new favourite thing, she decided, before sleep won.

CHAPTER TWELVE

IT HAD BEEN going so well—*so well*. The sex was hot... more than hot. It was as if the pair of them were teenagers. Since the Axe Me Another frantic bonking incident, as Jackson affectionately referred to it, they'd never stopped. They'd christened all the rooms in the house bar Zoe's. The shower was Jackson's particular favourite. He loved to soap up her boobs while they stood under the spray, he turning the shower to cold to shock her just after they'd heated each other to the point of combustion. Name anywhere, they'd done it there: her car; his car, twice. There was even a stack of mops in the downstairs cleaning closet that was still blushing.

It wasn't just the sex, though. They were together in every sense of the word. Jackson was romantic, which she'd never expected but readily appreciated. He'd leave her little notes around the house, stuffed in her locker at work or in the lunches he made her take to work in case she forgot to eat—which she did, of course.

I always called you Trig because it was our thing. A reminder of when we first met.

You're such a good auntie. Zoe and I heart you mucho.

See you tonight, baby, miss you already.

Eat your greens, Dr Bakewell.

Their work colleagues were surprisingly un-shocked. When she'd told Amy, she'd just laughed. 'I knew it,' she'd said. 'About time mate. Man, it's so good to see you happy.' Lucy had laughed, wondering at how things had changed.

They'd had an offer on Harriet's and Ronnie's house; a young couple had offered the asking price. She'd even found a tenant for her place. She hadn't told Jackson yet, but she reckoned that, after the lease expired, she'd sell up too. There'd be no point in having the place, and she no longer thought of it as home.

Zoe was thriving too, growing every day. She talked more and more all the time. She loved living with Jack-Jack and 'Luby', as she called her. Lucy had worried about whether the pair of them together would confuse her, but she didn't seem affected. In fact, she seemed thrilled to see the pair of them together. Jackson told her it was because kids were smart, and happy parents meant happy children. It was true, she came to realise as the days went on: they were all really happy. She should have known it wouldn't last *for ever*.

It was a Friday like any other. They were both on the late shift, Zoe sleeping over with Sheila and Walt, who were doubly elated at the news that Lucy was now even more part of the family than before.

I can't wait to sleep in tomorrow…shattered. Then I'm going to do that thing that makes your toes curl. Then breakfast.

I'm thinking of pancakes at that place we like after we pick Zoe up.

Lucy laughed to herself, tapping out a response as she sat in the break room, resting her tired feet. She had five minutes left on break, and a ton of paperwork to get through. There were also a couple of patients she wanted to check on before she left.

Sounds good. I love pancakes. And you.

He typed back almost instantly.

Don't play with me, woman. Or I'll do it twice. With more tongue. Love you too.

She almost choked on her coffee. It was criminal how sexually combustible this man made her. She couldn't get enough of him. Harriet and Ronnie wouldn't be in trouble when she finally saw them again, that was for sure.

Promises, promises. See you soon.

See you soon.

A second later, another message popped up.

I'm going to marry you, Luce. Real soon.

What?
She read the words again and saw that he was typing again. She held her breath, waiting for him to take it back.
He wants to marry me? No. It's too soon. It's...too much.

She was an aunt, a carer, a lover. She was his...but wife? Harriet had been a wife, their own mother too—look how they turned out.

Her old shields, stiff from lack of use these last few months, clanged back into action, raising up around her with a rusty screech. She felt her heart race as she saw the three dots bounce in the corner. He was still writing.

Don't freak out. We can talk later.

Talk later? Seriously? He'd told her something like that on a text and then expected her to work the rest of her shift? Her head was an utter mess. She wished that she didn't react this way, that she didn't want to run, but the second she'd read that text with their six-month review looming... It was too much. It felt like too much. She needed things just to slow down. They were about to cement their care for Zoe, which was a formality, but still. Marriage was binding: *for ever.* That suddenly felt like a threat, not a promise.

She tapped back.

You bet your ass we will.

His reply was instant.

Are you annoyed? I'm sorry, I know I should have said it to your face, I just couldn't hold it in any more. We'll talk tonight, okay? I have to go. A&E is slammed. Trust me, Luce. You said you were done running. Love you.

Fine.

That was all she could bring herself to write back. It felt as if he'd dropped a bomb at her feet. What should she do—run, seek cover, throw it away? The old Lucy would have without a second thought with not so much as a glance over her shoulder. He knew that. He'd dropped a grenade, and she was standing there, left to stare at it, knowing in all probability it was going to detonate and take off her face. She *was* angry. He was ruining it, changing things. They were going well, doing okay. Surely they could just go on as they were? Why change anything?

In a couple of days, after the six-month review, they were going to tell Sheila and Walt they were thinking about adopting Zoe. That was spinning her head already. Yeah, she wanted it, but it felt so final. Marriage would mean something else to risk losing. She couldn't take any more pressure. He loved her—*loved her.* She should be happy, right? She loved him. That hadn't and wouldn't change, but things were good as they were.

She cared about him, a lot. She loved waking up with him every day, sharing a bed. Falling asleep listening to his heartbeat was one of her new life's pleasures. She finally understood what Harriet had been on about. She got it. She was in this, but it was still so new, so precious, so fragile. They were exclusive, raising a kid under the same roof. That was commitment, more than she'd ever given anyone. More than she'd ever thought she would. She didn't want to go back to sleeping across the hallway.

Then she thought of what came next after someone said the 'M' word. They already lived together, but that was part of the arrangement for Zoe. It had lessened the blow of their grief, and had been a necessity. It had been thrust upon them, but now—this was different. It would be on them. If this next step failed, if she couldn't give him what he wanted, what then? 'For ever' was a long time, and look where it had got her sister and her parents. The one thing she'd learned was that love did not conquer all.

She saw the time on her phone and cursed.

Looks like my break is well and truly over.

Putting her phone back on silent and shoving it into her pocket, she speed-walked back up to the ward.

When rounds were over, Lucy headed for her office.

Nearly there, she told herself as she reached for the handle. *You can hide out here, do your paperwork. Catch your breath.*

'Dr Bakewell?'

So close.

Amy fell into step alongside her, following her into the room and taking a seat opposite hers.

'Well.' Lucy huffed. 'Come right in.' She slumped down in her chair. Amy was glaring at her from across the desk. 'What?' she snapped.

'Exactly. That's what I want to know. What's up? You've been like Mary Poppins lately, and today you've been biting people's heads off.'

'I have not!'

'Yeah, you have. None of the other staff dare mention it, but you've been worse than your old self—Medusa with a side of mean. What's going on?'

Lucy clenched her jaw and started shuffling papers on her desk.

'I'm not going till you tell me.'

Lucy tried to stare her down, but Amy just laughed. 'Nice try, mate. Your snakes don't scare me.'

'Fine.' She put down the papers. 'First of all, Medusa is

better than Mary Poppins, so that's a rubbish insult. Second, I'm okay.'

'No, you're not. So, what's going on? Is it the adoption thing?'

'No. Yes. I don't know.' She bit the bullet. 'Jackson just told me he wants to marry me—by text.'

Amy's eyes bugged out.

'Exactly—you get it. It's bad, right? I mean—what is he thinking?' When Amy didn't answer, Lucy looked at her expectantly. 'Seriously, tell me—what is he thinking?' Her friend smiled with a slow, knowing grin. 'Why are you smiling?'

Amy leaned forward, resting her elbows on the desk. 'I'm thinking that for a smart, driven woman, you're pretty dumb.'

'Oh, well, thanks! I—'

'He told you he loves you because he does. He told you he wants to marry you because he does.' Her eyes narrowed, a look of wonder crossing her features. 'You really don't see it, do you?'

'See what? How soon this is? How crazy?'

'Love is crazy, Lucy. What you have been through is nuts. Anyone else would have crumbled, but you two—you make each other stronger. That man has hankered after you ever since he came here. The whole hospital can see it, and you really can't?'

'No.'

'Still?' Amy's tone was incredulous.

'No, I mean I can see it.' To her horror, a tear slipped down her cheek. She stopped its descent with a shaky hand. 'That's the problem. It's not just my life—it's three lives. I don't know how to do this, Ames. I never wanted to be in something like this, something that I could stuff up. I could lose it all. Nothing good ever stays. We were fine as we were.'

They were interrupted by a sharp tap on the door. 'I'll get it,' Amy said softly. After talking to the nurse, she closed the door again.

'There's a consult in A&E. You want me to take it?'

Lucy was already on her feet. 'No, I'm good.' She wiped her eyes. 'Do I look okay?'

Amy took a tissue from her pocket and rubbed at Lucy's cheek. 'You're good.'

'Thanks.' She smoothed down her uniform and fixed her hair. 'Tell the staff I'll try to keep the hissing to a minimum but, if the name Poppins is used in the same sentence as my name again, all bets are off.'

She was halfway out of the door when Amy spoke again.

'Being scared of losing something is normal, you know. Not reaching for what you want in case the worst happens is all well and good, but it's not a life either. I don't want that for you, mate. Not now, when you've seen how great it can all be. You've lost enough already. You didn't have a choice then. You do now. Life is fleeting, just like happiness. You have to go for it while you can.'

'Hey!' Josh greeted her with a wide grin. The place was rammed, the staff rushed off their feet—a typical Friday afternoon. 'What brings you down here?'

'Paeds got paged. One of your patients?'

He shook his head, nodding to Triage Four. 'In there.'

Jackson was standing by the bed when she got there, suturing an arm laceration.

'Hey.' She didn't look at him for long, but she felt his eyes watching her as she introduced herself to the teenaged patient. 'Hi, I'm Dr Bakewell. How are you feeling?'

'Pretty rough,' the teenager croaked. Aside from his arm

lac, he had two black eyes forming, an obviously broken nose and a rather nasty lump on the side of his head.

'This is Lachlan, fifteen.' Jackson told her. 'Came off his skateboard at the top of the slope at the skate park. Ambulance brought him in, parents are on the way. I sent his friend to go get a drink.'

'He's scared of blood!' Lachlan laughed. 'Ouch.'

'Try to stay still,' she urged, shining a torch into his eyes. 'Normal pupillary response; did he stay conscious at the scene?'

'Ambulance said he was when they arrived but his friend Joe said he did knock himself out.'

Lucy nodded, checking his chart. 'Let's get him a head CT. No broken bones.' She donned gloves, removing the gauze to check his nose. It was cut on the bridge, the skin split but intact. 'Landed on your face, eh? Did you land the trick?'

Lachlan grinned. 'Yeah, stacked it straight after, though. My board broke on the railing.'

'No helmet either,' she chided, inspecting his head. He had a cut in his hairline that had already been glued. 'Do I need to lecture you about being safe over looking cool?'

Lachlan groaned. 'No. My mum always tells me. She's going to go mental when she gets here.'

She locked eyes with Jackson. 'Parents worry. I'm pretty sure she'll just be happy to see you, know that you're doing okay.'

She saw his eyes soften, and returned to Lachlan's face. 'Let's get you up to CT; we'll make sure your head injury is okay. Your nose is going to need some TLC, and you'll feel bruised and battered for a while.' She applied fresh dressings as Jackson finished sewing up his arm. Noting her instructions on his chart, she motioned for a passing porter to come over. 'Once we've done that, we'll get you up on the children's ward.'

'I have to stay overnight? Aww, man! The footie's on tonight.'

Jackson cut in. 'Leeds fan, eh? Good man. Your room will have a TV. We have that channel.'

'Safe.' Lachlan held out a fist, and Jackson bumped it gently with his gloved hand.

'I'll see you soon, Lachlan.'

Jackson was hot on her heels when she left the cubicle.

'Lucy, wait.'

'It's busy, Jackson, we can talk later.'

He blocked her path, taking off his gloves and shoving them in the adjacent bin. 'Fine.' He headed to the sink to wash his hands. 'Whatever.'

'No.' She joined him. 'It's not "whatever". Just not now.'

They both reached for the same paper towel, ripping it in half. Jackson grabbed another, his jaw taut. 'You talking about our talk, or us? I knew I shouldn't have said it. I knew you'd do this.'

'Do what?' she countered. 'You told me you want to get married in a text. I deserve a minute to process it!'

'You're not processing it, Luce. You know how I feel. You've known for a while, and I know you feel the same. You're just going to use this to push me away. I'm not demanding we do it tomorrow, but it is something I want. I thought you might too.'

He dropped the used towels in the bin, and she blocked his exit.

'That kid, in there?' She dropped her voice. 'His mother waved him out of the door and he ended up in hospital. She got a call telling her that someone she loved, someone she tried to protect and loved, was hurt, despite everything she did to keep him safe, despite everything she taught him. He knew to wear a helmet. She taught him to be safe, to look both ways when crossing the road, to chew his food. She taught him to be out in the world, and he ended up here.'

'And he's fine. He's on his way upstairs; he's alive and being looked after.' He scanned her face, his eyes widening with realisation. As usual, he saw through her shields. 'That's what this is about? Harriet and Zoe? The adoption plan?'

'It's not the adoption. I want Zoe. I like our life. I just…'

'You don't want more? I'm in this with you. I'm scared too, but we love each other, Luce. I will never not want this, want more.'

'I'm not scared.' She breathed. 'I'm terrified!' They were drawing attention now, her raised voice turning people's heads. 'I have to go, Jackson. We're at work.'

He grabbed her hand and wound his fingers around hers, grounding her frantic feet.

'I love you.' His voice was low in tone but not conviction. 'I'm here. I'm not going anywhere. Nothing has changed since this morning. I get that you're stressed. I'm sorry I didn't tell you in a better way, but I'm here—*for ever.*'

'You can't know that. Don't promise me what you don't know.'

His expression was so sad, she could barely hold his gaze.

'Oh, darling.' He squeezed her hand. 'My brave, stubborn heart. Tomorrow, I can't promise. You've got me there, but all of my todays are yours—yours and Zoe's. I will love you today and today and today, for as long as we've got. But you have to let me. You have to trust me. I want you to be my wife. I want to shout from the rooftops that I'm your husband.'

'Jackson, we have incoming!' Josh hollered, coming

round the corner on fast feet. 'Sorry.' He winced, seeing them together. He looked back at Jackson. 'Two minutes out.'

'I'm coming.' Jackson dropped a kiss on her forehead. 'Think about it, Lucy.' She stared up at him blankly, stunned by his words.

He loves me. He wants me as his wife.

The second he'd said it out loud, her heart had felt it. Felt the solidity of his truth. 'I'm yours, and you are mine. Don't shut that out, not when we're this close. Love trumps tomorrow.'

With a rueful smile, he left her there, standing by the sink, motionless in a sea of busyness.

Love trumps tomorrow, he'd said. She thought about it the whole way back to the ward. She allowed herself to digest the conversation.

When I get back to the ward, that's it—back to work, snakes at the ready, shields up.

Holding her ID badge to the admission panel, she shrugged her shoulders back and held up her chin.

The letter from Harriet was in her locked desk drawer. Pulling it out, she pushed her paperwork to one side, smoothing out the pages.

She'd read it a lot over the last few months. She used it to hear her sister's voice in her head and remind herself why she was doing this. Ronnie and Harriet had known just what they were doing. She'd kicked and scratched her way through things, but they knew. It seemed everyone knew. They'd known when Ronnie had been alive, even when they'd been tearing strips off each other, when she'd declared him to be the most annoying man on the planet.

Rereading the letter for the hundredth time, she longed

for her sister. She wished she could talk to her now about Jackson, about how scared she was. If Harriet were here now, she'd tell her how proud of her she was. How jealous she was of her ability to have leaped to form a family after living through the loss of their parents.

'I thought I was the brave one,' she said to the photo of Harriet sitting on her desk. 'Look at me now, eh? I know you said in your letter I'd be mad, but I'm pretty sure you're raging up there, or wherever you are.' Her pager went off; Lachlan was there. 'Oh, what does it matter?' She huffed, locking the letter back up. 'Tomorrow comes, no matter what you do. Screw today.'

Heading to Lachlan's room, she shoved her head back in the game. Taking a deep breath, she knocked and went in.

'Hi,' she said to a woman sitting next to his bed. 'Lachlan's mother, I assume?'

'Yes—Julia. His dad's just gone to get us some coffees.'

'Nice to meet you. I'm Dr Bakewell. Have you been updated?'

His mother, a small, rather worried looking woman who was the double of Lachlan, nodded back. 'The nurse said something about a scan.'

'That's right.' She looked at Lachlan. 'Your head injury has been checked over and we're satisfied it's just a concussion. Your laceration was glued in A&E, the cut on your arm has been cleaned and stitched and your nose isn't broken, but it will be very bruised and sore for a while.'

'That's it?' his mother checked. 'Nothing's wrong with his head? He knocked himself out.'

'I know, but he's fine. We'll keep him overnight to observe him, but tomorrow he should be well enough to discharge. You'll need bed rest at home, and no skate...'

His mother burst into loud sobs.

'He's really okay?' She sobbed.

'He's going to be fine,' Lucy said softly. 'We will take excellent care of him, I promise. He'll be home tomorrow.'

'Oh, God!' she cried, tears rolling down her cheeks. 'Thank you, thank you.'

'Mum…' Lachlan groaned, trying to reach for her hand. 'Don't cry!'

'I can't help it,' she managed to get out. She saw him reaching for her and clasped his hand tight between hers. 'If I wasn't so happy, I would be really mad, Lachie.'

Lucy stepped back, watching the teenager's bottom lip wobble. 'I know, Mum, I'm sorry. I swear, I'll always wear my helmet from now on.'

She kissed his hand, cradling it in hers and reaching over to brush back his hair from his face.

'You'd better, my boy. I can't function without you, okay? You're my world. I need you around.'

Lachlan sniffed. 'Love you, Mum,' he croaked.

'Love you too.' She smiled, her watery eyes bright. 'You're a pain in the bum sometimes, but I need you.'

Lachlan laughed. 'I need you too.'

'I'll…er… I'll let you have some time.' Lucy left the room, her legs shaking with every step.

I can't function without you.

Her kid hadn't worn a helmet. Something so basic, ignoring a request that could have caused a different ending— an ending she'd experienced first-hand, four times over. Watching them together in that room, so happy and elated to have escaped that, all she could think of was her people, her family: Zoe and Jackson.

For most of her life, she'd not only worn a helmet, she'd been too scared to get on her skateboard. Lachlan's mum had taken all the precautions, had had all the worry. She'd taught her son and he'd still got hurt. But she didn't regret being his mother, did she? She'd run to him, told him how important he was to her. She'd run to his side and stayed there, just as Jackson had for Lucy. No matter what she did or said, he was there, not fearing tomorrow.

She stood outside the room, heart pounding, and asked herself a question she hadn't dared ask before: if Jackson was hurt, would she regret it? Would she run to him, or run the other way?

She remembered his promise to her.

All of my todays.

For once in her life, she let the tears fall freely. Because she finally realised, no matter what happened down the road, no matter when tomorrow dawned, she loved him. If he had to leave her and this world, it wouldn't matter to her whether they were wed or not. But it would matter to him.

Lifting her tear-streaked face to the ceiling, she smiled. 'Okay, guys. You win.' She went to pull out her phone. 'It's time to get on that freaking skateboard.'

'Lucy!' Amy shouted, running down the corridor towards her as the nurses' station buzzed into life. Her pager went off in her pocket. 'Emergency!'

The warning siren went off around them and both women took off running.

CHAPTER THIRTEEN

THE SECOND LUCY got there, she knew something was really wrong.

There was a huge flurry of activity as her team gathered at the nurses' station. Her number three, Dr Adebi, was shouting orders at the rest of the staff, calling them out name by name. Once they got their instructions they rushed off, professional and nimble, eager to get on with their designated task.

'What's the emergency?' Lucy asked, running to his side. Dr Adebi turned to her once the last of the staff was sorted, but his words were half-drowned out when the lockdown alarm sounded again. An announcement asking people to stay calm and remain where they were rang out on repeat.

'We're getting reports of a man with a weapon in the hospital. A porter was injured in the back delivery bays. Security is trying to track the man down. Porter was stabbed in the stomach once, and once in the arm as he tried to stop the guy.'

'Lockdown procedures need to be initiated immediately, no one in or out.'

Dr Adebi nodded, pointing to the ward doors. 'We already locked it down, SCBU too.'

'Shutters on the windows facing the corridor?'

Dr Adebi shrugged, his eyes wide. 'I'm not one hundred

percent. I told the nurses to take the children who could be moved to the day room at the end of the hall, as per your protocols. Lunch is done, so we should be able to hole up for a while.'

She patted his arm. 'Go and round on the patients, make sure all observations are carried out on time. Nothing gets missed.'

He gave her a solemn nod and got to it. She picked up the phone, checking with maternity and SCBU that everything was locked down and all people accounted for. She knew they'd already locked down A&E. She felt better, knowing Jackson was safe, somewhere close. She hoped his parents weren't seeing any of this on the news. They'd been through enough worry.

The ambulances would have been diverted to other hospitals already. The other staff were coping well, pulling together as a team. The wards worked in conjunction with each other, all following the protocols and procedures. Now all they had to do was reassure the parents, carers and patients they had with them on the ward. Heading to the TV room, she pushed down the feelings of worry she had for the hospital and its inhabitants. Ensuring her patients were calm and still getting the best care was paramount.

'Right,' she said with a broad smile, taking in the sight of children in chairs, their parents' laps and wheelchairs and closing the door behind her to help muffle the sounds outside. 'Who fancies a movie, eh? We have headphones!'

She didn't hear a thing for the next hour. All the updates were the same: no one in, no one out. All non-emergency surgeries were cancelled. One of her patients was locked down in the post-surgery recovery room after having had a hernia repaired, and young Ada's parents were distraught at not being able to be there for their cute little five-year-old. Lucy had allocated one of the healthcare assistants to keep an eye on them. She knew what it was like to wait for news, and she looked after the parents and guardians just as well as she did the children.

Amy came to find her just as she was going on her rounds again.

'Ada's fine. The OR nurses got one of the tablets. I put the parents in one of the side waiting rooms so they could talk to her in private.'

Lucy patted her hand gratefully. 'You're a star; they should feel so much better after seeing she's okay.'

'Yeah.' Amy smiled, but it didn't last. 'I'll be glad when this thing's over. I heard from one of the OR nurses that someone else has been stabbed.'

'Someone on the staff?' Lucy asked, appalled. Amy shrugged.

'I don't have the details; it was pretty hectic there. They were getting him up to Theatre; she didn't have time to stay on the line.'

'Right,' Lucy replied, pulling out her phone.

She typed out a message to Jackson at super-speed.

Are you okay?

Then she got back to work, Amy in tow.

'Hey, Nathan, how's the apocalypse going?'

Nathan was one of her older patients, at sixteen, and secretly one of her favourites.

'Not bad. I finally kicked that level's butt last night.'

'Yeah,' she teased, washing her hands in the little sink near his bed. 'The night staff told me. No wonder you look tired. Three a.m.?'

Nathan winced. 'Can't believe they grassed me up.'

'They didn't, I read it on your observation chart. My team don't sweat the small stuff, but you do need to get your rest. Can I check your sutures?'

Nathan groaned, putting his game on pause. 'Fine,' he droned. 'But…' His smile turned mischievous. 'Since my parents couldn't get in today, you can't tell them that I didn't do my homework yet. Deal?'

Lucy pretended to ponder his bribe. 'Is it biology?'

'No, English lit.' Lucy's eyes flicked to the small stack of paperbacks Nathan had brought with him when he'd come in for his small bowel surgery and nodded. She wouldn't have been able to concentrate in his shoes, with all the excitement going on around him. If killing some zombies distracted him from being in hospital on lockdown when he should have been at school, that was fine with her.

In a kinder world he'd have been hanging out with his mates and not dealing with Crohn's. This operation wasn't the first he'd had. He lived on a special diet and had to endure a colostomy bag. He was a happy teenager who worked hard. One bit of homework missed was hardly going to derail his life. He read in the evening; she'd seen him plenty of times. They'd even swapped books before, ones she'd loved at his age.

'Fine, deal. What do you say, Dr Ackles?'

Amy laughed as she wrote on his chart. 'A day off on doctor's orders? They can't be mad at that.'

Donning gloves, Lucy gently removed the dressings, checking over the operation site. 'Good, it's healing well. No sign of infection or swelling. The surgeon said it went well.'

Nathan smiled. 'Yeah, they managed to save more than they thought, which is good, because I am sick of seeing you guys.'

Lucy pretended to be wounded, miming the removal of an arrow from her heart. 'Ouch,' she laughed. 'Cheers, Nath. We love you too.'

'When do you think the hospital will be open for visitors?' he asked as she finished up.

'Tomorrow, I would have thought,' she said, making sure she didn't show how uncertain she was. 'You have your phone, right, to video call your parents?'

Nathan nodded. 'Yeah, I told them to stay at work. I think they were planning to stage a vigil outside at one point!' He huffed, his trademark teenage eye-roll evident. 'I heard Isaac say the police were here. They would have freaked.'

'Hey.' She laughed, getting his attention. 'Don't knock it. Believe me, having parents that care and fuss like yours do is not a bad thing. It's nice having someone that cares for you.'

One of the nurses knocked on the door and Amy went to see what they wanted. When she came back, her face was white.

'What?' Lucy asked, knowing instantly that something was wrong.

'Nothing.' She went to open the blinds she'd closed for the examination. 'Good news, actually—the lockdown is being lifted.' She let the light into the room, making Nathan squint and hiss theatrically. 'Dr Bakewell, I need a word outside, please.'

Lucy passed Nathan his controller. 'See you later.' She followed her colleague outside. 'What's up?' she asked straight away. 'Did they get the guy?'

'Yeah.' Amy breathed. 'They got him, but you need to go to Jackson, Lucy.' She watched Amy's lips form more words, and then she was running.

Not again, her voice was screaming in her head. *Not again. Why us?*

She ran down corridor after corridor, barrelling past people, banging on doors, demanding that they let her through, screaming that the lockdown was over and to let her get past. Her phone was at her ear, but all it was doing when she called Jackson was ringing out, ringing out again and again.

Finally, she was there. Josh saw her running and came over. He took her to one side, towards Resus Two.

God, no, not that room. That was the room they'd taken her sister and Ronnie to. That room meant death.

Josh kept talking, his voice hushed, his arm around her shoulder as he laid out the details for her.

The guy with the knife had gone to A&E; he had walked right through the hospital and not been stopped. The security team had still been scrambling to get a description since the first alarm had been raised. In the chaos, he'd slipped by everyone. The loading bay doors had CCTV, but he'd been obscured by a delivery van. The bloke had walked right past people into A&E, where Jackson had been working. The lockdown between departments had still not been in full effect, the chaos still fresh. Jackson had blocked his path and challenged who he was. When he'd seen the blood on his clothes, he'd reacted.

Jackson had tried to protect everyone.

The attacker had lunged. Lucy couldn't get a breath big enough to fill her lungs as she listened, and it looked as if they were walking straight to the room she'd never wanted to set foot in again.

Not Jackson, she thought. *Not now. Please. It's not fair. Not that room.*

They were almost there, her steps slowing as Josh kept talking about how the man was in custody, how Jackson was a hero. How bad it could have been. She didn't want to hear any of that. She didn't want to hear that Jackson was a hero. He was already *her* hero. He was hurt, or worse, and life was changing again. She'd run from him, from his love, for so long. They could have had more todays. She had so much to say. She'd barely begun loving him.

Zoe... Zoe couldn't lose another person.

They were almost at the doors now, and she didn't hear or see anything else—not the lighting, not the patients or the staff, dealing with the aftermath of the last few hours. All she saw was those big wooden doors, the ones she'd pushed through half a year ago. She couldn't feel Josh's arms around her shoulders. She didn't hear him talking or see the faces they passed as she tried to put one numb body part in front of the other. Her phone was still in her hand, which was useless, because she couldn't reach whom she wanted to talk to. It was too late for him just to pick up the phone and for everything to be normal.

'I can't do this again,' she said. 'I can't. Not again.' When they passed the doors, her knees buckled. Josh took her over to a set of chairs and sat her down. He kneeled in front of her, calling a nurse to bring them some water.

It was then she truly understood. She loved him—today, tomorrow, for ever. She was completely in love with Jackson Denning. She loved him enough to run down that aisle, with him holding her hand. She'd walk through fire for him. She'd been over-the-top obsessed, to the point of losing her mind, with him since the day she'd seen the big lug howling and clutching his bruised nether regions.

He'd always been there—in the background, in her face, in her thoughts. Pushing her to be the best at work, if only to one-up him. They made each other better, and she didn't know another man walking the earth who could handle her like he could. Who could understand her and be part of her family. He was always challenging her, annoying the hell out of her. He made her feel alive, sexy. He saw her like no other did. He'd always seen her as if she was transparent under his gaze. He loved her, and she jolly well loved him too. Of course she should be his wife...in this life, in every life.

It was then she realised that Josh hadn't taken her to his side. He hadn't taken her to that room, the one she'd once barged into, looking for her sister, for Ronnie. Looking for proof that what she knew in her head wasn't true. She turned to look at the wooden barrier between Jackson and her. It was still. No one was coming or going. No one was barking orders or running in with crash trays.

'I never told him,' she said, her tears taking over. 'I know the answer now, and I'll never get to tell him. To see his stupid grin.'

'What?' Josh asked, his voice finally filtering through to her ears again. 'Lucy, I think you're in shock. Please drink this.' She pushed the cup away with a shaky hand. She felt sick and dizzy, so dizzy. Her head was spinning. She'd run again when he'd needed her. He'd spilled his guts and she'd left him hanging. It was too late. He was gone. He'd never know now.

'Lucy!' Josh boomed. 'She's passing out! Hold her head!' Arms scrambled around her as her sight turned to pinpricks, surrounded by black. 'Can we get some help here? Lucy,' she heard Josh say to her, 'we've got you.'

And then she let go and succumbed to the nothingness.

When she woke up, she was in a side cubicle in A&E, the curtains drawn around her. She sat up with a jerk when her memory slammed into action.

'Careful,' a deep voice said. Her head whipped to the side and she looked straight into Jackson's big, brown eyes. 'Take it slowly.'

He was lying in a bed next to hers, his bare chest sporting

a dressing. He had a split lip, and a deep bruise was forming around his right eye.

'Jackson!' she squeaked, her voice strangled. She pulled her blanket back and went to him. He reached for her hand as she sank to the chair next to his gurney. He pulled it to his lips and kissed it, wincing when it touched his injury. 'I thought you were…were…'

She started to cry then. Relief and shock flowed out of her. He pulled her closer, his other hand coming up to grab her cheek.

'Trig, I'm fine. I'm okay, Luce.' He looked down at his chest. 'The guy stabbed me. I clocked him the second he walked in, but security was thin on the ground. He was looking for another patient. Some ridiculous gang territory thing.'

She didn't care about any of that, she just cared that he was there.

'Shh,' he soothed her. 'Don't cry, darling, please. It'll drive me crazy. I can't get to you properly like this.'

She laughed, and it sounded hysterical between the sobs.

'You're lying there and you're worried about me,' she keened, leaning forward and kissing him. He made a pained hissing sound but, when she pulled back, he leaned his head closer to keep the contact. He kissed her softly, one kiss on each corner of her mouth and the tip of her nose.

'That's how this works,' he said once he'd let her go enough to look her in the eye. 'I'm fine.' He winked at her with his good eye. 'You're not getting rid of me that easily.'

She got his double meaning, and she didn't need to think twice about anything now. She knew she would never run from this man again. Almost losing him had woken her up. Life was short and cruel. She didn't want to miss a minute of it, good or bad, light or dark.

'I love you and I want to be with you. Yes…in every single way!' she blurted. 'I panicked when you said it today. I wanted to run, but I will never do that again.'

'Luce, you don't have to say this. You don't have to pity me or feel bad.'

'I don't. I already knew the truth; I just didn't want to face it. I thought I'd never get the chance to tell you. I thought I'd never get to say it.

'I love you. I love you, Jackson, body and soul. I swear, I would go through a lifetime of pain and lonely tomorrows for ten minutes being loved by you today. I'm sick of hiding in my half-life. I want us to be a family, a proper family. So, marry me, and yes—that's what I want to say. A question and an answer, no more time wasting.'

He didn't say anything at first. She studied his beautiful, broken face for clues.

Was she too late? What if he'd realised she wasn't worth it after all?

'Took you long enough,' his deep voice teased. 'Get in this bed, right now. I need you close.'

She scrambled in carefully, feeling the warmth of him against her. She kissed his cheek over and over when he tried to smile and whimpered at the pain it produced.

She held his face close to hers and said over and over, 'I love you…for ever.'

'Wow,' he mumbled from under her. 'I should get stabbed more often.'

'Not funny.' She scowled.

'I love you too, Luce,' he said in her ear as she held him tight. 'I always have.' His grin lit him up from the inside. 'We're getting married, Trig.'

'You bet your lanky behind we are, Sasquatch.'

EPILOGUE

Two and a half years later

'HEY!' JACKSON MET them at the front door, taking her shopping bags out of her hands as he always did. They walked down the hall to the kitchen and he leaned down for a kiss on the way, as if he couldn't wait any longer. 'Missed you,' he mumbled into her ear. Even after all this time, she still shivered when he did that. She still found him as hot as the day they'd met. The late August weather was fine, the sun blazing high in the sky.

'Did you get everything you needed?'

Lucy puffed her fringe out of her eyes, heading straight to the fridge to get them both a cold drink.

'We sure did, eh, doodlebug?'

Zoe was trying to get up on one of the stools on the island, her face like thunder.

'Mummy made me go to loads of shops. It was so boring.' Jackson lifted her up, making her laugh as he blew raspberries on her cheek.

'Oh, no, not shopping!' he teased. 'Did you get your school uniform?'

'Yes.' She grinned, brushing her blonde hair back with a little hand and reaching for the juice Lucy had put on the counter. She slurped when she drank, her eyes on the back door. 'Can I play outside now?'

Lucy was busy unpacking groceries from one of the bags. 'Till lunch, of course.'

'Yes!' Zoe punched the air, and it immediately reminded Lucy of Jackson. She was a Mini Me of him, all guns blazing, just like him. She wasn't one for shying away from things, and it thrilled Lucy to see it.

Jackson caught her mid-air as she shuffled off the stool, brandishing sun spray.

'Aww, Daddy!'

He laughed, putting her on her feet and getting down to her level to spray the sunscreen onto her skin.

'Aww, Daddy, nothing. It's hotter than Hades out there, and you're built like a child of the corn.'

'A what?' she asked, her little nose scrunching up in confusion as he lathered her up.

'Nothing. Have fun.' He dropped a kiss on her forehead and Zoe took off for the garden.

Just before she barrelled out to the swings she loved, she turned back to them. 'Don't forget to show Daddy your surprise!' She beamed, and then they were alone.

'Surprise, eh?' he fished, coming up behind her as she put the last of the food away. He tried to peek into one of the other bags but she swatted his hand away.

'Hey!' Lucy admonished. 'I wasn't going to show you till later. She snitched a tad early.'

He came round behind her, wrapping her in his arms, nuzzling at her neck. He knew that drove her crazy. Hell, one more rub of his stubble and she'd give away all her secrets.

'That's my girl. What is it? Come on, spill.'

She pretended to be annoyed with him, but she was too excited. She didn't keep a thing from him any more, not since that day when she'd thought she'd lost him.

The last couple of years had been amazing. It had been

hard work, sure, and exhausting. Somewhere along the way, they'd gone from Jack-Jack and Luby to Mummy and Daddy. Zoe knew all about her parents. Their pictures still hung in pride of place in their home. She'd heard the stories and, when she'd started calling Jackson and Lucy 'Mummy' and 'Daddy', they knew that she'd decided that for herself.

Zoe was a mix of all four of them. She had her mother's looks and soft blonde hair and Ronnie's calmness. Jackson always ribbed Lucy that Zoe had inherited her stubborn streak, and Lucy saw his loyalty and open-hearted love shine out from their little girl. It had been a journey, but she loved where they were going. Living for today, it turned out, was a hell of a lot of fun.

'Come on, wifey, show me!' Jackson had started to tickle her sides and she yelped as she jumped away from him, grabbing one of the plain bags.

'Fine!' She pretended to huff. 'Before I show you, though, promise not to freak out.'

Jackson scoffed loudly. 'Pot…kettle…?'

'Shut up!' She giggled. 'Fine.' She came to stand in front of him, holding out the bag to him. He grabbed at it, a daft look on his face, like a little boy on Christmas morning. She pressed her lips together to keep the smile off her face as she observed his confused frown.

'What…?' His voice trailed off as he unfolded the small, white cotton garment. '"My big sister is…"'

'"Awesome",' she finished. 'Zoe picked it out.'

He held it up, the bag falling out of his grasp to the kitchen floor.

'This is a onesie,' he said.

'Yep.'

'For a baby.'

'Yep.'

'You—you let Zoe buy this?' he stammered, his gorgeous face a maelstrom of emotions.

'Yep.' She smirked. 'Well, I reckoned we'd need it.' She came round the island to stand in front of him. 'You know, in a few months.' His eyes bugged as his jaw dropped. 'Freaking out?' she teased.

'We're having a baby?' His voice cracked. 'For real?'

'For real.' She laughed. 'Just our timing, too. One kid goes to school full time, and we start all over again. Are you happy?' she asked, watching him look at the little outfit in his hand as if it might vanish.

'I'm not happy,' he said, lunging forward and picking her up in his huge, muscular arms. 'I'm freaking ecstatic! Zoe!' he shouted, and she appeared at the back door. 'We're having a baby!' He yelled, twirling Lucy round on the spot.

Zoe rolled her eyes, a classic Lucy move.

'I know, silly! I'm the big sister!' She put her hands on her hips, nodding to the clothing in his arms.

Jackson and Lucy laughed out loud. 'Good point. Get over here, smarty-pants!'

Zoe ran over with a giggle, and Jackson reached down and scooped her up.

'My girls.' He grinned, showering them both with kisses. 'I love you,' he told them both. 'So much.'

'We love you more,' Lucy told him. Hugging them both to her, she wondered at how life could change so much. How tragedy could rip people apart and change them. It could alter their landscape for ever, but sometimes lead to something new and unexpected—something great that might never have made them so happy without going through the deep, dark sorrow first.

That night, with Zoe fast asleep after their busy day, and Jackson kissing her still-flat tummy before carrying her to bed with love and lust written all over his gorgeous face, she reminded herself never to forget how lucky she was. She liked to think that, wherever they were, the people they had lost would be watching and be happy for them…at peace. It gave her the strength to enjoy every moment and take the rough with the smooth. Squeeze every drop out of life and follow her gut in her personal life as well as in her career.

Months later, she proved just that to herself, and to the love of her life. As she cradled Zachary Ronnie Denning, exhausted from labour and eager to show Zoe her little brother, she didn't hesitate to enjoy every single second. He was perfect, just like Zoe. A child she'd made from love with Dr Denning, the man whom she'd once jokingly threatened to sterilise to do the women of the world a favour.

'I love you.' Jackson beamed, that grin bowling her over.

'Pack that grin up, Denning. I just had your baby. You'll make me want another just to make you do it again.'

'Deal,' he retorted, making her laugh. 'We can fill the whole house with kids.' He looked at Zachary. 'He's amazing, isn't he? He has the Denning chin.'

She rolled her eyes at him. 'Let's hope he doesn't go paintballing and fall in love with a stubborn woman, eh?'

His low, rumbling laugh surrounded her as he hugged them both to him. 'I hope he does. I'll tell him it's the best thing his dad ever did, being shot in the groin by his mother.'

'Worth all the todays?'

He bent to kiss her just as the door opened. Zoe ran in, followed by two very excited grandparents.

'All the todays for ever,' he whispered. 'Fighting and loving you is what makes life worth living.'

'Deal?' she joked.

'Hell, yeah.' He growled. 'Bring it on, Trig.'

* * * * *

MILLS & BOON MODERN IS
HAVING A MAKEOVER!

The same great stories you love,
a stylish new look!

Look out for our brand new look
COMING JUNE 2024

MILLS & BOON

COMING SOON!

We really hope you enjoyed reading this book.
If you're looking for more romance
be sure to head to the shops when
new books are available on

Thursday 20th
June

To see which titles are coming soon, please visit

millsandboon.co.uk/nextmonth

MILLS & BOON

MILLS & BOON ®

Coming next month

ER DOC'S MIRACLE TRIPLETS
Tina Beckett

'There's something I need you to know.'

Seb sat in silence, staring at her face as if he didn't want her to say another word. But she had to. He deserved to hear the words so that he could make whatever decision he felt he needed to. So she pushed forward. 'I'm pregnant.'

'Pregnant.' A series of emotions crossed his face. Emotions that she couldn't read. Or maybe she was too afraid of trying to figure them out. 'But the last attempt failed.'

Even as his words faded away, an awful twist of his mouth gave evidence to what he was thinking. That the babies weren't his. She hurried to correct him. 'But it didn't. I assumed when I started spotting that I'd lost the pregnancy, because it was the pattern with the other IVF attempts. And I didn't go to have it checked out right away because of all the stress. I waited until you were gone to try to sort through things.'

'So you didn't lose the baby?'

His words were tentative, as if he was afraid that even saying them out loud might jinx everything. She got it. She'd felt the same way when they'd done the ultrasound on her and told her the wonderful news.

'Babies. I didn't lose the babies…plural.'

He sat up in his chair. He was shocked. Obviously. But was he also happy? Dismayed? Angry? She could no longer read him the way she'd once been able to.

'You're carrying twins?'

She slowly shook her head, unable to prevent a smile from reaching her lips. 'There are three of them.'

Continue reading
ER DOC'S MIRACLE TRIPLETS
Tina Beckett

Available next month
millsandboon.co.uk

Copyright © 2024 Tina Beckett

afterglow BOOKS

Afterglow Books are trend-led, trope-filled books with diverse, authentic and relatable characters and a wide array of voices and representations.

Experience real world trials and tribulations, all the tropes you could possibly want (think small-town settings, fake relationships, grumpy vs sunshine, enemies to lovers).

All with a generous dose of spice in every story!

OUT NOW

Two stories published every month.
To discover more visit:
Afterglowbooks.co.uk

afterglow BOOKS

FAKE FLAME

ADELE BUCK

 Opposites attract

 Fake Dating

 Spicy

OUT NOW

To discover more visit:
Afterglowbooks.co.uk

LET'S TALK
Romance

For exclusive extracts, competitions and special offers, find us online:

f MillsandBoon

X @MillsandBoon

◉ @MillsandBoonUK

♪ @MillsandBoonUK

Get in touch on 01413 063 232

For all the latest titles coming soon, visit
millsandboon.co.uk/nextmonth